Cardinal

By SARA MACK

Always follow your cardinal rule!

Cardinal

ISBN-13: 978-1517055295
ISBN-10: 1517055296

Cover art by Cover to Cover Designs
Photograph by Mandy Hollis of MH Photography
Edited by Red Ribbon Editing Services

Dedicated to

All readers who ask for more

Table of Contents

Chapter One

Do you know what I hate?

Having the rug pulled out from under me.

I also hate the sinking feeling my stomach gets when something bad happens. I hate when panic sets in, and the back of my neck breaks out in a cold sweat. I hate the feeling I might throw up at any minute, and I hate that I always fall for lies.

Fuck you, Ross. I mean, Derek.

Reaching for one of the earrings he gave me, I rip it out of my ear. "Thanks a lot asshole!" I throw it at him and it bounces off his chest. I grab the other earring and do the same. "You're a real piece of work, you know that?" I get in his face. "Why the fake name? Were you worried you'd get caught? Karma sure is a funny bitch."

"I don't have time for you right now," my married boyfriend snaps.

"Perfect!" I yell. "Because I don't have any more time for you." I start to walk away, then stop. "I suggest you leave before the Dayton brothers kick your ass." My ex, Kyle, and his brother, Kevin, look ready for a fight.

I almost make it to the other side of the room before I hear a fist connect with a jaw. Staring straight ahead, I keep walking and try to calm my racing pulse. When I make it to the dance floor, I pick up my guitar; before all hell broke loose, Kyle and I had just finished playing a song for Kevin's wedding. I send a silent message to my friends: *Sorry about the additional entertainment, guys.*

After I put my acoustic back in its case, I decide leaving now would be my best option. I feel tears coming on, and I don't get those often. Keeping my head down, I make a beeline for the door. Unfortunately, Kevin is on his way back from disposing of Derek, and he intercepts me. He places a hand on each of my shoulders to stop me from walking.

"Jen." He tries to catch my eyes. "Where are you going?"

"Home," I say. "I don't want your night ruined any more than it has been."

"C'mon." He squeezes my shoulders. "My night isn't ruined. Yours shouldn't be either; that guy's a prick. You deserve better."

I force a smile. I've been friends with Kevin for the last five years, after I accidentally rear-ended his car when mine slid on ice. "Don't try to sugarcoat it. My romantic life is in the toilet." He should know. He set me up with his brother, Kyle, and that relationship lasted three years before it tanked.

Kevin grimaces. "You don't have to leave."

"I know, but I need to."

Just then, Kyle and Addison walk up to us. My eyes bounce from Kyle's swollen cheek to Addison's pale complexion. She must be traumatized because Kyle got hit and her husband's a bigger dick than she thought. "I don't know what to say," I tell her. "I didn't know."

"It's okay." She looks sympathetic. "He gave you his middle name. Even if he was honest, what were the odds of your Derek being the same as mine?"

I feel the need to tell her everything I know. Maybe it's to assuage my own guilt; I'm not sure. "We met on New Year's Eve, but he didn't call for months," I say. "We've been seeing each other since the end of February."

"You don't have to explain." Addison steps forward. "My marriage was hurting well before New Year's Eve."

"Still," I sigh. "I feel awful. I just ... I just want to go home."

After I say goodbye, I make it outside into the cool night air. You would think the month of May would be warmer, but it's still spring in Michigan. Shivering, I quickly find my car, put my guitar in the trunk, and then slam the door shut. It's always good to take out your aggressions on inanimate objects. They can't hit back.

During the drive home I try to bury my thoughts, but my emotions won't have it. Tears escape the corners of my eyes and they make the white traffic lines blurry. How is it I have the most shittastic luck when it comes to men? Is there a sign on my forehead I can't see? It must say "Assholes Apply Here. Employment guaranteed." Thankfully P!nk comes on the radio and distracts me. I turn up the volume and shout along to "Blow Me (One Last Kiss)". It's cathartic.

When I reach my exit, I pull off the expressway and concentrate on driving through the sleepy little town I've lived in my entire life. When I park in front of my apartment building, I turn off the ignition and wipe beneath my eyes. No one should be around to see my mascara-streaked face, but I still don't want to look like Alice Cooper. Even if one of my neighbors did question me, I doubt they would actually care. They'd just think I'm the girl from D3 who always stays out too late. Judging by some of the looks I get, my neighbors think I party. My reality is much more tame. I tend bar for a living and work late hours. Sue me, nosey people.

Once I make my way inside, I kick off my heels, toss my purse on the table, and head straight for the bathroom. Turning the water on full blast, I take off the blue party dress I bought especially for the wedding tonight. I hang it on the back of the door and run my fingers over the fabric. Will I ever wear it again?

If I do, it will only remind me of Douchebag Derek and the fact that I slept with a married man.

After a moment, I decide yes. Even though my heart stings, I, Jen Elliott, will wear this dress again. Maybe not anytime soon.

But I will.

Stepping into the shower, the hot water pulls the curls from my hair and a few angry tears from my eyes. It turns my skin pink, and I stand under it long enough to wrinkle my fingers and toes. When the water runs cold, I get out and wrap myself in a towel. What I wouldn't give to start over.

I'm not talking about the shower. I'm talking about going back in time and correcting a few things. I run my hand over the steam-covered mirror and stare at my foggy reflection. Apparently, I'm destined to be single bartender for the rest of my life. There are worse fates.

Right?

My destiny doesn't feel too glamorous, not that it ever did. Sighing, I dry my hair and then find my bed. I slide beneath the sheets and hug a pillow to my chest. I have to get some sleep. I have to work tomorrow.

I have to forget Derek tomorrow.

I have to pick myself up and start over again ... tomorrow.

Chapter Two

When I pull into work the next day, my boss is outside unlocking the door. Frowning, I park in my usual spot and cut the engine. I've worked at Jay's Sports Bar for four years, and this is the first time my boss has been late. Since she owns the restaurant, Norma always arrives an hour earlier than the rest of us to get her paperwork done.

"Hey," I call to her when I step out of my car. "Everything okay?"

Startled, Norma drops her keys and a few papers. She turns around and holds one hand to her chest. "Oh, Jen. You scared me."

Confused, I walk toward her. "Didn't you hear me pull in?"

All five feet of my sixty-year-old boss looks worn and frazzled as she bends down to pick up what she dropped. "I guess my mind isn't where it's supposed to be."

I smile and crouch down to help her. "Well, it is Sunday. We should be home relaxing." I pull a few papers into a pile and can't help but notice they're all the same. My eyes catch a few words printed on each piece and my stomach starts to knot. Swallowing, I ask, "What's going on?"

Norma looks defeated as she takes the papers from my hands. "Jay's is closing," she says, her voice barely audible. "Leon is sick. Real sick."

I blink a few times. Leon Jay, Norma's husband, has been battling emphysema for as long as I can remember. "I thought he was feeling better," I say.

"He was. Now ..." Her voice fades. "He's not."

My heart goes out to her. I know how much she loves her husband and his condition has been tough on both of them, especially since she's still working.

"We're running out of money," she says as we both stand. "We've had some unexpected medical bills; things our insurance won't cover." Norma hands one of the letters back to me so I can read it. "A few months ago, Applebee's expressed interest in opening a restaurant in the area. They offered to buy us out." She hesitates. "We agreed."

My eyes scan the letter, but I can't concentrate. "When is this happening?"

"It was supposed to happen at the end of the year."

"But?"

"We officially close tomorrow."

Questions bounce around my brain. "Why so soon?"

"More time is needed for renovations," she explains. "This is an old building, and it needs some repairs."

The words "first opportunity to apply" jump off the paper at me, and my shoulders sag. "None of us have jobs, do we?"

Norma closes her eyes. Somehow, when she opens them again, she looks years older. "They said our staff will have the first chance to apply, but you're right. Employment isn't guaranteed."

Now my stomach truly sinks. I need to start job hunting. I glance down at my feet, at the invisible rug that's being pulled from under me for the second time in a matter of hours. Tension fills my body and Norma must notice, because she tries to ease it.

"You know you're like family to me," she says with a sad voice. "It was a hard decision to sell this place, let alone share the news before I was ready. You need to know I'm going to pay you for the next six months, through the date we were supposed to close. It's the least I can do."

I give my boss a resigned smile. While her gesture is nice, the $7.40 I make an hour is nothing without tips.

"I can't tell you how sorry I am." Norma looks pained. "I've been dreading this day."

Even though I'm the furthest thing from happy, I can't be mad at Norma. I understand why she made the decision she did; family comes first. I set my hand on her arm to try and comfort her. "It's okay. Your husband is the most important thing."

She pats my hand.

A car door slams behind me and I realize my coworkers are starting to arrive. I look at the letter, then back to my boss. "Am I free to go?" I don't think I want to relive this conversation.

"Sure," she says and squeezes my fingers. "If you need a letter of recommendation, please let me know."

I nod and, defeated, turn and head back to my car. First Derek, now my job. What else can go wrong?

~~~~

Later that evening, after I spent the day driving around to find job applications, I stop at Starbucks for comfort food. I figure I deserve it after the last two days. Armed with a caramel Frappuccino and a double chocolate chunk brownie, I pull up to my apartment building only to discover I can't enter the parking lot. Two police cars and three fire trucks block the entrance.

You have got to be kidding me.

The flashing lights are blinding as I drive by. I park down the road and get out of the car to walk home. As I get closer, I can smell smoke. There was a fire? I hope no one got hurt. Thoughts begin to swirl in my mind: I straightened my hair this morning. Did I turn off the flat iron? What if I caused this? I was a little distracted because I woke up to a Derek/Ross text:

I want to see you.

Fat chance, asshole.

I reach a group of people huddled on the sidewalk wearing sweats and pajamas. "What happened?" I ask.

"Fire." An older woman I've seen in the laundry room turns around. "It started a few hours ago over on the end." She points. "Building D."

Figures. It's my building. At least I'm not responsible; my unit is in the middle.

"Did they put it out?"

"Yes, but rumor has it the indoor sprinkler system caused more damage than the actual fire." She looks around the group. "Before we evacuated, our units were soaked."

My mouth falls open. "So everything is wet?"

"Likely so."

Oh no. The last thing I can afford right now is to replace my things.

Overwhelmed, I step away from the group and sit down on the curb. I hold my head in my hands and stare at the pavement. My life has gone from normal to insane so fast I may have set a Guinness Record. I must have royally pissed off the universe, although I don't know how. My breathing becomes erratic as I realize everything I love is converging on ruin.

"Miss?"

I look up to find a fireman standing beside me.

"Do you live here?"

I nod while I consider asking him to save me from my life. He's a hero. That's what they do.

He crouches down to my level. "Chief says all residents are clear to go inside and get what they need for the night. Your landlord has opened the clubhouse as a temporary shelter."

I squint. "How long will it be until we can stay in our apartments?"

"Things are pretty messed up." He frowns. "I guess it depends on how fast the building gets cleaned and inspected."

That's not good news. Slowly, I stand. The firefighter helps by steadying my elbow. "Thanks," I say.

"Do you need any other help?"

I let out a sarcastic snort. "You have no idea."

He chuckles, then steps away. "My name is Peyton, if you need anything."

"Thank you, Peyton."

He winks at me and I notice his eyes. They're a stunning shade of blue. As he turns and walks over to another group of people, my frazzled mind does the most inappropriate thing possible: it wonders what he looks like under all that gear.

Really, Jen?! I chastise myself. This is not the time or the place to think about guys. Given my most recent romance, I should swear them off all together. With my luck, he probably has a wife, a girlfriend, *and* kids.

Just then, my phone rings in my bag. I reach for it and swipe the screen to answer as I walk. "Hey, Peter."

"Hey, Little J!"

I roll my eyes at my oldest brother's nickname for me. Actually, all my brothers call me that. After Peter, there's Josh and then Adam. I'm the youngest and the only girl.

"Pete. I'm not a kid. Stop calling me that."

"You will always be Little J," he says. "Anyway, listen, I need a favor."

"Not now," I snap.

"What's wrong?"

One of the fire trucks starts to pull away from the scene, and it's loud. I cover my other ear with my free hand and talk over the noise.

"I lost my job, my boyfriend is married, and my apartment almost burned down!"

"What?!" he exclaims. "Start from the beginning."

I catch him up to speed as I pace in front of my building. Other tenants push past me to get their things, but I'm nervous to go inside and see the damage.

"Are you serious?" Pete asks. "Where will you stay?"

"With mom and dad." It's not my first choice, but it beats bunking at the clubhouse.

"You should stay with me."

I scoff. "I can't just drive to Chicago."

"Why not? You have no job, no house, and no man."

I'm silent.

"Every Christmas you say you'll visit and you never do."

That's true. It's been years since I've been to Chicago. My brother comes home for the holidays and we see each other then. Even though I always promise to visit him, I don't. A trip to the city would seem like a vacation. In my line of work, I don't get paid days off.

"There's nowhere for me to sleep," I say.

"I have a spare room."

"What about Juliana?"

Juliana is Pete's permanent girlfriend. At thirty-two years old I don't think he'll ever get married – or grow up. My brother works as a bouncer and religiously plays Call of Duty. Jules doesn't seem to mind, however. She's been with him for years.

"You know she loves you," Pete says. "Besides, I'm at her place more than mine. Come out here, Little J. Escape for a while."

That does sound enticing. I sigh. "I can't right now."

"You can."

"I don't think so. I need to find a job. Are you going to pay my bills?"

"If you need help, yes."

"I won't take your money, Pete."

"Would you stop being so complicated?" He sounds like our dad. "Get your ass in the car and drive west. I'm trying to make you feel better and you're not making it easy."

A few of my neighbors walk out the door with their arms full of clothes and toiletries. The sight depresses me. I don't want to be a nomad. I also don't want to be a jobless twenty-six year old staying with her parents. Maybe I do need a change of scenery.

"Fine," I say quietly.

"Fine? You're coming?"

"Yes."

"Awesome." I can sense his smile through the phone. "When are you leaving?"

I look up at my building. "After I pack, I suppose. It shouldn't take long if everything is ruined."

"So, I'll see you in five or six hours?"

I walk up the steps and open the door. "I'll call you along the way."

Chapter Three

"Eeeeeep!" Juliana throws her arms around my neck. "You're here!"

I stare at my brother over his girlfriend's shoulder. I can't return her hug. I have a suitcase in each hand, a bag over my arm, my guitar strapped to my back, and eyelids that weigh more than bricks.

"I'm here," I choke out.

Pete grins. "Don't strangle her, Jules."

Juliana steps back and hangs on to my arms. "We're going to have so much fun!" she gushes. "I made us a pedicure appointment, I added you as my guest at the gym, there's a party tonight at Latson's –"

"Whoa," I say. "It's the butt crack of dawn. How did you do all that?"

"Online, silly."

Oh. Of course. Silly me.

"I think Jen needs some sleep," my brother says as he reaches for one of my suitcases. "Is this everything or is there more in the car?"

"No, this is it."

I was able to pack most of my clothes into two large suitcases since everything in the closet stayed dry. I tried to bring as much as possible because my landlord has no clue when cleanup will begin. When I talked to him before I left, he said he would call when he had any information. He also reminded me to contact my insurance company to make a claim for my belongings. I hope my parents will help, since my furniture is ruined and I left town before meeting an adjuster.

"Come see your room," Juliana says and takes my other bag. "I tried to spruce it up a little, but we may have to go shopping."

I look at my brother, confused.

"She's been up all night," he says.

Juliana elbows him. "You can't invite her to stay with you and expect her to live in a pig sty."

"Thanks," I say. I can only imagine what he had piled in there.

I follow them through the living room and down the hallway. The apartment is decorated differently than I remember. It looks more modern. A few pieces of abstract art hang on the walls and the furniture is plush and overstuffed. The entertainment center looks like it was forged from steel. I assume the changes are a reflection of Juliana's taste more than my brother's. I've never known him to decorate with anything other than old road signs and bean bag chairs.

"If the closet isn't big enough we can get a dresser," Juliana says as we enter my new space.

"I'm sure it will be fine."

"Well ..." She walks around the bed and opens the closet door. "I had to put Pete's stuff somewhere."

Half the closet is packed full. From where I stand I can see multiple shoe boxes, stacks of papers, and a couple of large plastic totes.

"Some of it is yours," my brother grumbles as he sets my suitcase on the bed. "All that stuff from your yoga phase for example."

Juliana makes a face. "Okay. So, there's like, two things in there that are mine."

I smile. Their bickering is cute. "Don't worry. I'll make it work." I drop my tote bag at my feet, then pull my guitar strap over my head and set the instrument against the wall.

Pete looks at my bag. "What's in there?"

"Just bathroom stuff and my purse."

"The bathroom!" Juliana exclaims. She drops my suitcase and sprints toward the door. "I'll clean out a drawer for you."

My surprised eyes follow her as she leaves the room. "She's excited," I say as I sit on the edge of the bed.

"Yeah, well." My brother smiles and joins me. "Her best friend moved away about a month ago. She's happy you're here."

I nod.

"So." Pete clasps his hands between his knees. "How are you?"

"Tired," I admit and roll my neck.

"Have you processed everything that's happened?"

"Not really." Instead of thinking during my drive, I turned up the music and turned off my brain.

"If you want me to kill him, I will."

My brow jumps. "You mean my cheating ex-boyfriend?"

"Yes."

I have no doubt my brother could – and would – toss Derek. It's what he does for a living. Pete cracks his knuckles for emphasis, and I notice his arm muscles flex against his shirt sleeve. "Have you gotten bigger?"

"A little." He shrugs. "Answer my question."

"You're going to crush Juliana!" I playfully shove him. She's so petite next to his huge, six-foot frame. "I don't know why she puts up with you."

He scowls. "What's wrong with being healthy?"

"There's a difference between being healthy and being Schwarzenegger."

Juliana appears in the doorway holding a hair dryer. "I take it you don't like big guys?"

To be honest, they intimidate me. "Obviously you do."

She grins.

"I prefer my men to be more defined," I say. "Not bulky."

"Good to know." Juliana wiggles her eyebrows before wrapping the dryer cord around the handle.

"Stop." My brother glares at his woman. "My sister is here to relax, not date."

"Whatever." Juliana rolls her eyes.

I laugh, but silently agree with Pete.

"Now, back to my question." He crosses his arms and looks at me. "Do you want me to kill him?"

I sigh. "Yes."

His face lights up.

"But, no."

His shoulders sag.

Scooting over, I wrap my arms around his waist and squeeze. "Thank you for wanting to, though."

"Did you at least bitch him out?" he asks, hopeful.

"Of course! You know who you're talking to, right?"

My brother pats my knee.

Juliana disappears from the doorway only to reappear seconds later. "The second drawer in the bathroom is yours."

"Great." I reach for my tote bag to find my toothbrush. "I'm ready for bed."

Pete stands. "We'll leave you alone for now. Sleep tight, Little J."

"Ugh," I groan at my nickname. "Don't call me that."

He snickers.

"I'll be at work most of the day, but I'll be back in time to get ready for Latson's," Juliana says. "Did you bring any party clothes?"

"I'm sure I have something." I glance at my suitcases. "What kind of place is it? A club?"

"It's an apartment upstairs."

I look at the ceiling. "Really?"

"Latson's a buddy of mine," Pete says. "We work together."

"Why is he having a party?"

"For the hell of it."

Good reason. "Well, if anyone needs to party, it's this girl." I point to myself. "Sounds like fun."

Juliana bounces on her toes. "Did I tell you how glad I am you're here?"

"I think more than once," Pete says and starts to push her out the door. "See you when the sun shines, Little J."

"Stop it!" I huff.

He laughs as they disappear down the hallway.

~ ~ ~ ~

"Baby girl. You gave me a heart attack."

"I'm sorry." I rub my eyes. "Yesterday was a mess."

It's eleven a.m. Chicago time which means it's noon back home. My cell was screaming from the nightstand before I blindly answered and was greeted by my frantic father.

"I saw the fire on the news. Are you sure you're all right?"

"Like I said, I wasn't there."

He pauses. "How's your place?"

"Ruined. Everything is soaked from the sprinkler system."

"Did you call your insurance agent?"

"Not yet."

I stretch my free arm over my head and my legs in the opposite direction. My dad starts to ramble about buying new furniture, and I turn my attention toward the sunlight streaming through the bedroom window. I wonder how warm it will be today.

"Jen?"

"What?"

"Are you listening to me?"

No. "Yes."

"What did I just say?"

"Umm." I bite my thumbnail.

He sighs. "So what made you decide to drive to Pete's?"

"He called at the right time and got on my case about not visiting."

"Ah," he says. Through the phone, I hear a door close and assume he's stepped outside. "I'm surprised you went. Did work give you some time off because of the fire?"

I close my eyes. "No. Jay's is closing, Dad. I'm out of a job."

"What?"

"My boss needs to spend time with her sick husband. She sold the restaurant."

He's quiet for a moment. "What are you going to do?"

"I have no idea." I roll over on my side. "I guess it's time to figure shit out."

"Jennifer Marie!"

"What?"

He chuckles. "You definitely have some shit to figure out."

"Right?" I pick at some fuzz on the comforter.

"Honey, listen," his voice softens. "You deserve a break. You've put in hundreds of hours at Jay's and you're always on your feet. You're one of the hardest working people I know. Take some time to regroup and focus on you."

"I feel like I should be job hunting."

"Are you going to go bankrupt in the next few weeks?"

"Probably not."

"Then, there you go. What do the kids say nowadays? You need to 'do you'."

I laugh. My dad is a high school English instructor and he tries to stay up on current slang.

My mom calls for my dad in the background. "Hold on," he says. His voice is muffled as he tells her I'm fine and with Pete. He returns to our conversation. "All right, baby girl. Your mom and I need to run errands. Promise me you'll keep us in the loop and tell us when you're headed home."

"I will. I may need your help with the insurance claim anyway."

"Okay. Try to relax and have fun. I'll talk to you soon."

We say I love you and goodbye, and I toss my phone aside. I flop back against the pillow. Maybe my dad is right. The time has come to 'do me'. It seems like I've been on the same path forever, caught in an endless cycle, unable to switch direction. I tend bar and fail at relationships. That's my life.

Pushing my hair off my forehead, I look around the bedroom, my eyes landing on my guitar. I can definitely spend more time working on my music while I'm here. That qualifies as 'doing me'. Glancing around again, I notice the sunlight a second time and make a mental note to get more vitamin D, too. Then, I snuggle into the blankets and figure a few naps might be in order. Slowly, a smile creeps across my face.

I can do whatever the hell I want.

My mind begins to swirl with possibilities. I can't remember when I've had this much free time. I can do whatever I feel like without worrying about a guy or a schedule. Despite all that has happened, it feels good. So good, I think I'll make it my rule.

My cardinal rule.

Starting today, Jen will only do what makes her happy.

Deciding coffee will bring me joy, I throw back the covers. Yawning, I make my way to the kitchen to peruse the countertop. I find a Keurig instead of a traditional coffee pot. *Score*, I think as I open the drawer beneath it and find the K-Cups. After I pop a Green Mountain Vanilla Crème into the machine, I search for a mug and come across a white board hanging on the refrigerator. There's a note from Pete:

If you want to eat, we need food. At the store.

Knowing my brother, he'll bring back nothing but vegetables and protein. Coupled with Juliana's gym comment, I realize staying here won't hurt my waistline.

When my coffee is done, I head outside to enjoy it. Sitting in one of the two chairs on my brother's small balcony, I take in the sights and sounds of the city below. Pete lives on the eastern edge of Lincoln Park, which isn't too far from Lake Michigan. It's the complete opposite of home, which is why he loves it. We grew up on a dead-end, dirt road with very few neighbors. Here, there are people everywhere. Most walk, some ride bikes. It looks like they are all wearing ear buds because I can see the cords. Car horns and a siren sound in the distance, and I mentally add exploring to my list of happy things to do with my free time. I like this atmosphere. It feels charged, but in a good way. Like everyone has somewhere important to go and something important to do.

I'd like to be one of those people.

After my coffee disappears, I head to the shower. I take my time soaping and shaving, and when the water runs cold, I pull back the curtain to grab a towel. Without the water in my ears I hear a weird thrumming noise. Confused, I make sure the faucet is off and I didn't screw something up. I mean, I only turned a knob, but the sound appears to be coming through the wall. Satisfied it's not the pipes, I wrap a towel around myself and crack the bathroom door.

It's music. My brother must be home.

Drying off, I secure the towel under my arms. I didn't think to bring my clothes with me; I'm going to have to remember I'm not living alone anymore. In a few steps I reach my room, and it hits me that the music is loud. I mean *loud*, as if I'm the one who is playing it. It's obvious that it's coming from the apartment above this one, not the living room like I thought. The lyrics to Buckcherry's "Crazy Bitch" ring crystal clear. The song reminds me of when my brothers got busted for playing it at home. My mother wasn't impressed by the use of the word fuck despite the catchy guitar riffs.

Since Pete's not here, I drop the towel and find my underwear, unable to stop my body from swaying to the music. Once the girls are secure, I turn around to find some clothes. It feels good to dance, so I roll my hips as I bend over to dig through my suitcase. When the chorus of the song plays, I stop searching to pull my hair off my neck and hold it on top of my head. I grind down to the floor and back up again. Then, I resume my seductive search by leaning over the bed and shaking my ass.

Apparently, my inner stripper wants to play today.

Finding a pair of shorts, I swing them over my head. They go flying because, let's face it, I'm not a real stripper. I turn around to pick them up and stop dead in my tracks.

There is a guy standing in the doorway.

Watching me.

Our eyes lock. He opens his mouth and says something, but all I can hear is the whoosh of my pulse and Buckcherry. As I step back, my mind registers the fact that his body takes up most of my exit and he has a sleeve of tattoos down one arm. As I try to find my voice he says, "Don't scream."

What the hell? Don't scream?

He holds his hands up in surrender. "I know Pete."

What? Creep! "Get out!"

"Okay!" He takes a step into the hallway. "Do you know when he will be −?"

"I said get out!" I pick up the closest thing to me and throw it at him which, unfortunately, happens to be a pair of balled up socks.

He dodges my attack and smiles.

"This isn't funny!"

His smile grows. "You're right. It's not funny." He turns to leave, but stops. His eyes give me an appreciative once over. "It's definitely somethin' though."

I march forward and slam the door in his face. Then, I grab my phone and text my brother.

Get home now!

Chapter Four

After I put on some clothes, I yank open the bedroom door to see if my uninvited guest is still around. He's not in the hallway, so I venture out to search the rest of the apartment. When there's no sign of him in the living room or the kitchen, I check Pete's room. I also look out on the balcony, just in case.

He's disappeared.

Sitting on the edge of the couch, I wait for my pulse to slow. I can't believe that idiot would just waltz in here like he owned the joint! Has he ever heard of knocking? Speaking of, I wonder if Pete forgot to lock the front door. I push myself off the couch to check. It's secure.

Creeper must have a key, unless he's Spiderman. Maybe he did come in through the balcony. I left the sliding door open.

Minutes later, my brother returns. I hear the deadbolt drop, then watch him open the door with his foot. One hand holds plastic bags while the other holds keys. His eyes dart around the room. "What happened?"

I walk toward him and reach for the bags. "One of your friends scared the shit out of me."

He looks confused. "Who?"

"How am I supposed to know? He was tall and had tattoos down one arm."

"That's Latson." Pete reaches for his back pocket and grabs his vibrating phone. He reads the message and types out a response. "I told him he could stop by to pick up my beer pong table for tonight."

"You have a beer pong table?"

"Yeah. It's in your room. Jules probably put it in the closet."

I carry Pete's purchases into the kitchen and set them on the counter. "Well, can you tell him you have company? I don't appreciate strangers staring at me in my underwear."

"Wait." Pete sets his phone next to the groceries. "Why did you answer the door in your underwear?"

"I didn't. I was getting dressed, I turned around, and there he was. How many of your friends have keys to this place?"

My brother frowns. "Only one." He grabs his phone and sends another message.

I open a bag and take out a package of chicken breasts. Beneath that is a package of bacon and under that is a steak. I was right about the protein. The next bag holds a bunch of bananas, two avocados, an onion, and some baby carrots. I scowl. "Where's the junk food?"

"Don't worry," Pete says. He peruses what he bought. "Here." He flips what looks like a granola bar at me.

"What is this?" I read the label. It's a dark chocolate and sea salt Mojo Bar made by the same people that make Cliff energy bars. I hold it by the end of the wrapper. "This is not junk food. I need you to tell me where the store is. I cannot survive on this stuff."

Pete rolls his eyes and reaches into another bag. He produces two Hostess apple pies. "I didn't forget your favorite."

"Yes!" My face lights up. I snag the pastries from his hand, tear one package open, and take a big bite. My mouth is filled with sugary cinnamon goodness.

"Geez." Pete shakes his head.

"I haven't had anything to eat yet," I mumble.

Pete's phone buzzes and he reads the message. "I'll be right back. I'm going to take the table to Latson."

I nod as I chew and continue to remove food from the grocery bags. I'm filling the refrigerator when my brother's cell goes off again. He left it on the counter and, curious, I glance at the screen. What I read makes me smirk. It's Pete's text thread with Latson.

L: Stopped by your place. Who's your friend?

P: My sister.

Then, a few minutes later:

P: She told me what happened. You're a dick.

L: Hey. I didn't know she was your sister. She's hot.

P: Don't even think about it asshole.

Then:

L: I still need the table.

P: Be there in a sec.

Hmm. Latson thinks I'm hot? I start to feel smug until my mind jumps to Derek, to the last guy who said that about me. Bastard.

I hope he realizes what he lost.

~~~~

"Will this work?"

Juliana looks me over. "Turn around."

I comply. I've paired my black skinny jeans with a hot pink tank top for tonight's party. It's layered down the front and has a sheer mesh back.

"Definitely," she says when I complete my circle. "I have the perfect shoes for you." She walks over to a duffle bag. "I didn't know what you would need, so I brought a few things. I hope you can wear a size seven."

"That's small," I say. "I usually wear an eight."

She produces a pair of open-toed, black strappy heels. "Well, give them a try. I think they're super cute."

They are cute. I sit down on the edge of the bed and take the shoes from her. To my surprise, my foot fits. Sure, my toes hang off the end, but if I scoot my heel back they're almost perfect. Since this party is in Latson's apartment, I decide to suffer for fashion. We'll probably be sitting most of the night anyway.

"Thanks," I say. "I didn't think to bring dressy shoes. Without these I'd be stuck with my flats."

Juliana smiles. "That's what friends are for."

We head to the bathroom to put the finishing touches on our appearance. I look at our reflections in the mirror. With these shoes on, I tower over Jules. "I'm a giant next to you," I laugh.

She winds a section of her auburn hair around a curling iron and frowns. "I'm used to it. Everyone is taller than me."

I apply some mascara to my lashes.

"Have you ever thought of using blue eye shadow?" she asks. "It would really make your eyes pop."

I stare at my pale baby blues. "No. I think it's too '80's."

"Here." She sets the curling iron aside and grabs my hand. She lowers the toilet lid and makes me sit. "Let me play. If you don't like it you can take it off."

I decide to let her experiment. I don't know any of the people going to this party and the chances of seeing them again are small. If I end up looking like Debbie Harry it will be okay. Plus, it feels nice to do girly things. Not that I don't wear skirts and paint my nails, but I haven't spent time with a girlfriend in forever. Most of my close friends moved away after high school, with the exception of Melanie. I talk to her from time to time, but it's usually online. We don't hang out often because she has a little one and another on the way.

Juliana paints my closed eyelids. "So," she says. "I heard you met Latson today."

I grimace. "You could call it that."

"Stop scrunching," she chastises. "Pete told me he scared you."

"Um, yeah. Creeper."

"You think he's creepy?"

"Wouldn't you? I thought I was alone and I wasn't. I turn around in the middle of my stripper routine and he says 'Don't scream'. Isn't that what rapists say?"

She giggles. "Your what routine?"

"I was kinda dancing in my underwear. There was loud music playing in the apartment above this one." I open one eye. "Don't tell Pete. I left out the dancing part."

She laughs. "My lips are sealed. No wonder Latson thinks you're hot."

"What?" I act surprised. I won't confess to reading my brother's text messages.

"Pete told me," she says. "He's not happy about it."

"Why? Is Latson bad news?"

"Not at all." I hear her put something down, then feel her finger smudge her work. "He's got a little money, he's eligible, and you can bounce a quarter off his ass."

I snort. "Have you tried?"

"No." I can hear the smile in her voice. "You can't tell me you didn't like what you saw."

"I didn't." It's the truth. "I was too worried about being attacked. I threw some socks at him and slammed the door in his face."

She laughs again. "Really? I wish I could have seen that. Doors tend to stay open for Latson."

I bet. Curious, I ask, "Is that his real name?"

"It's his last name."

"What's his first?"

"He only shares that information with a privileged few." I feel her back away. "All right. Open your eyes."

I raise my lids and squint at the light. "How does it look?"

"I think it looks great."

Standing, I face the mirror. The smoky hue surrounding my eyes makes them look twice their size. "Where did you learn to do this?"

"You pick up a thing or two working at a salon." She grabs the curling iron again. "If you're thinking about doing something new with your hair –"

"What's wrong with my hair?"

"Nothing." She shrugs. "But, I'm a stylist. If you want to take advantage, let me know."

I pull my straightened dark brown locks over one shoulder. I have a lot of changes going on in my life right now. I think I'll keep my hair the way it is.

I keep Juliana company in the bathroom while she finishes up. During the process, loud music starts to play above us.

"See? There." I point up. "That's what I was talking about. How do you and Pete put up with the noise?"

"We're usually at my place. Besides, the owner tends to warn us when he's having parties."

I groan. "It's coming from Latson's?"

She nods.

"I was dancing to his music earlier?"

She nods again.

That's not awkward or anything.

Finally, she's ready to go. We emerge from the bathroom to find my brother sprawled out on the couch.

"It's about time." He raises the remote and turns off the T.V. "I was going to leave without you." He stands as I turn to grab my purse off the table. "Jen. Where is the back of your shirt?"

I look over my shoulder. "It's right here."

He lets out a heavy sigh.

"Do you want her to wear a turtleneck?" Juliana asks.

"No. It's just..."

I set my hands on my hips. "It's just what?"

"Haven't you shown enough skin today?"

I scowl. "It wasn't intentional."

He doesn't look amused.

"Can we get out of here?" I ask. "There's a party going on and I need a drink."

"I second that." Juliana loops her arm through mine.

The three of us leave the apartment and take the stairs up one floor. When we get to the top, I see a hallway similar to Pete's. Three apartment doors span one wall while, opposite of my brother's floor, the other wall is empty. I assume this is how Latson gets away with loud parties. No one lives across from him. He must warn his neighbors on either side like he warns Jules and Pete. I can't imagine they would be happy with a bunch of people over all the time.

Juliana's arm remains entwined with mine and I let her pull me toward the door that's propped open. When we step over the threshold, my jaw drops. I expected a replica of Pete's place. This looks nothing like the apartment my brother rents.

Juliana grabs my attention. "Nice, huh?"

I nod. "Is it always like this?"

"Do you mean crowded?"

"No. Big."

She smiles. "Latson owns all the apartments on this floor. He knocked down the walls in between to create a suite."

He renovated an entire floor? I look around the room. He has enough money to do that but he can't he afford his own beer pong table?

Speaking of, the game is in full swing to my right. Behind the two teams bouncing ping pong balls back and forth I see the kitchen, which is separated from the living room by a breakfast bar. There must be an island past that, because people have congregated there. In front of me is a living area with a sunken center; you have to walk down two steps to get to the main floor. Couches and chairs have been pushed to the perimeter and a DJ is set up at the far end near the sliding balcony doors. As Aerosmith's "Walk This Way" morphs into Rihanna's "Umbrella", my eyes continue to roam. A fireplace is tucked away in a corner a few feet from a mounted flat screen and then, further to my left, I see a hallway.

"Pete!"

I turn to see a guy clap my brother on his shoulder.

"Hey, Carter."

"Juullles." He draws out Juliana's name, then kisses her on the temple. He pretends to whisper in her ear. "When are you going to dump this loser and go out with me?"

She laughs. "Carter, this is Pete's sister, Jen. Jen, meet persistent Carter."

Carter looks at me, intrigued.

"Hi," I offer.

He flashes a white smile to match his surfer boy looks. "Hello." He takes a step toward me, then hollers over his shoulder. "Felix!"

I see a guy with tan skin grab his red party cup and leave the side of the beer pong table. He stands beside Carter. "What's up?"

Carter gestures toward me. "Did you know Pete had a sister?"

Felix looks me over and one side of his mouth quirks up. "No." He reaches for my hand. "Mucho gusto."

The tone of his voice makes me blush. Is he really Spanish or is he pretending? Lucky for me I remember details – and Ms. Ciccone's high school class.

"El gusto es mio," I say and bat my eyelashes. There's no harm in having a little fun.

Felix looks impressed. Still holding my hand, he steps closer. "Quiero hacer el amor contigo."

I burst out laughing. "Maybe another time."

"Okay!" Pete puts both his hands on my shoulders and steers me away from his friends. He pushes me toward the kitchen while telling them, "That's enough."

"Hey!" I pout.

"We've been here two minutes," he grumbles.

Pete lets go of my shoulders when we make it into the kitchen. As he reaches for a cup, I ask, "Do your friends always ask random girls to make love?"

"Just Felix," he answers. "And, yes, that line has worked way too many times."

Pete gives me the cup in his hands, then passes one to Jules. He gestures toward the counter. "Pick your poison."

I walk over to scan the selections. Every type of liquor is here, from high-end to low-brow. Some bottles are unopened and brand new, while others are half-full or near empty. I decide to make a Kamikaze, since a bottle of Grey Goose is right in front of me. I eyeball two shots of vodka, add the triple sec and the lime juice, then take a drink.

So. Good.

Juliana tugs my arm. "We have to dance!"

I look at her over the edge of my cup. "We do?"

She nods. "Listen."

I take another drink. The song is "Kiss" by Prince. I agree. "We *so* have to dance."

We leave my brother in the kitchen and head to the makeshift dance floor. Once my feet hit the carpet I'm reminded that my shoes are too small. I can feel the fabric under my toes because they hang off the end. Regardless, I toss my purse on a nearby couch and follow Jules to stand among the other girls dancing. We sing the lyrics in our high-pitched Prince voices, stand back to back and rub up against one another, then turn around to drink and dance at the same time. When the song ends, my Kamikaze is gone.

"Need another?"

The voice in my ear sends a shiver down my spine. The tone is rich and smooth, and my eyes jump to Juliana's. Judging from her expression, I know who is standing behind me.

Slowly, I turn and face Latson. He's wearing a plain white tee and dark jeans. The tattoos that run down his right arm I recognize. It's the way his shirt pulls across his chest and the pools of melted chocolate for eyes that I don't recall. His eyelashes rival my own in length, and his hair is styled in the front but cut short on the sides.

Hello.

Despite his looks, he is still the guy that was watching me dance in my skivvies. I clip my words. "I can get my own drink. But thank you."

He gives me half a smile, which reveals a dimple. "Can you now?"

Holy perfect mouth. "Yes. I'm a bartender."

He raises one eyebrow, then holds his hand out toward the kitchen. "Then, by all means, help yourself."

I give him a curt nod and walk away. I can feel eyes following me, but I'm not sure they're his. They could be Juliana's, wondering where I'm going. I make it to the edge of the living room, to the first step, when my too-big toes for my too-small shoes catch on the carpet. I stumble.

Shit!

I right myself and resist the urge to look back. I keep walking and pretend like it didn't happen. Of course I would trip!

When I make it to the kitchen, I take my time fixing my drink to shake it off. *The lighting in the living room is dim*, I rationalize. Chances are no one saw my grace-less exit.

With my cup full again, I head out to find Jules. She's half-dancing, half-talking to a girl I don't know. As I make my way over to them, someone grazes my elbow. I turn and find myself staring at Latson.

"What?" I ask.

"I'm disappointed," he says.

"Why?"

"Your moves." He flashes a cocky grin. "Especially that last one. They're nowhere as good as what I saw this morning."

Jackass! He hasn't earned the right to tease me. I step closer to him and try to turn the tables. "That's because what you saw this morning is for private audiences only." I look around the room. "This is a public place."

He looks surprised before I walk away. I make sure to measure my steps so I won't trip again. Successful and smiling, I make it to Juliana, who introduces me to Gwen, a bartender who works with my brother. She seems sweet, and the three of us spend the next hour talking, drinking, and dancing.

Eventually, nature calls. "Guys," I say. "I need to use the bathroom. Where is it?"

"Down the – ahhhh!" Gwen laughs as Carter swoops in behind her. He spins her around and then sets her on her feet. She brushes her hair out of her face. "It's down the hall on the left."

"Got it."

I weave my way through bodies until I reach the hallway I spotted when we arrived. I'm surprised there isn't line for the bathroom. In fact, the hall is empty and all of the doors are closed. I head to the left and open the first one I see. Whoops. That's a closet. Gwen could have been more specific, but, then again, she's had a few shots. There is only one other door to choose from, so I open it and step inside. I feel around for the light switch and when I flip it, I'm not prepared for what I see.

Well.

This is unexpected.

Chapter Five

I glance around the room.

Posters of something called Minecraft hang on the walls. I've never heard of it, but the pictures make it look like some sort of pixelated video game. A blue striped comforter covers a twin bed, and a small entertainment stand holds a television and a gaming system. Cords snake across the carpet to two controllers that lay next to a Nerf gun on the floor. The top of the dresser is covered in action figures, and a small basketball hoop hangs over one of the closet doors.

I blink. This is a kid's bedroom.

Why does Latson have a kid's bedroom?

I quickly turn off the light and step into the hallway. I'm about to piss my pants. I decide to try the door across the hall. Where there's a bedroom there is usually a bathroom nearby. Lucky for me, I'm right. I rush inside and close the door. Apparently Gwen can't tell her right from her left. I'm going to have to show her that trick where you make a letter L with your left thumb and forefinger as a reminder.

When I head back to the living room, I spot Juliana and she makes a face. "Where were you?"

"I told you I needed the bathroom."

She jerks her thumb over her shoulder. "The bathroom for parties is over there."

I look over her head. She's pointing to the hallway on the opposite side of the apartment.

"No one told me there was a designated toilet." My expression twists. "Gwen said 'down the hall' and I picked one."

My brother comes up behind Jules. He hands her a cup, wraps his arms around her waist, and sets his chin on her shoulder. He looks at me. "Having fun?"

"If you forget about tripping in front of the host and venturing into prohibited territory, then yes," I say.

The music slows down and Juliana's eyes get that 'I'm-buzzed-and-I-want-to-rub-up-on-my-boyfriend' look. She turns around in Pete's arms and I decide I don't need to watch them get cozy. More party goers have the same idea as the two of them, so it's easy to find a place to sit. I wander over to an empty loveseat to wait out Ed Sheeran's "Kiss Me". As the song plays I can't stop my fingers from strumming invisible strings. I love Ed. Hearing him makes me itch to pick up my guitar and play.

A pair of legs rounds the couch and I look up as Latson sits down. He flashes a sexy smile in my direction and my heart stutters.

Damn it. The last thing I need is to be attracted to this guy.

He settles against the cushions all confident-like and I cross my arms. He looks at me and I look at him until I raise an eyebrow in question.

"You don't dance to slow songs?" he asks.

"Only with the right person," I respond.

"And where is he?"

I decide to mess with him. "How do you know he isn't a she?"

Latson smiles and shakes his head. "Is he a she?"

I shrug, trying to be nonchalant. "Maybe they should be. Good men are hard to find."

Ain't that the truth.

42

Latson's eyes light up like he wants to say something smart, but he doesn't. Instead, his gaze darts to the hallway I just explored. "Were you looking for one earlier? A good man, I mean."

He saw me? I don't want him to think I spy on people like he does. "I got lost, I swear. Gwen gives bad directions."

He laughs, then leans forward to rest his elbows on his knees. This closes the distance between us and his leg ends up pressed against mine. He shoots me another lethal smile. "Well, if you ever want a private tour let me know."

My mouth tries to fall open, but I catch it. I'm sure he's used this line on women before and I'm sure it's worked. Especially if he looked at their lips the way he's looking at mine.

Before I can think of a witty comeback, a girl wearing a tiny, form-fitting mini dress throws her body in his lap. I lean back as she winds her arms around his neck.

"I'm sorry I'm late," she coos. "Work ran over."

I take in her unnatural cranberry red hair and six-inch high stilettos. Hmmm. Where does she work?

"Heidi." Latson adjusts her weight on his legs. "This is Jen." He nods toward me. "Jen, Heidi."

I assume Pete told him my name. I like the way it sounds when he says it, but I don't like that he used it to introduce me to his girlfriend. He was just hitting on me. Are all the men I meet cheating pigs?

Heidi dismisses me with a flip of her hair and turns her attention back to her man. She whispers in his ear, and I roll my eyes and push myself off the couch. I take a few steps before Latson says, "Wait."

I turn to see him slide Heidi off his lap. She looks pissed. He walks over to stand in front of me. "Where are you going?"

"Away," I say.

"Why?"

"Because I just got rid of a cheater." I take another step. "And I don't plan on getting mixed up with another one."

~ ~ ~ ~

The following afternoon I find myself thinking about something I never considered before.

How to hurt Juliana.

Option number one: throat punch her. From the arc trainer next to mine, she's just the right height for my fist.

Option number two: pull the cord to her ear buds. When they fall, they might tangle around her feet and slow her down.

Option number three –

"You're doing great!"

Jules gives me an enthusiastic thumbs up and I give her a weak smile in return. I can't believe I let her talk me into going to the gym. I've never worked out before and trying to keep up with her pace feels like torture. When she introduced me to the arc trainer, she said the machine was great for cardio. She said nothing about the possibility of a having a stroke. I never run, and this machine is making me. Sweat runs down my forehead and down my back; hell, it even runs between my boobs. I glance down at the workout top Juliana made me borrow and frown at the growing stain. How is anything getting down there? The girls are pushed together so tight they look like I've had plastic surgery.

Finally the machine beeps, letting me know it's time to cool down after forty-five minutes of insanity. I look at Juliana. She fans herself and slows her steps. I slow down too, but my hands remain glued to the machine. They're sealed to the handles with a layer of sweat. I can't let go and keep moving. I'll lose my balance for sure.

Once we're finished I step off the arc on to wobbly legs. I grab my water bottle and chug. Juliana takes out her ear buds. "How do you feel?"

I swallow and wipe my mouth with the back of my hand. "Like road kill."

"Excellent!" Juliana gives me an energetic smile instead of sympathy. "Let's give your legs a rest and work on arms."

Oooo. Let's.

We walk over to the free weights, which happen to be stacked in front of floor to ceiling mirrors. Jules reaches for the five pound weights and hands them to me. Then, she grabs the ten pound weights for herself.

"Okay. Follow along in the mirror."

I do as I'm told and the whole time I question why. This hurts. As my biceps start to quiver, I assess my situation. I know Jules wants a workout buddy, but I'm not sure I'm the best girl for the job. Sure, there's a little extra junk in the trunk I could stand to lose. But I'm not a big fan of sweat. Or fatigue.

Or the cramp forming in my side.

I'm formulating a plan to break the news to Juliana when a guy walks up and selects a set of heavier weights. He steps back and places them on the ground, then reaches behind his head to stretch. The bottom of his t-shirt rises, revealing the waistline of his gym shorts and that deep V you read about in romance novels.

I miss a step following Jules. Holy abs, Batman. I start to reconsider my stance on working out.

By the time we return our weights to the rack, thirty minutes have passed. We've been at the gym for almost two hours; it has to be time to leave. Excited by the idea of a hot shower, I consider skipping to the locker room despite feeling tired. After I drain my water bottle, I ask, "Is it time to go?"

"Almost." Juliana starts to walk away. "There's another machine I want you to try."

Argh! "Are you trying to kill me?"

She laughs. "No. It's one of my favorite machines and it's rare to find it unoccupied. Let's go before someone claims it."

Her ponytail bobs as she power walks to a piece of equipment in the corner. When we reach it I read the name: Hammer Strength Leg Press. To me, it resembles something out of the middle ages.

"This one is great for your quads and glutes," she says. "You sit here." She plants her ass in the seat. "Then, lean back."

Juliana looks like she's lying on the ground in a chair that's been tipped over. She raises her legs in the air. "You place your feet here," she sets her shoes against a rectangular black plate in front of her, "and push."

My hands land on my hips. "You look like you're at the gynecologist."

"Ha!" She laughs before unlocking the machine and completing two sets of ten reps. When she finishes, she pauses to breathe before doing more.

"Your turn," she says and slides out of the seat.

Feeling wary, I trade places with her. I mimic Juliana, and when I set my feet against the plate, my knees are a centimeter from my chest. I'm crunched into a ball. I grab hold of the handles to unlock the machine like she did, and the weight falls against me. I straighten my legs to push it back up.

Holy hell this is heavy.

"Good!" Jules encourages me. "Try to do ten."

I'm on number three when she looks up and gets sidetracked. "Oh, there's Carly from the salon. I need to see if she can switch shifts with me. I'll be right back."

Yes! There's no way I'm doing ten leg presses. Even though I finished with the arc a while ago, my legs still feel like Jell-O. I finish the fourth press, then let my knees fall against my chest to rest. This is crazy. I look up and notice the weight of the plate is written next to my toe. One hundred and ninety pounds. No wonder I can't do this!

After I breathe for a couple of minutes, I push against the plate to lift it so I can get out of the machine. It barely moves.

Oh no.

I try again, but my legs are so wasted I don't have the strength. Not even enough to push the weight an inch higher so I can lock it into place and crawl out. I wait a second and try again. Nothing happens, except my legs shake.

This is not happening.

I'm stuck.

I'm stuck in a Hammer Strength leg press!

I lay my head back and close my eyes. Okay. It's not a big deal. Juliana will be back in a minute and she'll help me. I just have to keep the weight from completely crushing my legs into my body. I can do this.

I can do this.

I can do this.

The weight grows heavier against my feet, and my thighs press uncomfortably against my ribs.

I can't do this!

My heart starts to pound. I will be the first person to be crushed to death in a leg press. I know it. It will make headlines.

"Looks like you could use some help."

Awww, hell. I know that voice.

I open one eye to find Latson standing over me. "What makes you think so?" I wheeze.

"Your face is beet red."

Shit.

Before I can ask, he steps forward and lifts the weight off of my feet. I lock the handles into place and roll out on to the ground. I don't care that the floor of the gym is infested with germs. I don't care that I'm lying on my side in too tight workout clothes in front of a hot guy. All I care about is the return of circulation to my legs.

Latson crouches down beside me. "Is it that bad? How long were you in there?"

I should lie and say an hour. "Only a few minutes."

He chuckles. "It's a good thing I found you."

"Are you stalking me?"

He smirks. "I joined this gym two years ago. No."

I decide to sit up and he helps me by pulling my wrist. Once I'm on my butt, I look at him. He's wearing navy blue athletic shorts and another plain white t-shirt. I grab the material with two fingers and pull. "Don't you own any other clothes?"

"What do you mean?"

"Every time I see you you're wearing a plain white tee."

He gives me the half smile with the dimple. "Sounds like you're the one stalking me."

I fight the blush rising in my cheeks. "Pfffft. In your dreams."

He tries to help me stand, but I manage on my own. As I brush my legs to get rid of any dirt, he asks, "Are you finished with your work out?"

I toss an irritated look at the machine that tried to suffocate me. "I'd say so."

"That's too bad. I could spot you." He smiles and takes a step. "You know, teach you to exercise the right way."

He looks casual, but his tone insinuates he's not talking about exercise. "I don't think Heidi would appreciate the lesson," I say.

Juliana comes up behind me. "How was it?" Then, she notices my company. "Ohhh. Hey, Latson."

"Hey." He crosses his arms. "Just so you know, I saved your friend from death."

"What?" She looks at me.

He snickers. "I'll let her explain. I gotta run. I need to get this work out in before the bar opens."

He waves and walks away as Juliana pins me with a stare. "What happened?"

I sigh. Of course he would mention my predicament. "Let's just say I need to work up to your level, Jules."

We start to make our way to the locker room when Juliana bumps my arm. "Look over there," she whispers.

"At what?"

"Latson."

Um, okay. My eyes sweep the gym floor when I spot him standing in front of the same mirrors Juliana and I used earlier. His back is to us as he balances a weight bar across his shoulders and squats. I can't deny it's a nice view. Muscular arms, tapered waist. Defined legs.

"Do you see it?" she asks.

"See what?"

"His ass."

My mouth falls open. "Jules!"

"I told you you could bounce a quarter off it."

I can't resist and sneak another peek. He bends at the knees again, causing his shorts to hug his body.

Yeah. You could probably bounce a lot more than a quarter off that.

Just then, his eyes find my reflection in the mirror. He winks to let me know I've been caught. I'm tempted to wink back, but I stop myself. He's involved with Heidi. Instead, I stand there like an idiot and stare.

Great. In addition to stumbling and getting stuck in a leg press, I've embarrassed myself in front of him yet again.

"Let's go," I grumble and head toward the locker room.

Chapter Six

"Thank you, Tricia. I'll wait for your call."

I hang up with my insurance agent and look out over the blue water of Lake Michigan. I watch it lap the shore for a few moments before wiggling my feet and burying them further into the sand. The sun has decided to shine and turn this spring day into an anomaly. The temperature hovers near seventy-five degrees, which is high for this time of year. The city is taking advantage of the warm weather, and I'm one of hundreds on this beach. I thought it would be a good idea to get out of Pete's apartment, explore a bit, and recover from my gym experience.

I also thought it would be a good idea to spend some time alone. I know I've only been here two days, but if I'm going to relax and "do me," I should start sooner rather than later. I'm not sure how long I'll be staying in Chicago without obligations.

My eyes scan the people around me and they land on a young mother, or maybe she's a babysitter, with a toddler to my left. They're wearing jeans, but building sand castles anyway. Farther down the shore a few high school kids toss a football and, past them, a couple stands near the water's edge. They grab my attention.

He's wearing a suit. She's wearing denim capris and flip flops. She gestures with her hands and he reaches out, catching them to stop her. He studies her face, says something, then leans forward and, I assume, whispers in her ear. I watch her take a step back with wide eyes. It doesn't appear things are going well.

A seagull swoops low over the water and distracts me for a second. I glance at the bird, then back to the couple. They stare at one another. The man looks tired and the woman shakes her head. Then, she wraps her arms around her waist and walks away. She heads in my direction, and I watch the man close his eyes before opening them slowly. I expect him to call her back, or run to her to make things right. Neither happens. When she's steps away from me, he turns and leaves without saying a word.

I feel awful for her. I know I'm jumping to conclusions, but, given my most recent dating experience, I feel like none of this is her fault. As she passes in front of me I ask, "Are you okay?"

She looks surprised I noticed her and stops walking. "My fairytale just ended," she says.

Her choice of words strikes me. I can sympathize. Before I tell her so, she brushes tears from her cheeks and continues on her way. I'm sure she doesn't want to discuss her life with a stranger.

My fairytale just ended.

I turn her statement over in my mind. Unfortunately, I know that feeling all too well. The feeling that something is meant to be, only it turns out the opposite is true. An image of my ex Kyle appears in my thoughts, and I pull my knees to my chest.

As much as I don't want to admit it, I truly thought he was the one.

For three years Kyle and I lived together in his cute little two bedroom ranch. It was my home for a long time, and I made the mistake of assuming it would be forever. I think it surprised him just as much as it surprised me when I walked out. I wanted a deeper commitment. A ring. When I brought up the subject he said he wasn't ready to take that step. I didn't understand why and I let my emotions get the best of me. Only after meeting Addison did everything become clear. As much as I wanted his heart, it never belonged to me.

Suddenly, inspiration hits. I open the notes app on my phone and start typing.

The sounds around me fade as a song forms in my mind. It comes to me quickly, faster than any song I've written before. Even the one I wrote for Kevin's wedding took longer than this. Probably because it was his gift and I wanted it to be perfect. Regardless, things can't always be perfect and this song won't be, but when I finish the lyrics, I fall in love with what I've created.

Standing, I wipe the sand from my jeans and find my shoes. I walk away from the beach and toward the sidewalk.

Thank you, mystery couple, I think. I can't wait to get to my guitar.

~~~~

"Heads up!"

A black t-shirt smacks me in the face.

"Hey!" I look at my brother. "What was that for?"

"We're short bartenders and I need your help."

"At work?" My face twists as I lean over to snag the shirt off the floor. "Why me?"

"Because you're great at it and I know you'd like some extra cash. Plus, it's Saturday. I don't want to leave you all alone."

"I'll survive," I say, although the idea of working appeals to me. More money has left my pocket than I anticipated. Juliana and I went shopping on Michigan Avenue the other day. It's hard to resist new clothes when someone gushes about how cute they look, especially when the outfit matches the new boots you just bought from Saks.

"Okay," Pete sighs. "We *really* need your help. A band is performing tonight and the bar will be packed. Both Mina and Maggie called off; they have the stomach flu or something. Gwen is the only one left and she can't handle it on her own."

"Why didn't you say so?" I straighten out the shirt in my hands. "Gwen I'll help. You on the other hand ... "

Pete rolls his eyes and I glance at the shirt. Scrawled across the chest, in fire-orange letters, is the word *Torque*. My brother wears a similar uniform, except his shirt has his first name on the sleeve.

Pete checks his watch. "Put that on. We need to get moving."

Leave it to my brother to wait until the last minute. "If I'm going to make any tips I at least have to comb my hair."

Pete sighs as I set my guitar down and leave the couch. I head to change, opting for black jeans to go with the black shirt, since I left my bartending skirts at home. In the bathroom, I brush through my hair and pull it back in a low, messy pony. I take a few minutes to fix my face and when I'm done, I have dark smoky eyes and pink, glossed lips. Hopefully this will be good enough for the atmosphere. I've never been to Pete's work before.

The drive takes us around thirty minutes with traffic. If the streets were empty, it would've taken us ten. Torque is located on the outskirts of a trendy area in Lincoln Park, or so my brother tells me. He said the bar started out small, but became popular by word of mouth. When we pull down a random side street and up to the entrance, the location is more discreet than I had imagined. Through the car window, I look up at the plain red brick building. Only a few tinted windows dot the exterior, and a small black awning stamped with the word "Torque" marks the door. No wonder this place relies on recommendations. How does anyone find it?

As Pete rolls to a stop in front of the entrance, I unfasten my seatbelt. "Where do you −?"

My question is cut off when my door unexpectedly opens. I turn to see a surprised yet familiar face. Once Felix takes me in, he rearranges his features to look suave. "Mi amor," he purrs.

He extends his hand and I let him help me out of the car. Once I'm standing on the curb, I shoot him a saucy, "Muchas gracias."

He grins at me.

I hear the other door shut and watch Pete walk around the hood of his car. He tosses his keys to Felix. "My little sister is filling in. Please behave."

Of course he would emphasize 'little sister'. I roll my eyes. "I'm grown, Pete. You behave."

Felix laughs. "This should be interesting. Have you told the boss who you've hired?"

"Just park the car," Pete says.

My brother starts to walk inside and I follow. Is his boss going to be mad that he brought me? Over his shoulder, I ask, "Are you going to get in trouble? And why are you making Felix park your car? It's rude."

Pete holds the door open for me. "It's not rude. It's his job. He's a valet."

Oh. So much for my earlier cut-off question. I was going to ask where he parks.

"Besides," he continues, "I hired him. I can fire him."

"What?"

Pete ushers me inside. "I'm a bouncer, but I'm also a manager. That's why I needed to find someone to cover the bar. The schedule is my responsibility."

My eyes narrow. *"I don't want to leave you alone on a Saturday',"* I mimic his voice. "You're so full of shit."

He grins. "Hey. I didn't know if you would want to work while you're here. I haven't forgotten my tactics from when we were kids. Remember when I tricked you into doing my chores because I told you I'd split my allowance?"

"Yes," I snap. "You're awful. Convincing a six-year-old to clean toilets because you, Adam, and Josh couldn't hit the broad side of a barn when you took a piss. You told me a nickel was worth more than a dime because it was bigger."

He laughs. "I paid for it, though. Mom grounded me for a week."

This is true.

My brother stops walking and grabs my elbow. "Little J, you're really helping me out. If I had any other alternative, I wouldn't have dragged you down here. The last thing I want to watch is my friends hitting on you."

I'm confused. "Do you mean Felix? He's harmless."

"And Carter. And Latson. And God knows who else."

I give him an exasperated look. "I can hold my own. A little innocent flirting never hurt anyone. It can make a girl feel good, you know."

Pete scrunches up his face like he tasted something sour. "I don't need my friends making you feel good."

I roll my eyes.

"Jennnnnnn!" Gwen draws out my name and rushes to greet me. "I'm so glad you're here! When I called your brother to tell him about Mina and Maggie I almost cried."

My forehead creases.

"Let me show you around."

Gwen grabs my wrist and I let her lead me around Torque. As we walk, I realize the outside of the building doesn't do the inside justice. It's much bigger than it appears from the street, with two levels and an elevated stage in one corner. The décor is urban, with exposed light bulbs, pipes, and wood beams. Mismatched chairs and high top tables are sporadically spaced, and a large horseshoe-shaped bar extends to the center of the main floor. As my eyes trace the upper balcony that wraps around the entire room, Gwen catches me staring.

"There are couches upstairs and two private lounges," she says. "The only bar is down here, but people can order drinks from the waitstaff if they're sitting up top."

I nod as she leads me behind the massive bar. She points out all the essentials: ice machine, dump sink, soda guns, syrup connections, keg coolers. She crouches in front of a locked cabinet and pulls a key ring from her back pocket.

"Here's where we keep the liquor for set-up and stock if we run low. There's more in the basement if the night gets busy, which I think it will with Riptide here."

"Riptide?"

"The band that's playing tonight." She smiles over her shoulder. "They're local but they're popular."

Gwen opens up the cabinet and starts handing me bottles to fill the wells.

"Premium on the left, house on the right," she says.

We spend the next hour prepping our work space. We laugh and make small talk as we tap kegs, fill napkin dispensers, stock glasses, and slice lemons and limes. I get to see a little of the basement on a search for maraschino cherries, and, as we stand and spear olives, the band starts their sound check. I hate to admit that I've missed working a bar, but I have. There's something about this atmosphere that excites me. The music, the party, the people. I know my feet and my lower back are going to ache in the morning, but right now I couldn't care less.

"Well, lookie who's here."

Gwen is in the middle of giving me a cash register lesson when we're interrupted. I look away from the monitor. "Hey, Carter."

His eyes light up. "You remember me." He leans over the top of the bar and grabs a stir stick from the container.

"How could I forget the man who's trying to steal my brother's girl?"

He gives me a wry smile. "That's just me giving Jules crap. Pete and I asked her out at the same time on a dare. She flipped a coin to decide who to see first and he won. The rest is history. I never got my chance."

"Awww." I fake sympathy and pout. "Poor Carter."

"Poor me is right."

"What-*ever*." Gwen draws out the word and rolls her eyes. "This guy is with someone new all the time. Don't let him fool you."

I level my eyes at Carter. "So, you're a player."

"No. I'm a bouncer." He wiggles his eyebrows at me. "It's not my fault if the ladies need help getting home from time to time."

I laugh.

"Carter!"

My brother's voice carries from the main doors. "Let's go!" he hollers.

Carter sighs. "Duty calls." He walks backward from the bar. "Save me a shift drink, Little J." He smirks as he puts the stir stick in his mouth to chew.

Ugh! Why did Pete tell him my nickname? I step to the side to look around Carter and find my brother across the room. "You're in trouble Peter Frances!" I shout.

My brother's eyes get big. He hates his middle name.

No. He loathes it.

Carter turns around and starts to laugh. "Frances?"

Pete's scathing look meets a smug one of my own. Ha! He wants to share embarrassing things about me? Score one for Jen.

It's not long before the bar is packed and I'm running my ass off. Gwen and Pete were right. It's a busy night. When the band takes the stage at nine o'clock, I feel like I'm attending a big-name concert, not working a local club. Applause and whistles accompany Riptide's opening song, and the energy doesn't stop through the band's first set. Their music is good, rock with a bluesy feel, and I fight the urge to dance by timing my drink slinging skills with the beat. At one point, Gwen and I end up facing each other and realize we're doing the same routine. We laugh.

When the band takes a break, our business picks up. I'm busy pulling a draft when a guy pushes his way through the crowd and slaps some bills on the bar top.

"Hey, Sweet Cheeks."

I meet his eyes. "Excuse me?"

"I have something extra for you if you hurry it up."

He pushes the money toward me and I scowl. This isn't the first time someone has tried to bribe me to serve them before others. "Not interested," I say. "These people were here first."

I turn and hand the beer to the person who ordered it, earning a two-dollar tip. I start to take the next order when Jerk Face interrupts.

"C'mon." He moves into my next customer's personal space. "You look like you could use the extra cash."

Whoa. What? I pat the growing wad of bills in my back pocket and get sarcastic. "I have enough money without yours. Keep it up and I won't serve you at all."

A group of people is next in line and they witness our exchange. One of them speaks up. "Dude. Leave her alone and wait your turn."

I shoot him a tiny smile and try to take their order again.

Jerk Face gets obnoxious. "This is bullshit. No wonder I haven't had a decent drink all night. You have no idea what you're doing." He looks me over with disdain. "Who did you fuck to get this job?"

The words *Listen here, Pencil Dick* race through my mind. If I were at Jay's I wouldn't hesitate to rip into this guy, but I'm a guest at Torque. The last thing I need is for Pete to get in trouble for bringing his foul-mouthed sister to work, regardless if I'm right and the customer is wrong.

Before I can say anything, a girl standing by the bar defends me. "You're a real asshole," she says and then meets my eyes. "Do you want me to get someone?"

"No. I've got this." Stepping forward, I rest my hands on the bar and lean toward the Douche with cool confidence. "You think I don't know my job?"

He snaps, "Did I stutter?"

"Hmm. Right." I play like I'm unaffected and tap my chin. "How about this. Since you're so thirsty, I'll make your drink right now." I gesture toward my defenders. "If these people think I can't do my job, the drink is free."

"And if they can?"

"You pay double."

"I'm not falling for that shit. They're already on your side."

"Then I guess you'd better find witnesses of your own. The faster you come up with some, the faster you'll get served." I step back and move to take other orders again. "Or, you could just wait for Gwen to help you over there." I jerk my thumb toward the opposite side of the bar. "It's your call."

Jerk Face Douche, as I'm now calling him, curses under his breath. He obviously felt I was inferior and would cave to his belligerent attitude. Not so. I can tell he doesn't like being challenged by me, especially since my new group of friends is staring at him with satisfied smiles. He turns around and quickly grabs a couple of random strangers. He tells them about the bet, leaving out the intricate details.

"Good then," I say and wipe my hands on a towel. "What'll it be?"

"Dirty martini," he says with a smug look.

Really? I think to myself. Number one, he in no way, shape, or form looks like a martini drinker. He resembles a rugby player. Number two, his choice makes it obvious he's never made a martini. It may sound like a complicated drink, but it's not.

Before I start, I meet the eyes of my support team to my left. Entertained, they give me encouraging nods. I grab a metal shaker and toss it in the air. It flips around twice before I catch it with one hand and set it on the bar. I fill it with a few ice cubes, then grab a bottle of dry vermouth from the cooler. I look at Jerk Face Douche. "Shaken or stirred?"

His eyes narrow. "Shaken."

He doesn't know the difference, I think. I move my hand to the neck of the vermouth bottle and toss it behind my back, catching it over my shoulder with the opposite hand. This earns me a few "ooos" from my audience. After I add a splash of vermouth to the shaker, I pick up a bottle of gin and repeat my theatrics, this time tossing the bottle higher and in front of me. I add some olive juice to the mix, then shake everything together. I find a cocktail glass and strain the martini into it, raising the shaker high above the bar so the liquid pours out in a precarious stream. I don't spill a drop. For my final act, I pluck two olives out of their container and then step back a few feet. I toss them into the drink one at a time.

Plunk. Plunk.

My skills earn applause from both sides. Little do these people know I only learned to flip bottles to fend off boredom. If some of my past jobs weren't so slow, I'd never have practiced with coworkers.

Stepping forward, I lift the glass and hand it to my customer in complete smart-ass mode. "Your dirty martini. As requested."

Jerk Face Douche turns to his witnesses, sees their nods of approval, and knows he lost. He slams thirty dollars on the bar and yanks the glass from my hand, spilling half of it, and stalks away.

I grin. *Go me.*

As I pocket the cash and step forward to continue working, Gwen sidles up to my side. "Slow down there, Coyote Ugly," she teases.

She has no idea I was trying to prove a point. "I was putting an asshole in his place."

"Oh. I thought you were trying to impress the boss."

"Who?"

"The boss." She nods over my shoulder. "You know. Latson."

What? I turn around and, sure as shit, from the far side of the bar, Latson is leaning against the wall with his eyes fixed on me. For some unexplained reason my pulse starts to race. I mean, he looks like sex on a stick, but I feel like I've been caught doing something wrong. I was showboating a little. At least I was good at it and didn't embarrass myself in front of him for once.

I offer him a small wave before I get back to work. Instead of waving back, or even smiling, he pushes himself off the wall and makes his way toward me. Now my heart wants to beat out of my chest. I can't tell if he looks angry or determined. Am I not supposed to be here? Is this why Felix wanted to know if Pete told him I was filling in?

I busy my hands until he reaches me. When he does, I look up and force a smile. "Hey."

His eyes bounce from my eyes to my lips and back again. "Come with me. We need to talk."

Chapter Seven

Nervous, I glance around the bar. "Now? We're really busy. I can't leave Gwen." *And I'd rather avoid you if you're mad.*

Latson looks past me to see my coworker with her hands full. He nods. "Fine. But you're not leaving tonight until we talk."

I've never seen him this serious before. Hoping to break the tension, I salute. "Yes, sir."

He almost cracks a smile before walking away.

The rest of the night flies by. Riptide plays until the bar closes, and I'm running the entire time. When the last of the patrons are ushered out the front door, Gwen and I start cleaning up the bar while the band breaks down their equipment.

As I return from taking a trash bag to the kitchen, Gwen surprises me by shouting, "Round up!" to no one in particular. Seconds later Carter appears, followed by Felix. They take seats at the bar as my brother wanders over, along with most of the other staff. Pete sits down in front of me, and eventually Latson appears and joins a group opposite us. He glances at me before one of the band members taps him on the shoulder to ask a question. I give my brother a curious look. "What's going on?"

"End of the night tradition," he says. "Time to unwind before heading home."

I walk over to Gwen. "What do I do?"

She hands me a stack of plastic cups. "Fill these with ice water. Most people just want something wet while they talk."

I do as I'm told and place the cups on the bar top. Carter takes one. "We didn't get our shift drink." He fake pouts.

"We were too busy," I say. "I don't think anyone got a break."

"Did you see this girl?" Gwen drapes her arm over my shoulders. "She knows her stuff. I'd like to learn a few of her fancy tricks."

"Tricks?" Felix gives me a sly smile. "What kind of tricks? Queridos sexy?"

My brother elbows him. I laugh and clarify, "No, no dirty tricks."

"Lemme guess," my brother says. "You went all Tom Cruise in *Cocktail*."

"Had to." I grab a cup of water for myself. "I needed to prove I knew my job."

"And that's why I recruited you." Pete smiles. "How'd you do?"

"You mean money-wise?" I think of the stack of bills in my back pocket. "I'm impressed." I know I made close to three hundred dollars.

"Good. Now you can't be mad at me for asking you to work during your vacation."

"True. But I *can* be mad at you for telling Carter my nickname." I stick my tongue out at him. "I'd be careful while you sleep."

"Your nickname is cute," Carter chimes in. Then, he looks at Pete. "Frances though..." He makes a face.

Pete rolls his eyes, then asks for a draft. Gwen gets it for him. As I sip my water, I look around the room. Everyone looks so comfortable; no one is rushing to go home. People joke with each another; the valets talk with the waitstaff who hangs out with the kitchen crew. No one appears excluded. I always wondered why my brother never considered another line of work. Now I know. Even though I'm an outsider, it feels like a big family here at Torque.

Half an hour later, when Pete finishes his beer, he asks, "You ready to go?"

"Yeah." It's late. Standing still for the first time in hours has allowed exhaustion to creep in. "Let me get my bag."

I walk over to where I stashed it beneath the register, and Gwen finds me for a hug. "Thank you so much for helping tonight. There's no way I could have done it without you."

"You're welcome," I say into her shoulder. "I had fun."

"Me too!" she exclaims.

Pete and I say our goodbyes to Carter and Felix, and I duck under the bar to join my brother on the other side. We start to leave when he gets distracted by another coworker who wants to say goodnight. I decide to keep walking until, about half the distance from me to the door, Latson steps into my path. He sets his feet and crosses his arms, like there's a problem. My walk slows. He notices and smirks, then crooks his finger for me to come here.

My knees go weak. How can he make that gesture look hot?

Putting on a confident mask, I make my way over to him. He cocks an eyebrow. "Were you going to leave without talking to me?"

"Nope," I lie.

"Huh. It sure looked that way."

"I was just about to find you," I fib. "What is it you wanted?"

He tips his head and eyes me skeptically. He knows I'm lying. I hold his gaze because I don't want him to see me sweat, which turns out to be a bad idea. Those eyes are criminal.

Seconds pass before he finally says, "I want you."

I think my heart stops. "What did you say?"

"I want you," he says again and steps toward me. "I want to hire you. I know the best when I see it and I need your skills here at Torque."

"Jesus." I let out an exaggerated breath.

"What's wrong?"

"Nothing." I'm quick to recover. The last thing I need is for him to know I misunderstood his words. "Thanks for the offer, but I'm not looking for work."

He frowns. "Why not? Pete told me about your job and the apartment."

He did? "Then you know I'm only in the city for a little while. As soon as I can go back home I'm leaving."

"But, you don't know when that will be," Latson says. "I think you could do well here. Pete said you need to replace your things."

I can't help my twisted expression. "My brother has a big mouth, doesn't he?"

Latson ignores my question. "I'm not talking about a full time job. We're closed Mondays and Tuesdays as it is. After watching you tonight I thought –"

"You thought what?" Pete walks up behind us.

"I'm trying to give your sister a job and she's being difficult."

"You what?" Pete scowls at Latson. "No way."

I stare at my brother in confusion. Why would he care? "Excuse me? You're the one who told him about my personal life."

"Only to explain why you're here and why he's never met you before." He looks at his boss. "Jen can't work here."

"Why not?" Latson and I ask in unison.

Pete turns to me. "For the same reason I told you earlier. This was a one-time thing. I don't need anyone messing with you."

I didn't plan on getting a job while in Chicago, but having my brother deny me the opportunity is annoying. "Like I said before, I can hold my own. Who says I'm going to get messed with?"

Just as I utter those words, Carter playfully pulls my ponytail as he walks by. "See you around, Little J."

The three of us look at him as he sends a smile in my direction.

"See?" Pete complains.

Latson looks lost. "What's the big deal?"

"I don't want her to get hurt," Pete says.

"Who would do that?"

My brother pins Latson with a stare, as if he knows something I don't. Then, he elaborates, "Jen needs a break. On top of the fire and her job, she just broke up with her prick of a married boyfriend."

Gah! How embarrassing! "Shut up!" I whisper-yell at Pete.

My reaction doesn't faze him. Instead, he keeps talking. "She shouldn't work here." He turns to me. "If you want a job maybe Jules can help you find one."

"I never said I wanted a –"

"Is it true?" Latson cuts me off.

"Is what true?"

"Your boyfriend was married?"

I let out an exasperated sigh. "Unfortunately, yes. Can we not talk about it? I'm trying to forget." I narrow my eyes at my brother. "Thanks for bringing it up."

"Sorry," Pete mumbles, although he doesn't sound apologetic.

Latson's expression morphs into one of concern. Whether it's true empathy or a farce, I can't tell.

"You need a distraction," he says.

"Well, yeah," I concede. "That's why I left home."

He takes a step, then another and another, until he closes the distance between us. If he moves again, we'll be breathing the same air. He stares down at me, and I feel myself getting lost. Is this his idea of a distraction?

Because it's working.

"You're not the kind of girl who is easily swayed," he says. "You're going to do what you want to do."

I nod. He's right.

"You just admitted you need something to take your mind off things," he continues.

"I did."

"You *want* a distraction."

"That's what I said."

"Something to keep you busy."

"Yes."

"To forget about him."

"Right."

"So, you'll work for me."

"Okay."

Wait. What did I just say?

Latson's face lights up. "Excellent."

My eyes grow wide. "Hang on. I –"

"Dude. What the hell?" My brother steps between us.

"You heard the lady," Latson says. "I'm trying to help. She accepted my offer."

My brother faces me. "You honestly want to work here?"

Do I? I mean, I just agreed out of the blue. My eyes jump between Latson and Pete. My brother looks stressed while his boss looks satisfied. It's too early in the morning to deal with these two.

"You know what? I'm tired. I'm leaving." I start to walk away and Pete follows.

"Jen."

I turn around at the sound of Latson's voice.

"I'd like an answer."

The confident way he looks at me tells me he knows the answer. He's certain I can't refuse. The responsible part of my brain I've been trying to repress while I "do me" is fighting to take over. The part that says I'd be an idiot to turn down a good paying job. My reason for saying no was because my time in the city is limited. If Latson knows that and doesn't care ...

I meet his eyes. "When do I start?"

~~~~

For the last few minutes, I have been mesmerized by jellyfish.

I didn't plan to spend my day this way, but I can't say that I regret it. Hundreds of delicate, deadly creatures float in front of me, and I am in awe. They look fragile, but they're not. They are transparent, yet complex. They have survived for more than 500 million years without brains or bones or blood.

At least that's what the sign at the Shedd Aquarium says.

When I woke up this morning, I decided to get out and be a tourist. I had no idea where to go, other than away from Pete's apartment. Since I accepted Latson's job offer my lazy days are numbered. I start work in forty-eight hours. I should have known my personality couldn't handle an undetermined amount of worry-free time.

As I continue along the glass wall that separates the sea life from myself, I'm thankful for the advertisement that brought me here. I never considered visiting an aquarium before, until I saw the sign on the side of a passing bus. The illusion that I am underwater with these creatures is relaxing and just plain cool.

"Um, excuse me?"

A small voice and a tug on the back of my shirt make me turn around. A little boy with a faux hawk and an Iron Man t-shirt stares up at me.

"I can't find my uncle," he says.

I glance around the area. "Where did you see him last?"

He points over his shoulder. "Back there."

I scan the exhibit space, expecting to see a frantic adult. Instead, I find relaxed people enjoying the display. His uncle must have gone to find security. At least, that's what I would do.

"I'll tell you what." I crouch down to the little boy's level. "Let's walk and find a nice security guard. I bet they can help us. Sound like a plan?"

He hesitates, then nods.

I don't want him to be scared, so I hold out my hand to introduce myself. "My name's Jen. What's yours?"

His fingers wrap around the tips of mine. "Oliver."

"Nice to meet you, Oliver." I smile and shake his hand. "I like your name."

He looks shy at my compliment before I stand to begin our search. There are exits at both ends of the exhibit, but I'm not sure which one will bring us closer to the main lobby. I decide to head in the direction Oliver pointed. Maybe we'll run into his uncle along the way.

"So, how old are you, Oliver?" I ask as we start to walk.

"Seven."

"Have you been to the aquarium before?"

He looks up at me. "Uncle Gunnar brings me every week."

Impressive, I think. "You two must really like fish."

"Yeah. The sharks are my favorite. Do you have a favorite?"

I think for a second. "I like the jellyfish. Oh! And the glow-in-the-dark seahorses."

Oliver crinkles his nose. "The sharks should be your favorite."

I smile. "Why?"

"They're like the superheroes of the ocean," he says. "There's good guys and bad guys, but mostly good." He looks serious when he gives me his reason.

"You're very persuasive," I say. "Maybe I'll change my mind when I see the sharks."

"You haven't seen them?"

"Nope. This is my first time here."

Oliver's soft brown eyes consume his face. He can't believe it. "You have to see them! I'll take you after we find my uncle. I can tell you about all the sharks, even the Great White. They don't have any Great White's here, but I know all about them. They're just like the one in Jaws."

The kid knows his predators. "You've seen that movie? Wasn't it scary?"

"Nah." He shakes his head. "All the blood was fake."

Alright, then. The music alone creeps me out.

We make it to the exhibit exit and head up the stairs to the next level of the aquarium. When we reach the top, I immediately spot two security guards having a discussion and point at them. "Let's go ask for some help."

Oliver walks with me over to the guards. When we get close, he grabs my hand, almost like he's nervous. I squeeze his fingers to let him know everything will be okay.

"Hi," I interrupt the men. "This little boy is lost. He can't find his uncle."

One of the guards leans down to look at Oliver. "I bet we were just talking about you. Is your name Oliver?"

"Yes," Oliver says.

The security guard smiles and then speaks into the radio on his shoulder. "Tell Mr. Latson we've located his nephew."

Wait...what?

A woman radios back. "What's your location?"

"Abbott Oceanarium North. At the stairs."

She responds. "He's on his way."

"Your uncle will be here soon," the other security guard tells Oliver. "Can you do me a favor, though, buddy?"

Oliver steps closer to my side.

"The next time you're anywhere with a crowd, make sure you stick by your uncle or your parents, okay? Not all people are as nice as this lady here." The security guard looks at me. "Thank you for your help."

"Of course," I say.

While we wait, Oliver starts to look around. He tugs on my hand. "Those seahorses you like are over there."

I turn around. "They sure are."

"Can we go see them?"

I look at the security guards. "Is that okay?"

They agree since we'll be in their line of sight. Oliver leads me over to the display and just as we get into a conversation about which color seahorse is the best, I hear a voice call out "O."

This is crazy, I think.

71

Oliver lets go of my hand and takes off. He runs toward Latson, who scoops him up and holds him tight.

"I told you never to wander away from me," Latson says against the top of his head.

"I know," I hear Oliver say, "but I was bored at the river stuff."

Latson closes his eyes and hugs his nephew. Tension leaves his body and relief takes its place. As I watch the two of them, my heart melts. I don't think I've ever seen anything so sweet.

When Latson opens his eyes, his brow furrows. He sets Oliver on the ground and crouches in front of him. "You scared me, O. You have to tell me when you want to see something else. If you run off again we're not coming back. Understand?"

Oliver looks at his shoes. "Yes."

Latson waits for his admonishment to sink in, then holds his fist out to Oliver. "Hey," he says.

Oliver looks up. He bumps his uncle's fist with his own, and all seems right again.

When Latson stands, he notices me. He does a double take and smiles. "Who's your friend?" he asks his nephew.

"That's Jen. She helped me. I told her I would take her to see the sharks. She has to like them better than everything else."

"She does?"

"Yes!"

"The kid is adamant when it comes to his favorite," I say.

Latson takes Oliver's hand and walks over to where I'm standing. "It sounds like you have a date with my nephew."

I smile. "I guess I do."

"How is that possible?"

"He's passionate about sharks. Besides, who could say no to that face?"

He chuckles. "I meant, how did he find you?"

I shrug. "Coincidence?"

"She looked nice," Oliver says. "That's why I picked her."

Latson tips his head and studies me. Then, he confers with Oliver. "I agree. She looks *very* nice. Not like a kidnapper at all."

I roll my eyes.

Latson steps toward me and asks, "Are you here alone?"

"Yeah. I figured I should see the city. You know, before I start my new job."

He gives me half a smile. "You'd better not be late."

Oliver pulls on his uncle's hand. "Can we go now?"

"Sure." Latson looks at me. "You ready?"

"Yep. I'm ready to be scared by *Jaws.*"

The two of them lead the way and I follow. As I walk behind them, I can't help but notice how similar they look. They have the same hair color, almost the same style, and they hold themselves in the same way. Their family genes are strong. An image of the kid's room I accidentally found at the party least week flashes in my mind. They obviously spend a lot of time together.

Latson looks over his shoulder. "Are you coming?"

"Absolutely." I catch up and ruffle Oliver's hair. "I don't make a habit of letting handsome men down."

"Really?" Latson grins. "I'll keep that in mind."

I shoot him an annoyed look. "I was referring to Oliver."

He covers his heart with his free hand. "That hurts."

Oliver laughs.

We make it to a set of elevator doors and stop walking. Oliver pushes the down button, and while we wait, Latson takes the opportunity to lean close to me. "Am I not handsome enough for you?" he whispers.

His breath warms my ear, and I try not to react. I refuse to swoon over his voice, his body, or his scent ... which happens to be amazing. It's crisp and woodsy, with a little citrus thrown in. What cologne is that?

Focus, Jen.

"You know you're covered in the looks department," I admit.

"Then what's the problem?"

He can't be serious. "Does the name Heidi ring a bell?"

"Yes," Oliver pipes up. "She's Uncle Gunnar's friend."

Whoops. Apparently I said that a little too loud.

"Thank you, Oliver," I say, satisfied. "Uncle *Gunnar* seems to have forgotten." It dawns on me that I now know Latson's first name.

More people join us to wait for the elevator, and Latson moves Oliver closer to us. He leans over again and says, "Why do you keep bringing up Heidi?"

I glance at him. "Because you're together."

"Who told you that?"

"No one. I saw the proof at your party."

Latson's confusion turns into a cocky grin. "I'm not with Heidi." He steps closer and brushes my arm with his fingertips. "Never have been, never will be."

Holy shit. It's hard to concentrate. I clear my throat. "Well, still." I look forward. "I'm your employee now, so ... "

The elevator door opens and we wait for the riders to file out. When we step inside, Oliver pushes the button for the lower level. More people enter the small space, and the three of us move over to make room. By the time the door closes, we're squashed in the corner. My back ends up pressed against Latson's chest while Oliver stands in front of me. I set my hands on the little boy's shoulders in an attempt to distract myself from the feeling of his uncle's hard muscles against my back.

As the elevator descends, Latson finds my ear again. "Do you have any more reasons to avoid letting me down?"

His breath against my skin causes heat to slide down my neck and leave goose bumps in its wake. I don't want him to notice, so I turn and peek over my shoulder.

"You're wearing another plain white tee," I sniff. "Obviously you don't own any other clothes. I can't be seen with you. Other than professionally, of course."

Latson laughs and I feel the vibration through my shirt. "You're going to have to do better than that," he murmurs.

His words sound like a dare.

Chapter Eight

Two days later, my brother leans over the bar above me. "Are you feeling any better?"

I finish tapping a keg and stand, holding my stomach. "Not really," I say. "What was in that pizza?"

Last night, Jules and Pete decided to forego the health food and introduce me to the world of Chicago-style deep dish pizza. It was all they promised it would be: thick, covered in chunky tomato sauce, and dripping with cheese. I'm not ashamed to say more than one piece went down without a problem.

"Just your standard stuff," Pete says. "Are you sure you don't want me to take you home?"

I know he would like that, seeing as how this is my first day as an official employee at Torque. "No." I shake my head despite feeling like my gut is digesting itself. "I don't want to make a bad impression."

My brother gets sarcastic. "I know the owner. You do, too. Latson will understand."

"Pete." I'm agitated because no matter what I do I don't feel good. "I've been lying around all day. Maybe if I move I will feel better."

Ever since I woke up this morning I've had this gnawing sensation under my ribs. It started out as a dull ache but got worse the longer I laid on the couch. Food doesn't usually bother me, so I'm not sure what is going on. All I know is that I'd like it to stop.

"Well, tell me if you change your mind," my brother says. "Carter can handle the door and the girls can handle the bar if you need to leave."

My eyes dart to my coworkers. Mina and Maggie talk while they set up. When Pete introduced us tonight I got the typical "new girl" once over. I've been in this situation before and I expected it; the last thing I need to do is leave early. I have to prove that I deserve the job I was given, even more so since I'm Pete's sister. Three main bartenders have been the status quo at Torque since it opened. Now that I'm number four, even for a brief time, I have to pull my weight. People don't like to have their hours threatened, especially when they rely on tips. Also, Pete let me in on some behind-the-scenes information: both of the girls calling off the other night didn't sit well with Latson. I'm sure they think he's looking to replace one of them, which makes my presence even more awkward.

I turn my attention back to my brother. "I'll be all right. This thing will pass sooner or later."

Pete looks uncertain. I shoo him away with a wave of my hand. "Don't you have somewhere to be? We open in, like, twenty minutes."

"Fine," he says and heads toward the main doors. Satisfied, I walk over to the register to count the change in the drawer. Just as I grab the stack of one dollar bills, a sharp pain flashes across my stomach. I double over as much as I can without anyone noticing.

Ouuuuuuch, I mentally groan. What is this? On my first break, I'm calling my mom. She'll know what to do. I know I'm an adult, but you never get over the need for motherly advice. Moms know everything.

"I've been thinking."

My head snaps up. Latson is standing opposite me wearing half a grin. "Did it hurt?" I ask.

"Funny," he says. He moves to the other side of the register, so he's closer to me. "Don't pretend like you didn't have a good time the other day."

"Who's pretending? Your nephew is adorable. I had a great time."

"Good."

After I got my full tour – and I mean *full* tour – of the shark exhibit, Oliver asked me to have lunch with him and his uncle at the aquarium cafeteria. While we feasted on chicken fingers and French fries, Oliver quizzed me on all the shark facts he taught me earlier. Then, we spent some time in the gift shop where Oliver tried to talk Latson into buying him a book about whales. Apparently he has all the books about sharks. When Latson said no, I fake pouted alongside Oliver until his uncle caved. When it was time to leave, Latson made a big deal about me following them home, which Oliver thought was hilarious until he learned I really am staying in the same building. When he found out I was neighbor Pete's sister, he hugged me. When that little boy's arms wrapped around my waist, my heart puddled for the second time that day. I don't think anyone has ever been that excited to be near me.

Another weird pain hits my stomach and I try to ignore it by shutting the register drawer. "So, about your thoughts?"

Latson steps back and takes off his leather jacket. He holds his arms out to the side. "Your reason for not letting me down has been negated."

Huh? I look at his shirt and it clicks. Instead of his usual plain white tee, he's wearing a navy blue one with white lettering.

"No pants are the best pants," I read, then raise an eyebrow.

"It's the truth," he says with a sexy smile.

I wish I didn't feel so shitty. I can't banter with him in this condition. All I can muster is a sarcastic, "Classy."

"You said nothing about class." Latson lowers his arms. "All you said was I couldn't wear white shirts."

"No. I said you shouldn't wear them all of the time."

"Stop trying to come up with loopholes." He walks up to the bar and sets his hands against the top. "You're out of reasons. Admit it."

I point at the word Torque scrawled across my shirt. "Still your employee," I say.

He smirks.

People start to enter through the front doors and they grab my attention. "Looks like I have a job to do." I glance over at Mina and Maggie to see if they're ready and catch both of them watching Latson and me. They have confused looks on their faces.

Great. Not only am I their manager's sister, it's obvious I know the boss.

Ugh.

I step to the side so Latson is out of my way. When I do, a horrible pain shoots across my belly. I clutch the edge of the bar for support as it crawls under my ribs and burns its way up into my chest. It hurts so much, I can barely breathe.

"Jen?"

I try to answer but I can't. All I can do is concentrate on taking short breaths as my body breaks out in a cold sweat.

"Jen. What's wrong?"

I have no fucking clue, but I think I'm dying. I try to send the message to Latson telepathically, because there's no way I can talk. A wave of nausea washes over me and suddenly the floor seems like a good place to be. My vision blurs as my knees buckle and I land on my hip behind the bar.

"Jen!"

I hear the scuffle of feet and feel someone grab under my arms before my head hits the tile. "Get Pete!"

I think that was Maggie. My eyes close. *God, I hurt. Make it stop.*

The next thing I know, I'm floating. At least it feels like I'm floating. I don't have the energy to open my eyes. I'm still trying to take little breaths, to try and keep my stomach and my chest from burning. It doesn't work. Nothing works.

"What happened?" It's Pete.

"I don't know. She passed out." Latson's voice is muffled and I realize he's carrying me. I hear a door. "Felix! Get my car!"

"Shouldn't we call 911?" Pete sounds panicked.

"Dorothy is faster," Latson says.

"You and that damn car. Jen!" Pete's voice is next to my ear. "Can you hear me?"

I nod because I can.

"What's wrong? Can you breathe? Open your eyes!"

I squint. "Stop yelling," I croak out. "My stomach is killing me. It hurts to take a deep breath."

"Is it the same thing as this morning?"

"Only a thousand times worse."

Latson holds me tighter, and I clench his shirt in my fist in response to the pain. Leave it to me to feel like I'm birthing an alien in his arms. I can't even enjoy the feeling of being held in them.

Before long I hear the rumble of an engine. Latson starts to walk and Pete stops him.

"Give her to me," my brother says. "I'm riding with you. Are you going to Mercy?"

"Yes," Latson says before handing me over.

I open my eyes as I'm jostled from one person to the next. Felix jumps out of a black muscle car and rounds the front, drawing my attention to the white stripes that run the length of the hood. "Is she going to be all right?"

"Estare bien," I mumble against Pete's chest. *I'll be fine.*

"Let's hope so," my brother mutters.

Latson opens the passenger door and pulls the seat forward. Pete sets me in the backseat. As he buckles me in he says, "You're killing me, Little J. You know that? You should have stayed home."

"So I could pass out all alone? No thanks." I wince. Damn pain.

Pete gives me a worried look. He knows I'm right.

The guys jump into the front seat and as soon as the doors slam shut, Latson tears away from the curb. "We'll be there in twenty minutes, tops," he says as he maneuvers through traffic.

I try to settle against the soft leather of the seat beneath me and pull my legs up to the side. Latson steers with one hand as he pulls his cell from his back pocket. He pushes a button and tells it to "Call Dad."

His phone responds. "Calling Dad."

"Are you sure?" my brother asks. "When's the last time you talked to him?"

"Two years ago," Latson answers.

~ ~ ~ ~

The lighting in the hospital room is dim. I blink to focus and search the walls for a clock. Hearing the slow tick, I find it by the television. It's almost two a.m. I've been here for seven hours.

My head rolls against the flat pillow and I look down. I still have my IV. I silently thank the nurse who injected the morphine into the tube to kill my pain. After that, I didn't care how many vials of blood they had to take. I didn't care that I had to put on a backless hospital gown. And I didn't care when they used the same tube to inject dye into my body for a CT scan. All that mattered was finding out what was wrong.

I look in the opposite direction and find Pete asleep in a chair beside my bed. His head is tilted at an odd angle, which makes his mouth hang open. If I had something to throw, I would totally try to make a basket. I lean over and tap his knee. "Hey."

His eyes fly open. "What?" He blinks. "You're awake."

"Yeah. Why are you still here?"

"Like I'd leave you." He straightens his body and yawns.

"Pete. I really appreciate it, but you can't sleep in that chair. You're three times its size. Go home. I need you to pick me up after surgery later."

He runs his palm over his tired eyes. "Nothing's changed, has it?"

"Not that I'm aware of."

I can't believe I have to have surgery. Stupid gallbladder. How can such a tiny organ cause so much pain? Apparently mine is inflamed and full of stones, one of which is blocking some sort of duct. It needs to come out. Thankfully the procedure is outpatient, and I won't have to stay in the hospital very long.

I smile innocently at Pete. "You're going to have to wait on me for the next five days. Instead of sitting here, you should make yourself useful and go to the store. I'll need plenty of apple pies and coffee."

"Nope." He leans forward. "You heard Latson's dad. You have to watch what you eat, at least for a while."

I frown. After my problem was diagnosed, I got a visit from my surgeon. Latson's father drew a diagram of what was happening, explained laparoscopic surgery, and told me how long it would take to recover. He was patient and reassuring. He also looked like an older, gray-haired, more distinguished version of his son.

"Why is it you listen to him but ignore me?" I ask Pete. "I told you to leave and get some sleep. Instead you chose to stay and remind me of my restricted diet."

"He's a medical professional," my brother says. "You're just my stubborn sister."

"Who you love," I say sarcastically.

"I ... " Pete's expression morphs from playful to serious. "I know I don't say it, but I do." He hesitates. "You scared me today. I'd be a mess if something happened to you."

I'm not sure how to react. This is a side of my brother I've never seen. "I didn't mean to scare you. Honestly, I scared myself."

I pull the blanket higher on my waist. "I'll try not to do it again, if that makes you feel better."

Pete smiles. "It does. Thanks."

It's awkward being emotional with my brother. Maybe he is finally growing up. He's a manager now, and his apartment looks different. I haven't seen him play a video game since I've been here. He's a health nut, and I've caught him staring at Jules like he can't live without her. Not that I didn't like the old Pete, but mature Pete is pretty awesome. Even if he is overprotective.

"Well," I say, "since I'm doing you the favor of not dying, could you do me a favor?"

"What's that?"

"Go home." I shove his leg. "Hug Jules. Get some rest. I plan on sleeping until they wheel me into the operating room."

He stretches. "Are you sure? I don't want to leave you if you're nervous."

I am a little anxious, but there's nothing he can do about it. "I'm sure. I'll see you tomorrow when they prep me for dissection."

He scowls. "That's gross. You're not a frog."

I grin. "I promise I won't *croak*."

Pete rolls his eyes.

"Hopefully the anesthesia won't make me sick. I mean, *green*."

"Stop."

"Just think. I'll feel *toad*-ally new again in a few days."

"Really?"

"Then I'll be able to *jump* right into work."

"You're pathetic."

I laugh. "I'll keep going if you don't –"

"Fine." My brother stands and holds his hands up in surrender. "I'm leaving."

"Say hi to Jules for me."

"Will do." He gives my shoulder a nudge before he walks toward the door. "I'll see you later. Go back to sleep."

"Okay. See you later."

The door closes behind him and I decide to get comfortable. I'm finally alone for a few hours. I've had someone poking, scanning, or talking to me since I fell over. I find the control pad that adjusts my bed and start to play with it.

"I forgot."

"Geez!" I jump as the door opens.

Pete points. "The nurse button is right there. Call them – or me – if you need anything."

I sigh. "I got it."

He waves. "Okay. Bye."

"*Gooooodbye,*" I drag out the word.

The door closes again.

That boy is worse than my parents. I pity his kids, if he ever has any. Which reminds me: I need to call my mom and dad before surgery. Pete called them when I was admitted, but I haven't spoken to them personally.

The door opens again.

"Now what?" I groan. "This is getting –"

Latson sticks his head inside the room and looks around. "Is he gone?"

My stomach does a little flip. "Yes," I say, uncertain. "Did you need Pete? He just left."

"No." Latson steps inside. "I came to see you."

Really? I take in my tall, handsome, tattooed neighbor-boss. He walks over to the chair my brother occupied and pulls it closer to my bed. "Is it just me or does Pete get weird when you're around guys?"

"He gets weird," I confirm. I gather my hair and pull it over one shoulder. I'm sure I look like crap with a capital C.

Latson gives me a lopsided smile and takes a seat. "So, how are you?"

"I'm good. Just a little clogged."

He laughs. "Sounds like a personal problem."

"It is."

"I hope it's nothing serious."

"Gallbladder," I explain. "Your father plans to take it out around noon."

Latson nods like he understands. "I'm sorry I left earlier. I would have hung around, but you had Pete. I knew you were in good hands."

I would never have expected him to stay and I find it odd he would think so. "I'm not your responsibility," I tell him. "You shouldn't apologize. You helped me so much."

Suddenly, it dawns on me how much. I remember the conversation from the car. "Have you really not spoken to your father in two years?"

Latson leans back against the seat with a resigned slump. "Yeah."

"Why?"

I realize I asked a very personal question when he lets out a heavy breath and runs his hand through his hair.

"I'm sorry," I say. "That is none of my business. In case you haven't noticed, I embarrass myself a lot. I trip, I get trapped in gym equipment, and I speak before I think."

He raises an eyebrow. "And you dance in your underwear."

My cheeks turn red. "That, too."

Latson leans forward and sets his elbows on his knees. "I'm kidding. You shouldn't be embarrassed about the dancing." He catches my eyes with his and smiles. "You're gorgeous."

Is it hot in here? I feel hot. I resist the urge to fan myself. "I don't know whether to thank you or punch you."

"Why would you punch me?" He looks shocked. "I complimented you."

"Because! You scared me that day. My goal wasn't to give you a free show."

"What was it?"

"To relax. Unwind. Be carefree. Forget."

"Did it work? I mean, until you saw me?"

"Well, yeah."

Latson looks impressed. "Maybe I should try it sometime."

84

An image of him doing the sprinkler or some other lame dance pops into my head. I laugh. "You'll have to let me know when the pressures of Torque get to be too much. I'll remind you about Stripper Therapy."

"It has a name?"

"It does now."

He chuckles. "I don't think I've ever met anyone who unwinds the way you do."

I shrug. "What can I say? I'm unique."

There's a knock on the door. Before I can answer, a nurse appears. "Oh, hello. I'm sorry to interrupt. I just need to check your IV." She rounds my bed. "Are you comfortable?"

"Yes," I answer. "Much better than when I first got here."

She smiles. She checks the tube taped to my arm and the level of fluid in the IV bag. "Is there anything I can get you?"

"A bacon double cheeseburger." Now that the pain has subsided and I've slept, I'm starving.

She shakes her head. "No food after midnight before surgery. I meant a blanket or an extra pillow. Or water. You can have that."

I frown. "Water it is then."

"I'll be right back."

She leaves and Latson watches her go. When the door closes, he turns to me. "If I could, I would sneak you in a burger."

I shift my weight in the bed. "I might have to take you up on that. I'm not supposed to eat like I used to, at least not right away. Pete's going to watch me like a hawk. I'm sure he'll have me eating tofu until I go back to Michigan." I make a face.

"That's no fun," Latson agrees. He pulls out his phone. "I've been meaning to get your number."

I'm skeptical and he notices. "For work," he clarifies. "But, now I have another reason. Covert ops." He flashes the one-dimple smile. "What is it?"

I want to give him my number. It makes sense. However, he's wearing a very non-business like expression. "This is for work only, right?"

"And the occasional smuggling of food," he says as he opens his contact list. He looks up at me expectantly and when I don't give him what he's waiting for his smile fades. "Why are you fighting my friendship?"

I try to answer and nothing comes out. I don't know what to say. There is no logical reason, other than Derek's cheating put a sour taste in my mouth.

A realization settles over Latson's features and his lips form a thin line. "You know, don't you."

His words are a statement, not a question. "Know what?"

"Who told you?" His tone is accusatory. "Pete? Or was it Jules?"

I'm lost. I can't answer him.

His eyes harden. "Or was it Google?"

Whoa. Where is this coming from? "I have no idea what you're talking about."

He stands. "Never mind." He shoves his phone in his pocket and turns to leave. "Let me know if you still want the job."

What the hell? Why is he mad?

He walks to the door and grabs the handle.

"Wait," I stop him. I'm so confused. "What just happened here?"

He yanks open the door. "Goodbye, Jen."

Chapter Nine

I pluck the guitar strings in a mess of notes. The lyrics I wrote at the beach came so easily. The music, on the other hand, is giving me a tough time.

"Everything okay in there?" Jules calls from the kitchen.

"Yeah." I lean over to look at my notebook and wince. "I can't seem to think straight."

"That's probably because you're hopped up on pain meds." She rounds the corner. "Are you sure you don't want something else besides green tea? Like food?"

I lift my pencil and shake my head. I'm sore. Five tiny incisions dot my stomach, ranging from my bellybutton to my side to just beneath my ribs. The thought of digesting anything makes me queasy. "I think I'll stick with liquids, at least for today."

Jules walks over and sets a steaming mug on the coffee table. "Well, you should try to get some chicken broth down later. Or one of those vitamin drinks Pete bought. You need nutrition."

I look up at her. I'd rather not choke down some chalky concoction, either. "I promise I'll eat tomorrow."

"Okay," she says as her eyes narrow. "Don't think I'll forget. While Pete's at work it's my job to take care of you." She takes a seat on the opposite end of the couch and tucks her legs beneath her. "What are you working on?"

"A song I came up with the other day. I was watching a couple and they were arguing. When the woman walked away, I asked her if she was okay. She told me her fairytale had ended. It struck me."

"I'll say." Jules reaches for my notebook. "May I?"

"Go for it."

I strum the strings while she reads my song. Since my mind doesn't want to come up with anything original, I start to play "Hey There Delilah" by the The Plain White T's. I hum the words and make it to the second verse before I realize the band's name reminds me of Latson.

Jerk.

I stop singing and just play. I don't know what got into him at the hospital. One minute everything was fine and the next he was pissed. Since then, I haven't spent much time awake to think about what he said. Do I still want the job? Honestly, I don't know. I don't know if I can handle working for someone who refuses to communicate.

"You're really good," Jules interrupts my thoughts.

I stop playing. "Thanks. I have fun with it."

"I'm sorry I can't help you with your new song." She slides my notebook back to me. "When it comes to music, I'm illiterate."

"That's okay." I smile. "You can be taught, though. Maybe you should ask Pete for a guitar for your birthday."

She tips her head, considering it. "I think the triangle would be better. Or the tambourine." Her eyes light up. "We could be a two-woman show! Jules and Jen. J and J."

I start to laugh, but stop because it hurts. "We could combine it and be Jenniferana. Or Juliffer."

"I like it." Jules grabs my notebook and rips out a clean sheet of paper. "I'm in charge of designing our album cover." She shoots me a sly look. "And hiring the roadies."

I get the feeling they would end up being Pete and his crew. "It's not like we don't know a bunch of guys," I say. I adjust the guitar on my lap. "Now all we need is a tour bus."

"Latson could help with that," she says as she sketches. "He has all kinds of connections." She looks up. "You know, he could help you write your song too, if you're stuck."

She must be joking. "I'm not that desperate."

Jules eyes me suspiciously and lowers her art project. "Do I detect a hint of irritation in that statement?"

I shrug.

"I thought you guys were getting along." She frowns. "Especially after you met Oliver."

"I thought so, too." I pluck a few strings. "But, he got all weird at the hospital."

"Weird how?"

"He asked for my number. When I hesitated to give it to him he got moody. He accused me of knowing something, but wouldn't tell me what it was. He said to let him know if I still wanted the job and walked out."

Jules chews on her bottom lip as I replay the conversation in my head. "He asked me if I found out from you or Pete. Then he accused me of Googling him." I scoff. "Like I would do that."

Jules sets her art project down. She leans forward to snag her phone off the coffee table. "Have you?"

"Have I what?"

"Googled him."

"No." I look at her like she's crazy. "I've been a little busy getting cut up and sewn back together. Why would I?"

Her expression tells me she thinks I'm the crazy one. "Two reasons. One, you know his first name. And two, he specifically mentioned Google. Aren't you curious?"

Now I am. "What are you trying to say?"

She flips her phone to me. "Here. Go for it."

"You're serious."

She nods.

Setting down my guitar, I start to type Latson's name, then stop. "I feel like I'm violating his privacy."

"Its public record," she says, then looks annoyed. "Although, most of the reports are false."

Okay. Now I need to know. I type 'Gunnar Latson' into Google and hit search. A sidebar pops up with pictures. I read the words beneath them aloud: "Gunnar Oliver Latson is an American musician best known as the lead singer, songwriter, and guitarist for the American rock band Sacred Sin."

My eyes snap to Jules.

"Keep going," she says.

I tap the link for the Wikipedia article. It says he was born in Peoria, Illinois, and he's twenty-eight years old. Further down, I find information on the band. Sacred Sin started as a garage band ten years ago, when Latson was eighteen. They hit mainstream radio a year later with their single "Easy", which I vaguely remember. I was sixteen at the time and wasn't following rock music. Back then, if it wasn't pop, it wasn't on my radar.

The website goes on to say the band was together for eight years, producing three albums and embarking on two nationwide tours. They broke up a couple of years ago.

"Why did they break up?" I ask Jules.

She gestures with her hand, rolling it in a "continue reading" kind of way.

I scroll down to a section entitled 'Personal Life'. "Gunnar Latson has been linked to supermodels Amberly Higgins and Vanessa Cromwell. He also dated professional beach volleyball player Kristi Owens and singer-songwriter Ariel Allyn."

I let out a low whistle. I assume one of his women was the reason for the band's demise. "Which one was the Yoko?"

Jules rolls her eyes as I continue. "In the spring of 2012, Audrey Latson, Gunnar's sister and band manager, died of a drug overdose leaving behind a five-year-old son."

I wasn't expecting that. A lump forms in my throat. Poor Oliver.

"The singer was granted temporary custody until allegations implicated him in his sister's death. Sacred Sin was dropped from their label, Snare Records, and a custody case was settled out of court. The terms of the settlement were never disclosed."

The news takes a moment to sink in. I lower the phone and look at Jules. "I know I just met him, but I can't believe he was involved in his sister's death. Which part of that was false?"

"None of it," she says. "Look up the other links. You'll see what I'm talking about."

I close Wikipedia and use my thumb to scroll through the search hits. Headlines like "*Sacred Sin Dropped Amid Controversy*" and "*Security Cameras Capture Gunnar Latson At Sister's Hotel*" catch my attention. Then, "*Agent Confirms Singer's Role in Manager's Overdose*" and "*Brother Sits Back and Watches Sister Die.*"

My stomach twists. "These are horrible."

I read further and it gets worse. "*Singer's Father Fights for Custody of Grandson – Accuses Son of Murder.*"

"Oh my God." I stare at Jules wide-eyed. "No wonder they haven't spoken."

"Are you talking about his dad?" She moves over to peer at the phone. "Yeah. It's not pretty. Yet ... " She pauses and cocks an eyebrow. "Latson broke his silence for you."

The weight of what he did settles on my shoulders. "Why?" I ask in disbelief. "Any doctor could have helped me."

"Apparently he felt you deserved the best. His father is the best."

My mind swirls. No one has ever put themselves out there like that for me. No one.

I hand her the phone. "I've seen enough."

She turns it off and tosses it aside. "Do you understand why he would assume the worst? He thinks you found out and hate him."

"First of all, I had no idea who he was to even think about researching his past. I was never a fan. Besides, even if I was familiar with the band, he's changed from those pictures." The few photos posted with the article showed a much younger and less tattooed version of Latson. Plus, he had a grunge look going on, with long hair that fell to his chin.

"Second, I'm not that judgmental. Obviously the allegations were false. He's not in jail and he gets to see his nephew."

"Correction," Jules says. "He has full custody of his nephew."

"See?" I point at her. "He shouldn't jump to conclusions. I never believe stories reported by TMZ."

"He doesn't know that," Jules defends him. "What would you think if your family turned on you? What's to stop him from thinking you would, too?"

"Because I'm Pete's sister and your friend. I trust you guys. You wouldn't let me around him otherwise."

Jules concedes my point with a nod. "Okay, maybe he did overreact. But, he's been through a lot."

"I see that now." I reach for the mug on the table and it pulls at my stitches. "Ow."

Jules hands it to me. "Once you're feeling up to it you should talk to him. Tell him I told you about his past. Working at Torque won't be easy if he thinks you're afraid of him."

I blow on the tea just in case it's still hot. "I would never be afraid of Latson. I've seen him with Oliver. He's a big softy."

"Isn't he though?" Jules squishes up her nose. "He's cute, talented, good with kids ... " She drifts off. "Husband material."

I almost spit out my tea. "Are you thinking of proposing?"

"No." She smiles. "But you might want to."

"Please. My track record is awful." I take another drink. "I'm not his type anyway. I'm neither a supermodel nor an athlete."

"But you're a musician."

I shake my head and ignore her. Then, a thought occurs to me. "Is this why Pete didn't want me working at the bar? Does he believe those rumors?"

Jules scowls. "Absolutely not. It has more to do with Latson's rock star past. Late nights, hard parties, trashed hotel rooms, groupies like Heidi. You get my drift."

My eyebrows shoot up. "Heidi was a groupie?"

"Was?" Jules pretends to gag. "She still is."

I try to laugh with my mouth shut so it won't hurt. I fail.

"I know! We should watch YouTube videos of the band." Jules stands. "I'll get my iPad."

She skips out of the room before I can stop her. I'm sure she's trying to bring out my inner fan girl. I should tell her only one singer makes me weak in the knees. Ed Sheeran. My Eddie. Well, technically he's not mine, but a girl can dream. If he showed up and asked me to run away with him, I would. He could teach me to play all his songs and sing me to sleep each night.

While Jules is gone I sip my tea like a good patient and stretch my legs out in front of me. My feet land by Jules' phone and my thoughts turn to what I learned. Not only did Latson lose his career, he lost his sister. That had to be devastating, especially to lose her to something like drugs, something that could have been prevented. I think of Oliver and my arms ache to hug him.

"What are you thinking?" Jules appears in the living room. "You look like you're lost in la-la land."

"I was thinking about Oliver. How could Audrey risk her life when she had a son? It makes no sense."

"I don't know." Jules gently pushes my legs over and takes a seat. "It was accidental, I'm sure."

Just then, there's a knock on the door. Jules shoots me a confused look and I shrug. She hands me her iPad and walks over to answer it.

"Speak of the devil," she says. "Mr. Oliver. What can I do for you?"

"I made a card. Uncle Gunnar said Jen wasn't feeling good. Mrs. Gibson helped me."

"He was adamant about bringing it down," I hear an unfamiliar voice say. "I hope that's all right."

"Of course," Jules says. "Come on in."

She steps out of the way to let Oliver and the woman inside. The couch is in view from the front door and Oliver's eyes light up when he sees me. "Jen!" he says and runs over. "I made this for you." He holds out a folded sheet of white paper.

I smile and take it from him. "Thank you. Is it a get well card?"

He nods. "I asked Uncle Gunnar if we could take you with us to the aquarium again and he said we couldn't because you were sick." He sits down next to me. "When will you be better?"

"Soon," I say. I look down at the card. The front is covered in multi-colored blobs that look like the letter S. They also have eyes. "Are these seahorses?"

He smiles. "Yep."

I open the paper and find "Get Well Soon Jen from Oliver" written in uneven capital letters. On the opposite side of the page is a blue fish. I can tell it's a shark by the crooked teeth.

"This is one awesome card," I say. How sweet is this kid? I wrap my arm around Oliver's shoulders and squeeze. "I feel better all ready."

He grins.

"Is this *Jaws*?" I ask and point to the shark. "He's scary."

"Nope. It's Bruce from *Finding Nemo*. Have you seen that movie?"

I shake my head.

"It's really funny," he says. He looks at the woman who brought him. "Can we watch *Finding Nemo* with Jen?" He turns back to me. "I have the DVD."

"I don't know about that," the woman says. "Your friend needs her rest."

Oliver's face falls.

"Actually," I say, "we aren't doing anything but sitting here. I don't mind if he wants to watch it. Jules?"

She shrugs. "Sounds good to me. I think we might even have some popcorn."

"I'll go get the movie!" Oliver jumps up.

"Hold on," the woman says. "I still have laundry to take care of upstairs. I'm supposed to be watching you, not these ladies."

"You can leave him with us, Mrs. Gibson," Jules says. "Go do what you have to do. He'll be fine here."

"You're sure?" she asks. "I don't want to impose."

"Absolutely."

Oliver leaves with his babysitter to get the DVD and Jules heads to find popcorn. "I'm making you chicken broth," she hollers to me from the kitchen.

Twenty minutes later Oliver returns with the movie. We hit the lights, get settled on the couch, and press play on the remote. Oliver sits next to me, sharing the bowl of popcorn with Jules as I now sip broth instead of tea. The opening scene shows a clownfish couple joking around at their new sea anemone home. They're expecting tons of fish babies. It's cute and playful, until tragedy strikes.

This is awful, I think. *We're not even ten minutes in.* I shoot Jules a worried look over Oliver's head. Should he be watching this? I know it's supposed to be a kid's movie, but come on. Oliver lost his own mother in real life. "O," I say. "I thought you said this was funny."

"It is," he says. "Just wait."

To the kid's credit, the story does get better as it progresses. Dory cracks me up, along with the surfer sea turtles. Oliver giggles uncontrollably at the sea gulls, then again when Nemo's new friends attack a little girl named Darla.

By the end of the movie I'm emotionally invested. I can't stop myself from tearing up. I glance at Jules and notice she's having the same problem. She wipes beneath her eyes as I try to blink my tears away. Damn Disney movies. Is it their goal to turn people into emotional wrecks? I remember when I saw *Bambi* as a kid. I was so scarred that I forbid my father to hunt that fall. Of course he didn't listen. When he brought home a doe I refused to eat the venison in protest.

When the movie ends, I look down at Oliver. He's sound asleep against my side. I could have sworn he was awake a second ago, when he scooted closer to me.

Jules gets up and turns off the TV. She glances from Oliver to me and whispers, "I'll go tell Mrs. Gibson the movie is over."

Oliver looks so peaceful I don't have the heart to wake him. "Tell her he's asleep. I doubt she'll be able to carry him. We'll take him home in the morning."

"You sure?" Jules asks. "I don't think you can stand without moving him."

I nod. "If you prop his feet up I think he'll slide down on his side."

Jules moves Oliver's legs and my idea works. He snuggles down into the couch cushions on his own. Jules finds a blanket for him while I stand and carefully stretch. I think about moving to my own bed, but don't want to leave the kid all alone. What if he wakes up in the middle of the night and freaks out when he's not in his room?

"I'm going to sleep out here," I tell Jules. "I don't want him to wake up and get scared."

"As long as you're comfortable." She gives me a warning look. "I don't need you busting a stitch."

She leaves to inform Mrs. Gibson of our plan and I head to the bathroom for another pain pill. After I drink half a glass of water, I crawl beneath the blanket I've been under all day and stretch my legs behind Oliver. Our heads are at opposite ends of the couch, so I can see his face when I lift my head off the pillow. By the time Jules comes back, I'm barely coherent. Pain medication, a healing body, and emotional cartoons don't mix. I'm exhausted.

"Good night," she whispers from the hallway. "Let me know if you need anything."

I wave with a floppy hand. "'Night."

~ ~ ~ ~

Around three a.m. something wakes me. I open one eye and look at the clock before lifting my head to check on Oliver. He's still asleep. I hear a door close and assume Pete is home. Slowly, I move from my side to my back to get comfortable, then close my eyes again.

Moments later, I can see light behind my eyelids. They flutter open. A shadow is standing over me, illuminated from behind. It takes a few good blinks to focus, and I realize it's Latson. He must have turned on the kitchen light. He wears an odd expression; one I can't place.

"What are you doing here?" I rasp in a sleepy voice. "Where's Pete?"

"In his room." He crouches down. "I came to get Oliver so you can go to bed."

"He's fine. Don't wake him."

Latson shakes his head. "The kid would sleep through an earthquake. Let me get him out of your way."

"He's not a problem," I say, but it's too late. Latson stands and scoops up his nephew, cradling him against his chest. The kid doesn't even twitch.

He takes a few steps, then looks over his shoulder. "Don't move. I'll be right back."

"Why?"

He doesn't answer. He leaves the apartment with Oliver and I'm left alone in the living room. I consider ignoring him and going to bed, but for some reason I don't. I'm curious to see what he wants.

I'm almost asleep again by the time he returns. When I hear the door open, my eyes meet his. He doesn't say anything. Instead, he walks over to me and moves the blanket. Then, he slides one arm under my knees and the other around my waist.

"What are you doing?" I whisper.

He picks me up. "Helping you. You just had surgery."

"I can walk," I protest, but wrap my arms around his neck anyway.

He looks straight ahead as he carries me down the hallway. I notice the muscles in his jaw tense, like he wants to say something but he's holding back. My guess is he doesn't want to be near me after our last conversation, but feels obligated because I spent time with Oliver. I try to relieve his conscience. "This really isn't necessary."

We reach my room and he sets me on the bed. He reaches for the covers and pulls them back. "Get in."

I roll my eyes, but do as I'm told. Once I bring the blankets to my chin, he starts to leave.

"Hey." I stop him. "Does this mean you're speaking to me again?"

He turns around with a resigned sigh. "That depends. Do you want me to speak to you?"

I prop myself on my elbow. "I shouldn't because you were an ass the other day. Just so you know, I did ask Jules about you, but only because of the way you acted. I had no idea about any of it."

He looks at the floor, then back at me. "And?"

"Yes, I want you to talk to me. And no, I won't be quitting my job."

His eyes lock on mine. He looks surprised, maybe a little relieved. "Okay," he says. He backs toward the door with a hint of a smile. "Goodnight, Jen."

"Goodnight."

He disappears down the hallway, and I carefully roll on my side to bury myself in the sheets. I'm glad we cleared the air. It reminds of my cardinal rule, to do what makes me happy. As my mind drifts, I recall Latson's goodbye and compare it to his goodnight.

I much prefer the latter.

Chapter Ten

"What? Your first day didn't kill you, so you're back for more?"

I look up at Carter as I pull the cork out of a bottle of merlot. It makes a loud *pop*. "Of course. You know I couldn't go another day without seeing your handsome face."

He grins. "You fit in here so well."

I wink.

"Seriously, though." He leans over the bar. "That was some pretty freaky shit last week. Are you sure you're okay?"

I nod. "I'm good as new, minus one unnecessary organ." And a few pounds, I mentally add. My appetite definitely took a hit after surgery.

Carter raises his hand over the bar top. "Well, I'm glad you made it."

"Me, too." I give him a high five.

"Did I hear the word organ?" Gwen appears at my side. "What are you two talking about?"

"Unnecessary things, like gallbladders," I explain.

"And kidneys," Carter chimes in. "You can live with one kidney."

"And lungs," I add, but then frown. "You can live with one lung, right?"

"I think so. I know you can survive with a partial liver," Carter says. "My uncle only has half of his."

Gwen looks over her shoulder. "I know I could make it with half of this ass," she complains.

I laugh as I glance at her butt. "I don't think your ass is an organ."

She ignores me. "Do you think I could get some of my butt fat sucked out and injected into my boobs?"

"You don't want that," I say and adjust my own. "Trust me. Some days I wish I could downsize these babies."

Gwen frowns. "Your boobs are perfect." She looks at Carter. "Aren't they perfect?"

He tries to hide his smile. "They look nice from here."

My expression twists, but not from embarrassment. "His opinion doesn't count. Men think all boobs are perfect. It's ingrained in their psyche."

"Whoa, whoa," Carter interrupts. "I beg to differ. All breasts are not made equal. Just like all asses are not the same. Gwen, here, happens to have a very nice ass."

"Thank you." She smiles.

"But, I see where she's coming from about her chest. Guys want a handful, or at least I do, and hers isn't –"

"Hey!" Gwen cuts him off by throwing a bar towel at his face. "Not nice!"

"Yeah." I glare.

"I'm just agreeing with her." Carter steps back. "She's the one who said she wanted to inject fat into other parts of her body."

"I'm *allowed* to say that," she huffs. "Not you."

"I thought you wanted someone on your side," he protests. "According to Jen all guys like all boobs. What I'm trying to say is – wait a minute." He stops.

"What you're trying to say," I finish for him, "is guys like boobs, period. They may have preferences, but they'll take what they can get. Hence, men think all boobs are perfect." I reach over the bar and sarcastically pat his arm. "Thanks for proving my point."

He looks speechless.

I turn to Gwen. "You, my friend, are stunning. Never forget it. There are plenty of men who will appreciate your body and not just settle for it. The hard part is finding one who wants your heart *and* your assets."

Gwen's expression softens. "I knew there was a reason I liked you." She hugs me. Then, she faces Carter. "You're lucky we're friends. Here's some advice: the next time a girl criticizes her body, just tell her she's hot and leave it at that."

Carter blinks. "How'd we even get on this subject?"

"We started to talk about unnecessary organs," I say.

"Whose organs are unnecessary?"

I look over to watch Latson approach the bar. This is the first time I've seen him since Oliver fell asleep with me on the couch. He's wearing another new t-shirt today. This one is red and says *I'm lost. Please take me home with you.* Although the statement is loaded with innuendo, I think about how I met Oliver and smile.

"Don't get these two started," Carter warns as Latson stops in front of us. "I'll be outside with Pete."

Latson looks confused as Carter walks away. "He said something stupid, didn't he?"

"He knows better now," Gwen says.

I grab another bottle of wine. Torque opens soon and we still have things to prep.

"Jen," Latson says my name. "I want to show you something. C'mere." He gestures for me to follow him.

"Are you sure? I still have set up to do."

"I've got it," Gwen says. "It's not much."

I set the wine down and, due to my healing torso, slowly duck beneath the bar. "I'll be right back."

She shoots me a knowing look. "Take your time."

I catch up to Latson's side as he walks. "What's going on?"

"Just something I thought you'd be interested in." He points at his shirt. "Did you see?"

"Yes," I laugh. "How apropos."

"I thought you might like it." He smiles.

We make it to the stage in the corner of the bar. It's set up for tonight's performance. Only a stool and a mic sit under the main spotlight, and a few guitars sit on stands in front of the house speakers. I trail behind Latson as he takes the stairs to the top of the stage. He walks over to one the guitars and pulls it off its stand. He turns around and holds it in front of him with two hands. "Do you know what this is?"

My eyes comb over the instrument. It's metallic mint green and rosewood, with a cream-colored pickguard and maple neck.

Holy shit. There's no denying that shape.

"That's a vintage '59 Fender Strat," I whisper.

He looks impressed. "You know your guitars."

I silently nod. Fender is an American rock icon. My fingers tingle at the thought of touching the strings. "Whose is it?"

Latson shrugs. "It's mine."

"You're kidding."

He shakes his head.

"Are you playing tonight?"

"Hell, no," he laughs. "Dean is. We played together in the Sin days. He's been working on some new stuff and asked to borrow a few things. Well, actually, his van broke down and his equipment is stuck somewhere on 94."

"That sucks. I hope he didn't leave anything like that on the side of the road."

"No, nothing like this." Latson lifts the guitar, looks it over, and then holds it out to me. "Want to try?"

Hell yes, I want to try! But, it's a $2500 guitar. And that's if it's brand-new-to-look-vintage. If it's really fifty-five years old, it cost thousands more. I take a step back. "I don't want to break it."

Latson sighs. "You won't break it."

"How do you know I even play?"

"I saw your acoustic when I picked up Oliver the other night." He closes the short distance between us. "I know Pete and Jules don't own a guitar. C'mon. You know you want to."

He flashes his panty-melting one dimple smile. Coupled with the instrument he's holding, it's too much. Way too much. I need a distraction. "Let me see it." I hold out my hands.

Satisfied, he gives it to me. As I pull the guitar strap over my head, I swear I feel dizzy. I'm holding a freaking vintage Fender Strat. The angels should start singing any minute.

He gestures toward the stool and I take a seat. I set the guitar across my leg and try to get comfortable. "Any requests?" I joke.

He flips a pick at me and, surprisingly, I catch it. "Impress me," he teases back.

Oh, lord. Okay. I'm holding a Fender. I should probably break out some Clapton. He's notorious for using a Strat. I rifle through songs in my mind. What wouldn't Latson expect?

Ah ha. I grin.

I position my fingers and effortlessly play the opening chords to "Enter Sandman."

"Metallica?" Latson looks suspicious. "You don't strike me as a metal head."

"I'm not," I admit, "but I can appreciate good songwriting." I tilt my head and think about what else to play until the song it took me the longest to learn jumps to the forefront of my mind.

I only intend to play through the first few lines of "Freebird" but, before I know it, one note morphs into the next. Latson doesn't stop me and his presence fades the longer I play. The spotlight shining on the stage is warm and bright, making the bar fall into darkness and my skin feel like I'm under the sun. I close my eyes and forget where I am; it's as if the only things that exist are me, the guitar, and the music. I'm not ashamed to say I'd stay forever in this spot if I could.

Despite my trance, halfway through the song, a metal chair scrapes against the floor and the sound pulls me back to reality. My hands still and my eyes spring open.

"Sorry," I mutter to Latson. "I got carried away."

He's looking at me like I've sprouted a third eye.

"Are you okay?"

"That was Skynyrd," he says like he can't believe it.

"Um, yeah." I start to hand him his guitar. "Thanks for letting me play. She's awesome."

"No." He pushes it back into my hands. "Keep going."

"With "Freebird"?"

"With whatever," he says. "I like watching you."

I raise an eyebrow, to keep my heart from racing. "You're the rock star. Shouldn't you be the one performing?"

He gives me a self-deprecating smile and doesn't answer. He crosses his arms. "So? What else you got? Who's your favorite to play?"

My face lights up and reveals my crush. "That's easy. Eddie."

"Vedder?"

"No. Not Pearl Jam. Ed."

"Sheeran?" Latson's mouth twists around his name. "Really?"

"What's wrong with Ed?" I defend my pretend boyfriend. "He's talented. He writes his own songs, he collaborates with other musicians, he –"

"He's a pansy," Latson goads me.

My mouth falls open. "He is not."

"Yes, he is."

"He's romantic! Not that you would know anything about that." My eyes bore into his. He can't mess with my Ed and get away with it.

"What did you say?" Latson steps closer and towers over me.

"You heard me. Garage band ex-rock stars don't know anything about romance."

I can see the wheels turning in his head. One side of his mouth quirks up. "That's what I thought you said."

He steps back and rolls his neck, as if trying to relax. "Enough about Ed. What else do you like to play?"

"Besides my music *boyfriend's* songs?" I stress the word.

He begrudgingly nods.

I readjust the guitar on my lap, then take a breath. I play the chorus of the new song I've been working on. The Fender must inspire me, because the next few chords I've been struggling with appear in my head. Yes! Finally. I play it one more time before I stop.

"Who was that?" Latson asks.

I smile. "Elliott."

"Who?"

I stand and remove the strap from around my neck. "Me. Jen Elliott."

"You wrote that?"

I nod.

Pounding footsteps pull my attention to the right as someone bounds up the stairs. "I need to know you," he says and makes his way toward me. He holds out his hand. "Dean McCarthy."

I take in his rugged looks. Mussed hair, five o'clock shadow. He must not have had time to get ready with the van breaking down. I tentatively shake his hand. "Jen."

"Is she new talent?" Dean asks Latson.

"Maybe," Latson answers. "I just heard her play."

"No. I was goofing around. Latson was nice enough to let me hold a classic." I hand him his guitar. "Thank you."

"How long have you been playing?" Dean asks.

"Since I was nineteen." That's when I inherited my brother Josh's guitar. He didn't want it anymore, and I couldn't let him give it away. I had always wanted to play, but he never had the patience to teach me. Plus, God forbid I touched his stuff.

"You're a natural," Dean says.

"Thanks."

People wandering in the front doors of Torque distract me.

"Shit!" I push past Latson. "I left Gwen alone and got stuck dicking around with you." I still haven't forgiven him for the Ed comment.

"It was good for me, too," he says.

Smart ass. I don't bother with the stairs and hop off the stage despite my almost-healed incisions. It's only a short drop. "I have to get to work. Nice to meet you, Dean."

"You, too," he says.

I speed walk to the bar and crawl underneath. "I'm sorry, Gwen."

"For what? Impressing us with your hidden talent? I swear we all stopped to listen to you. Well, most of us."

I frown. That's both embarrassing and weird.

She misunderstands my reaction as offense toward the people who didn't drop everything for the Jen show. "Heidi was the only one who wasn't impressed," she explains.

"Heidi? What's she doing here?"

"Dean's playing. He's a former member of Sacred Sin. You do the math."

"Ah." Cue groupies.

Some girls step up to the bar and order. As I make their drinks, I think. Apparently everyone at Torque is aware of Latson's past. After I start a tab for the girls, I ask Gwen, "Am I the only one who didn't know about Latson and the band?"

"You didn't know?" She looks shocked. "He only hires people he trusts. I'm surprised you got in."

"Well, I am Pete's sister."

She smiles. "Pete's a good guy."

As the night wears on, Dean blows me away with his set. He's an incredible guitarist, and it's a miracle he complimented me. The crowd is full of energy for him, even though it's not as packed as when Riptide was here. Everyone who came tonight easily fits between the bar and the stage, including Heidi and her entourage. She has five girls with her who are acting like they're here to see Elvis. I mean, I get it – Dean's wicked talented – but, they're dressed to the slutty nines, and they've even designated one of the waitstaff as their personal server for the night. Poor Kenzie.

"That's it!" She slams her tray down on the bar top. "If that red-haired bitch looks down her nose at me one more time I'm going to punch her! Or pour a drink over her head. She's asked me a thousand times where Latson is. *I don't know where he is.* What does she want from me?!" Kenzie lets out a frustrated breath and blows her bangs out of her eyes. "I need another Sex on the Beach."

I start making the drink. "I'm sorry. The night is almost over."

"Thank God. She'd better tip well or I *will* find Latson to straighten her ass out. She's got me running around here like her BFF's are royalty."

The crowd bursts into applause as Dean finishes a song. I look past Kenzie to see him nod thanks and grab a water bottle off the stage. He takes a big swig. I'm not sure if he's done playing or if he has a finale planned.

"Thank you so much, guys," Dean says into the mic. "You don't know how much your support means. This is a new road, but one I hope you'll travel with me. Branching out on your own is a scary thing when you're used to having friends behind you."

People whistle and clap.

"Speaking of," he looks around, "tonight was made possible by someone you might know. He's here somewhere ..."

The crowd goes nuts, especially Heidi and her friends. Latson appears from the side of the stage and walks toward Dean. He squints into the spotlight and holds up one hand in a wave. They share a manly one-armed hug before stepping apart and exchanging some words. I notice Latson has changed his shirt. He's back to the plain white tee. I have to admit it suits him. His tattoos stand out against the color, and he looks every part the rocker with his dark denim.

"What do you think?" Dean leans toward the mic. "Can we convince him to join me for a reunion? One night only?" He laughs.

People start to chant Latson's name. It doesn't take much convincing though, as he willingly grabs the Fender. The crowd goes ape-shit crazy.

"No way." Gwen grabs my arm. "He never plays." She meets my eyes. "Never."

Anticipation runs through me as Dean moves to the side and swings the acoustic he was playing in front of him. As he messes with the tuners, Latson steps up to the mic and grabs it with both hands. He says four words that put everyone on their feet: "This one's called "Easy"."

Holy hell. His voice. Amplified it's...it's... I look away from the stage.

I'm in so much trouble.

Dean starts to play, and Latson joins him. The crowd continues to cheer. The song stays instrumental for a few moments before I hear:

"It's supposed to get better, not worse
It's supposed to hurt less, not more
But I can't stop loving you
There's nothing I can do
Nothing about us is easy."

The song is a ballad, but it has a hard edge to it. A vague memory hits me full force. Yep. Summer of 2005. I walked in on my brother, Adam, making out with his girlfriend to this same song. Shirts were off, hands were places. No wonder I repressed it. Now, hearing the song live, Latson's voice is trying to make new memories for me.

"What do you think?"

I hear Pete over the music and the crowd. I find him, Felix, and Carter standing near Kenzie. As I glance around, all the employees I can see have stopped to enjoy the show. Gwen sings along, Kenzie sways, and Felix is playing air guitar. It makes me smile.

"I think it's great!" I shout to Pete.

He gives me a thumbs up, and I let myself be a fan.

When the song ends I clap with everyone else. Performing the song that started their career was the perfect end to Dean's show. The people can't get enough. I put my thumb and forefinger in my mouth and whistle. The sound is loud and sharp, and it carries through the bar.

As the noise dies down, I start to clean up. We'll be closing any minute. I move along the bar, grabbing empty glasses with my fingertips. With four in each hand I carry them over to the dump sink and start tossing out the used ice and drink stirs.

"Okay, okay. One more." Latson's voice echoes.

I hear shrill shrieks and assume they're from Heidi and her crew.

"This one ..." He pauses. "I didn't write this one."

I dump the last glass and stand up straight, curious. Latson pulls his guitar strap over his head and sets the instrument on its stand. He returns to the mic, then holds up a hand to block the spotlight shining on the stage. He squints as his eyes roam the room, until they find me.

"Today ... today I was told I know nothing about romance."

I freeze. I hear more shrieks for the word romance and a few boos for the awful person who told him that.

"I know, right?" He shifts his gaze downstage to the dissenters. "She's crazy," he mouths and makes a swirling motion with his finger. People cheer and his eyes land back on me. "So, this song is for that person. She knows who she is."

Oh no.

Latson takes the microphone off the stand and says a few private words to Dean. Dean nods and smiles, then starts to play. IIe strums and plucks the strings of his guitar in a familiar, upbeat tempo, and all the blood drains from my face.

I know this song. By heart. I know the chords. I know the transitions. I know when it was written and what album it's on. When Latson opens his mouth and sings the first line, I mouth it with him.

It's "Little Bird" by Ed Sheeran.

I'm rooted in place, my pulse keeping time with the music. As Latson sings he works the stage, his eyes occasionally jumping to where I stand. It's obvious he didn't just learn this song for my benefit. He anticipates each line and clips his words in all the right places. Ed is a pansy my ass! What a liar.

I decide to focus on that, his lie, to get through this without literally swooning. It's tough when he's singing about mouths reading truths, missing you, and lips tasting like strawberries. As long as he stays on the opposite side of the room, I should be fine.

He hops off the stage.

Fuck.

He tries to make his journey casual, by stopping every now and again to sing a few notes. As he gets closer to me I can't decide if I want to throw myself at him or hide. He focuses on my face, and it's obvious who he's singing to now. My eyes dart to Pete. His smile is rapidly fading.

I don't know what to do. The song is coming to an end and all attention is on us as Latson takes his final steps. He stops directly in front of me, and I think I might overheat. His chocolate brown eyes bore into mine as he sings the last line of the song. I can't breathe.

The crowd erupts in applause. They start to converge on Latson. He continues to stare at me as random hands pat him on the back for a job well done. Ignoring them, he lowers the mic and leans over the bar top.

"How's that for romance, Little Bird?"

Chapter Eleven

"I knew it was you," Gwen whispers. She's found me standing in the corner, in the farthest spot behind the bar.

"No shit, Sherlock," I respond over the rim of my cup. "Everyone knows it was me."

For this evening's round-up drink, I've opted for something with a little kick. The first time I worked here, I chose water for Torque's closing time tradition. The second time, I never made it that far. The third time ... well, I need something to calm my frazzled nerves. Or my raging hormones. I'm not sure which is higher.

"I meant I knew *before* he sang." She rolls her eyes. "You're the only one who would tell Latson he isn't romantic." She turns and glances around the bar. "What an insane night."

I follow her gaze. No one wanted the impromptu Sacred Sin semi-reunion to end, and my brother and Carter, amongst others, had a hard time getting people to leave. Now, an hour after closing, most of the staff has finally taken a seat. They've given up trying to throw Heidi and her friends out. They're busy at the opposite end of the bar, fawning over Latson and Dean while obnoxiously giggling.

Ugh. The giggling.

I take another drink.

"He doesn't look interested, you know," Gwen says.

I avert my eyes. "What?"

"Latson. He looks like he'd rather descend to the seventh circle of hell than put up with them."

I look at him again. He's talking to Dean, despite Heidi trying to weasel her way between his legs. He's sitting on a stool, and she keeps touching his knee. I mentally smile when he grabs her hand and shoves it away.

"You should go save him," Gwen suggests. "Put her in her place and claim your man."

I make a face. "He's not my man."

"Please." Gwen gives me a blank look. "Denial looks awful on you."

Pete approaches the bar. "Are you ready to go?"

I nod.

"What are you drinking?" He reaches out, snags my cup, and smells it. "Whiskey?"

"And Coke." I grab the cup back. "Is there a problem with that?"

He scowls. "You're not supposed to have either."

"I can eventually."

"Eventually is not a week after surgery."

I quickly down the rest of my drink. "Pffft. Surgery was eight days ago." Not only will the alcohol relax my mind, it will soothe the tiny twinges of pain I'm starting to feel. Maybe working a full shift tonight wasn't the best idea.

Pete shakes his head. "I swear ..." He starts to walk away. "I'm going to get the car."

"'Kay." I toss my cup in the trash. Grabbing my bag, I duck under the bar and notice my shoe is untied. I fix it, then stand. "See you tomorrow, Gwen."

She grins. "'Night."

Is something funny?

I turn around and run smack into Latson's chest. He catches me by my arm and his woodsy scent invades my senses. "Are you leaving?"

"Yes."

"I'll give you a ride."

What kind of ride?

Sweet Jesus. Did I just think that? "No," I say. "Pete's getting the car."

He steps closer. "I think we should talk."

I think so, too. However, in my periphery, I catch a glimpse of Heidi staring at us. "I think you're busy. You shouldn't leave your adoring fans."

He nudges my arm, pulling me closer still. "Forget them."

That would be easy to do, but whatever is going on here is already conspicuous enough. "You know I can't leave with you. Pete will bust a nut. We can talk tomorrow."

Latson looks uncertain, like I'm trying to brush him off. I'm not. I'm trying to avoid questioning stares and a lecture from my brother.

"I promise," I say. "Cross my heart and hope to die, stick a needle in my eye."

Latson wasn't expecting my rhyme and tries not to smile. "What are you? Seven?"

I shrug and he sighs. "I'll walk you out."

He lets go of my arm and sets his palm against my lower back, guiding me toward the door. I didn't expect his touch and his hand burns a hole through my shirt. I know he's held me in his arms before, but this feels different. This feels intimate and possessive, and I'm not the only one who notices.

"Bye Little J," Carter says as we pass him. He takes one look at Latson's hand and does a double take. "Or is it Little Bird now?"

Ah, Christ. "It's Jen," I say and keep walking.

Latson holds the door for me as we step outside. When we get to the curb and separate, he pulls his cell out of his pocket and looks at the screen. "It's after four a.m.," he says.

I nod.

"Four hours ago, today became tomorrow."

I'm confused. "What?"

Pete's car rounds the corner and Latson doesn't explain. As my brother pulls to the curb, he steps forward and reaches for the door. He starts to pull the handle, then stops. "Don't fall asleep when you get home."

My forehead creases. "I think I'll do what I want."

He opens the door an inch. "Today is tomorrow. You said we could talk." He meets my eyes with a sincere expression. "Don't fall asleep when you get home."

Now I get it ... and there goes my pulse. I have no idea what he's planning, but damn it if I don't want to find out.

He opens the car door, and I get inside. Pete pulls away as soon as the door shuts behind me. We make it one block before he asks, "Do you want to tell me what's going on?"

My head falls back against the head rest. "I wish I knew."

As Pete drives, I stare out the window and wonder what is happening. Latson has hit on me since the day I met him, but it's always been fun and something I could handle. Tonight went to a whole new level. He used music to get to me and it worked. Am I ready to have his babies? No. But the idea of playing house is starting to grow on me.

"He's not good for you."

I look at Pete. "You keep saying that. I thought he was your friend."

"He is," he gives me a warning look, "which means I know a lot about him. Just like I know Carter and Felix. Guys talk. Trust me. He's not for you."

"You need to elaborate." I cross my arms. "What are you saying? He's abusive? He's into drugs? He has a foot fetish? What?"

"No." Pete shakes his head. "Relationships aren't for him. I know you, and you're not into casual. He doesn't do long-term commitment."

"Long-term? Like weeks or like marriage?"

"Marriage."

I snort. "You're one to talk. Have you looked in the mirror lately? If marriage were the basis for a relationship, Jules should have left you years ago."

"What makes you think we're not married?"

"Um, because you're not." I look at him like he's lost it. "I don't remember a wedding."

Pete sighs as he turns the wheel. "That's because you weren't there."

I blink. "I'm sorry?"

He gives me a resigned look.

"You're married?!"

"Since March."

"How ..." My face falls. "Why didn't you include us? Mom and dad are going to be so hurt." *I'm* hurt.

"We had a scare," Pete says. "Jules found a lump. Cancer runs in her family."

My stomach knots. Jules looks so healthy. "Is she okay?"

He nods. "The tests turned out fine, but it was a huge reality check. We decided there was no point in waiting, so we went to the courthouse. I mean, why plan a party for a year when the important part of the day is the actual marriage?"

I'm stunned. I lean over and try to see his left hand under the passing street lights. "Where's your ring?" Come to think of it, I haven't seen one on Jules, either. I know I would have noticed a diamond.

"We don't have rings," Pete confesses. "Jules didn't want to discuss her health when asked why we did what we did. We've decided to keep it between us for a while. Things happened fast. No one knows we're married."

I frown. "That is unacceptable, Peter. Jules deserves a gorgeous ring, even if she's not wearing it." My eyes get wide. "And you need to get down on one knee and propose like a gentleman!" I shove his arm. "You were raised better than that, jerk face."

"I know." He looks sheepish. "That's the favor I was going to ask you when I called a few weeks ago. Remember? I dropped the subject when I found out your life was falling apart. I was going to ask you to help me pick out a ring."

I smile. "Well, nothing is stopping us now. Let's do it soon. I want my sister-in-law to be legit."

"She is legit. I have the license to prove it."

"You know what I mean."

We turn into the parking garage, then get out of the car and make our way upstairs. Outside the apartment door, I grab Pete's arm and pull him into a lopsided hug. "I'm really happy for you. I love Jules. Mom and Dad do, too. I'm glad she's okay."

He hugs me back. "Me, too."

"Her proposal needs to be epic."

"I have some ideas." Pete steps back and puts the key in the lock. "But I might need some help there as well."

"Count me in." I grin.

He starts to open the door, then stops. "You deserve epic things, too, you know. That's what I meant about Latson. If you decide to get involved with him, I worry that won't happen for you."

I sigh. I've learned all things epic don't revolve around men. "If I were to get involved with him I would have no expectations." If my last two relationships taught me anything, it's not to bank on a future.

Pete looks like he disagrees, but lets it go. We head inside and say goodnight. When I get to my room, I shut the door and drop my bag on the floor. My brother is married. Married. It explains so much, like his mature behavior and concern about me. Especially when I was sick. I'm sure my health only reminded him of his wife's issues.

His wife. Gah! I love it. I can't wait until they decide to share the news.

Kicking off my shoes, I start to get ready for bed. I pull the rubber band out of my hair, shake my head, and hear three taps in the process. Glancing around the room, I wait and hear it again. It's coming from the window. I walk over and tentatively lift the edge of the blinds. Someone is standing on the fire escape. All I can see is a shoe and a knee, and I remember what Latson said. It has to be him. How did he get home so fast?

Opening the blinds, I crack the window. He crouches down with a mischievous smirk. "Come out here with me."

"Did you grow wings and fly?" I look over his shoulder. "Didn't I just leave you on a sidewalk?"

"I left right after you," he says. "Dorothy is fast."

I remember the name of his car.

"C'mon," he says and holds out his hand.

There's nothing to stop me. There are no prying eyes here, and I do want to talk to him. Pushing the window open, I set my hands on the sill and hop up. I get one knee on the ledge then reach out, so Latson can help me crawl through. He ends up holding both my hands as he pulls me to stand in front of him.

"I haven't snuck out a window since high school," I say.

"It's good to know you have a wild side."

"So wild," I joke and remove my fingers from his. I slide them into my back pockets.

He walks over to the edge of the fire escape, and I follow. He sits down, hanging his legs over the side. I sit beside him and do the same. The rough metal of the platform digs into my legs through my jeans, but I don't mind. Once my eyes catch the view of the sleeping city, I'm kind of swept away. The twinkling lights and the muted sounds hint at the energy it holds during the day. It's a different world up here in the dark.

"Where are your shoes?"

I stop my swinging legs and look at my socks. "I was getting ready for bed."

"I told you not to fall asleep."

My eyes swing from my feet to his face. "You're not the boss of me."

A slow smile takes over his features.

"What?"

"Nothing."

"Tell me."

Cue the dimple. "Well, you do work for me, so ... I am the boss of you."

He thinks he's clever. "Very funny. That title only applies inside the walls of Torque. Outside, I'm just Jen and you're just ..." I look him over. "You." *A very handsome, talented you wearing the Take Me Home t-shirt again,* my mind adds.

"I'm glad you said that." Latson moves over and ends up an inch closer to me. He produces his phone. "Can I get your number now?"

"Sure." I recite my cell. He enters it, then says, "I'll text you so you have mine."

I don't think twice about it.

As he's busy tapping letters, I look over the city again. "Is that what you wanted to talk about? You could have asked for my number through the window."

"I thought the fire escape would be romantic," he teases. "I am, you know. In case you didn't get the message earlier."

"No, I got it," I say. Every inch of me got it.

He puts his phone away. "So, what did you think?"

"Of the message?"

He nods.

I assume he wants me to tell him I dissolved into a puddle of goo, so I decide to mess with him. I let my voice get breathy and lower my lashes, channeling my inner Marilyn. "I ... I think ..." I turn toward him and slowly run one finger over the tattoos on his arm. "I think you're an amazing singer."

At first he looks puzzled, but then his confusion melts into satisfaction. I purposefully bite my lower lip and try to look seductive. He follows suit. His lowers his eyelids and stares at mouth, playing along. "Tell me how amazing I am."

"Soooo amazing," I repeat. I take my time trailing my finger back up his arm and pick up my breathing as I do. I lean forward, like I want to whisper in his ear. "I have something else to tell you. I can't keep it inside. Not anymore."

Latson meets my eyes and brings his hand to the side of my face. "Tell me, baby."

I arch an eyebrow and bring my lips to his ear. "You're a fucking liar."

He quickly leans back and I poke him in the shoulder. "Why did you pretend to hate Ed?! You. Don't. Mess. With. Ed!" I poke him in between each word.

Latson laughs and grabs my wrist.

"You suck," I say.

He pulls me close. "I've been told I suck quite well, actually."

It takes me a second to recover from his comment. I frown. "Talking about your sexual escapades will not get you into another woman's pants."

"Who's talking about sex?"

"You are."

He grins. "No. I was talking about popsicles."

I narrow my eyes.

"Look who has the dirty mind," he muses. "Maybe you're the one trying to get into my pants."

I need to redirect this conversation. "Fess up," I say. "Tell me about Ed."

He releases me a little. "I pretended not to like him because I could tell you did. It made you mad." He turns my wrist over and kisses the inside of it. "You're cute when you're angry."

What just happened?

I pull my arm from this grasp and lean back. "I'm cute when I'm angry? That's your excuse? I'd rather you think I was cute when I'm not pissed off."

"I already do, but ..." He winks. "Noted."

Okay. He's kissed me and called me cute. He can't be that desperate to hook up with someone. I'm sure Pete has warned him off me, just like he's warned me off him.

Latson changes topics. "Honestly, though. What did you think? You play. Could you tell I haven't performed in two years?"

I'm surprised. "No, not at all. You rocked that stage."

"Yeah?"

"Don't play dumb. You owned the crowd. If I had a quarter of the talent you have ..." I shake my head. "I wouldn't be standing behind a bar."

Latson looks intrigued. "You don't like your job?"

"It's not that. Bartending pays the bills."

"But?"

"But, it's not a career. I can't be seventy and slinging drinks from my Amigo."

He laughs. "Then what would you rather do?"

"That's just it. I don't know." I shrug. "Even as a kid, I didn't know. After graduation, I got a job at a diner and my future was written." I remember the constant questions from my parents and relatives. They always wanted to know when I was going to get a "real" job.

Latson nods in understanding. "I never knew, either. At least your parents didn't pressure you. Mine were set on Columbia, followed by med school. I dropped out after the first semester." He pauses. "Scratch that. I didn't even make it through the first semester. I only left the dorm for parties and band practice."

I raise my eyebrows. "I take it your dad wanted you to follow in his surgical footsteps?"

"He didn't think I'd amount to anything as a musician." Latson smirks. "I got to prove him wrong. For a few years, anyway."

I don't know what to say. I know his father is a sore spot.

"Have you considered playing?" Latson asks me.

"You mean professionally? No."

"Why not? You could do local gigs."

I laugh. "I'd never be able to support myself. No one would show up."

"I'd show up," he says and my pulse quickens. "You could always start at Torque," he adds. "The stage is yours. Just tell me when you want it."

I can't lie. Performing there would be a rush. However … "I don't think so. I'm nowhere near your level or Dean's."

"You underestimate yourself," Latson says. "You feel the music. It means something to you. Dean said it best: you're a natural."

Music does mean something to me. How many hours have I spent playing for fun, or to calm my nerves, or to forget something bad? "It's my escape," I confess.

Latson gives me a small, commiserative smile. "I know what you mean."

A few silent moments pass before he looks down, his eyes landing on my hand. The heel is pressed to the fire escape and my fingers are curled over the edge. Slowly, he reaches over and traces two fingers over my skin. It's the lightest of touches, yet heat blazes up my arm.

"You know," he says, "I have a room upstairs I think you might like."

Where did that come from? We were just sharing our pasts. I bite my lip.

"Do you want to see it?" he asks.

His eyes meet mine and they smolder. I never thought I would use that word, but it's the only word to describe them. They burn. He can't be asking what I think he's asking.

Can he?

"I … I still work for you," I stutter.

"You're still hung up on that?" His fingers travel to my wrist. "Outside of Torque, I'm me and you're you. You said it yourself."

Shit. My mind races. "Oliver's sleeping."

Latson's gaze goes back to his fingers, and his voice drops to a whisper. "So many excuses." He leans toward me. "Why don't you want to see my guitars?"

I snap out of it. "What?"

His pulls his hand away. "I have a room full of guitars upstairs." He raises an eyebrow. "What did you think I was talking about?"

I can't believe I fell for that. "You're an asshole."

He pretends to be shocked. "You were thinking dirty again, weren't you?"

"Ugh!" I jerk away from him. "You're impossible."

He laughs. "I couldn't help it. You dished it out first, so I had to give it back."

Whatever.

As my racing heart returns to normal, it takes my remaining energy with it. Working a full day after being off, along with the night's crazy emotional highs, has left me drained. It has to be after five a.m. by now. I try to stretch my back by twisting to the side. "My bed is calling me," I say.

"My bed is calling you, too."

I shoot Latson an annoyed look. "You can stop now." I start to stand. "Unless you want a zombie working the bar tomorrow, I need sleep."

Latson gets to his feet and follows me to my window. "We wouldn't want that. I can't hit on you if you're not in the mood."

I snort. "Why don't I think my mood would stop you?" I crouch down, sit my butt on the window ledge, and swing my legs inside.

Latson kneels down. "I meant what I said about performing. You'd be great. Think about it."

It would be impossible not to. "Thanks. I will." I hop down into my bedroom and turn around. "Have a good night. Or morning. Or whatever it is," I say.

He gives me a small smile. "You, too."

His legs disappear when I close the blinds. As I finish getting ready for bed, my phone beeps and I dig it out of my bag to silence it. I see Latson's earlier text:

Here is my number. You should save it under 'Ed' so you'll confuse me with your boyfriend.

He wants me to confuse him with Ed? I text back: *Ed doesn't like to share.*

Minutes later, after I've crawled beneath the covers, he sends another message.

Then you should dump his ass.

I text back. *For who? You? Pete said you don't do commitment.*

He replies: *I think I should start.*

Chapter Twelve

I scowl at my phone. I'm pretty sure I made the same face this morning when my brother farted during breakfast. I had to stop myself from asking Jules why she agreed to marry his gross ass, but I kept my mouth shut. She doesn't know I'm aware of their secret.

"Looks like there's a problem."

I stop reading Tricia's email and glance up. "Hey, Dean."

He takes a seat at the bar. "Everything all right?"

I turn off my cell and slide it into my back pocket. "My insurance agent has no news for me." I wipe my hands on a bar towel. "What can I get you?"

"Insurance agent? Were you in a wreck?" He settles on the stool. "I'll take a Two Hearted Ale, please."

"No. There was a fire at my apartment building." I walk over to the cooler and grab his beer. "I've been waiting to find out when I can go home." Setting the edge of the bottle cap against the edge of the bar, I slam my hand down to open it, then give it to him. "I've been crashing with my brother for the last three weeks."

Dean looks curious. "Where is home?"

"Michigan."

Latson walks up behind Dean and claps him on the shoulder. "We're still on for tonight, right?"

Dean nods as he raises his beer to his lips.

"What's tonight?" I ask.

"Small gathering at my place." Latson meets my eyes as he leans against the bar. "You're coming."

"I am?" This is the first I've heard of it.

"Yep. Pete, Jules, Gwen, Carter, Felix ... they'll all be there. When Dean's in town we hang out."

News to me. *Oh! I hope Heidi's invited*, I think sarcastically.

"What's up with your shirt?" Dean eyes Latson. "I've never seen you wear purple."

Latson looks down at his chest. Today he's sporting a dark purple tee that reads *Will do nude scenes*. "I thought you quit doing porn," Dean jokes.

"I'm trying to send subliminal messages to someone. She's being stubborn," Latson says.

Dean immediately assumes it's me and tips his bottle in my direction. "Could this be the same someone who doubted your romantic tendencies?"

"The very one."

My mouth falls open.

"You're working hard for this girl," Dean says. "Are you sure she's worth it?"

"She's starting to crack," Latson replies. "She has this weird hang up about me being her boss."

Dean shrugs. "Then fire her."

"Oh, I've considered it."

He *what?* I put my hands on my hips. "I'm standing right here."

They both ignore me.

"So, what time tonight?" Dean sets his bottle on the bar top.

"We close early, so around ten," Latson says. "Unless you want to leave now. I have some things to pick up."

"Sounds good. Let me finish this." Dean indicates his beer.

Latson looks at me. "Are you hungry?"

I glance over my shoulder to see if someone else is behind me. "Are you talking to me? I thought I was invisible."

"Yes, I'm talking to you."

I could use food, but I decide to get sassy. "Are you buying?"

"That depends." Latson tries to look innocent. "Are you putting out?"

I pick up the bottle cap from Dean's beer and throw it at him. It bounces off his shirt, under the word *scenes*. "Is that all you think about?"

Latson and Dean look at each other. Dean says "Yeah" as Latson says "Pretty much."

I sigh. Men.

Two guys approach the bar and I move over to help them. As they decide what they want, I hear Latson tell Dean, "She didn't say no."

Dean laughs. "Way to stay optimistic, bro."

By the time I finish with the guys, Latson is gone. I serve a few more drinks before Dean empties his bottle and sets it on the bar. I grab it as I walk by.

"You know," Dean says. "You should give him a shot."

I stop. "Why's that?"

"Because he hasn't fallen for someone in a long time."

I'm skeptical. "Nothing has happened between us to make him fall anywhere."

Dean gives me a pointed look. "Trust me. Something did."

"Um, Miss?"

A customer interrupts us for service, and Dean stands. "I'll let you get back to work. See you later."

Yeah, I mull over his words. *See you later.*

~~~~

After the bar closes, Pete and I head home to change and grab Jules for tonight's soiree. My brother doesn't bring up his feelings on the topic, and I don't ask. I'm not sure if he feels better about me spending time around Latson because of our talk, or because he'll be in attendance. Regardless, back at the apartment, I take a few minutes to comb through my hair until it lies in waves around my face. I touch up my lips and eyes before changing into jean shorts and my black White Stripes tank top. I want to look like I care, but not too much. This is the second time I've hung out with these people socially; they're becoming a bigger part of my life than I had planned. I'd rather they see me in something else besides the standard Torque attire.

When the three of us are ready, we head upstairs and Pete knocks on Latson's door. It cracks open, and one tiny, brown eye appears. It grows wide when it sees us, and Oliver throws open the door. "Hi!" He immediately reaches for my hand. "Jen's on my team," he announces as he pulls.

"Team?" I ask.

"For war," he states.

I let him drag me over the threshold, then look back at Jules and Pete. "War?"

"You'll see." Jules smiles.

I follow Oliver as we pass through the living room. I notice Dean and Felix are sitting on one of the couches, and Gwen and Kenzie are here as well. They say hi, and I wave with my free hand as Oliver keeps walking.

"O." I hear Latson's voice. "Don't forget to show her how to reload."

I look over my shoulder and catch a glimpse of Latson standing in the kitchen. He holds up what looks like a Nerf gun and gives me a challenging nod.

What is going on?

Oliver and I make it to his bedroom, and he shuts the door. I look around, remembering the action figures and the Minecraft poster. "Okay." He lets go of my hand and skips over to his bed. "I have almost every gun. I even have the Zombie Strike Crossbow."

He picks it up and shows me. "But it only shoots two darts at a time, so you'll probably want one of the other ones."

I look over the arsenal of Nerf weapons laid out on his comforter, then back at him. He's wearing a black tactical vest over his pajamas. The top half of the vest is filled with individual spongy darts, while the bottom holds two clips full of them.

"What's our mission?" I ask, playing along.

"We have to take out the other teams. We shoot at everyone else until we win. But, we can't shoot them in the face." He looks serious. "That's Uncle Gunnar's rule."

"It's a good rule." I pick up one of the guns. "It sounds like you two play this a lot."

He nods. "When Uncle Dean visits I get to stay up past my bedtime. When I was little we had Nerf wars at the hotels and sometimes on the bus."

He must mean the band's tour bus. An image of Latson and Dean chasing a giggling Oliver pops in my head, making me smile. Suddenly, I'm excited to kick some butt. I select the gun closest to me. "How does this one work?"

"Just pull the trigger." Oliver takes it and demonstrates. The gun whirs as a dart smacks the wall. It travels faster than I expected.

"This one uses batteries," he explains. "Some of the others are manual."

"I think I like this one," I say. "What happens when I'm out of darts?"

"Here's how you reload." He shows me the button to eject the clip and then shoves it back in. Then, he grabs another plastic rectangle full of darts and hands it to me. "Put this in your pocket."

I do as I'm told. Oliver hands me my weapon, picks up one of his own, and walks toward the door. He puts on his game face and turns the knob. "It's go time."

I stifle a laugh. This kid is so cute, it's ridiculous.

As we creep down the hall I realize the apartment is eerily quiet. Everyone must be lying in wait. Are they hiding or will they be in plain view? Can we run anywhere or are certain places off limits? I should have asked my seven-year-old partner these things before we started.

All of a sudden, Oliver drops to the ground and a bunch of darts whiz past my head. I duck and see Carter run from one side of the room to the other. I jump out of the way, pressing my back to the wall, as Oliver fires a couple rounds. What the hell? Where did Carter come from?

Oliver starts doing some sort of belly crawl across the carpet, and I crouch down as we advance. Once we're out of the hallway and into the living room, I can see where a few people are hiding. Jules' knee is sticking out from behind the loveseat, while the top of Kenzie's head is visible behind the breakfast bar. I'm just about to wave Oliver over to our right, when Felix jumps out of the closet by the front door and starts firing. My adrenaline spikes and I shoot a few darts in his direction without aiming. One of them hits him in the arm, while Oliver catches him multiple times in the shin. Felix yells, "Noooo!" as he makes a big show of crumpling to the ground. I realize this is all for Oliver, and I fight a grin. These people are awesome.

Over to our left Dean has jumped up, and he and Jules, along with Pete, are firing at each other and ducking behind the couch and the loveseat. Carter darts out from somewhere and runs into the kitchen; I'm trying to figure out who's on what team. Or does it matter? Gwen appears from the opposite hallway, shooting first into the kitchen as Carter and Kenzie spring into action, then at us as she skips out of the way. I fire back and hit her in the ass when she turns around. "I told you my butt was too big!" she hollers as she lies on the ground.

Laughing, I advance with Oliver and start shooting randomly at anything that moves. Nerf darts are flying everywhere. Latson makes a show of leaping into the room through the open balcony doors, and he starts firing like Rambo. Oliver aims for him and pulls the trigger, only to find he's out of ammo.

"Shoot!" he says as he reloads.

I squeeze off a few rounds but miss, discovering that I'm out of ammunition, too. I dodge my way across the room, barely making it to the opposite hall. I eject my empty clip, letting it fall to the floor, and put in the new one. I lean around the corner, prepared to fire, when I'm confronted with Latson a few feet from me.

"Ahhh!" I jump. I didn't expect him to be so close. I turn tail and run down the hallway, to avoid being shot at close range. Of course Latson chases me and shoots me twice in the back. Holy mother! Those little darts sting!

I turn around and start firing, not caring that I'm supposed to fall down dead. I'm not aiming; I just want to hit him. As he stalks toward me, I nail him in the chest, the stomach, and the thigh before I accidentally shoot him somewhere I shouldn't. He stops walking and winces, sucking in a breath and biting back a curse.

I freeze. Oh, shit.

I shot him in the balls.

"Are you all right?" I ask.

He stares at me through narrow eyes.

"I'm so sorry! I didn't mean it."

His mouth twitches.

"What can I do?"

He chokes out a laugh. "You shouldn't ask me that question."

I lower my gun and give him a stern look. "Are you really hurt?"

He stands up straight. "It was a dart, not a sledgehammer." He starts to walk toward me. "I'd run if I were you."

Aw, crap. I look around. There's nowhere to go unless I choose one of the doors in the hall. Even then, I'd still be cornered. I decide to cower against the wall and accept my fate. I slam my eyes shut and flinch. "Just shoot me and get it over with."

The buzzer from the intercom sounds, interrupting us. I open one eye as I hear Carter verify a delivery man is downstairs bearing take-out.

"Saved by food." Latson grins. "C'mon. Let's eat."

I relax and let out a breath. That was close.

We walk into the living room with our guns by our sides. People are crawling around on the floor picking up darts. I'm just about to help, when Latson turns his wrist and shoots me in the leg.

"Ow!" I yell and jump, shoving his arm. "That's NOT romantic!"

He leans toward me. "Neither is shooting me in the junk."

Before I can respond, he brings his hand to the back of my head and plants a quick kiss on my temple. My cheeks flush as a shiver runs down my spine. He leaves me to meet the delivery man, and I glance around. Did anyone see that? It doesn't appear they did.

"Good job, Jen!" Oliver comes running. He holds up his hand for a high-five. "We won!"

"We did?" I slap his hand.

"Yeah. I was the last man standing."

I smile. Of course he was.

It's not long before food is spread out over every kitchen surface. There are Coney dogs with all the fixings, chicken gyro sandwiches, fries, and onion rings, along with a grilled cheese pita for Oliver and a huge antipasto salad. I immediately go for that, since my gallbladder-less self shouldn't eat the other items in front of my health conscious brother. Despite my taste buds yearning for a gyro, I try to be excited about the lettuce.

"Excellent choice," Pete says as he stands beside me and heaps salad on to his plate.

"Yeah, yeah." I roll my eyes.

When Pete moves on, Latson takes his place. "Hey," he says, trying to be inconspicuous.

"Hey."

His eyes dart to a paper bag tucked in a corner by the refrigerator. "That's for you," he whispers.

I raise a questioning eyebrow.

He nudges my arm with his elbow, indicating I should check it out. I wander over slowly, taking a bite of my salad as I go. When I make it to the bag, I reach in and pull out a small container. I open the Styrofoam and my mouth instantly waters.

It's a bacon double cheeseburger. He remembered my hospital request before surgery. My gaze jumps to his. Is it wrong I want to hug him for buying me ground beef?

"Covert ops," he mouths and jerks his chin, telling me to find a place to hide and eat. I whisper a grateful "Thank you", then silently disappear from the kitchen. I balance my burger on top of my salad and lean over my plate to hide it. I make my way toward the balcony doors and slide outside in attempt to be stealthy.

No one joins me for a full five minutes. I enjoy as much of the burger as I can. To be honest, it tastes like heaven, but sits a little heavy in my stomach. I finish only half, which is enough, before Jules and Gwen decide to step outside for some fresh air. We talk about the summer weather, and then Jules moves on to sandals after noticing Gwen's cute purple wedges. During all of the talk, I try to think of something nice I can do for Latson. It was sweet of him to think of me.

"Jen," Carter sticks his head outside, "Latson and Dean are looking for you."

My brow furrows. "For what?"

"Jam session."

My interest is piqued. Jules and Gwen follow me inside where I spot Latson standing in the middle of the room. He's holding an acoustic guitar in each hand.

"There you are." He feigns ignorance as to what I was doing outside. "Here. We're going to entertain our friends."

I reach for the neck of the guitar and realize it's my own. "How did you get this?"

"I have a key."

My expression twists. "That's not stalkerish or anything."

He shakes his head. "I asked Pete to go get it."

I turn around and find my brother talking to Felix across the room. I catch his eye and point to the guitar, silently asking *"You went and got this?"*

He nods and shrugs.

I'm always down to play, so I find a seat on the couch next to Dean who is tuning his own instrument. "Are you sure you want me to join in?" I ask. "I'm not in the big leagues like you."

"You could be," he says, which makes me smile. I'll gladly take that compliment.

Latson sits across from us as everyone else, including Oliver, finds somewhere to sit or stand. He strums the strings of his guitar and looks up. "Any suggestions?"

Dean looks at me. "You know Skynyrd. How 'bout ..." He strums the first unmistakable chords of "Sweet Home Alabama."

Latson waits a moment then jumps right in. I wait until I can catch up. By the end of the first verse I'm there, keeping time and singing right along with them. Both Latson and Dean shoot me a look, but keep playing. Am I not supposed to sing? I keep going anyway. Halfway through the song everyone in the room is either clapping or singing along except for Oliver, who has no idea who Lynyrd Skynyrd is. We finish out of sync and sloppy, but our friends don't care. We still get applause.

"What's next?" I ask. This is way too much fun.

"You choose," Dean says.

I think for a few seconds, then start "Closing Time" by Semisonic. No one joins in, so I stop playing. "Do you know it?"

"I know who I want to take me home," Laston quips.

Smart ass, I think. I catch Pete giving me a questioning look; if he knew the song he'd understand. Still, I sass, "You're already home," and start the intro again. This time the guys join me, and when we get to the bridge, Latson kicks it up a notch. He rocks it with a louder, harder edge. It forces me to think faster and throw more of my upper body into playing, which I love. We end up locking eyes, and it feels like he's challenging me. I keep the pace and even manage to throw in a couple chord changes of my own.

This earns me an impressed nod, and I feel high. I've never played with anyone who loves music as much as I do.

We finish to more applause, although I'm sure these people would applaud anything Latson and Dean play. Dean holds out his fist and I bump it with my own. "Niiiiiice," he says, drawing out the word. "What else do you know?"

We toss around song titles for a minute before settling on "Wonderwall" by Oasis. This song plays out just like the last with Latson and I vying for the upper hand. Other than Dean, I wonder if anyone else notices the unspoken competition. It's as if we've stepped into a modern version of dueling banjos and Dean, like a patient parent, plays backup to our rivalry.

When the song ends Latson shoots me a wry smile. He shakes his head like I'm wearing him out, and I laugh.

"Can you guys play "First Love"?" Kenzie asks. "That's one of my favorites."

Latson looks at me. "I don't think Jen knows it."

"That's okay. I can sit one out."

"You're sure?"

I nod. "Go ahead. I've never heard it." *Liar*, I chastise myself. I downloaded all of Sacred Sin's music this morning. "First Love" is off their second album.

The guys get ready to start and I relax. I like to play, but I like to be entertained, too.

At first, I have no problem enjoying the song with everyone else. Then, around the second verse, Latson decides it would be fun to mess with me. He catches my eyes every time he sings certain words; specifically you, me, love, and tease. I try to avoid his gaze and find myself fixated on his arms, at the way his biceps flex and his muscles strain beneath his tattoos. I admire the way his fingers move on the strings and, the longer I stare at them, the more I imagine them moving over me. I close my eyes to erase the thought and then open them to see him giving me a sexy smirk. Am I that easy to read? It's obvious he knows what he's doing.

And damn if he isn't good at it.

By the time he finishes the song I've pictured him kissing me three times. It feels like the temperature in the room has gone up ten degrees. The guys decide to take a break, and I decide to head to the kitchen for a bottle of water. Singing has made my throat dry.

Okay. A certain someone's antics have made my throat dry. There's no use in trying to delude myself.

When I can't find any bottles on the counter, I open the fridge. It seems less intrusive than rummaging around the cupboards for a glass. I push a carton of milk and some orange juice out of my way as I search.

"Making yourself at home?"

I stand up straight. Latson is hanging on the refrigerator door wearing a "you've been caught" look.

"I just need some water."

He points to the bottom drawer. "In there."

"Thanks." I grab a bottle.

He shuts the door as I back away and twist the cap. He leans against the fridge in front of me. "That was a lot of fun back there." His eyes dart toward the living room.

I nod as I drink.

"We should do it again sometime."

I nod again.

"Except alone."

I swallow.

"And naked." He wags his eyebrows.

Oh my God. Really? I cross my arms over my pounding heart. "Haven't you realized it's going to take more than talk to get me naked?" Although, right now, this tank top is feeling like a snowsuit I'd like to rip off.

"A date it is, then. Tomorrow at seven. Don't be late." He gives me a confident nod and walks away.

I have no words. My throat is dry again. I take another drink.

I'm screwed.

Chapter Thirteen

What do you wear on a date with an ex-rock star?

I send Jules a picture captioned *How about this?* I've paired khaki capris with a flirty black top. It says "I'm fun," but in a reserved way.

Absolutely not, she sends back. *Are you going to a luncheon?*

That's the problem, I type. *I don't know where I'm going.*

It's true. All I know is I need to be ready at seven o'clock and I'm running out of time.

I wish I could be there to help, she sends. *Damn job. Let me see your dresses.*

I sigh and head over to the closet. I have two sundresses, both of which Jules talked me into buying the first week I was here. One is sky blue with a lace overlay, thin straps, and a sweetheart neckline. I would say it's beach wedding appropriate. The other is a deep red and gold paisley print, more bohemian, with a halter top and deep V-neck. Both dresses fall just above my knee and show off plenty of leg. I take a picture of each and send them to Jules.

#2!! She responds almost immediately. *There's some jewelry in the bedroom. See if my bangle bracelets are there.*

CARDINAL

I walk across the hall to Pete's room and find a jewelry box on the dresser. I pull out several bracelets, try them on, and decide on an intertwined set that looks like hammered brass. As I put everything back in its place, I'm grateful for Jules. Without her I'd be wearing shorts and flip flops tonight.

I pause to consider the thought. Maybe that's what I should be wearing. I mean, does a flirty dress send the right message? I have no idea what Latson hopes to gain from this date, aside from the obvious. Hell, I don't know what I'm looking for, either. What I do know is it never crossed my mind to back out. Whether I'm seeing him to tease him or for something more, I'm not sure. But, whatever it is, it makes me happy.

Cardinal rule.

About an hour later, and not a second after seven, there's a knock on the door.

"Punctual, isn't he?" My brother glowers over his glass. Of course he would make it back from the gym in time to harass me.

"You said you were okay with this," I huff as I walk past him. "I thought we were making progress." After last night's party, Pete conceded Latson and I do have something in common – music.

He finishes his protein shake. "That was before I saw what you're wearing."

I make a face. *God forbid you ever have a daughter,* I think. "I'm wearing perfectly acceptable date attire," I say. Sure, I'm not wearing a bra because my dress ties around my neck and has no back, but it's tight enough to keep everything in check. Other than that, I'm wearing Juliana's bracelets, strappy sandals, and my hair in loose curls. It's not over the top by any means.

When I get to the door, I compose my expression and pull it open. I expect to see Latson in all his cocky, t-shirt-wearing glory. Maybe he decided on one of those fake tuxedo tees to dress things up, or maybe he chose a plain white one to get me going.

I'm wrong on both counts.

Standing in front of me is one of the most handsome men I've ever seen.

Latson is wearing a lethal combination. Dark jeans. A fitted black tee beneath a black sport coat. Just trimmed, styled hair that looks like I ran my fingers through the front of it.

And his signature sexy smile.

He looks like he stepped off the pages of an Abercrombie catalog.

"Hi." His eyes drink me in. "Did you wear that dress just for me?"

"No," I tease him to calm my pulse. "This is how I always look on a Monday night." I glance over my shoulder. "Right, Pete?"

"Don't involve me in this," he warns from the living room.

I turn back to Latson. "Yes, I wore it for you."

His eyes darken and he loses a bit of his playful attitude.

" ... and any other guys we happen to come across tonight," I add. "I figure why not? Maybe I'll meet a hot waiter."

"I heard that!" my brother yells.

I smile innocently as Latson shakes his head.

It's probably not wise to stress Pete out with my comments, so I step into the hallway. "Bye!" I wave before shutting the door. I check the handle to see if it's locked and when I move to the side, Latson's hand brushes along the small of my back and lands on my hip. I try not to react as he ushers me toward the elevator. "Where are we headed?" I ask.

"To a restaurant I think you'll like." He pushes the button for the ground level. While we wait, he leaves his arm around my waist and runs his thumb over the bare skin just above my dress. He leans in close. "Unless the place has hot waiters," he whispers. "Then we're leaving."

I look at him out of the corner of my eye and try to breathe normally.

We make it to the parking garage where he opens his car door for me. "I'm glad you get to ride in the front this time." He smiles.

"Me, too," I say as I sit down and swing my legs inside. He rounds the back of the car as I look around the interior. I know nothing about cars, but I can appreciate a classic when I see one.

I'm busy running my hand over the cream-colored seat and inhaling the smell of leather when he gets behind the wheel. "What kind of car is this?"

"A 1970 Chevy Chevelle."

"She looks high maintenance. How long have you had her?"

"Since high school." He turns the ignition and she rumbles to life. "My dad saved her from the junk yard. It took us almost three years to restore her."

He backs out of the parking space, and I study his profile. It sounds like he and his father were close. He's never directly mentioned his mom. Is she still part of his life?

"Tell me about your family," I say, curious. "We should do the whole getting-to-know-you first date thing."

"Really?" He raises an eyebrow as he steers with one hand. "You don't know enough about me?"

"I know next to nothing about you." It's true. Internet aside, I know he owns a bar and he's good at sarcastic banter.

He sighs like he's humoring me. "What burning questions do you have?"

"Well ..." I tap my chin. "I know a little about your dad. When was the last time you talked to your mom?"

He looks both ways before pulling out of the parking garage. "A week ago Friday."

I like his answer. That was the holiday weekend. "Did you take Oliver to visit for Memorial Day?"

"No." He glances at me. "It was my birthday."

What? My eyes grow wide. "I missed your birthday? Why didn't anyone tell me?"

"You were recovering from surgery," he says like that's an acceptable excuse. "It wasn't a big deal."

It is a big deal. I'm sure everyone knew but me.

"What's wrong?" Latson asks.

"I wish I would have known. I feel bad."

"Why?" His tone turns suggestive. "What would you have given me?"

140

"Stop," I chastise him. "I'm being serious."

"So am I."

He grins and I shake my head. "Anyway ... what gifts did you get?"

"None." He stops at a light. "My mom thought it was her birthday."

I frown.

"She has dementia." He gives me a sad smile. "When I showed up with a cake she thought it was for her."

Oh no. "That's ..." I trip over my words. "I'm sorry."

"It's okay." Latson steps on the gas. "She lives in an assisted living home and she seems to enjoy it. She's not the same, but she's still my mom. A few times she's mistaken Oliver for me and me for my dad." He meets my eyes. "I don't mind, though, because it means she still remembers something."

I swallow the lump in my throat. "Does anyone else visit? I mean, do you have help?"

"I take O to see her once a month. My dad goes and sometimes Dean drops by."

That makes no sense. "Why would Dean visit?"

Latson slows the car and turns a corner. "My parents raised Dean. We were a foster family, and he was a placement."

I stare at him in awe. "That's so cool."

My response takes him by surprise.

"Your parents fostered," I explain. "I bet you had kids around all the time. Mine wouldn't even consider an exchange student."

He chuckles. "Yeah, well. There was never a dull moment."

"I would have given anything to have another girl in my house," I sigh. "Pete, Josh, Adam ... I love them to death, but all they did was eat and make messes. Both of my parents worked, so my brothers got stuck watching me. They didn't appreciate it. I spent many an afternoon playing Barbie dolls by myself."

Latson pouts with fake sympathy.

"All they knew how to cook was macaroni and cheese, pizza rolls, and toast. Sometimes the mac and cheese was served on the toast."

"It had to get better as they got older," he says.

I give him my 'oh please' look. "It did, but only because I got older, too. I didn't need them as much."

"Poor Jen. I know deep down inside they cared. Hell, they fed you. They could have let you starve."

I roll my eyes.

"And I'm sure they gave your boyfriends hell when they came over."

"As a matter of fact, they didn't," I say. "Pete and Josh were out of the house by then, and Adam was ready to leave. My dad was the one who stepped up for me."

"Good 'ole dad," Latson says as he makes another turn. "I can relate. Mine was really protective of Audrey."

I'm a little stunned he mentioned his sister. We've never discussed her, not that we've had the opportunity. I want to tell him I'm sorry about her too, just like his mom, but it feels like I'd be overstepping. I don't know if the topic of Audrey is, or will ever be, up for discussion.

Not much later we make it to our destination. Latson pulls to the curb in front of a valet stand, next to a sign that reads, "Geja's Café. Fondues and fine wines." A valet opens my door and helps me out of the car, while Latson rounds the front and hands another his keys. Once that's taken care of, he wraps his arm around my waist again, and we walk down a small flight of stairs to the restaurant.

"Fine wines," I muse. "Are you trying to get me drunk?"

"Possibly." I get the lopsided dimple smile as he opens the door. "Honestly, I was thinking more about the atmosphere when I picked this place."

We're greeted by a hostess who finds our reservation, then leads us through the restaurant to a table for two in the back. It's set in an alcove with thick, tapestry-like drapes flanking each side.

It's intimate, as is the entire restaurant. The room is candlelit, the tablecloths are a rich, deep red, and the walls alternate between old-style brick, red paint, and shelves upon shelves of wine. Spanish-style classic guitar fills the room, and it appears only couples are dining tonight. The place oozes romance, and I can see myself getting swept away if I'm not careful.

The hostess leaves us with menus as we settle in our seats. As I reach for mine, I wonder how many times Latson has been here. Specifically, how many women has he wined and dined this way.

"What do you recommend?" I ask as I open my menu. "I've never had fondue before."

"Never?"

I shake my head. "You must come here a lot. Name your favorite."

Instead of taking the bait and telling me, he picks up his menu as I continue to peruse mine. There are so many options and they all look delicious, especially the desserts. I want to try one of everything, but I don't want to order the most expensive item available.

"We should get the Premiere Dinner," Latson says, pulling my attention away from the chocolate covered fruit. I look up and my jaw drops.

"What are you wearing?" I blurt out.

"What?" He looks confused. He's leaning back in his seat wearing a pair of black framed glasses. They're just nerdy enough to be hot, especially on him. Paired with the jacket, the hair, and the lighting he's gone from Abercrombie model to Clark Kent.

"What's with the glasses?" I ask.

"Oh. They're for reading. The print is small." He takes them off and slides them into an inside lapel pocket. "I guess you're learning some of my secrets tonight."

"I guess so." I blink. I want to tell him to put the glasses back on. Not that he doesn't look good without them, it's just ... wow.

Our waitress appears and Latson orders the dinner he mentioned for both of us, along with a bottle of red wine. Once she's gone, he says, "I hope that's okay."

I nod. I was checking out what he ordered as he spoke. I've got four courses of deliciousness headed my way. "Is that what you usually get when you come here?"

"I haven't been here in years."

"Please," I scoff. "This isn't your go-to date spot?"

He frowns until the realization hits. "You're trying to figure out how many women I've fondued."

I laugh. "I don't think fondued is a word. But, yes, you're right."

A gentleman arrives with our wine. He presents the bottle, uncorks it, and then pours us each a glass. When he leaves Latson asks, "Do you really want to know how many women I've fondone?"

I smile. "Yes. I fondue." Don't ask me why. It won't do me any favors to know I'm one of many. However, I'd like to know what I'm getting myself into. After Derek, it's better to be safe than sorry.

"I'll only tell you if you tell me," Latson says. "You need to spill some secrets, too."

"That's fair," I agree. "I'm sure you've got me beat by a mile anyway."

He smirks, sits back in his chair, and starts to count in his head. He makes a show of it, squinting, then shaking his head no as he mentally adds and subtracts. I pick up my wine and take a sip. An image of him wearing nothing but his glasses and a pair of boxer briefs jumps in my head. *Hello.* I take another drink.

Then another.

And another. He's still counting.

Jesus. Does he need a calculator?

Finally, he looks at me and smiles. "I'm sorry to disappoint you. My answer is four."

"Four?" I set my glass down. "That's it?"

"What did you expect? I'm a guy from Peoria who owns a bar."

"You're also Gunnar Latson, lead singer of Sacred Sin, who dates supermodels and pop stars."

"Ah. You've visited Wikipedia."

"Well ..." I shrug.

"Listen." Latson leans toward me. "I'm not saying I haven't made out with a bunch of girls. Or messed around with them, or flirted with them, or thought about taking them home. What I am saying is, full-blown relationship wise, I've only been with four people."

I lean closer to him. "Then why is there a rumor going around that you don't do commitment?"

"Because that's what I said." His hand finds my knee beneath the table and gives it a gentle squeeze. "I have Oliver to think about. I'm not willing to risk committing to someone who only wants me for one thing. It will confuse him. Especially when it doesn't work out and they leave."

I pause. His words make sense. Latson has a huge responsibility when it comes to his nephew. "So, obviously, I'm in the 'thought about taking them home' category?"

"No." He squeezes my knee again. "You're in a category all your own."

Before I can ask him what that is, we're interrupted by our waitress bearing our appetizer. A tray of assorted breads and fruit is set on the table, along with a creamy cheese fondue. As I reach for a chunk of bread, Latson grabs my wrist.

"Nope. No food until you tell me how many."

"How many?"

"Guys," he says. "You agreed."

Ugh. He's right. I have to stop assuming things about him because, unfortunately, I've got him beat in this area.

"Six," I mutter.

"What was that?"

"Six." I look him in the eye. "The number that comes after five."

His eyebrows shoot up. I can't tell if he's shocked or amused. I feel the need to clarify. "There were two high school boyfriends, a couple mistakes in my early twenties, a three-year relationship, and then the cheating douche Derek."

Latson studies me like he's trying to solve a puzzle. Then, a slow smile spreads across his face. "You're full of surprises. You know that?"

I am?

He lets go of my wrist. "Thank you for being honest with me."

It never crossed my mind to lie. "It's all I've ever been."

He smiles again and reaches for a grape. "Let's eat."

~~~~

After dinner, back in the car, I know I ate too much. It was hard to resist all that food. In addition to the bread, we had salad, lobster, beef, chicken, shrimp, vegetables, and then chocolate dipped marshmallows and strawberries for dessert. If I ever go to Geja's again, I'll need to fast the whole day prior.

"I'm so full," I say as Latson drives. "Remind me not to eat tomorrow."

He laughs. "Do you want to go somewhere and walk it off?"

"Please." Not only does moving sound good, but I'm not ready for this night to end.

When we weren't tasting everything on the table, Latson and I were talking. He's easy – easy to get along with, easy to get sarcastic with, and easy on the eyes. We also share the same sense of humor. When I challenged him to a duel with my fondue fork, he didn't hesitate. Our little war earned us some annoyed looks from one of the more romantic couples, so we stopped fighting and cracked a few hushed jokes at their expense. From then on we engaged in more mature behavior.

Much more mature.

There's no denying there's chemistry between us. Not only did his hand find my knee more than once, his eyes found mine, his fingers found mine, and his thumb? It found the corner of my mouth when I had a little bit of chocolate left there. It's a good thing I don't have a heart condition, or I would have passed out when he traced my bottom lip before wiping the dessert away. I'm smart enough to know moments like that don't happen very often. Like I said, I'm not ready for our date to end because I'm curious to see what else might happen.

The longer we drive the more the city grows. The buildings get taller and the streets get busier. I vaguely recognize the area as the same route I took when I drove to the aquarium, although we don't make it that far. Soon, we're out of the car and walking toward Millennium Park.

"Have you been here yet?" Latson asks as we stroll along the sidewalk.

"No. My tourist stops have only included Shedd and the beach." I step closer to him to avoid a passing cyclist. "And the hospital."

He chuckles. "Yes. That's definitely a landmark."

We stop at a street corner to wait for the light. Other people join us and some continue around us as the red hand blinks and the timer counts down from ten. Dusk has settled over the city, yet it seems alive as ever. When traffic stops and our mob moves, Latson weaves his hand through mine to keep me beside him. We're headed toward two tall illuminated structures which, once we get closer, I realize are fountains. Water pours from the top of each tower into a large pool that extends between the two. Adults wade ankle deep as kids chase each other and splash around.

"In the daytime the fountains have faces projected on them," Latson says. "Water shoots out the middle, and it looks like the mouth is spitting. Oliver thinks it's hilarious."

"I bet." It would be fun to bring him here. I can see myself playing in the water right alongside him. We'd have a blast or, at least, I would. "The next time you guys visit let me know. I'll tag along."

Latson's hand tightens around mine. "You really like O, don't you?"

"Um, of course. Your nephew is the coolest seven-year-old I know." He's also the only seven-year-old I know. But, he's a good kid. He made me a get well card for crying out loud. Aside from wandering away from his uncle once, I've never seen him act out. Even when he was told to go to bed the night of the Nerf war he didn't complain.

"He thinks you're pretty cool, too," Latson says. "In fact, I think he might have a little crush on you."

Awww. How sweet. "You just made my day."

Latson stops walking. "Our date did nothing for you?"

"No." I bump his arm with mine. "I meant it added to my already good day."

He smirks and we round the fountain, passing by a building with a patio and outdoor seating. I assume it's a restaurant. Further along we come across a sculpture that looks like a giant metallic bean. I want to stop and take a closer look, but we pass by that, too. I get the feeling he's leading me somewhere. "Where are you taking me?"

"You'll see." He nods, indicating our stop is up ahead.

I follow his eyes and can't miss it. We're approaching a huge outdoor amphitheater. Exposed steel arches form a trellis over the most grass I've seen anywhere in the city. Gigantic pieces of metal that look like boat sails surround a massive stage to our left, and, in front of us, people use the lawn to enjoy the evening air. Some sit on blankets, others stand and talk. I catch a few throwing a Frisbee. We pass a sign that says we're at the Great Lawn, part of the Jay Pritzker Pavilion.

"Wow," I breathe as Latson continues to lead me on to the grass. We stop in the center, hundreds of feet from the stage.

He smiles. "Imagine what it would be like to play here."

"Have you?"

He looks down, then back at me. "Maybe."

"This is ..." I let go of his hand and take a few steps. "This is unbelievable. How many people can it hold?"

"Thousands. There are a lot of free concerts in the summer."

My eyes get big. "Did you say free?"

"I take it you'll be adding some entertainment to your tourist to-do list?"

"Absolutely."

I look around some more. It would be a thrill to play here. I hope Latson knows how lucky he is to have done it. I can picture the view from the stage – the crowd and the lighting. I can imagine the energy, hear the applause, and see a guitar in my hands. I can feel a pick between my fingers and sense the anticipation of striking an opening chord. My skin breaks out in goose bumps and I shiver.

"Are you cold?" Latson appears by my side. He starts to take off his jacket.

"No." I shake my head. "Places like this they..." How do I put it? I don't want him to think I'm weird. "Places like this give me chills. But good chills. Excited chills."

He steps closer, intrigued. "Why?"

"Because it's music," I say. "It's creativity. Its escape. It's sharing a piece of –"

Before I can think his hands are on me. One slides around the back of my neck while the other wraps around my waist. He pulls our bodies together, my palms landing against his chest, and he kisses me.

He didn't ask and he doesn't hesitate. He just kisses me.

All of the innuendo, everything he's ever said, is delivered through his mouth and his hands. I melt into him, clutching his shirt to bring him closer, and he responds by finding my lower lip and gently biting it. My knees go weak and I lose track of time. This is the best kiss I've ever received. Outside, under a warm, dusky night, in front of a stage with a handsome musician. My pulse races with the perfection of it.

When he pulls back he rests his forehead against mine. "If I don't stop now I won't."

I catch my breath. "Then why did you kiss me?"

"Remember when I said Oliver had a crush on you?"

I nod, biting my lip to suppress a smile.

"His uncle does, too."

Chapter Fourteen

It's like we just discovered kissing exists. My back is flush against the wall outside Pete's apartment as Latson's mouth leaves a warm trail up the side of my neck.

Earlier, when we left the park, I made him stop at the metallic bean so I could get a closer look. It turns out it's not supposed to be a bean at all but a sculpture called Cloud Gate. You can walk beneath it, and the mirrored surface distorts your reflection in all sorts of ways. The unique images didn't hold Latson's attention like they held mine; while I was looking up I saw him brush away my hair before I felt it. Standing behind me, he pressed a kiss to my shoulder, then glanced up and caught me watching him. His eyes held mine as he made a path with his lips, grazing my skin, to just beneath my ear. When his hands circled my waist and pulled me close, I couldn't take it and turned around to kiss him. Since we were in a somewhat secluded spot, we stayed there.

We stayed there until a security guard told us we had to leave.

Now, back at the apartment, we're all over each other again. His mouth leaves my neck and follows my jaw, and I push off the wall to get closer to him. As I slide my hands over his shoulders, I silently hope my brother doesn't appear. It makes me wonder why Latson stopped the elevator on Pete's floor instead of his own.

"Damn," he mutters against me. "I should have asked Diane to keep Oliver overnight."

"Diane?"

"Mrs. Gibson," he clarifies.

Oh. We're here because Oliver is home with his sitter. Since the sarcasm stopped once the kissing began I say, "That's okay. You weren't going to get lucky after the first date anyway."

He leans back, playful. "You're telling me if I asked you to come upstairs you'd say no?"

I'd so say yes. What is wrong with me? "That's right," I lie. "You have to work for it. The chase hasn't been long enough."

"Oh, really?" He zeroes in on my mouth. "I've been chasing you ever since you got here."

His admission causes butterflies to take flight in my belly just like they did when he confessed his crush. He places a slow, deliberate kiss on me, and my hand slides around his neck to keep him close. The other runs down his chest, over his stomach, and lands on the waistband of his jeans. He backs out of my reach, and my eyes fly open.

"Uh uh," he says. "You don't get to feel me up."

"I was feeling down, actually."

Latson groans, making me laugh. He steps forward and I step back. He sets his hands on either side of my head, against the wall, boxing me in. "I'm tempted to pick you up and carry you out of here."

My pulse pounds. That would be okay.

Really.

"But since our places are occupied," he leans forward, "I'm going to go home. So I can think of ways to chase you."

"Make 'em good," I tease. "I can run fast or I can run slow. It all depends on you."

He searches my face for a moment before flashing his sexy smile. "Little Bird, I don't care how fast you run. Just as long as it's toward me."

My heart doesn't know what to do with itself and I feel a little dizzy. He kisses me again, and a thought pops into my head. Dare I think it?

I'm sorry Ed, but you may have to move over.

When Latson walks away he does so slowly – and backward. "Goodnight," he says.

"'Night. Thank you for dinner."

"Anytime." He makes it to the stairwell door and cracks it open. "Don't stay up too late thinking about me. I'll be the one above you, all alone, in a big, cold bed."

He attempts a sad puppy-dog face and I laugh. "You're the one with a kid at home."

"You're the one with a brother."

Touché. "Go work on your chasing skills. I'll talk to you later."

"Count on it." He smiles before disappearing. I wait a few seconds and when I'm sure he's gone, I let out a sigh. A big, relaxed sigh. A slightly dazed sigh.

A holy-shit-this-night-was-amazing sigh.

I open Jules' clutch – yet another item borrowed – and hunt for my key to Pete's door. He had an extra made so I could come and go, and tonight I took it off my key ring because I had too many keys to fit in the purse. Where in the hell is it? There's, like, two pockets in here. I pull out my driver's license, my debit card, a little cash, my phone, and my lip gloss. I could've sworn I put it in here. Giving up, I put everything back and knock on the door. I impatiently tap my foot while I wait for Pete. When he doesn't answer, I knock again. He's probably asleep. I take out my phone to call him and when I hit the wake button, there's a message I missed:

I'm with Jules if you need me.

Great. I'm locked out. I start to dial his number when I remember someone else has a key. A certain someone I was just kissing.

I make my way upstairs with a smile. Latson will probably assume I'm lying to see him, but that's okay. Two can chase, right? When I reach the top of the stairwell I open the door only to hear voices. I stop short and peer into the hallway. Latson is talking to Heidi. I'd recognize that red hair anywhere.

"You came here to complain?"

"You had a party and didn't include me." She pouts and tries to set her hand on Latson's chest. "What's going on?"

He moves out of her way. "I thought Dean would have invited you."

"Well, he didn't." Heidi crosses her arms. "Has he found out if he's going on tour?"

"Ah," Latson snickers. "The real reason you're here comes out."

"Just tell me."

"No. He hasn't heard."

"If he goes will you go with him?"

"No."

Heidi tips her head and sticks out her hip. "It's because of that girl, isn't it? Julia or Genevieve or –"

"Her name is Jen."

"What-the-fuck-ever." She rolls her eyes. "Is that where you were tonight? With her?"

Latson looks irritated. "That's none of your business."

"It is," she insists. "You know I promised Audrey –"

"You didn't promise her shit." Latson stands to his full height. "You need to stop using that excuse."

Heidi tries to look innocent. "She was my best friend. I told her I'd look out for –"

"Stop." He cuts her off again. "The only one you've ever looked out for is yourself."

Heidi steps back like his words hurt. "I care about Oliver."

"No. You use him to stay close to me." Latson leans forward. "I've told you before. You need to stop hanging on to something that doesn't exist. The band is done. I'm not going back to that life; you won't get your minute of fame from me. Move on."

Heidi's back stiffens. "Did it ever occur to you that I stay close because you remind me of your sister? Because I miss her?"

Latson's laugh is sarcastic. "Maybe you should have thought about losing her before you did lines together."

Heidi's eyes grow wide. "That's not fair! When she and I ... you know it was once or twice. It wasn't a problem then. Levi is the one who ruined her, not me."

"And we all know who introduced them, don't we?"

"Why are you being so mean?" Heidi hisses. Then, her voice turns venomous. "It's Jen, isn't it? She's putting thoughts in your head because she doesn't like me."

"We've never discussed you."

"She's a bitch," Heidi says. "I can't believe you hired her and I can't believe you let her spend time with Oliver. Audrey would hate her."

Latson's eyes flash. He sets his jaw and steps into her personal space. "My sister would have loved Jen and you know it. I won't let you talk trash about her."

"You won't *let* me?" Heidi looks unimpressed. "You don't control me, Gunnar."

"But I do," Latson says. "Utter one more word about Jen and you can kiss following Dean's tour goodbye. All it takes is one call from me and you'll be thrown out on your ass so fast you won't know what hit you."

"You wouldn't."

"Oh, but I would."

Heidi's eyes narrow. "Fine. It's only a matter of time before you find out what she really is anyway. I'm just trying to warn you."

My mind reels. What does she think I am? We haven't said one word to each other since we met. The idea of her running her mouth when she knows nothing about me pisses me off. I think it's time to end this conversation and put her in her place.

Stepping into the hallway, I open the door with enough force for the two of them to hear it. Heidi quickly turns and Latson's eyes swing to me as I walk toward them.

"Speak of the devil." Heidi looks smug. "Eavesdrop much?"

"Only when I hear my name and bitch in the same sentence." I stop walking a few feet in front of her. "Is there something you would like to say to my face? Because I'm all ears."

Heidi looks shocked for a second. Then, she flips her color-treated hair over one shoulder. "You don't know who you're messing with, little girl. You're in my territory now."

Confusion creases my brow, and I glance at Latson. "What in the hell is she talking about?"

He lets out an exasperated breath. "I don't know." He brushes past Heidi and to my side. "What do you mean 'territory'? Are you an animal?"

I can't resist and clap my hands. "Oooooo! Are you going to piss a circle around Latson to claim him? I'd love to see that." I start to open my purse. "Hang on. Let me get my phone so I can take a video."

Latson covers a laugh as Heidi's face turns red. "You think you're funny?" she snaps. "Why don't you just tell him what you want and save him the trouble? Then we can all go on our way and pretend like you don't exist."

What have I ever done to this woman? Sure, I may have given her an irritated glance or two, but nothing to warrant her shitty behavior. "I don't know where you got the idea that I want something. I don't want anything." I look at Latson and his eyes dance. He's clearly enjoying this. My gaze falls to his mouth and I decide to mess with Heidi a little more.

"Wait," I say, holding up a finger. "I changed my mind. There is one thing I want." Reaching over, I grab Latson's shirt and pull him to me. I find his mouth with mine and press my body against his. He leans into my kiss and reciprocates, his hands sliding around my waist and down to my ass.

"Just like I thought," Heidi snipes. "You're nothing but a gold digging attention whore."

Latson's lips leave mine and he growls, "That's enough." He steps back and takes my hand, pulling me toward his place. "Go home, Heidi. If you want to know about Dean, ask him yourself."

Without another word he opens his door and ushers me inside. He lets the door close behind us, and I catch a glimpse of Heidi's angry expression before it shuts all the way. If she hated me before, she loathes me now.

"Well, that was fun," I joke. "I'm sorry, but I couldn't stand there and say nothing."

Latson walks toward me. "Why were you standing there?"

"I'm locked out. I forgot my key and Pete is with Jules." I reach for my phone. "See?"

He takes my cell and glances at the screen, then gives me a sly smile as he slides it into his back pocket.

"Um ... can I have that back?"

"Maybe."

He moves closer and reaches for my purse. I give it to him, along with a questioning look. He sets it on the table in the entryway, then threads his fingers through my empty hands. Gently, he winds my arms around my back and pins them there, bringing his chest to mine. "I like how you stood your ground with Heidi."

I look up at him. "I like how you defended me."

He starts to walk forward, pressing me back. "I like that you like how I defended you."

I smile taking careful steps. "I like that you like my like of your defense."

He pauses and squints. "This is getting complicated."

I laugh.

We keep walking. As we do, I realize the lights are off in the apartment with the exception of a lamp in the living room and a kitchen light. As we pass the dining table, I see Latson's jacket tossed over a chair, and his wallet and keys next to a note. I assume it's from Mrs. Gibson, which reminds me of Oliver. I stop walking. "Is Oliver asleep?"

"Funny you should mention him." One side of Latson's mouth quirks up. "You're not the only one who's been abandoned tonight."

He leads me over to the table to read the note, but doesn't let me go. Someone named Nathan is staying at Mrs. Gibson's house, and the boys were begging for a sleepover. Despite it being a weeknight, she caved and will drop the kids at school in the morning.

"Who's Nathan?" I ask.

"Diane's grandson."

I look at Latson and he looks at me. "So, we're all alone?"

He nods and my pulse quickens. His breathing increases too, because I can feel the rise and fall of his chest. He leans forward and brushes his nose across my cheek until his mouth finds my ear. "I was headed outside to your window when Heidi knocked on the door. I was going to ask if you wanted to have a sleepover of our own."

My breath hitches and a warm anticipation starts to spread through my veins. "Hmmm," I tease. "I'll have to check with Ed. He doesn't like to share, remember?"

Latson frowns. "Again with Sheeran?"

I nod with a smile and he pauses to think. Then, he cocks an eyebrow.

"When's the last time he kissed you?" he asks.

"Ummm ..." He's got me there. "Never."

Latson gives me his sexy smirk before lowering his mouth to mine. He takes his time teasing my lips, first the top and then the bottom, by slowly pulling each one between his own and sucking on it. No one has paid such delicate attention to my mouth before and the feeling is incredible. When he finishes his individual attention, he takes my lips together, parting them with his tongue and branding me in his own way. A whimper escapes my throat, and I feel Latson smile before he pulls back.

"That's one for me and zero for Ed," he says as I catch my breath. "When's the last time he touched you?"

I shake my head. "Never. He's touched me with his words, though. That should count."

"Maybe," Latson concedes. "But, what if you could have the real thing?"

Before I can answer, he releases my hands. He runs both of his up to my shoulders and focuses on my eyes. "I haven't forgotten about the chase," he says. "I said I didn't care how fast you ran and I meant it." He turns his hand over and trails his knuckles over my collarbone. "If you decide to stay with me tonight I'll still chase you. Nothing needs to happen that you don't want."

My heart races and all I can think is I *want*. His brings his hands to my waist and leans in close, following the same path over my collarbone with his lips. I reach for him, to wind my arms around his waist, his neck, anything, but he suddenly backs away. He smiles as I frown.

"I think that's two for me and zero for Ed." He grins as he pulls my phone from his pocket. "Would you like to tell him it's over or should I?"

"You're an arrogant ass," I laugh as I swipe my cell from him.

He shrugs. "My point has been made. I'm better than your imaginary boyfriend."

He definitely better than anything imaginary. Hell, he might be better than anything I've ever had.

Just then a phone rings and it's not mine. Latson glances at his cell before picking it up and answering. "Hey, buddy."

I decide to walk over to my purse to give him some privacy.

"What are you doing up? It's after ten," he says. "Yes. I know school's over next week. You still have a bed time."

I smile as I put my phone away.

"Jen," Latson whispers and I turn around. *"Where are you going?"* he mouths.

"Nowhere," I whisper back.

"What, bud? No, you cannot have that game. We've talked about this before. You know –" He's cut off. "Oliver. It's too late for this discussion." He sighs. "Yes. We can talk about it tomorrow."

Latson paces back and forth as he talks to his nephew. Watching him makes me wonder how hard it was to go from fun uncle to father figure and having to set rules and boundaries. The realization hits me that he went from single rock star to single dad in the blink of an eye. The situation had to be a huge change.

"I love you," Latson says. "Sleep tight."

"Wait!" I whisper-yell and wave my arms to get his attention. "Tell Oliver I said hi."

Latson smiles. "Hey, O? Remember when I told you I was going to see Jen tonight?" He waits. "Well, she said to tell you hi."

I walk over to him as he ends the conversation. "Okay. I'll tell her. I don't – I can ask. Buddy, she might be busy." Latson winks at me. "We'll see. Goodnight. I'll pick you up from school." He hangs up the phone.

"What was that about?" I ask.

"Oliver would like to know if you're free next week."

"For?"

"The end of the year first grade picnic."

My heart melts for the kid a little more. "When is it?"

"Thursday afternoon. You don't have to go."

"Are you kidding? Of course I'll go. I have nothing else to do."

Latson's arms circle my waist and he pulls me close. "You have me to do."

My heart skips. "Oliver asked first. I can't see you next Thursday."

He leans in and rests his forehead against mine. "Sneaky kid."

"Are you jealous?"

He looks up. "I have been. The night he fell asleep with you on the couch? I've never been so jealous of a seven-year-old in my entire life."

I want to grin. Instead, I tip my head and run my finger along his shirt collar. "Is that why you felt the need to carry me to bed?"

Latson's eyes grow dark. "No. But I feel the need to carry you to bed right now."

He tightens his hold around my waist and presses my body to his. I can feel the need he's talking about.

Holy shit. It's an impressive need.

"I thought you said we didn't have to do anything I didn't want."

He blinks. "I did. I'm sorry."

He tries to step back, but I hold on to him. "That's not what I meant." I stand on my toes and find his ear. "I meant I don't want you to carry me to bed. I can walk."

He buries his face against my neck. "You're killing me."

Latson starts to walk backward, pulling me along with him. His mouth assaults my skin, kissing and nipping wherever he touches. I close my eyes and run my fingers into his hair, behind his head, to keep him in place. We make it into the hallway, the one where I shot him during the Nerf war, and his hands slide from my waist, to my hips, to my ass. When we stop walking, one of his hands disappears and I hear a door open. He steps back and takes my hand, leading me into his room.

The lights are off, but the moon is high in the sky. Its light shines through sliding glass doors illuminating an impressive master suite. It's big, bigger than any of the rooms in Pete's apartment, and I remember Latson renovated the entire floor. In addition to a California king, there's the typical furniture – a large dresser and two end tables. There's also a seating area, with an entertainment center and a loveseat. I can also see a set of double doors which I assume lead to a closet. Or maybe it's a bathroom.

We stop walking next to the bed and Latson wraps me in his arms. He runs his fingers up and down my back and asks, "Are you sure?"

I want to tell him my freaking blood is on fire, of course I'm sure. Rather than do that, I reach between us and pull at the bottom of his shirt. "I want to see you," I whisper. Without question, he reaches for the back of his collar and pulls the shirt over his head. He crumples it in his hands and tosses it on the floor as I stand there and stare.

Good lord.

I go for his abs first. There's no other choice when there are so many of them. I set my hands flat on his stomach, then run them over his defined muscles. I feel his breathing catch as I take my time tracing them before moving higher on his chest. His skin is so smooth I start to worry about my own. Pushing the thought aside, I step closer and start to follow my fingers with my tongue. Yep. I literally lick him.

He groans and grabs hold of my waist, pulling at my dress and lifting my skirt. "How does this thing come off?" he murmurs as he tries to figure it out.

I stop treating him like an ice cream cone and move back. I step out of my shoes before reaching behind my neck. "It's pretty simple." I smile.

He smiles back, but doesn't let me continue. He turns me around and then gathers my hair in one hand. I feel the tie on my dress loosen, then watch as the top half falls away. Suddenly, his mouth is on me, devouring the nape of my neck and traveling down across my shoulder. His touch feels warmer than before as he gently grips my hair and pulls, tilting my head in the opposite direction of his lips. His free hand sends a shiver down my spine as it slides around my middle, just grazing the bottom of my breasts. I think he realizes they're free, because it takes only a second for his hand to find one and consume it.

It's not long before my dress is gone and I'm lying on the bed. He stands over me, his feet still planted on the floor, and his eyes rake over my body as his hands skim every part. My nerves jump into overdrive when he gets to my pink bikinis and stops. He threads his thumbs under them at my hips, pauses to kiss around my belly, and then slides them slowly down my legs. When they're off, he stands and spins them around one finger. "I think I've seen these before."

I'm confused. "What? How?"

He grins and lets my underwear fly off his finger. "I believe you called it Stripper Therapy."

Oh my God. He's right. I didn't even realize I put on the same pair. Wait. "You remember what I was wearing?"

He leans halfway over me and lifts my legs, running his hands down the back of them. "Every detail of that performance is burned into my mind."

Everything inside me tenses. My eyes fall on his jeans and I set my feet against the front of them, curling my toes over the waistband. "Why are you still dressed?"

He undoes the button, and I help him shove them off with my feet. When he's standing there in his boxer briefs, I have a flashback to dinner. *My glasses fantasy can totally come true.* When he rids himself of his Calvin's, I make a mental note to make that fantasy come true. This man is gorgeous.

I push myself sideways, further into the center of the bed and toward the pillows.

"Where are you going?" He grabs my ankle and pulls me back.

"Not far. I just –" Sweet mother! His hand slides between my legs causing my back to arch and my hips to jump. As my limbs go limp and my mind clouds over, I've never been so happy that he picked up a guitar and mastered it than I am right now. All rational thought leaves my mind as his movements bring sensations that build and build until my body lets go and hums.

When I come down from the high, my eyes flutter open to see him backing away. Now it's my turn to murmur. "Where are you going?"

He kisses me and smiles. "Don't worry. I'll be right back."

When he leaves, I want to complain about being cold without him near, but I can't. The view I get when he walks away is priceless. Shoulders: strong. Back: toned. Waist: tapered. Ass: perfect. I bite my lip to suppress a grin. I can't wait to get my hands on every inch of him.

Latson makes it to the doorway and reaches inside to flip the light switch. He enters the bathroom and stands there, butt naked, and starts to rummage through the medicine cabinet. I think I know what he's looking for, so I slide myself up toward the head of the bed.

When he turns off the light and returns to me, he wastes no time covering my body with his. He plants kisses along my chin and down my neck, and I zero in on his shoulder with my lips. As my hands explore his back, he leans up on his elbows and holds a condom between his fingertips. "Sorry. I don't keep these handy anymore."

I tilt my head. "There's one in your hand right now."

"I meant in a convenient location. It's been ..." He looks down and then back at me. "It's been awhile since I've had anyone in my bed."

"Are you blushing?" I tease.

He shakes his head and gives me his lopsided dimple smile.

"You are blushing!" I grin. "Give me this thing." I steal the plastic from him. As I tear it open, he brings his hands to the sides of my face and gently pushes my hair behind my ears.

"Jen." His eyes focus on mine. "I don't know what this is."

"It's sex," I laugh.

His eyes grow intense. "Hell, yes." He flexes his hips against mine, giving me a taste of what's to come. My laughter fades into a moan.

"God. I love that sound," he breathes. "What I meant is I've never wanted anyone the way I want you."

Speechless, I get lost in his gaze, in his burning expression and beautiful eyes.

"I don't know what that means, but I want to find out," he says. He runs his thumb over my lower lip. "Are you okay with that? Jumping into the unknown?"

I've never been one to back down from a challenge. I lift my head, plant a slow kiss on his lips, and then whisper against them.

"Geronimo."

Chapter Fifteen

Sunlight warms my face and I open one eye. I take in the room around me and wonder what time it is. I should probably get back to Pete's in case he comes home. The last thing I need is a lecture on what he would perceive as the walk of shame.

I bury my head into a pillow at the thought. Closing my eye, I allow myself a few more minutes of peace. I have no idea what will happen once I get out of this bed. Under the sheets, everything makes sense. My naked back is pressed to Latson's chest, and his arm is draped over my side. My muscles are blissfully sore, and I feel warm and wanted. I'm me and he's him, and we're two people that really like one another. I don't regret what happened.

However, outside of the blankets, he's my boss and my brother's friend. I didn't think about that last night. I was wrapped up in doing what made me happy, caught in the whirlwind that is Latson. I got lost in his kisses and touches and words. Do I want it to continue? Yes. But I'm pretty sure I'll need to quit my job for that to happen. When I do, my brother will know something big went down. I hope it won't create a problem for Latson, especially with Pete.

The thought of a potential shit storm makes me groan into the pillow. I curse my over-analytical mind. Leave it to reality to crush my high. *Forget it,* I think. *Relax. Remember your rule.*

Latson's arm tightens around me, and he finds the crook of my neck with his lips. He gives me a sleepy kiss. "Why are you making strange noises?"

"I'm sorry I woke you." I roll on my back and look at him. He couldn't be more adorable if he tried. His hair is sticking up in all directions, probably from me pulling on it, and his eyes are tired. "I was thinking about my rule."

"What rule?" He frowns. "Please tell me it doesn't pertain to guys you sleep with."

I smile. "It does and it doesn't."

He drags his hand over his lazy eyes, trying to wake up. "Care to fill me in? I don't want to break this rule."

"It's not for you. It's for me."

He raises a questioning brow and I elaborate. "When I came to the city, I promised myself I would only do what made me happy. I made it my Cardinal rule. After everything in my life fell apart, I had to do something to stay sane."

Concern crosses his features. "Are you saying last night didn't make you happy?"

"Absolutely not." I roll to my side and prop my head on my hand. "I haven't been that happy in, oh, I'd say *ever.*"

He gives me his signature smirk before giving me a hungry kiss. "But to keep the happy, I need to quit my job," I mumble against his lips. "Pete will probably flip out, and I don't want it to affect your friendship."

Without warning he rolls over and pounces on me, causing me to yelp. He covers my body with his, twisting the sheets around us. "This is what you think about first thing in the morning?"

I laugh. "I can't help it."

He hovers above me, leaning on his elbows. "We need to redirect your train of thought."

"I'm serious," I say. "I can't sleep with my boss."

A slow smile spreads across his face. "I know you can, because you did."

I try to kick my feet, but get nowhere. "This is an important issue!"

"Only if you make it one." He kisses my forehead. "No one will care if we're seeing each other except for Pete. Do you really want to quit working at Torque?"

"Well, no," I confess. I like it there. The money is good and the people are better.

"Then stop trying to create a problem. I don't want you to quit. I like the thought of seeing you every day." His voice gets low and seductive. "I can control myself. Are you saying you can't?"

I roll my eyes. "Of course I can."

"Like you said, outside of work we're us. Inside, we can be professionals unless we're alone."

"What?"

He leans down and whispers in my ear. "Don't think I haven't thought about taking you over the bar."

A shiver runs up my spine. "Really?"

"Really."

I have to admit that's something I've never done – and would totally love to do. "Fine." I pretend to be stern. "But we should set some rules. You can't come within five feet of me while I'm working."

"Three," he counters.

"No touching."

"Can I touch you with words?"

I sigh. "Are you making fun of me?"

"Not at all." He tries to look innocent.

"I don't want the other staff to think I'm getting special treatment," I explain. "I got enough suspicious looks the day I started."

"That's understandable," he says. "Although ..." His fingers trace a pattern over my skin, along the edge of the sheet trapped between us. "You will be getting special treatment."

He nudges the fabric down, and I squirm beneath him. "I'm trying to have an adult conversation with you."

"And I'm trying to act like an adult with you."

His lips replace his fingers as he moves down my body, pulling the sheet off and exposing me along the way. "Just so we're clear," he mumbles against my belly, "I can't think straight around you. It's worse when you're naked beneath me."

My body warms to his touch. "That sounds like a serious problem." I run my hands into his hair. "Maybe I should avoid you altogether."

He nips my hip in admonishment, and I twitch. "Not an option."

He sits back on his knees allowing his eyes to rake over me. I'm not used to being scrutinized nude in the daylight, so I cover myself with my arms. "Stop staring."

Slowly, he crawls back up my body, taking my wrists and pinning them beside my head. "Again, not an option." He leans in and kisses my neck. "You're beautiful. You'll be lucky if I let you wear clothes when we're alone again."

I laugh. "I think you're just happy I agreed to stay the night."

"No." His eyes immediately snap to mine. "I meant what I said. I've never wanted anyone the way I want you. I don't know if it's your smart mouth, your talent, or your heart that makes me want you more, but you haven't left my mind since day one. Yes, I'm glad last night happened, but I'd feel the same if it hadn't. I don't think you understand what you've done to me."

My expression softens as I take in his words. "What did I do?"

"You made me feel."

He releases my wrists, and I rest my hands on his arms. "Feel? I don't −"

"I've been numb," he says. "I knew I was, but I didn't care. A month ago I never would have performed in front of a crowd. I wouldn't have asked a woman out on a date, and I sure as hell wouldn't have talked to my father. Those things happened because of you."

A tiny smile dances across my lips. "Well ... you're welcome."

"Now," he focuses on my mouth, "can we stop talking? I don't get many Oliver-free mornings, and I'd like to enjoy our time while we can."

"So, that's how this is going to work?" I tease. "While the little kid's away ..."

He flashes a wicked grin. "... the big kids will play."

~ ~ ~ ~

The following afternoon, I give my coworker a concerned look as she hobbles the length of the bar. "Gwen. Are you limping?"

"Yes." She frowns. "I sprained my ankle yesterday."

"How?"

Her face turns red as she reaches me. "Promise you won't laugh." She hands me her purse to stow beneath the cash register and lets out a big sigh. "I tried to rollerblade."

I instantly hide a smile. "Oh no. What went wrong?"

"Everything!" She tosses her hands in the air. "I finally got this guy in my building to ask me out, and he decides to take me rollerblading. Me! The least athletic person on the planet. I should have known he would want to do something outdoorsy with his perfect tan and his strong legs and the kayak strapped to the top of his Jeep."

I pat her shoulder in sympathy as she leans on the bar and holds her head in her hands. "Why didn't you suggest dinner or a movie instead? Outdoorsy guys have to eat, too."

"I was so excited he asked me out I didn't think about it. I figured I could do it; I mean, I used to roller skate when I was little."

I smile. "So, what happened?"

She peeks at me from beneath her hands. "I put the rollerblades on, stood up, and started rolling backward. The parking lot was on an incline, and I didn't know how to stop. I was picking up speed and a car pulled in, so I ditched."

My eyes grow wide. "Did the car hit you?"

"No." She shakes her head. "But the driver got out to see if I was okay. Talk about embarrassing. Then, Logan came gliding over all professional-like to see if I was hurt. He helped me up, and I couldn't put pressure on my foot." She gives me a miserable glance. "We spent the next six hours in the ER. He got to witness a nurse bandage my scraped elbows and knees. I felt like a ten-year-old. It was incredibly sexy." She pauses. "Not. It was my first date in over six months and I ruined it."

I shouldn't tell her I had a date, too. Not only did it go well, but I'm not sure I'm ready to spill about Latson. I have, however, had my share of bad dates in the past. "Listen. If this Logan gives up on you because you fell over, he's not worth the trouble. If he doesn't check on you in the next twenty-four hours, forget him. We'll find you someone new."

"Good luck with that." Gwen stands up straight. "I've been trying to find someone new for freaking ever." She ducks beneath the bar. "Where are we at with set up? I don't know how much help I'll be tonight, but at least I'm a body."

"Maybe you should go home," I suggest.

"I wish I could, but I need the cash." Gwen gimps over to look at the wells I've stocked with alcohol. "I'll just stay immobile on this side and you take the other."

"If that's what you want," I say skeptically. I feel bad for her. It's obvious she's in pain. "Do you have any medicine?"

"Generic oxy." She pats her pocket. "They're my new best friends."

"Do I have to remind you two that Torque has a strict no drug use policy?"

I turn around and come eye to eye with Latson. My stomach flips. It's the first time I've seen him since we got out of bed yesterday morning. I can tell he's joking with his words, but I can also sense some emotion behind his question. "Gwen twisted her ankle," I explain. "It hurts."

He frowns. "What happened?"

"It's a long story." Gwen waves her hand as if to say 'forget about it'. "Rest assured I'm only popping doctor prescribed meds."

Latson nods toward her feet. "Are you sure you're okay? I don't want you hurting yourself any worse."

Gwen hops over to me and puts her arm around my shoulders. "Jen's got my back. We make a great team. She'll work this side, and I'll work the other. Besides, I need her dating advice."

Latson's eyebrows shoot up. "You do?"

Gwen nods. "She's going to help me find someone new if Mr. Outdoors doesn't work out."

Latson looks at me and tries to hold back a smile. "Well, I've heard she's pretty good in the dating department."

The tops of my ears start to get hot. "Don't you have some work to do or –"

"Oh, hey. That reminds me." He steps back. "What do you think of my new shirt?" He looks down at his chest and points. My eyes travel from his face to his pecs. *I licked it so it's mine* is printed in bold white letters.

The heat from my ears travels to my cheeks. "You ..." I close my eyes to keep my composure. I didn't expect him to be this blatant. I open my eyes to Latson's crooked smile. "That's a little unprofessional, don't you think?"

"Why? Oliver says it all the time."

My eyes bug out of my head. "He does? Why would he say that?"

"So I won't steal his Oreos." Latson looks at me like I'm overreacting. "He likes to lick the filling before he dips them in milk." He turns to Gwen and shrugs. "I guess she's never eaten an Oreo."

Gwen looks at me. "Haven't you?"

"Of course I have. The statement just seems a little ... I don't know. Inappropriate."

Latson tsk-tsks. "Jen. Are you thinking dirty thoughts again?"

Gwen shoots me a questioning look. "Again?"

"No. I –"

"You can admit it," Latson says. "I'd like to know what's going on in that head of yours."

He purposefully bites his lower lip as he smirks, drawing my attention to his mouth. Thoughts of kissing him cloud my mind, so I get sarcastic to push them away. "I bet you would."

Latson backs away from the bar. "I won't keep you ladies. I'm getting dangerously close to violating the three foot rule."

Gwen's confused. "The what?"

"It's five feet," I remind him.

"I believe we negotiated three." He grins. "Oh, and I already talked to Pete. I'll be driving you home later."

He will?

Latson looks at Gwen. "Speaking of home, let me know if you need to leave early. Don't overdo it."

"Got it, boss," she says as he turns and walks away. When he's out of earshot, Gwen lowers her arm and wobbles a few steps away from me. "Correct me if I'm wrong, but something happened between you two."

I debate telling her. Pete, Jules, and Heidi already know we went out. Latson isn't acting shy about us, although he is being vague. "He's full of innuendo," I say, playing along. "You know that."

She narrows her eyes. "What's the three foot rule?"

I decide to busy my hands and grab some cocktail napkins to place around the bar top. "It's five feet, and it's a good distance to prevent touching." I try to change the subject. "So, what do you think Logan is doing right now?"

She doesn't fall for it. "Touching?" Gwen's mouth falls open. "Something did happen!"

I shake my head like she's being silly. "I want to talk about Logan."

"Liar." Her eyes light up. "Tell me what happened."

I try not to laugh. "No."

"Yes!" She points at her ankle. "I'm in pain. Humor me. I'll make it easy for you and play the opposite game."

"The what?"

"It goes like this: I ask a question and you give me the opposite of the truth. That way you don't have to actually say what happened."

"Have you lost your mind?"

"Have you lost yours?" She leans close so she can whisper. "Something happened with that fine specimen of a man and you don't want to talk about it? C'mon!"

It would be a girlie thing to do. Obviously I didn't talk specifics with Pete. I told him the date went well and to be prepared – I was going to see Latson again. Jules has family visiting from out of town, so I only shared a few brief texts with her, although she wants details when her sisters leave on Friday.

"Okay," I concede. "You can ask a few questions."

Gwen smiles. "You can trust me. I'll share a secret of my own to prove it, too. No opposites."

I raise an eyebrow. "You didn't hurt yourself rollerblading?"

"Ugh! No, that's true." She shakes her head. "I slept with Carter."

My jaw drops. "You what? When? What about Logan?" I hiss.

"Please." Gwen rolls her eyes. "The Carter thing happened over a year ago."

I'm floored. They get along like brother and sister. I would never have guessed.

"Your turn," she says. "I already know something happened, so when?"

I think about how to answer in an opposite. "Um, not Monday night?"

"The day after the jam session? I knew something was up! The way you two played guitar together ..." She drifts off with a dreamy look. "Okay. Did you run into each other in your building?"

"Yes."

"So, no." She puts her finger to her chin. "Did he send Oliver over to lure you to his place?"

"What? No. I mean, yes."

I start to move around the bar to finish setting up before the doors open. Gwen limps a few steps behind me. "Was this a planned event?"

"No." I toss the empty napkin box in the trash and realize I never cut the lemons and limes. They're still sitting on the cutting board. I pick up a knife and start slicing.

"Was it a date?" Gwen sounds surprised.

"No."

"It was a date. This is *huge*," she emphasizes the word. "He never dates. Never. Never ever ever –"

"Stop," I laugh. "I know. We discussed it."

"Was it romantic? Did you kiss? Did anything naked happen?"

"It was horribly boring and no." I'm starting to like this opposite thing.

Gwen looks excited. "This is so much better than my date! Was it mind-blowing? It had to be with someone like him."

"What do you mean 'someone like him'? He's a guy like any other guy."

"No. He's a mysterious, reserved, apparently uber romantic, sexy ex-rock star. That's not any other guy."

I smile. She's right. "Well, if you put it that way, it was awful. Hideous. Worst time of my life. You couldn't pay me to do it again."

She squeals. Really, really loud. I catch Latson's eye from across the room. He stops talking to Felix and Kenzie, and they all give us puzzled looks. I stop cutting fruit and point at Gwen with the knife. "Ssshhh! People are staring at us!"

She slaps her hand over her mouth. "Sorry!" comes out muffled.

I go back to slicing. "I'm glad you're excited, but the world doesn't need to know."

"I'll try to contain my enthusiasm," she says. "This is really awesome news, though. I'm happy for both of you."

"Thanks. It happened kind of fast."

"Fast is better in my book," Gwen says. "Life is short. You should live it up while you can."

I slide a chopped lemon to one side of the cutting board and then look at her. "I hope you're right."

During our shift, business is steady, but not overwhelming. Gwen and I talk in short bursts, until she falls silent because of her pain. She looks like she hurts more and more as time goes on. By midnight, I'm tired of watching her try to hide her grimaces and scowls.

"That's it," I say. "You need to go home."

To my surprise, she doesn't fight me. "You're right. It's only getting worse. The medicine isn't helping."

"I'd say all the movement isn't helping."

She starts to hobble her way over to me. "I'll go tell the boss I'm done for the night."

"No. I'll go. You don't need to walk any more than necessary." I crouch under the bar and come up on the other side. "I'll be right back."

Gwen teases me. "Suuure. Use me to go see your boyfriend."

I smirk, then start to pick my way around people, tables, and chairs. I head to the rear of the bar where Latson's office is located. As I knock and hear "It's open," I realize I've never been inside before.

I crack the door and peek around the corner. "Hey."

Latson looks up and smiles. "Hey."

He's wearing his glasses, and my stomach flutters. My gaze leaves him for a moment to look around the office. It's full of the standard stuff, including the calendar for this month's entertainment written on a big white board. My eyes study the concert posters hanging on the walls until they land on handmade drawings pinned to a bulletin board behind the desk.

"Did Oliver make those?" I step inside and shut the door behind me.

Latson looks over his shoulder. "Yeah." He faces me again. "Did you come to look at my art gallery?"

"No, but it's a perk." I walk over to get a better view. I hesitate when I get next to his desk. I'm not sure if I should go behind it. "Do you care if I –"

"Get over here."

He stands and reaches for me, pulling me into his arms. "I've been dying to touch you all night."

I wrap my arms around his waist and snuggle against him. "This violates the five foot rule."

"It's three, and I don't see you complaining."

I stifle a laugh. He runs his thumbs over my lower back as we stand pressed together. I take a deep breath and inhale his scent. "Why do you smell so damn good?" I ask. "It's distracting."

He kisses the top of my head. "I think you answered your own question."

His hand leaves my waist and removes his glasses, then appears under my chin. I lift my face toward him and as soon as our eyes meet, he lowers his mouth to mine. It's a heated kiss, like we haven't seen each other in days, and I'm quickly forgetting the reason I came in here. It doesn't take long before his hands are in my hair and mine are digging into his back through his ridiculous I licked it shirt. Latson's hands travel to my waist and he turns us, backing me against his desk. Gently, he lifts me up to sit on the edge, and I wrap my legs around his hips to pull him close. Just as my hands find the bottom of his shirt and slide underneath, the office door opens.

"Hey! I finally heard from –"

Dean's excited voice echoes and I nearly jump ten feet in the air. Latson catches me before I fall off the desk and laughs. "Dude. Ever heard of knocking?"

"I've never had to before." I can sense Dean's amusement. "I see things are progressing nicely. Hi, Jen."

I turn my red-stained face toward Dean. "Hi." I start to stand.

"Don't leave because of me," he says. "Actually, I'm glad I caught you two together."

"What's up?" Latson asks as he helps me hop down.

"I finally heard from Roxanne. I'm in." Dean's smile could light up a stadium.

"Yeah?" Latson leaves my side to give his brother a high-five and pull him into a one-armed hug. "That's great, man."

"I got the first five months of the tour, the North American leg."

"You're going on tour?" I move closer to the guys. "Congratulations."

"Thanks. I'm opening for Ariel."

I remember the Wikipedia article and glance at Latson. "As in Ariel Allyn? Didn't you two date?"

"A lifetime ago." Latson wraps his arm around my waist. "When do rehearsals start?"

"Next week. I've got Drew on drums and Paul on bass." Dean looks at me. "That's where you come in."

"Me?" I'm confused.

"I need the rest of my band." He pauses. "I want you on guitar. What do you say?"

Chapter Sixteen

"I ..." I stutter.

There's no way I heard him right.

"I've never played for an audience bigger than a wedding." I gesture toward Latson. "You want him, not me."

"He won't come." Dean crosses his arms. "I asked him months ago, when I first started working this gig. I asked him again the night we played on stage. His answer was still no."

"Why?" I look at Latson. He looks apprehensive, possibly torn. "You should go." I nudge him with my elbow. "You love to play."

He shakes his head no. "I have Oliver. He doesn't need to live on the road."

"It's only five months, right?"

"You don't ..." He sighs. "I'm not traveling with a seven-year-old, and I won't leave him behind. He deserves better."

Latson's arm leaves my waist and he heads behind his desk. Did I upset him? I didn't mean to.

"Jen." Dean redirects my attention. "What do you think? How does touring sound?"

"I don't ..." Again with the stuttering. I don't understand why he would want me. I don't know any of his songs. I've never performed on stage. I own a used acoustic guitar. "I need some time to think about it. I've never done anything like this before."

"I get it." Dean steps toward me. "But, keep in mind, everyone has to start somewhere." He pulls his phone from his pocket. "Why don't I send you the information and you can look it over? What's your email address?"

I give it to him, along with my number. He types them into his cell. "Check your email when you get home and let me know if you have any questions. Rehearsals start in a week, so I need an answer soon. Within twenty-four hours, if you can manage it. If you say no, I need to go to Plan B."

"What's Plan B?"

"Begging."

My forehead pinches. "Begging? As in begging me?"

"I really want you to say yes. You're good, and I don't say that lightly. When I heard you play before my show I knew. Then, at Gunnar's, you nailed it. You can do this. You *should* be doing this. Not bartending."

Wow. I'm just about to thank him for his compliment when Gwen limps through the open door. "Did you forget about me?"

Aw, crap. "I'm sorry. I got caught up." I turn around to face Latson. "I came in here to tell you that Gwen needs to go home. She's in a ton of pain."

He nods, his eyes never leaving the paper in his hands. "Let me know if you can make it in tomorrow," he says.

"I will. Thanks." Gwen looks at me. "Maggie is covering for us, so ..."

"I'm right behind you," I say and start to leave. I glance at Dean. "I'll let you know soon. Thanks for the opportunity."

"You're welcome."

As soon as I'm out the door I hear Latson's voice snap. "Thanks a lot, asshole. You could have told me you were going to ask her."

Dean's voice bites back. "She deserves it."

"I agree, but we just started –"

"Jen."

My eyes jump to Gwen.

"Come on." She waves me forward. "Maggie's going to kill us."

I nod and pick up my pace.

~~~~

The ride home with Latson is quiet. He seems lost in his own world, so I don't say anything. I know he's not happy with Dean, but it's not my place to question him. Especially since I overheard what was said.

With nothing else to do, I stare out the window and contemplate going on Dean's tour. I imagine accepting his offer. I have to admit it gives me the good chills. It also makes me nervous as hell. I have to be the least qualified person to round out his band. What makes him think I won't embarrass him? I guess if I'm terrible at rehearsals he could let me go. The idea of being fired from a job I was handpicked to fill makes me feel a little leery. Trying and failing would be a nightmare.

But, then again, at least I could say I tried.

By the time Latson pulls into our building I've decided on one thing: to read Dean's email. Talking in circles is useless, and I need all the facts before making a decision. When Latson parks and turns off the engine, I reach for my bag, then the door handle. "Thanks for the ride home."

He gives me half a smile and then holds out his hand. I set my bag down and thread my fingers through his. "Thanks for letting me pout."

"Why are you pouting?"

"Because you're going to say yes." He runs his thumb over the back of my hand. "You're going to leave."

I tip my head and scrutinize him. "What makes you so sure?"

"Because I won't let you stay."

I frown.

"C'mere." He pulls me closer by pulling on my hand. I slide over next to him, but it's not good enough. With some maneuvering, I end up sitting in his lap, facing him.

"You have too much talent to let this pass you by," he says. "Didn't you say you were tired of tending bar? It's time to be a rock star."

I laugh. "That's stretching it a little, don't you think?"

"Nope." He runs his hands over my arms. "You'll be great."

I lean forward and hold my face inches from his. "I still think you should go."

"Jen, I –"

"I understand about Oliver," I cut him off. "I do. But, other people tour, and they have families. It's five months."

"Remember that when you're missing me." He gives me a gentle kiss, then rests his forehead against mine. "I have more reasons than Oliver for saying no."

"Such as?"

He sighs and lets his hands fall to my thighs. He leans back against the seat and looks out the window. "Audrey."

I set my palms against his chest and wait for him to explain.

"I won't put myself in a position to re-live the past," he says. "Too many things would be the same."

He looks like he wants to say more, but changes his mind. I wonder if he's talked to anyone about his sister. I doubt his past comes up when he's hanging out with Pete and the guys. I lean forward to get his attention and softly ask, "Do you want to talk about it?"

He runs his fingers in circles on my legs. "What's there to talk about? My sister died on our second tour. I can barely escape the memory without my music. It would be impossible to shake if I went with Dean."

My breath catches. "I'm sorry. I didn't know."

"Don't be." Latson's sad eyes find mine. "What happened has nothing to do with you."

My gut tells me he's wrong. "I think it does." I sit up straight. "We're together, right?"

He nods, yet looks confused.

"Then your hurts are mine. Just like if I were upset. Wouldn't you want to make me feel better?"

"I would."

"See?" I lean toward him and set my hands on either side of his face. "Listen to me. I'm sorry. I can't imagine what losing Audrey was like for you and your family."

Latson sighs and gives me another soft kiss. "Thank you."

"Any time."

He covers my hands with his and moves them to his chest. "I wish I could go back," he says. "There are days when I question everything. You should know that about me, for when I act like an ass again. Because it's going to happen, just like it did at the hospital."

I squeeze his fingers. "Not if I can help it. What are you second guessing?"

He lets out a sarcastic laugh. "You don't want to know."

"I do."

"There's no fixing the past."

"True, but you can feel better about it." I decide to share my own revelation. "Take my ex, Derek, for example. He was a massive mistake. Huge. But I feel better about what happened because he led me here. Had things not happened the way they did, I'd be four hours away dating a lying bastard. You and I would never have met."

Latson raises an eyebrow. "Is it wrong to be happy he was a lying bastard?"

"Not at all." I smile. "Now, tell me one of your regrets."

He gives me a resigned look. "I don't think –"

I bring my face close to his. "Tell me."

"Okay," he concedes. "Fine." He looks at our hands. "I regret asking Audrey to manage the band."

My stomach knots. "Because of what happened?"

"Because she had a degree in finance and was headed to New York City. If I hadn't asked her to manage us instead of money, Heidi wouldn't have introduced her to Levi. She wouldn't have started using, and she'd be here right now."

My eyes grow wide. "So, yes, then."

He sighs. "She should have gone to Wall Street. Instead, she got in Dean's beat-up Chevy with me."

"Hold on," I say and sit back. "Did you force her into the car against her will?"

"No."

"Then it wasn't your choice. It was hers." I tip my head. "You guys were successful. You got a record deal. That's nothing to regret."

Latson looks like he doesn't buy it. "It's not that simple. There's more to it."

"I'm sure there is. Maybe you should tell me."

He grimaces. "Not today."

Just then, his phone sounds. I pull my hands from his and shift my weight to the side so he can get it out of his pocket. "It's Dean." He reads the message: "Tell your woman to check her email." His eyes light up. "I like the sound of that. Your woman," he repeats.

I try not to smile, but fail. I like being called his. However, I wish Dean wouldn't have interrupted us. I want Latson to share more of his past, to get it off his chest. I feel like he hasn't talked about it enough.

"Where's your phone?" he asks and grabs my ass, feeling around the pockets. "Let's see what Dean sent."

I twitch and laugh. "Hang on." Leaning over, I find my bag and pull it up on the passenger seat. I root around for my cell. "You seem excited about this. Or are you faking?"

"It's a great opportunity." Latson doesn't answer my question. "You deserve to play, and people deserve to hear you."

I roll my eyes. "I'm not so sure they should pay to see me. What if I embarrass Dean?"

"That won't happen."

"How do you know?"

"Because music is a part of you. You love it too much."

I find my phone and open my email. There are a few messages from Dean. "Which one should we look at first? 'Schedule' or 'Details'? Or 'Sorry, here's some more I forgot?'"

"Doesn't matter. Pick one."

His hands move to my thighs as I open the most recent message. "Sorry, there's one more thing I forgot," I read aloud. "Please say yes." I give Latson a confused look. The message is followed by a bunch of worried smiley emoji's.

"Jesus," he groans. "He's already resorted to Plan B."

I shake my head. "Let's try Details." I touch the screen. "Here we go." I lean forward so Latson and I can read the email together:

Jen –

I'll try to break everything down. Basically the tour runs from late June until mid-November. We'll be opening for Ariel, but you already know that. If you're not familiar with her music, I would suggest some quality listening time. You never know what she may want to talk about, and it's always a good idea to be friendly with the headliner.

I stop reading and look at Latson. "You were friendly with her," I tease.

He squeezes my legs. "Stop. That was years ago."

I turn back to Dean's email.

Speaking of music, I know you're not familiar with mine. Attached you will find the MP3 files for all ten of my songs. We only have 30 to 45 minutes each night before Ariel, depending on the venue. Each one is different. Regardless, we'll need to do around eight songs per set. I would recommend downloading the files to your phone or iPod, to listen before rehearsals.

I make a face and think *well, duh.*

The label will cover our travel expenses like transportation and room & board. I hope you like busses and hotels. Some food may be covered; it depends what we're attending. You will get paid $200 per show. I know it doesn't seem like much, but with 63 shows on the schedule, it adds up.

"Sixty-three shows?" My mouth falls open. "Is that normal?"

Latson nods. "If you're in front of someone like Ariel, yeah."

I do the quick math. That's over twelve grand. Twelve thousand dollars in five months to play guitar? With basically no expenses? I hate to say I'm driven by money, but I'm starting to really like this idea.

"Let's look at the schedule," Latson interrupts my thoughts.

I close the email and go to the next. A list of cities and dates pop up. My eyes widen as I read them: Los Angeles. Anaheim. Houston. Vegas. New Orleans. Nashville. Atlanta. Tampa. Raleigh. New York. Boston. D.C. Detroit. The list seems endless.

My pulse starts to race. "I've barely traveled out of my home state. This is ... it's ..."

"An amazing chance for you."

I was going to say overwhelming, but the look in his eyes makes me bite my tongue. He's looking at me but through me, like he's focused on a memory.

"The first time you step on stage, any time you step on stage, it's electric," he says. "You'll feel it in your bones, in your veins. Performing is one of the best things that ever happened to me. There's no better rush, no bigger high." His gaze finds my face. "I don't know how else to describe it, but it will be like that for you, too. The music will take over, creating you instead of you creating it. The feeling won't come close to your imagination, but it will try."

I'm moved by his passionate words. I know it's killing him not to play. It's almost as if he wants me to do it for him, so he can experience it again.

"You'll know what I'm talking about, after your first show in L.A."

I toss my phone onto the seat beside us and set my hands against his chest. "You really want me to go, don't you?"

"The truth?"

"Always."

"I want you to go for you, and I want you to stay for me." He tucks a piece of hair behind my ear. "I have to listen to my head and support you, because if I listen to my heart …" He hesitates. "I'll never let you go."

My breath hitches. If anyone had those feelings for me before, they never said them. Latson doesn't want to let me go while every other man has watched me walk away. I can feel my heart rearranging itself, to make a permanent place for him. "I'm kinda falling for you, too," I confess.

His eyes grow intense as he slides his hand around the back of my neck and pulls me close. "I'm going to have a sign made that says you belong to me. You'll need to carry it with you everywhere you go."

I smile. "That might be difficult. How about you loan me one of your shirts? As long as it smells like you, I'll wear it all the time."

He makes a sound low in his throat and brushes his lips against mine. "I like the idea of you wearing me."

I close my eyes as his mouth skims over my chin, traces my jaw, and lands on my neck. "I do, too."

"Maybe you should get my name tattooed somewhere," he says between kisses. "So it's permanent."

I laugh. "That takes wearing you to a whole new level."

"I'm surprised there's no ink on this body."

I lean back a bit. "Is that a problem? I never planned on getting a tattoo."

He cocks an eyebrow. "Never?"

"Never."

He glances at his arm, covered from wrist to shoulder. "Why? Do they turn you off?"

I shake my head.

"Do they turn you on?"

I bite my lip and slowly run one finger up his arm. "You have no idea."

His eyes flash as his hands slide to my hips. "I'm going to miss the hell out of you," he breathes.

Have I decided to go? In a roundabout way, I guess I have. I know I have his support no matter what I decide and that means the world to me. "You said you wouldn't let me stay."

"Can you blame me?" His hands leave my hips and start to untuck my shirt. "I get to date a hot musician who wears my clothes."

His fingers brush my bare waist, sending a wave of electricity over my skin. "It seems like you want me to wear no clothes."

"Only when you're with me."

He pulls my shirt over my head, and I wrap my arms around his neck. I'm still sitting on his lap, and my head falls back as his tongue traces the edge of my bra. "We need to make the most of our time," he says, his voice muffled. "Starting now."

"Umm hmm," I agree.

His hands travel up my back as he continues to kiss me, pulling my bra straps down my shoulders. "Backseat?" he murmurs.

I lift my head and start to scoot off his lap. "I thought you'd never ask."

Chapter Seventeen

"I'm having second thoughts."

I pull my eyes from the sparkling diamonds in front of me to look at Pete. "Stop. Jules is going to love the ring you picked out for her."

"Mr. Elliott," the sales woman interrupts. "Remember, here at Tiffany's, we have a thirty-day refund policy. If your fiancée prefers a different style, you can always exchange your purchase."

"Thank you," Pete leans forward to read her name tag, "Ellen. I hope that won't be necessary. I've spent too much time here as it is."

I roll my eyes at my brother as I go back to looking at the jewelry. We've been here less than two hours. I've had fun standing in for Jules and trying on different rings for size. The one my brother chose is a one-carat square diamond on a plain platinum band. It's beautiful and elegant, just like Jules. She's going to love it.

"Here you are, sir." Another sales associate delivers two months' of his salary in an unmistakable blue bag. "Good luck with your proposal." She smiles.

"Thanks," he says and takes the dainty handles. "Although, her answer is a sure thing."

My eyes meet my brother's and we start to laugh. The sales ladies give us curious looks. We didn't tell them he had already tied the knot.

As we leave the store, I sigh. So many pretty things in one place. It reminds me of the last diamonds I wore – the earrings Derek gave me. I wonder if anyone picked them up off the floor at the wedding reception. I'm sure they weren't cheap. Or, maybe they were fake. He said they weren't, but he certainly was.

"Now we need to come up with a way to break the news to Jules," Pete says as he holds the door open. "You said her proposal needs to be epic."

I walk past him and out into the hustle of Michigan Avenue. Little does he know I have news of my own. I haven't told him about the tour yet. I was going to bring it up this morning after breakfast, but he suggested ring shopping before I could. I didn't want to ruin the trip, in case he got pissy about me taking off across the country with three guys I don't know.

"You said you had a couple ideas," I say. "What are they?"

"At the top of the Ferris wheel on Navy Pier, or on the observation deck of the Willis Tower."

My brow furrows. "Does she like heights?"

He shrugs. "I thought those were unique places. I don't want to do it at a restaurant or rent a scoreboard. Jules doesn't do sports. She does fitness."

"What about sky writing?" I ask. "You could hire a plane and have it pull a banner over the lake."

He frowns. "I just dropped some serious cash on this ring." He holds the bag with one finger. "I think hiring a plane is out of my price range. Unless you know a pilot."

Unfortunately, I don't.

"Any other ideas?" Pete asks.

I tilt my head in thought as I keep up with foot traffic. "When did you want to do this? I need some time to think."

"I'm not in a big hurry. But I'd like to do it before we head home for Christmas."

I smile. My parents are going to be so excited. "I can come up with something before December. Especially if I'm going to be spending a lot of time on a bus."

"Why would you be on a bus?"

We stop at the edge of the sidewalk to wait for the street light. I guess now is as good a time as any to tell my brother I'm leaving. I look up at him. "I have some news."

His questioning look doesn't hide his annoyance. I'm sure he assumes what I have to say is bad. "What did he do?" he asks.

"Who?"

"Latson."

"Nothing! He's being very supportive."

"Of?"

I take a deep breath. "You know Dean?"

Pete nods.

"He's going on tour. He's opening for Ariel Allyn, and he wants me to play in his band."

My brother's eyes grow wide. "*The* Ariel Allyn?"

"Is there another?"

In one quick swoop, Pete wraps me in a bear hug and lifts me off the ground. "You're going to be famous!"

People standing next to us start to back away. "Put me down," I laugh. "I'm not going to be famous."

"You never know," he says as my feet touch the sidewalk. "When did this happen? I knew you could play after Latson's party, but damn. A tour? Have you told mom and dad?"

"Not yet. It just fell in my lap last night."

The light changes and we start to walk across the street. "So, spill," Pete says. "When do the shows start?"

"Late June in L.A."

"So, you'll be here a couple more weeks?"

"No. We need to rehearse. I leave after Oliver's school picnic." I was relieved when I got home and finished reading Dean's email.

193

Our flight leaves next Thursday evening. I have a date with a certain little boy, and I didn't want to let him down.

"When it rains, it pours, huh?" Pete bumps his arm against mine. "New boyfriend, new career, new sister-in-law." He lets out a low whistle. "Maybe you should thank me for making you come out here."

I bump his arm back, but harder. "I would have had the sister-in-law regardless, but I do thank you." I smirk up at him. "I might even miss you while I'm gone."

"You'd better." Pete's walk slows a little. "I know all of us will miss you. How long will you be on the road?"

"Until November. I'll be back before Thanksgiving."

He nods. "This is big." He stops walking. "I'm proud of you, Jen."

"Don't be proud yet. I haven't done anything." I step out of the way of passing pedestrians. "I didn't compete for this. Dean handed it to me. It could be a disaster."

"Nah." Pete shakes his head. "You'll do fine."

"C'mon." I grab his wrist and pull him along. "Latson helped Dean write a few of his songs, and he said he'd work with me before I go."

"Work with you or work on hooking up with you?"

I shoot him a sarcastic look. Does he think that hasn't happened yet? "Do you really want to know?"

He closes his eyes. "Never mind."

We walk half a block in silence before I say, "I'm surprised you're on board with this. Aren't you worried about me? What happened to Protective Pete?"

"He's still around." My brother gives me his fatherly stare as we get stopped at another street crossing. "But this is a professionally run organization. You'll be surrounded by people, and Dean's not trying to get into your pants."

"You're right." The light changes and we start to walk. "However, I will be spending months on a bus with him and two other guys."

Pete's expression changes. "Wait. What?"

I skip ahead of him, dodging a few people so he can't lecture me.

"Come back here!" he shouts and tries to catch up. It's not easy to for him to work around people with his big body. "Little J!"

I laugh and start to run. I'm going to miss teasing him while I'm gone.

~~~~

"Let's take it from the top of "The Short Life"," Latson says as I reposition my fingers. We ran through the ballad a couple of times before switching gears to the faster paced "To Hell and Back."

As he plays next to me, I concentrate on the chords, waiting for my turn to join in. We're sitting in the infamous guitar room, the one he mentioned during our fire escape talk. He wasn't lying; he really has a room full of guitars. In fact, it's set up more like a mini-studio, with soundproof insulation on the walls and a mixing board in the corner. There are at least fifteen instruments in here, including the Fender, along with a few amps and mics.

He nods as he comes to the end of the first verse, indicating it's time for me to play. The first part of this song features the lead alone, then the rest of the band joins in. Latson sings the chorus, since I don't know all the words yet:

"I'm down so low, you're up so high
A million miles an hour
The speed you fly
Never catching up, never slowing down
Short is the life
We're burning into the ground."

At first I keep up, but then I start to stumble through the rest of the song. I find myself paying more attention to the words than the notes. I try to focus, but this is the third time I've heard the lyrics. Before the song ends, Latson stops playing and gives me a curious look. "What's wrong? Did your fingers seize up?"

"Of all of the things you make me do, the worst of them is missing you," I quote a line from the song. The words are so sad. "Who is Dean missing?"

Latson shrugs one shoulder as he shifts his weight. "He lost a sister, too."

"The song is about Audrey?" I don't know why I'm surprised. "I thought it was about a woman."

Latson acts nonchalant. "Audrey was a woman."

"You know what I meant." I reach over and set my hand on his arm. "If you would rather I learn this one on my own that's okay."

He shakes his head. "It's fine. When Dean started to write the song it was originally about an old girlfriend."

Oh. "When did that change?"

Latson gives me a pointed look. "After our sister killed herself."

His words make me do a double-take. "I thought you blamed someone named Levi for her death."

He lets out a heavy sigh. "Hang on." He sets his guitar down and then heads over to the corner where the mixing board sits. There's a small desk there too, and he opens the top drawer. When he returns to me, he's holding a picture. "This is us," he says as he hands it to me.

The picture is of a group of people standing outside a tour bus. The girls have their arms wrapped around one another, and the guys try to look like hard asses by striking rocker poses. I find Latson standing next to Dean in the back; his hair is longer and he has his fist in the air. Dean is sticking his tongue out and giving the camera the bird. My eyes skip over the people I don't know and land on the girls. I recognize Heidi, even without her red hair. She's blonde in this picture and has her arm around another girl's waist. Their heads are tipped together, but I know it's Audrey without asking. She has the same color hair as Latson, except it's wavy. I can see Oliver in her, especially in her eyes and mouth. She has cheekbones some women would die for.

"There's Audrey and Heidi," Latson points, "and Paige, Lauren, and Shannon. They were all friends with my sister. If you ever get bored, ask Dean about Shannon." He wags his eyebrows. "That's a good story."

"Is she the old girlfriend?" I ask, referring to the song.

"Possibly." He smiles and moves on. "There's me, Dean, Rob, Mike, Luke ..." His tone changes. "And Levi."

I look at the guy he obviously hates. He's tall, taller than Latson, and casually dressed like the rest of them. The exception to his appearance is his brown hair is styled, while the other guys have messy mops on their heads. He has piercing blue eyes, but they look smug, like he's hiding something. He's also standing at the edge of the group, like he's included but not accepted. "He looks shady," I say. "I didn't know he was in your band."

"He wasn't. He was our agent." Latson leans back in his chair. "Heidi kept running into him at shows and she introduced him to my sister. What started as a working relationship turned into more."

"More?"

He nods toward the photo. "You're looking at Oliver's dad."

What? I study Levi closely. I see nothing of Oliver in him. "Is it weird that I never gave a thought to who his father was?"

Latson shrugs. "It's just as well. Oliver never knew him. Levi stayed with Audrey through the pregnancy, but as soon as she had O, he left. He didn't want anything to do with a baby."

"That's awful." How could anyone leave O? Or Audrey? She's gorgeous and, from what Latson told me earlier, really smart. Or was she?

"Please tell me she didn't OD because of this asshole." I hold out the picture.

"Levi introduced her to drugs," Latson says. "Hell, we all tried something at some point." He studies his hands. "She stopped using when she found out she was pregnant, but started again after he left. It didn't help that my father practically disowned her after he found out she had a baby and no husband. She named Oliver after my dad to try to smooth things over." Latson looks me in the eye. "It didn't work."

It's hard for me to imagine the kind doctor who helped me abandoning his only daughter. "So, she committed suicide? I mean, things sound like they were shitty, but she had you and Dean and –"

"I don't think she meant to," Latson says. "Dean and I got her into rehab, and I kept Oliver while she got clean. When she was sober, I talked her into terminating Levi's parental rights."

"And then?"

"He started coming around again." Latson scowls. "He wanted her, but not his son. She fell into old habits; her tolerance level wasn't what it used to be." He sighs and rubs the back of his neck. "You know what happened next."

I look back at the picture and the smiling faces. Everyone looks so unsuspecting. They look like they're ready for the time of their lives, like nothing bad could possibly touch them. I can tell they felt invincible.

"It was her choice," I eventually say. "You did everything you could."

"Did I?" Latson gives me doubtful look.

"Yes." I turn my body toward his. "You intervened. She got well."

"She didn't stay that way," he mutters.

"What were you supposed to do? Monitor her every move? Set up shifts with Dean? You two did –"

"This is getting us nowhere," Latson cuts me off. He sits forward and picks up his guitar. "Do you want to try those two songs again or move on?"

There he goes, shutting down like he did in the car. He may not think he wants to talk about what happened, but he keeps revealing bits and pieces. I'm not sure how much is left to the story, but I wish he'd let it out.

Setting the picture aside, I pick up my guitar as well. "Show me the other songs and then we'll go back to the first two. That way I'll know what to concentrate on when I practice later."

Latson studies me for a few seconds before leaning forward and kissing me.

"What was that for?" I ask.

"For not pushing. I changed the subject and you let me."

I lift my hand and play with his hair. "I can be patient. You'll discuss it when you're ready."

"I'm surprised I'm discussing it at all. I think this tour is messing with me."

My expression softens. "It probably is. Dean is going without you."

"You're going without me."

I freeze. "If it bothers you that much –"

"Don't say you'll stay." Latson's eyes grow dark. "Not because of me."

"I wasn't." I smirk. "I was going to say if it bothers you that much, you'll have to make time to come out and see me. A visit or two won't hurt, will it?"

He circles my wrist and lowers my hand, bringing my fingers to his lips. "I'm so glad you said that. I didn't want you to think I was stalking you across the country."

I laugh. "I see. How many trips were you planning?"

"That's for me to know and you to find out." He kisses my fingertips. "But, there will only be a few. I have some things that need my attention here, like a bar and a kid."

"Being responsible is so overrated," I tease.

"You're right." He inches closer. "Now you know why I wanted to be a musician and not a doctor."

I kiss his nose. "I'm happy you're a musician. I'm also happy I'll get to see you. Thanks for fitting me in."

"I think it's you who will have to fit me in."

I shake my head, although he would know a touring schedule better than me. "We'll make time," I promise.

"Good," he says, "because we'll need to be alone when we're together." Smiling, he leans over his guitar to kiss me again. This time, when his lips meet mine, they stay there. Our kiss deepens, and our guitars bump together.

"Um, there's something in the way," I say.

Latson takes quick care of the situation. "There shouldn't be anything between us." He slides his hand around the back of my neck to bring me closer.

"You're right," I murmur before my mouth is occupied again. There will be too much distance between us soon enough.

Chapter Eighteen

Eight days later, the sound of hyper first graders echoes in my ears. I put my hand to my forehead to block out the sun and search the playground for Oliver. The weather decided to turn full-on summer for his last day of school.

Eventually I find him at the water balloon station. The kids are paired up on the grass and tossing balloons back and forth like an egg toss. Sporadically spaced around the playground are other activities, like sidewalk chalk, bubbles, tug-o-war, and a bounce house. Parent volunteers man each station, and Latson was assigned to the shoe pile. I was given the ice cream table, and my pre-made sundaes keep melting into mush before they're eaten.

"This is pointless," Erica, Donovan's mom, says as she presses whip cream onto my cups of vanilla soup. "Although, the kids don't seem to care."

I add some chocolate sprinkles to our concoctions and look out over the covered pavilion in front of us. Kids are sitting at picnic tables and slurping their ice cream with laughter. Some have vanilla mustaches from drinking the dessert instead of using a spoon. It makes me smile. "As long as they're happy," I say.

She agrees and keeps whip-creaming. She stops when we finish enough sundaes for the next rotation of kids. I stick my spoon back in the dish of sprinkles and my eyes roam the playground for Latson. He's all broad shoulders and khaki cargo shorts, his arms flexing as he helps another mom chuck small shoes and sandals into a mountain of footwear. After the last shoe hits the pile he looks over and waves. I wave back.

"So," Erica fans herself in the heat, "how long have you been dating Oliver's uncle?"

When she introduced herself as Donovan's mother, I introduced myself as Oliver's friend. She grew concerned about Mrs. Gibson and asked if I was his new nanny. I told her I was seeing Latson to clear up any confusion.

"A few weeks," I say.

"Well, between you and me," she steps closer, "I know some PTA moms who are going to be disappointed."

I frown. "Why?"

"Have you seen your boyfriend?"

Yes, I think. *I saw a lot of him this morning after he dropped Oliver off at school.* I'll never be able to look at his shower the same way again.

Erica glances over my shoulder at a group of ladies gathered on the sidewalk. There's not a lot to monitoring the chalk station, and they're staring in Latson's general direction.

"The one on the far right, Natalie Spencer, she's Max's mom," Erica says. "She's been after your man since she got divorced last year. And the one in the middle? Jackie O'Rourke? She's been eyeing him since Oliver first started at this school."

She's serious. "They really talk about him?"

Erica nods. "I'm surprised he's not a permanent agenda item. The PTA meetings usually start out like an episode of *Cougar Town*."

I laugh. I wonder if Latson knows.

Speaking of, out of the corner of my eye, I catch him walking my way. He grabs the bottom of his shirt and wipes his forehead with it, earning a collective gasp from the chalk moms. I stifle another laugh. I'm tempted to tell him he's the PTA hottie.

He makes his way over to me with a smile. "Can I get a water?"

"Sure." I open a cooler under the table marked for volunteers. I hand him a bottle and watch a bead of sweat roll down his temple before I brush it away. "I'm glad I got the job in the shade."

"Lucky." He smirks before downing half the bottle. "I'm surprised how bad little kids shoes stink in the heat." He makes a face, then looks down. "How are your feet?"

I look at my exposed toes in my flip flops. "They don't smell."

"I meant are they cold," he says. "You're getting on a plane in a few hours."

"I know," I sigh. "It's hard to believe I'll be in L.A .tonight."

The past week has flown by so fast my nerves haven't been able to keep up. It's been both a blessing and a curse: while I haven't had a chance to be anxious, I know, sooner or later, reality is going to bite me in the ass. I've been going through the motions to make sure I stay busy, so I won't second guess my decision. Keep working: check. Spend time with Pete and Jules: check. Try to learn Dean's songs: check. Try to pack everything I own: check. Spend quality time with Latson: check. And last, but not least, attend Oliver's picnic.

Check.

"Yoo-hoo! Lat-son!"

I look to my right and see Natalie wave as she comes over. When she makes it to us she flashes a perfect, white smile. "Sorry for interrupting, but I've been meaning to ask ... who are you requesting for Oliver's teacher next year? It's a toss-up between Littlejohn and Hunter for Max."

She bats her eyelashes and I take in her denim capris, flowy tank, and cute wedges. Her brown hair is layered in a trendy cut, and she looks like she could be in her late thirties.

"I'll let the school decide," Latson responds. "He's a little young to have a preference, I think."

"But he'll want to be with his friends." She lets out a tittering laugh. "Max and Oliver are like two peas in a pod."

They are? I glance at Latson and recognize the knowing gleam in his eye. He can tell she's flirting. "He talks about a lot of kids," he says. "I'm sure some of them are bound to be in his class."

Natalie shrugs and moves closer. "It doesn't hurt to be sure. I can submit the form to the office for you. It would only take a few seconds. I could also sign him up for t-ball with Max for the summer. We could carpool. What do you say?"

Latson gives me a wide-eyed look, as if saying, *Can you believe this?* A snicker gets caught in my throat, and I cover it with a fake cough.

He takes another drink of water, then leans in to give me a wet kiss on the cheek. "I'd better get back." He looks at Natalie. "I think we're all set, but thank you."

His tone indicates he's talking about more than class selection and sports. He winks at me then walks away, finishing his water as he goes. When the bottle is empty, he shoots it like a basketball at a nearby recycling container. It goes in.

Natalie turns to me, her shocked expression full of questions. "You know him?"

I give her a sweet smile. "Yes."

The top of her ears turn pink. "Well, I ... I ... didn't realize." She stiffens her spine and holds out her hand. "Natalie Spencer, PTA president. You are?"

"Jen Elliott." I shake her hand. "Girlfriend."

She nods, then turns on her heel and walks away, struggling to keep a slow pace back to the other moms. I look at Erica and she laughs. "You should have seen her face when he kissed you. No amount of Botox could have hid that reaction."

I shake my head. This is the last place I expected women to vie for Latson's attention. Torque and the gym I understand. But an elementary school?

My thoughts are interrupted when the kids in front of us start to leave. Per my instructions, I round the front of our table and hold out a container of disinfecting wipes for them to take as they walk by. Behind me, Erica grabs another stack of plastic cups. "Ready to make some more slop?"

"Ready as ever," I say.

By the end of the afternoon, the kids are tired, sticky, and sunburned. Oliver says goodbye to his teacher and his friends, and the three of us head to Latson's car for my trip to the airport. Since I have to be there early to get through security, we decided to leave straight from the picnic. After shutting the car door, I turn around to look at O in the backseat. "Did you have a good time?"

"Yes!" He grins. "I did so many flips in the bounce house I almost threw up!"

My face contorts. "Gross. That doesn't sound like fun to me."

He giggles. "Uncle Gunnar? Can Donovan spend the night? He wants to come over and his mom said maybe."

"Not tonight, buddy," Latson says as we leave the school. "After we take Jen to the airport we're going to dinner, remember?"

"Oh, yeah!" Oliver looks excited. "We're going to Medieval Times."

"What's Medieval Times?" I ask.

"It's where you eat with your hands, and there are knights and horses. They have battles right in front of you."

"That sounds much better than puking," I say. "Make sure you take pictures and send them to me."

"I will. Uncle Gunnar? Can I use your phone?"

Latson's eyes find Oliver in the rearview mirror. "Sure, dude." He looks at me. "You might get a bunch of blurry texts later."

I smile. "I look forward to it."

Latson pulls away from the school, and we discuss Oliver's summer vacation plans. Along with more aquarium time, he'd like to visit the zoo, go swimming, see his buddies, and have more Nerf wars, for which he says he'll need some sort of new gun.

"You have forty guns," Latson says. "That's enough."

"You're lying," Oliver's little voice accuses. "I have eighteen; I counted. You have more guitars than anything and you don't even play with all of them."

My eyes grow wide and swing to Latson. This is the most attitude I've ever heard from O. "I think you just got told by a second grader."

He smirks. "He's not a second grader yet."

"Am, too," Oliver interjects.

"We'll see once I get your report card," Latson says.

Their back and forth banter is sweet, and a pang of sadness hits. I'm going to miss this over the next few months. I'd love to take O to the zoo or to the beach. We never did get to the park to play in the fountains. Suddenly, I want more time. I stare out the window and swallow.

We pull into O'Hare International Airport, and Latson finds a parking space. Dean is supposed to meet us inside, along with Pete and Jules. I grab my guitar, swinging the case over my head and shoulder, and then my carry-on bag. Latson pulls my two suitcases from the trunk. I'm only working with what I brought to Chicago, so there wasn't much to pack. As we make our way to the crosswalk to head to the terminal, Oliver decides he wants to help. Latson lets him drag one of my bags, and the sight is too freaking cute. Maybe I'm being overly sentimental, but I let the boys walk ahead of me so I can take a picture.

Once I get checked in, we walk to the security screening point. There, I find Dean, Jules, and Pete standing off to the side.

And, unexpectedly, Carter, Felix, and Gwen.

"You guys!" I say in surprise and hurry my steps. "What are you doing here?"

Carter opens his arms wide, and I step into them for a hug. "Little J. Do you think we'd let you leave without saying goodbye?"

"I said goodbye last night at work." My voice is muffled against his chest.

"It's not the same." He holds me tight. "I forgot to tell you. If you need a bodyguard, let me know. I'll be there in a heartbeat."

Aww, I think. Before I can respond, he steps back and hands me off to Felix.

"Mi amor," Felix says with a pout. He catches my hand and kisses my knuckles. "Como voy a vivir sin ti?"

I give him knowing look. "You've lived without me before. I'm sure you'll manage."

He grins. "Be careful out there." He wraps me a quick hug before Gwen pushes him out of the way. She holds on to my shoulders and looks me squarely in the eye. "You must call or text me," she demands. "I want all the details. I want pictures of roadies. I want pictures from the stage. Oh! I want pictures of you *on* stage."

I laugh. "Okay, but only if you promise to take care of my boys." My eyes jump from Carter to Felix, then to Latson and Oliver who are talking to Dean. "You don't have to worry about Pete. Jules has that covered."

"You're damn right I do," Jules says and walks over. "Don't worry about us back here. Concentrate on you." She leans into my side. "And, remember, if you need someone on the tambourine, my offer still stands."

"Got it," I say. "You guys will probably get sick of my daily updates. I've never met Paul or Drew, and I doubt Dean and I have much in common. I'll need someone to talk to."

"We're here for you twenty-four, seven," Jules says and Gwen nods. "Any hour of the day or night. Don't hesitate to call."

"Thanks." Even though I assumed as much, it's still reassuring to hear the words.

Jules' eyes focus on something over my shoulder, and I turn around to see my brother. He doesn't say anything; we've talked about this opportunity so many times over the last week there's nothing left to discuss. Without words, I step up to him and we give each other an insane squeeze. "Love you," he says against my hair.

"Ditto," I say into his chest.

After I step away from Pete, Oliver skips over and tugs on my hand. "I made you something."

"You did?" I crouch down to his level. "What is it?"

He holds out a piece of paper that's been folded a dozen times. "It's a picture."

"You made me my own Oliver art?" He nods as I carefully take the paper and open it.

It's a drawing of three stick figures. Each one is labeled above their head: "Uncle Gunnar," "Me," and "Jen." My heart melts as I notice the little Oliver figure stands in the middle, holding hands with his uncle and me. I'm wearing a colorful triangle-shaped dress, and there's a guitar in my other hand. Latson is wearing shorts and has three straight lines for hair. A bright yellow sun sits at the top of the paper, and there's green grass at the bottom.

I hold it out so we both can see. "I'm going to hang this up wherever I go," I tell Oliver.

"You will?" He gives me a tiny smile. "I thought if you missed us, you could look at a picture. That's what I do when I miss my mom. It makes me feel better."

My breath catches. He's such a well-adjusted kid. It's easy to forget everything he's been through. I look over his sweet drawing again, now aware of the meaning behind it. "Thank you," I say softly. "I'll look at it every day."

He looks a little sheepish as I ruffle his hair.

"Hey."

I stand up at the sound of Latson's voice. He gestures for me to follow him, and we walk a few steps away from the group. He takes my free hand, threading his fingers through mine.

"Dean's ready whenever you are," he says. "He didn't want to interrupt your goodbyes to tell you."

"So he made you do it?"

"I volunteered." Latson gives me an uneasy smile. "I wanted a few minutes alone with you."

I don't like his expression. "Is everything okay?"

He nods. "Do you like Oliver's picture?"

"I love it," I say. "He's so thoughtful. You're doing a good job with him, you know."

Latson ignores my compliment and runs his thumb over the back of my hand. "You remembered to pack my shirt, right?"

"Of course." Latson gave me one of his white tees that suspiciously smelled like he dropped a whole bottle of cologne on it. "Everything in my suitcase is going to smell like you."

His smile grows more genuine. "I may have added another one to your bag. I hope you don't mind."

I wind my hand, the one that holds Oliver's picture, around his waist. "I don't, but I wish you had crawled inside instead."

Latson lets out a breath and rests his forehead against mine. "How did this day get here so fast?"

"I don't know," I say. "Time always does the opposite of what I want."

We stand there in silence before he brings his hand to cradle my face. He kisses me, catching my mouth with his and taking his time to brand every part. When I think the kiss is over, he surprises me by capturing my lips again.

And again.

"I want that burned into your memory," he whispers. "No one else gets to kiss you. No one."

"Okay," I breathe. Like the thought would cross my mind. "I'm going to miss you."

"Not as much as I'll miss you."

"Jen?" I hear Dean. "You ready?"

No, I think, but "yes" comes out of my mouth. Latson squeezes my fingers before letting me go. Reluctantly, he gives me his lopsided dimple smile. "Go be a rock star."

~~~~

After a four -hour flight, we land at LAX. I spent most of the trip with my eyes closed and my ear buds in, listening to a continuous loop of Dean's songs. Before the plane took off, he showed me an itinerary for the coming days. Scheduled in amongst rehearsals and photo shoots are appointments for costuming and radio interviews. It was a little nerve-wracking to see what lies ahead, so instead of watching the in-flight movie, this newbie decided to be proactive and practice playing guitar in her mind. The music took me to another place, and it also helped block out the cries from a screaming toddler a few rows back.

"Roxanne will meet us by the baggage claim," Dean says as we walk down the jetway.

"Who's Roxanne?"

"She's my agent-slash-manager." He smiles. "She'll be joining us on the tour, so you won't be stuck alone with us guys."

The news will make my brother happy. "Is that routine?" I ask. "I mean, she's not just doing it for me, is she?"

"No," Dean says. "Managers usually accompany their talent."

I nod. Okay. Good.

We exit our gate to a long line of people waiting to board our empty plane. The airport is teeming, as I assumed it would be. Dean seems to know where he's going, so I walk beside him without question and glance around. Maybe I'll see someone famous. All I end up seeing are a blur of faces until my eyes zero in on a Starbucks.

"Can we stop?" I ask, my eyes darting to the coffee shop. "The pretzels on the plane really didn't do it for me."

"Sure." He pulls out his phone. "Let me tell Roxanne."

"You have to check in?"

"She has a car waiting. It's courtesy to let her know we'll be a few minutes."

Holy crap. I didn't realize. "I'll make it fast," I promise and start to walk away. I thought we would be taking a cab.

"Wait." Dean follows me. "You're not the only one who's hungry."

Of course the place is crowded and the line takes forever to move. I don't want to leave a bad impression with Roxanne by making a pit stop, but I really am starving. I consider getting a smoothie, but throw health out the window and end up ordering a S'mores Frappuccino instead. I get a zucchini walnut muffin too, and Dean opts for an iced coffee with milk. When our drinks are prepared, the barista calls out, "Jan and Dean!"

"Jan and Dean?" I frown. "Wasn't that a real group?"

Dean laughs. "Yeah. It was two guys from the sixties."

I shrug and go retrieve our drinks. I'll be Jan as long as I can claim my Frappuccino.

We make our way to the escalators, then down to the baggage claim. It seems like everywhere I look there's a driver holding a sign. I read a line of them: Ryan, Stephens, Reid, McCarthy. That's us. A tall man wearing a blue suit holds the sign and looks bored while a petite woman with a raven-colored pixie cut stands beside him consulting her phone.

"Rox!" Dean shouts and waves.

She looks up and waves back. "'Bout time!"

Dean weaves around people to get to his manager and when he does, he hugs her. Then, he steps back and introduces us. "Jen, Roxanne Hughes. Rox, Jen Elliott. Rhythm guitar."

Roxanne extends her hand and I shake it. "I've heard good things about you." She looks me over from head to toe, appraising my appearance. "This is good," she says to herself and then looks at Dean. "Nice window dressing. You needed some spice for the men in the crowd. Now you can appeal to more fans."

Wait. What?

My eyes swing to Dean. "That's why you asked me out here? To sex up your band?" Disbelief washes over me. I can't believe I fell for this. "You brought me across the country to look pretty?"

Dean's complexion pales. "No! You're mad talented." He gives Roxanne a hard stare. "Why would you say that? You just met her."

Roxanne looks stunned, but in a phony way. "I wasn't trying to be nasty. I'm your manager; I look at your image from every angle. Despite her inexperience, she *will* help." Her eyes focus on mine. "I'm sorry, but it's true. It's the nature of the business."

I want to throw my Starbucks at her. I picture it splattering against her chest, and I'm surprised by my visceral reaction. It must be because I've been pent up in a flying metal tube for the last four hours.

"Jen." Dean can tell I'm annoyed. "Gunnar would never support this if he thought I was messing with you. Don't be upset. Rox is just –"

"Telling you how it is," she cuts him off. "I've been planning this tour non-stop since we were given the green light. It's Dean's second chance and everything needs to be analyzed." She extends her hand again. "Let's start over. I've heard great things about your playing and nothing about your looks."

I narrow my eyes.

"Jen." Dean looks desperate. "It's true."

I believe him. I really do. It's Roxanne I'm not sure about. My shoulders relax a little and I focus on Dean's manager. "Did he tell you this was all new to me?"

"He did."

"Okay. Then you know I have no idea how the business works," I stress the word. "If he gains new fans, that's fine. But it won't be because I'm window dressing. I didn't come out here to parade around. I came to play." I don't need her thinking she can dress me up like a doll.

Roxanne's professional expression turns into an approving one. "Good." She steps to my side, wraps her arm around my waist, and starts to usher me toward the baggage carousels. "I was worried when Dean said you've never toured. The last thing I have time to do is babysit you. I don't need you breaking down on me."

"You were concerned?"

"The pressure can be stressful," she says. "There are new people and new temptations. You're in a new place every other day. I don't need you getting emotional. My instincts tell me you'll only do that when necessary. You won't allow anyone to run over you. That's important."

"I wasn't planning any emotions other than nerves."

"Trust me," Roxanne leans closer, "there will be plenty of feelings. Just try to act on them in a positive way. Remember, there are cameras everywhere. Are you on social media?"

I think I know what she's getting at. "I'm not going to make a fool of myself, if that's what you're worried about."

She gives me a curt nod. "Not anymore."

We step up to a conveyor belt of traveling bags. "Let's get your stuff and get moving." Roxanne consults her vibrating phone. "Paul and Drew are already at the hotel."

Once we find our belongings, we walk outside to where our driver parked a sleek black town car in a reserved space. He helps load everything into the trunk, and then I get in the back with Roxanne while Dean sits up front. Once we leave the airport the ride is stop and go. Traffic is unbearable, even after seven p.m. I stare out the window and pick at my muffin, realizing the time difference. In Chicago it would be after nine. Since I'm trapped in the car, I find my phone and send a group text to my brother, Jules, Gwen, and Latson to let them know I landed safely.

By the time we pull up to the hotel, it's late evening. Roxanne gave me her contact information, I've given her mine, and we've gone over our agenda for the next few days. I also received a message from everyone back home. Oliver sent me a picture of a horse's rear end and one of his own nose. Latson said it was his attempt at a selfie. I also got a nice shot of the two of them wearing paper crowns. It made me smile.

While we're unloading our bags, Roxanne hands a key card to Dean and then one to me. "You're both on the same floor as Paul and Drew," she explains. "I'm one below. Feel free to call if you need anything."

We head inside and when the elevator stops at her floor, Roxanne says goodnight and she'll see us at rehearsal tomorrow.

When we get to our level, a guy walking past the elevator door stops in his tracks.

"Well, I'll be damned." He grins. "You made it."

"Hey, Drew." Dean steps out of the elevator and they give each other a one-armed man hug. "Jen, this is Drew. Drew, Jen."

"Hi," I say as I struggle to pull my suitcases around Dean's.

"The new guitar player, right?" Drew asks. "Here." He leans forward to grab one of my bags. "Let me help."

"Thanks." I smile and move to the side. Drew is slightly taller than me with clear blue eyes and a little scruff on his chin. I catch a glimpse of a tattoo peeking out from beneath his shirt sleeve. It looks like a skull. "You're the drummer."

He nods. "My reputation precedes me. What rooms are you two in?"

"Ummm ..." I twist the key around in my hand. "408."

"410 here," Dean says.

"I'm across the hall with Paul, 409 and 411." Drew starts to walk. "Welcome to home sweet home."

We make it to my door which isn't far from the elevator. When I step inside my room, I find the typical hotel set up with a king size bed, a dresser with a television, and a small desk with a coffee pot sitting on the corner. I pull my suitcase over near the window and set my guitar case on the bed. Drew stops just inside the doorway. "Do you guys have plans? Paul and I were going to head downstairs for a beer."

My stomach growls. "If there's food involved I'm in," I say. "Just give me a second to get situated."

"Great. I'll let him know and be back in a few."

He closes the door, and I lift one of my suitcases on to the bed to unzip it. As soon as I open my bag I see the shirt Latson added to my things. Smiling, I unfold the *I licked it so it's mine tee*. I start to laugh when I see a few changes. Latson used a black Sharpie and crossed out the words "I" and "mine", so the shirt now says *Latson licked it so it's his*. Of course it smells like him, and I hold it to my nose and breathe deep. I needed this. Between the flight, meeting Roxanne, her stupid comment, and the long drive, it calms me. I know what I'll be sleeping in tonight.

Just as I start to unpack, my phone rings.

"Excellent timing," I say. "I just found your stowaway t-shirt."

Latson laughs. "What do you think? I thought maybe I could make a bunch and sell them."

"Don't you dare."

"So, how are things going?"

"Good, I guess." I sigh and plop down on the bed. "Roxanne's different. How was Medieval Times?"

We get lost in conversation and I sit there, sorting through clothes, before the adjoining door between my room and the next opens. Apparently, my side wasn't locked. Dean sticks his head around the corner. "Cool. Our rooms are connected."

"Is that Dean?" Latson asks.

"Yep. Do you want to talk to him?"

"No. I'll catch up with him later."

Dean continues to stand there and I feel awkward. "Hey," I say. "You can't just come in here whenever you want. What if I was changing?"

He looks surprised. "It didn't even cross my mind. Sorry."

"What's your ass sorry for now?" Drew appears behind him. "Are we ready to go or what?"

"Who is that?" Latson asks.

"Drew," I say. "We're supposed to go downstairs for a drink. I was just –"

"Jennnnnn!"

This must be Paul. He strides around both Dean and Drew and over to me. "Would you hurry it up? I'm fucking thirsty."

He jumps on to the bed with both feet and hops up and down, throwing me off balance. "Stop!" I laugh.

"Are they all in in your room?" Latson sounds annoyed on the other end of the line.

"Yes, and they're uninvited." I move the phone away from my mouth. "Go. I'll catch up." I wave them away.

"Okay, okay," they mumble and walk back into Dean's room. "We'll save you a seat."

Once they leave I lock the adjoining door. It's like living with my brothers again. "They're gone," I say. "Where were we?"

"I think you were going out."

Latson sounds disappointed and my stomach sinks. "I'm not going out. I'm going to eat. There's a difference."

"I know." Silent seconds pass before his tone changes. "Don't let me keep you. Go. Meet the band. I have to get Oliver to bed anyway."

He's not fooling me. I know the guys bug him, but there's nothing I can do. "Tell O I said goodnight." I reach for my carry-on bag and find his drawing. I need a place for it. "I'll call you after rehearsal tomorrow."

"Sounds good," Latson says.

When we hang up, I prop Oliver's drawing on the bedside table, so I can see it all the time. I take a picture of it, then send it to Latson. Maybe it will make him feel better.

So you can tuck me in too, I type.

I wish, he sends back.

Chapter Nineteen

"Stop! Stop! Stop!"

Dean waves his arms like he's directing air traffic. My hands still and my guitar goes silent.

"Jen! Move!"

I look up just in time to see a huge inflatable heart falling toward my head. Paul's big hand wraps around the top of my arm and yanks me out of the way.

"Sorry!" I hear someone from backstage shout. "The rigging on that one is a bitch!"

I watch as the heart hits the ground and bounces back up. I was almost attacked by one of Ariel's stage props. I look above me again to see a sea of hanging hearts in various sizes, colored red, pink, and purple. She's certainly going all lovey-dovey for one of her numbers.

"We should move," Paul says. "It's not like we don't know our fucking places. We're not jumping around like fucking River Dance."

Ah, Paul. If I've learned anything about him in the last ten days, it's that he doesn't hold back.

"Sure," Drew huffs from behind us. "Move farther away and leave me lost in the goddamn glitter." He brushes his head and sparkles go flying. "Tell me why we're here again?"

"We're here," Dean's voice echoes through the speakers, "because we need to be. They said we could rehearse, so we're rehearsing."

I take a step away from Paul and stare out into the empty abyss of the Staples Center. The tour begins tomorrow night, and Roxanne secured us some stage time while the crew runs through Ariel's set changes. What sounded like a great idea at first has turned into a comedy of errors. In addition to the falling heart, we've been blinded by stage lighting and bombed with glittery chunks of confetti. The pyrotechnics that exploded a half hour ago almost made us piss our pants. As I look around, I start to wonder if we should cut our losses and call it quits.

"Now what?"

Drew's groaning question makes me turn around. The hearts above us start to ascend and large tie-dyed panels are wheeled into place around the stage. They surround Drew, and he tosses his drumsticks over his shoulder, defeated and annoyed.

"I feel like I've stepped into some trippy dream," I say to Paul. "Hearts and tie dye. Is Ariel sixteen or twenty-five?" I've yet to meet her or any of her people, but I am familiar with her music. To me, she seems like a mix of Britney Spears and Katy Perry. Sexy and sweet with a little raunchy thrown in.

Just then, the lights go out and black lights illuminate the stage. Everything glows, including us.

"Your dream just got a fuck-ton trippier," Paul jokes and starts to pluck a familiar bass line. It's "Purple Haze" by Jimi Hendrix. I laugh and try to join in, but I'm terrible.

"Guys. Let's focus," Dean says. "Let's take it from the top of "Out of the Blu."

"I need out of the black," Drew says. "I can't find my sticks."

Dean lets out a frustrated sigh. "Take five."

I walk back to my side of the stage to wait out the latest special effect. Standing in place I rock back on my heels, thinking about the last week and a half. It's been a blur and my fingers are blistered, but I wouldn't trade this crazy experience for anything. I never thought I'd be standing on stage in an arena that can hold 18,000 people, yet here I am. Playing tomorrow both excites and terrifies me. It's a heady feeling. I'm still nervous, but not as much as I was when I left Chicago.

When the lights come back on, movement off stage catches my attention. Roxanne is headed our way with her arms full of paper.

"How's your rehearsal? I hope you're putting in quality time."

I want to tell her if she's worried she should stay, but I don't. Even after a week and a half I still can't read her very well. Is she our friend? Our boss? I'm still not clear on whether she works for the record label or Dean.

Roxanne shifts what looks like posters in her arms. "I brought the final product of your last photo shoot." She stops walking and stands near the front of the stage. "I think you'll be pleased."

We all walk toward her, and she hands us each a copy. The glossy posters are longer than they are wide with a sepia-toned background. Each of us is pictured in black and white, and we're standing side by side but looking off in different directions. We never posed this way, so I know the photographer took our individual shots and Photoshopped us. Dean is first in line and he stands casually. He's holding the neck of his guitar with one hand and looking down at the ground with a smile. Drew is next, and he wears a more serious expression. He has his arms crossed and most of his back to the camera, so you can see his drumsticks sticking out of his back pocket. Paul wears his usual cocky smirk as he holds his bass over one shoulder, and then there's me.

I'm last in line, but I wear the biggest grin. My eyes are closed as I hold my acoustic in front of me like I'm playing. My hair whips around my face, but it doesn't obscure it. I think I remember this shot. At one point during the session, the photographer's assistant turned on a big fan and it felt like I was stuck in a hurricane. I started laughing because I thought it was silly; a stylist spent an hour meticulously curling my hair only to have it ruined in an instant. Plus, I'm not a model. The fan reminded me of a fashion shoot.

Paul reads aloud from the top of the poster and embellishes the band name just a little. "Dean McCarthy and the motherfuckin' Union."

A small smile plays over Dean's lips as he looks over the design. "Joining Ariel Allyn on the Renegade Tour," he adds.

"Here." Roxanne starts to hand out equal stacks of posters. "Every one of you needs to sign all of these."

"Why?" I ask as I receive mine.

"We'll be shipping them to radio stations and doing online giveaways through Dean's website. People who purchase a VIP ticket to the show will also get one."

I look over the picture again. Cool. I get to autograph something.

When Roxanne's hands are empty she reaches into the over-sized canvas tote she always carries and pulls out two packages of Sharpies. She hands them to Dean. "I'm giving the swag to you now because I have a dinner meeting with Ariel's manager. We need the posters signed by tomorrow and there's five hundred here."

"Okay." Dean juggles the items in his hands. "I say we set this stuff down and –"

"PA-SSSSSSHHH!"

A pop followed by loud hissing noise makes us all jump and duck. I turn around and see plumes of white smoke being shot into the air at the back of the stage. There must be twenty air-pressured jets shooting the mist sky high. It's so loud we can't do anything but stare until the test is over. When the jets stop, a damp fog drifts over us.

"All these effects can't be safe for the dancers," I think out loud. "Someone is going to fall and kill themselves."

"That's why they make more money than you," Roxanne says matter-of-factly. "They're trained for this."

I meet her eyes and frown. The woman doesn't have a filter.

"Let me explain why." She holds both hands in front of her, palms up, and shifts them like a scale. "Headliner, opening act. Established musician, former guitarist starting over. Practices that have taken place since the tour was established, one week of rehearsals. Do you see a theme here?"

Way to make me feel small, Rox. "Thanks for clearing that up," I say sarcastically.

She doesn't react to my tone. "Well," she claps her hands together, "I'm off. I need to meet Mason and discuss uploading your merchandise to the tour store. I also want to add a link on Ariel's webpage. I swear, you'd think these things would be easy, but ..." She drifts off. "Anyway, I'll see you all bright and early. Remember you have a radio interview at ten. I need you alert and happy, so turn in early, okay? This could be the last decent night of sleep you get for a while. Call me if you need me."

She walks away and our collective group of eyes follows her. Once she's out of sight, tense voices can be heard from the opposite direction. Our attention shifts to the left, and we see some arguing crew. Drew clears his throat.

"I say we ditch this joint. Let's find some drinks, sign this shit, and celebrate. The tour starts in twenty-four hours." He looks around the group. "Who's with me?"

Paul's hand shoots up first and mine follows. Dean gives us an exasperated look. "Guys. I think we should run through the set at least one more time."

I walk over and nudge his arm with my elbow. "We got this." I sound more confident than I am, but I think a break is in order. I can tell we're starting to stress, Dean more so than the rest of us. We've been going non-stop since we flew into L.A. "Let's relax," I say. "All of these stage surprises have us on edge."

Dean remains silent.

"C'mon." I give him an exaggerated pouty face before Drew and Paul do the same.

"Fine," Dean concedes. "I could use some Jager."

"Hell yeah!" Drew throws his fist in the air. "I dub this the first official party of the Renegade tour. Let's go."

It doesn't take us long to leave our instruments and find the exit. As we step out into the summer night Drew says, "There's a restaurant Mona told me about near L.A. Live. The Yard House. She said they have good food and it's in walking distance."

Paul looks doubtful. "You want to go somewhere our stylist recommended?"

"Would you rather pay for beer or cab fare?"

"Beer," Paul says.

"That's what I thought."

Drew and Paul lead the way as we walk up some stairs and round the side of the Staples Center. Across the street is the Nokia Plaza. It's lit up like Times Square by a huge LED screen and multiple smaller screens attached to six tall pillars. Latin music spills into the air from the open doors of a bar named The Conga Room and, after we walk across the space, we pass a Starbucks. My stomach growls for a Frappuccino, but I keep moving. Soon, I spot awnings printed with the Yard House name.

Glancing at Dean, I ask, "Is it weird we're carrying our own promo material through downtown L.A.?"

He laughs. "If we were smart we'd start handing it out." He looks at the people milling around. "Roxanne might kill us if we returned less than five hundred posters, though."

"She's ..." My voice fades. "Are all managers like her?"

Dean raises an eyebrow. "You mean direct and to the point?"

"I would have said crass and bossy, but yeah."

He smiles. "I wouldn't know. My only other manager was Audrey, and she was family."

We arrive at the restaurant doors where the logo boasts "Great Food, Classic Rock, and the World's Largest Selection of Draft Beer." We follow Paul and Drew inside. After Paul flirts with the hostess, we end up seated at two small tables side by side. Dean and I are at one, and Drew and Paul are at the other. A waiter arrives to take our drink order, and I opt for a Gin and Ginger. Drew high-fives me over the back of my chair. "First official party." He winks.

"Is this you guys?" The waiter eyes our posters.

"Yep," Dean says. "You coming to Ariel's show?"

"As a matter of fact I am. I got my girlfriend tickets for her birthday."

"Great. What are your names? I'll give you a shout out tomorrow night."

"You will?" The waiter looks surprised. "That would be awesome. I'm Chris and my girlfriend's name is Whitney."

Dean smiles. "I'm Dean. Nice to meet you." He shakes Chris' hand, then looks back at the menu. "I'll take a Surly Furious, please."

"Got it," Chris says as my eyes dart to an ad on the table for the hoppy beer.

"What? No Jager?" I tease, remembering the liqueur Dean said he needed.

"Not when there's decent ale around."

The waiter leaves to get Paul and Drew's order, and Dean reaches for a package of markers and rips it open. "Better get started," he says and flips me a pen. We spread out the posters and start signing them. I follow Dean's lead and scrawl my name above my head. After signing a few, I find my cell and take a picture. I caption it #signingswag and send it to Latson. Then I post it to Facebook, Instagram, Snapchat, and Twitter. I have to remember to do all four, since Snapchat and Twitter are new to me. Roxanne made me get the apps, so I was available to potential fans.

When Chris brings our drinks, he tells us they're on the house. I surprised the drinks are free and accept mine with a grateful "thanks." Dean thanks him as well before answering his vibrating phone. "Hey." He takes a drink of his beer. "Yeah. Where are you?" He waits for their answer. "The Marriott by L.A. Live? We're across the street, at the Yard House." He sets his glass down and picks up a pen. "Sure. We just got here." He signs his name. "Okay. See you in a few." He hangs up.

"Expecting someone?" I take a sip of my drink.

"Just Heidi."

I nearly choke. "Heidi? As in red-haired, bitch-face Heidi?"

Dean smirks. "Gunnar told me about your confrontation in his hallway. Did you not expect to see her on tour?"

I'd forgotten about that part of the conversation. "Does she know I'm here?"

"I didn't tell her."

"Why?"

"Because it's none of her business who's in my band."

This ought to be interesting. "She's going to be pissed when she finds out. You might lose a groupie."

Dean shrugs. "It's nice to have the girls around, but they're not necessary. I let Heidi and her friends tag along because their reaction to the band stirs up interest. If she wants to play dirty, however, she can go. It makes no difference to me."

"It might get dirty," I warn him. "She hates me. I don't know what I did but –"

"You stole my brother's attention." Dean talks as he autographs. "Heidi's been after Gunnar since his voice changed. I think she thought the two of them would bond over Audrey's death, but it didn't happen. No matter how hard she tries, he doesn't want her."

I think about what he said. She does act like a spurned lover.

Dean continues. "You know why I call Gunnar my brother, right? I was a foster kid."

"I know." I smile. "Latson told me. He told me about his – your – mom, too. I'm sorry she's sick."

"You and me both."

"Hey." I feel a tap on my shoulder. "Can we get some of those pens over here?"

I grab a few and turn around to hand them to Drew. "Thanks," he says. "Oh, and here's a tip. The more you drink, the less you'll feel the carpal tunnel."

I laugh.

Dean and I continue to sign until the Eagles "Hotel California" comes on. He starts to sing and I join him, until footsteps and laughter interrupt our duet. I look up to see Heidi and her entourage approaching. They're wearing tight, skimpy outfits with little strappy tank tops and heels. Heidi's all big smiles and swaying hips until she sees me. Her eyes narrow and her walk slows, yet she makes it to our table. She looks down and picks up one of the band posters.

"What the hell?" she hisses and turns to Dean. "Please explain why this bitch is here."

"I think it's obvious." Dean remains nonchalant. "She's in my band."

"Since when?"

"Since I asked her."

"She has no talent!"

"Says who?"

"Says me!"

I pick up my glass and take a drink. This is entertaining.

"You must not have ears," Paul says from behind me. "She's fucking talented. And, hey, by the way, long time, no see."

Heidi shoots him an evil glare. "You didn't call me, remember?"

My eyebrows shoot up.

Heidi turns her attention back to Dean. "I didn't sign up to watch her on stage."

"Then look past her and at me," Drew says over my head. "I'll be the one behind the drums."

"Or," Paul stands, "you could not show up at all. It wouldn't hurt my feelings any."

Heidi scowls and focuses on me. "You've got them all wrapped around your little finger, don't you?"

I shrug. I refuse to get riled up. Instead, I grab a Sharpie and remove the cap. I sign another poster and ask, "Should I make this one out to Heidi or do you prefer another name?"

She slams her hand down on the table and leans into my space. "You don't get it, do you?"

"I'm sorry. I guess I don't. Do you want me to sign your hand instead?" I move quickly, getting a J and an E on her skin before she yanks her hand away.

"You ..." she seethes. She points at me and looks at Dean. "I'm not putting up with this!"

"No one said you had to." Dean raises his glass. "Why don't you take a seat and relax. Jen won't talk to you if you don't talk to her. Right, Jen?"

I nod.

"Ugh!" Heidi huffs and stomps off to an empty table. One of her girlfriends follows her, while the other three remain by us.

"Wow." A nameless woman steps forward. "Hi. I'm Brooke." She extends her hand to Dean. "I don't want to get off on the wrong foot. I have no idea what's going on, but I'm super excited to hear you guys play. So are Kate and Lisa." She looks over her shoulder at the other two girls.

Dean shakes her hand. "That's good to hear. Are you familiar with our music?"

Brooke blushes. "Um, no. Not really. Heidi just said she was following a band and we could come along. Maybe meet the guys and help out and ... I don't know. Have fun, I guess."

"Well, ladies, you've come to the right place." Paul grins and pulls over two empty chairs. "You're more than welcome to join us." He looks around. "I don't see another empty seat. One of you will have to sit on my lap."

One of the girls, Kate or Lisa, I'm not sure who, happily volunteers. *Jesus*, I think. *So it begins.* I've yet to see any "rock star" behavior out of any of the guys; I suppose it had to start sometime. As Paul plays Bad Santa, I roll my eyes and go back to what I was doing. I silently wonder how interesting things will get once we're out on the road. I have no idea how big the tour bus is. Should I invest in sound-proof headphones?

"Don't worry about Heidi," Dean interrupts my thoughts.

"Do I look worried?"

"I don't know. You're making some kind of face."

I laugh. "I'm just thinking, that's all."

"About?"

I glance back at Paul, Drew, and the girls. Their flirting makes me miss Latson. Not that I haven't missed him every day, but this kind of throws it in my face.

"Hellooo," Dean says. "What are you thinking about?"

I sigh. "That there's only one lap I'd like to sit on."

Dean gives me a knowing smile. "You guys will be together before you know it."

"You promise?"

"Promise."

~ ~ ~ ~

"God, I wish you were here."

I stare at my reflection in the dressing room mirror as I hold my phone to my ear. I'm trying to remain calm, but we go on for the first time ever in about an hour.

"You're going to be fine," Latson reassures me through my cell. "I know it. I can feel it from two time zones away."

I let out a heavy breath and blow my side bangs off my face. Mona, our stylist, intricately curled my hair to the left, since I decided to grow a zit on that side of my forehead. I know it's from stress, but come on. Did it have to show up on opening night?

"Take a picture of yourself and send it to me," Latson says. "I want to see you before L.A. does."

"Okay. Hang on." I put his call on hold and do as he asks using the mirror. I send the picture as a text message and then go back to the call. "Done," I say.

It takes a minute before he receives it. "You look amazing," he says. "Where's the sign that says your mine?"

I laugh. "It will be spelled out in lights over my head on stage."

I have to admit that Mona did a great job despite my new friend Zitty McZit. She gave me cat eyes with thick, black liner, and she made my lips look pouty with two shades of lipstick and some sort of gloss. My cheeks look perfectly pink, and the clothes she picked out are cute ankle boots, tight jeans, and a sheer white peasant blouse. I'm wearing a black mid-riff tank underneath it, and my hair falls in waves down my back.

"I miss you," I say. "I could use a kiss for encouragement right about now."

"If I was there to kiss you I wouldn't stop. You'd be late for the show."

"I'd be willing to risk it."

Dean gags from behind me. My tone must give me away. "Are you two getting all mushy? We're taking good care of her, G!" He yells so Latson can hear.

"Tell Dean to worry about himself," he says.

A guy wearing a headset knocks on the open door. "D.U.? You have five minutes until meet and greet."

"Thanks," Dean says.

I meet his eyes. "D.U.?"

"It's short for the band name. It's easier."

"Oh."

"Still learning the ropes?" Latson asks.

"Yeah. They don't give all the secret codes to the new kids."

Roxanne comes speeding around the corner. "Why are you all still in here? Meet and greet. Now. Walk."

"Gotta go," I say to Latson as I hop off the stool. "Wish me luck."

"You don't need it," he says, "but break a leg anyway."

I fall in line behind Rox, Dean, Paul, and Drew. We make a few turns down a couple of hallways before we're led into a small conference room. There are no tables or chairs, just a group of about twenty people wearing lanyards and holding stuff like cameras and papers. Roxanne stops us before we get too close.

"These are the VIP people who paid extra for close seats. They get to meet you now and Ariel after the show. So be nice, smile, and sign whatever it is they want you to sign."

We nod and she releases us. The guys wave and greet the fans like the pros they are, while I do my best to fit in. A few cameras flash and Dean's name is shouted before Roxanne and another attendant start to let people forward. The first two ladies look like sisters and wear huge grins as they ask Dean to sign t-shirts. They each pose for a picture with him and then make their way down the line. We each sign their shirts and they want pictures with all of us, which surprises me. I mean, who am I? They haven't even heard me play.

At the end of the session I meet a girl who came to see the show with her mother. She looks about twelve years old and asks me to sign her backstage pass.

"Sure. What's your name?"

"Amanda."

"It's nice to meet you, Amanda." I sign my name next to the words "Renegade Tour." "Are you excited to see Ariel later?"

She nods. "And you, too."

"Me? No one knows me."

She blushes. "I didn't know girls could play in rock bands. I always thought they had to be pop singers."

"Oh, no," I say. "Girls can be band members. They can play any instrument they want."

"What do you play?"

"The guitar."

"That's cool." She looks at her pass I just signed and smiles. "Thanks. I haven't heard any of your music yet, but I'm sure I'll like it."

"I hope so," I say as her mother asks us to stand together for a picture.

We finish the meet and greet with time to spare since not everyone who purchased a VIP ticket showed up. Roxanne explained some people buy the tickets just to meet the headliner, but she hopes that will change the longer we're on tour.

"You have half an hour before show time," she announces. "Make the best of it."

Without consulting the guys, I decide to go back to the dressing room to busy my hands. I need something to pass the time to keep my mind off what I'm about to do. Even though I'm using another guitar on stage courtesy of the label, I brought my own with me tonight to keep me sane. It's comforting to hold something familiar before doing something that's the exact opposite.

I'm almost to the room when the same guy wearing the headset from earlier stops me. "Are you Jen Elliott?"

"Yes."

"There's someone waiting for you in your dressing room."

Immediately my thoughts jump to Latson. "Thank you." I grin and pick up my pace. Maybe he was lying when he said he was two time zones away. When I make it to the room, I expect to see him standing there with his lopsided smile and open arms. Instead, who I see stops me dead in my tracks.

"So." Ariel Allyn flips her hair over one shoulder. "You're the one dating my ex."

Chapter Twenty

"Uh ..." I stutter. I'm flustered by the famous celebrity pop star standing in front of me.

"You know," she turns toward the mirror and checks her bright red lipstick, "Gunnar's phone call surprised me. I didn't think he'd keep my number."

Wait. "Latson called you?"

She nods and turns to me, then pulls at the top of her strapless leather bustier. In fact, her entire outfit is leather. She's got the body to pull it off, too. She reminds me of Anne Hathaway when she played Catwoman, but without the mask and ears.

"I don't know who thought this was a good idea," she says as she adjusts her chest. "I've got more double-stick tape going on than 3M."

I suppress a laugh as her eyes comb over me.

"I'm jealous," she continues. "You don't have to worry about flashing an arena."

"True." I take a few steps toward her. "But that doesn't mean I won't find a way to embarrass myself."

She gives me half a smile and starts to back away from me. "Well, you've made it this far. You must've done a few things right." She turns around and reaches for a guitar case propped against the wall. I don't remember seeing it before.

"Whose is that?"

"Yours," she says before placing it in my hands. "It was delivered to me with strict instructions to make sure it got safely to you."

I'm confused. I take the case from her and set it on the vanity in front of the mirrors. Popping the latches, I open the lid to a familiar sight.

"No way," I breathe as I stare at the Fender. It's Latson's. The same guitar he let me play the night of Dean's show. There's a folded piece of notebook paper tucked in the strings, and I wiggle it free.

So we can be on stage together.
She's yours now. I know you'll take good care of her.
You've got this, Little Bird. Knock 'em dead.
— Latson

I'm speechless. His gift is unexpected and over the top. Slowly, I run my fingers over the strings.

"Do you like it?" Ariel asks.

"Very much."

"Then it looks like my job here is done. I'll leave you two to get acquainted."

"Thank you." I meet her eyes. "You didn't have to be Latson's delivery service."

She smiles. "He thought if he sent it to Dean you might accidentally see it and ruin the surprise."

"I don't ruin surprises," Dean's voice sounds as he enters the room. "Ariel. How in the hell are ya?"

She opens her arms wide and squeals. "C'mere! I need hugs!"

Dean wraps her tiny frame in his big arms. "Thank you so much for this. We'll make you look good, I promise."

"No worries. When that Australian boy band canceled I knew who I wanted to open for me." She steps out of his embrace and hangs on to his hands. "I'm so glad you're here! It's almost like old times."

As the two of them reconnect, Paul appears by my side with his bass. "Hey. You want me to help you tune that thing?" His eyes dart to the Fender.

"Yeah." I lift it out of the case. I swear the air around me changes the moment I slide the strap over my head. I position my fingers on the strings and Paul strums an E. With his tone as a reference, I strum the same note and then adjust the tuner. We go through all six strings and play the beginning of our opening number for good measure.

"Sounds good," Ariel says. "I'll be watching you guys." She starts to leave, but stops. "Oh, and I'll see you after the show. You're coming, right? Never mind. I just made it mandatory. I'm at the Ritz. In the penthouse." She gives us two thumbs up before disappearing out the door.

"After party?" I ask the guys.

Drew stops doing push-ups and wags his eyebrows. "Oh, yeah."

Why is he on the floor? "What are you doing?"

"Pre-show ritual," he huffs. "Gotta get the blood flowing."

Good to know.

I run my hand over the smooth face of my new guitar before I decide to give Latson a call. I want to let him know I got his gift. It's unbelievable, and he shouldn't have done it. I no more than tap his name on the phone when headset guy returns for a third time. He must get exhausted running back and forth all night.

"D.U. The stage is ready when you are."

I swallow and hang up.

"Okay." Dean looks at us. "Ready?"

Drew gets to his feet, and Paul slams the last of his Red Bull. They both walk toward Dean, so I do the same. We end up standing in a circle, and Dean puts his fist in the middle. Paul follows suit and so does Drew. I place my fist in last. It looks small next to the others.

"Tonight is the beginning of something I thought I'd never see," Dean says. "I wasn't sure I'd set foot on a tour again, let alone one this big. You all made that possible. We've put in the hours and we've practiced our asses off. Now, there's only one thing left to do." He looks each one of us in the eye. "Go out there and kill it."

"Hell yeah!" Paul pumps his fist in the air.

"Kill it!" Drew does the same.

"Let's do this!" Dean says with the most excitement I've ever seen from him. He high-fives me, and then we file out the door.

When we get to the side of the stage, the place is swarming with crew. They descend upon us, attaching receiver packs to the backs of our clothing and helping us place our ear piece monitors. Dean and Paul are given their guitars, and another crew member tries to hand me mine until he sees the Fender in my hands.

"Change of plans?" he asks.

"Yes. Sorry. Is it a problem?"

"Nope. Here." He hands me a few extra picks, and I slide them into my back pocket. "You're all set."

I give him a nod of thanks and suddenly Roxanne is in my face. "Nervous?"

"A little bit, yeah."

"Well, snap out of it. You're stepping on stage in less time than it takes to pour a cup of coffee."

My expression twists. "Gee. Thanks for the pep talk, coach."

She gives me the first genuine smile I've ever received from her. "You don't need any talk from me. I saw the effect you had on that girl at the meet and greet. I don't know what you said to her, but she was grinning from ear to ear. I like it." She leans closer. "Now go out there and show the boys how it's done."

I'm starting to like Rox a little more now.

Drew walks on to the darkened stage and I go with him. I find my place and plug into the sound system as he gets settled behind his kit. Paul joins us, and my eyes catch the first arena audience I've ever seen.

Now would be a good time to remember how to breathe.

My hand clutches the neck of my guitar as I stare. I can see the arena isn't full by any means; however, a lot of people have found their seats. Other concert-goers wander the aisles trying to find their section and, closer to the stage, I see people returning to their friends carrying plastic cups. Drew hits the bass drum a few times and does a quick fill, testing the sound of his equipment. This gets the attention of the audience and, realizing something is about to happen, a small cheer erupts. The sound sends chills down my spine.

Paul gets my attention from across the stage. He tests a few chords, and I respond back on the Fender. Satisfied with the sound coming through the amps, he starts the bass line that will weave into our first song. In this big space, with this many speakers, you can almost see the notes vibrate through the air. On his cue, Drew jumps into the mix, pounding the drums in a familiar rhythm. Each hit resonates deep in my chest and I close my eyes, listening until the hair on the back of neck stands on end. It's time for me to add the hook.

Taking a deep breath, I think of Latson and his faith in me. I think of Oliver, my brother, Jules, and everything that's brought me here. I open my eyes and see Dean standing at the side of the stage, ready to make his entrance. I strike my first note.

And find absolute heaven.

~~~~

"Break free of the bonds
Break free of the chains
Own the blood
That runs through your veins
Love's bigger than you
And it's bigger than me

We're breaking free, baby
We're breaking free."

I finish singing the chorus with Dean. "Breaking Free" is the last song of our set. As the final notes of our instruments fade, Dean sings the ending lines solo:

"There's so much more out there to see
If love breaks one of us, let it be me."

The crowd cheers as his voice drifts away.

"Thank you!" Dean says into the mic. He wipes the sweat off his forehead with his arm. "We've had a great time with you tonight, L.A. Now, who's ready to see Ariel Allyn?" He puts his hand to his ear and the crowd roars. He looks over his shoulder at us, grins, and faces the audience once more. "That's what we thought. It won't be long now."

He lifts one hand above his head in a wave, our signal to join him at the front of the stage. The guys and I leave our places to form a crooked line with him in the middle. Dean speaks, his voice echoing through the speakers. "Thanks for a great show, Los Angeles! We'll see you all again real soon." I watch him take a small bow over his guitar and see Drew wave his sticks in the air. Paul and I wave too, and I know my smile consumes my face. So much adrenaline is pumping through my veins right now, I don't know what I'll do to contain myself once we're off stage.

Speaking of off stage, as we exit, I catch a glimpse of Heidi and her friends near the front row. They're being so loud they're impossible to miss. Heidi must catch me watching because she shuts up for a second. I'm not close enough to see her eyes but I'm sure they're shooting daggers at me. It doesn't matter. Nothing can ruin this high.

Nothing.

As soon as we're out of sight, the crew descends upon us again. We're stripped of everything technical and electronic, and even the Fender finds its case. I'm confused as to how it got backstage, but I'm so geeked about the show I don't care. People rush everywhere to transform the stage for Ariel, and I realize I should get out of the way. Dean is talking to Roxanne, so I start to head in that direction. Suddenly, strong arms wrap around my waist, stopping and startling me.

"You blew me away out there."

His voice melts over my skin, warm and soft beneath my ear. I turn around and throw my arms around him. "You're here!"

Latson grins before ducking his head to catch my mouth with his. It's a greedy kiss, one I've missed, and I pull him closer by the back of his neck. He holds me tight, clutching my waist, as I press the length of my body against his. "Surprise," he says when we take a breath.

This night couldn't get any better. "How long have you been here?"

"Since we talked on the phone. I was in a cab when you called."

"Why didn't you tell me?"

"Because I didn't want to distract you. Dean needed you focused."

"He knew?"

"Who do you think sent me this?" He holds up a backstage pass. "It pays to grow up with the lead singer."

I look at the plastic and get hopeful. "Please tell me that's good for tomorrow, too."

"Definitely. Oliver is staying with Mrs. Gibson until you leave for Anaheim."

I bounce up and down on my toes, then pull him toward me and kiss him again. I get to keep him for two whole nights.

"So, how do you feel?" Latson searches my face. "How was your first show?"

"It was ..." I can't find words. I don't think anything I say will do the experience justice. "It consumed me."

He gives me a gentle, knowing smile and brushes his thumb across my cheek. "You were incredible."

Dean appears beside us. "I see you found each other." He looks pointedly at me. "I promised you'd be together soon."

"You did," I say. "Thanks for delivering."

"C'mon." He waves us forward. "Let's get out of here."

"Where are we going?"

"Up to the label's private suite. Ariel said we could watch her perform from there."

He walks away and my jaw drops. I had hoped I would get to see some of Ariel's show, especially after being attacked by her props. I assumed if I did it would be from the television in the dressing room or some other obscure location, not a suite. Excited, I start to follow Dean until Latson takes my hand and stops me.

"Hey."

I face him. "What's up?"

"Do you really want to watch Ariel?"

"Yes. Don't you?"

He looks confused. "Isn't there anything else you'd rather do?"

"Like what?" I know this scene is nothing new to him, but it's shiny and sparkly to me. "I've never seen her perform before. I've also never been in a private suite. It sounds like fun."

Latson looks disappointed, then shakes the expression away. "You're right. Let's go."

"What is it? What's wrong?"

"Nothing." He starts to walk. "Sometimes I forget our experiences are different. Just because you're on tour doesn't mean you've seen it all."

We make it out of the backstage area and into the hallway I took from the dressing room. We look left and right until we see Dean waving to us from an elevator. Once we make it inside, Latson's fingers tighten around mine.

"So, what'd you think?" Dean turns toward Latson. "Did you notice we changed the end of "Over-Exposed"?"

"I did," he says. "I know that transition was bothering you. The show was epic, man. A great start."

"I thought so, too." Dean runs his hand through his hair and gives Latson a resigned smile. "It felt like Vegas. Remember?"

Latson's eyes go blank for a second. If I didn't know him so well I wouldn't have noticed. He quickly adjusts his features and nods. "Yeah. I remember."

The elevator stops and we exit. I let Dean get a few steps ahead of us before I ask Latson, "What happened in Vegas?"

"We opened our first tour there. It was Sacred Sin's first concert as a headliner."

Mentally, I frown. I understand why Dean would compare his first concert with the Union to his first with Sin, but didn't he realize it would bother Latson? I try to lighten things up. "I bet it was a rush," I say and then pull on Latson's hand. He leans over. "But nothing compared to tonight," I whisper. "Hands down, Vegas blows L.A. out of the water."

He kisses me.

When we arrive at the suite, Roxanne, Drew, and Paul are already congregated by a small bar just off the entrance. The room is filled with people I don't know, some of whom are already seated outside on the suite's private balcony. The place resembles a tiny apartment, with a bathroom, the wet bar, and a bunch of overstuffed furniture. A flat screen mounted from the ceiling in one corner broadcasts the empty stage below, and a variety of hors d'oeuvres are set out on a small dining table.

"There they are!" Paul gets loud. "Get your asses over here and do a shot with us." He hands Dean a glass filled with amber liquid, then me, and then Latson. "Gunnar! How in the hell are ya?" Paul thumps Latson on the back. Then, he holds up his glass and we all follow suit. "To the Renegade tour! May the groupies be hot, Betty be swift, and the music rock!"

"Hear! Hear!" Glasses clink together.

I sniff my shot before I send it down my throat. It smells like whiskey; I bet it's a Three Wise Men. I toss it back and grimace. Yep. I was right.

I hand my glass back to the bartender. "Who's Betty?" I ask no one in particular.

"The tour bus." Latson stares at his empty glass. "We always named them Betty."

Jesus. Couldn't they have come up with another name?

"Let's go get seats," I suggest and pull on his arm. "I'd rather sit out on the balcony than in here."

"Gunnar? Is that you?"

A man dressed in a button down and jeans approaches. His dirty blonde hair is styled, and he flashes a perfect white smile.

"Caleb," Latson says. I can sense the irritation in his tone, and, judging by the size of the Rolex on Caleb's wrist, I assume he's with the record label.

"Holy shit." The man shakes his head in disbelief. "Where have you been?"

"Oh, you know. Here and there."

"I thought you fell off the face of the earth."

"Nah," Latson gets sarcastic. "I just disappeared from music."

Caleb's smile disappears. "You know my hands were tied."

"Yep. That's what you said two years ago." Latson sets his shot glass down on the bar and pushes it forward with two fingers. "It's good to know you're sticking with the same story."

The record exec looks uncomfortable as Latson turns to me. "Let's find those seats you wanted." He sets his hand against my back and starts to usher me toward the balcony.

"Jen Elliott, right?"

I give Caleb a questioning look. "Yes?"

"I caught your set. Dean was smart to bring you aboard. I look forward to working with you."

I cross my arms. "And you are?"

"Oh, forgive me." He plasters on a smile and extends his hand. "Caleb Jackson. I work for Snare Records."

I shake his hand to be polite. "I thought Dean hadn't signed with a label."

"He hasn't. Not yet. But we're interested. If the tour goes well, I think we can offer him a pretty sweet deal."

"I wouldn't know anything about that," I say. "I'm just here to play."

Caleb tilts his head toward me. "I like your attitude."

Latson presses his hand firmly against my back to get me moving and I nod goodbye to Caleb. As we walk toward the sliding doors that lead to the seating, Latson says, "If Dean signs with that asshole I'll kill him."

I glance back at Caleb who's now talking with Roxanne. "Why?"

Latson's hard eyes meet mine. "Caleb is Levi's brother."

Chapter Twenty One

Lying on my side, I prop my head against my hand and stare at Latson. He's sleeping on his back with the starchy white hotel sheets pushed to his waist. My eyes roam upward, over his bare chest, his face, and his arm that's slung over his head against the pillow. He looks peaceful and content, a far cry from what he was last night. I thought after we left the concert and got away from the record people he would relax. He didn't. He seemed just as stressed during Ariel's after party.

I wanted to talk about what was bothering him, but the Ritz wasn't the place. The atmosphere was too loud and too busy; there were people everywhere. Dancers, friends, band members, crew, roadies, and, of course, Heidi. Avoiding her death stare was impossible whenever she was in the same room. When we left the party and got back to my hotel, I could tell how tense Latson was by the way he kissed me and the way his hands roamed my skin. He was rough and demanding, which I didn't mind because I've missed him and I wanted him as much as he wanted me. As time passed, the more tender he became. Before we fell asleep he was back to the sweet, teasing, unhurried Latson I remember.

Without warning, his eyes open and he blinks a few times. "Hey." He starts to smile but ends up covering a yawn. "I felt you staring."

"You did? How?"

"It's a side effect of living with a kid." He reaches for me and I slide over, winding myself around his body. "If I'm asleep and Oliver's awake, he'll stare at me until I wake up, too. It's like a sixth sense."

I remember staring at my sleeping parents when I was young, especially around the holidays. "I used to do that. My brothers would always send me into our parent's bedroom because I was the youngest. I finally put a stop to it when I was twelve. I mean, Pete was eighteen for crying out loud."

Latson laughs.

"What's so funny?"

"I can imagine your little determined face."

"Well ..." I drift off. "My brothers had to grow up sometime. I know they were excited about Christmas morning, but come on."

Latson squeezes me in a one-armed hug. "I started to get excited about Christmas again after my sister died. I wanted to make the first one special for O. Now, I get just as excited as he does. There's something to be said for playing the man in red."

I never thought about it that way before. I've never been around a kid to surprise on Christmas, and my eyes light up. "Can I help this year? I can be an elf."

He scrutinizes me. "Hmmm. You're a little tall and your ears aren't very pointy. I guess it depends on how you look in green tights."

I shove his chest. "You know I can totally rock green tights."

He smiles and leans down to kiss me. "I'm sure you can."

When he settles back against the pillow, I snuggle closer to his side. "I'm glad you're in a better mood. I don't like it when you're grumpy."

He exhales with a heavy sigh. "I didn't want to see any of those people last night. I only wanted to spend time with you."

My face falls. I should have realized the environment would be difficult for him. "I'm sorry. I shouldn't have dragged you where you didn't want to go."

He runs the tips of his fingers up and down my back. "Don't apologize. I shouldn't have let things get to me. Last night was *your* night."

I give him a tiny smile, and he pushes my hair behind my ear. "So. You've been christened. First show, first suite, first after party. You're officially a rock star."

I laugh. I'm not, but I felt like one. "You were right. Nothing compares to performing. I'm glad you talked me into it."

He shakes his head. "You would have done it regardless. Pete or Jules would have convinced you. Or your parents. Have you talked to them? What do they think?"

"They sounded thrilled over the phone. They're planning to come to the last show, since the tour ends in Detroit. You should come, too, and meet them."

Latson's brow jumps. "You want me to meet your parents?"

"Well, yeah. I've already met your dad."

He's silent as he studies me.

"What?"

"I'm a tattooed ex-musician raising his nephew. What are they going to think?"

"They're going to think you're stepping in for the father Oliver never had." I push my body up and partially over him, so we're face to face. "They're also going to realize you employ my brother, who makes a decent living. I guarantee they're going to think I'm happy and you're amazing."

A slow smile spreads across his lips before they're inches from mine. "In that case," he kisses me, "I'll definitely meet your parents."

"You will?" I whisper. The thought gives me butterflies. "I guess this means we're serious, then."

"Were we ever not?" His hands slide down my back and find the bottom of my shirt. They slip underneath and start to trace my spine. "The minute I saw you dancing I was serious about you."

"No." I smirk. "You were horny. There's a difference."

He laughs. "Is that why you think I asked you to work for me?"

"No. You needed me because I have mad bartending skills."

His eyes light up and he shakes his head no. My mouth falls open. "I do have mad bartending skills!"

"You do. But my real motivation ..." He stops following my spine and removes his hands from beneath my shirt. He runs them up into my hair, cradling the back of my head. "My real reason was to get close to you. I had to find a way to spend time with you, to get to know you."

I study his chocolate brown eyes and my heart pounds. "Let me guess. Next you're going to tell me you lost Oliver at the aquarium on purpose."

"Hell, no. Running into you there was a coincidence. A very lucky coincidence."

"You're telling me," I say. "I think O stole my heart the minute I heard his little voice. If he had asked the wrong person for help ..."

I shudder at the thought before Latson pulls me close. "I think fate stepped in that day."

"Or maybe it was Audrey."

I hadn't thought of the possibility until now, and Latson's expression softens. "I wouldn't put it past her."

I smile before his lips gently brush over mine. Before we can take things further, my phone sounds with a reminder.

"Ugh," I groan. "I have to get moving."

"What's on the schedule for today?"

I roll off him and on to my back, reaching for my cell. "Brunch with Roxanne. She wanted to get together after the first show to discuss any changes."

"Are you meeting anyone else?"

I silence the reminder. "The guys will be there. Why?"

"Not Caleb?"

"No, not that I'm aware of. Last night was the first time I'd ever heard of him." I sit up and set my phone back on the table next to Oliver's drawing. "He really gets under your skin, doesn't he?"

Latson scrubs his face with the palm of his hand. "Yeah. He does."

I pull my legs beneath me and adjust my expression, to let him know I'm waiting for an explanation. He rolls his eyes.

"I told you Caleb is Levi's brother."

"So, he's guilty by association?"

He sighs. "He's also the record exec who had the final say in dropping my band from the label. He chose to believe the tabloids and his asshole brother instead of me."

I vaguely remember some of the headlines I read during my Google search. "How did the press get wind of the situation anyway?"

"Levi. He hates me just as much as I hate him. He was there when I –" Latson catches himself, his mouth forming a thin line. "Levi twisted the truth and took it to people who would listen. Then, my dad got involved and wanted custody of Oliver." Latson grimaces. "So, yes. Caleb getting under my skin is an understatement. He ended my career."

The more I learn about Latson's past the more I think Audrey ended his career. Everything he's dealt with has stemmed from her decisions. I keep my mouth shut, though. Bad mouthing his dead sister is probably not the best idea.

Instead, I crawl over to his side and hover above him. "People are shitty and I hate that you've been hurt."

"I hate that we're talking about this." He sits up straight and reaches for me. "I have one more night with you. Let's not ruin it by talking about my past."

I agree and end up in his lap. "No parties after the show tonight either," I add. "Just us."

He smiles. "Just us. On a date."

I shoot him a curious look.

"I thought we could sight-see, if you're up for it," he says. "How much of L.A. have you visited since you've been out here?"

"Lemme think." I set my finger against my chin in pretend thought. "Barely any."

"Good. After you play we're headed to see the Hollywood sign."

"Yeah?" I can't stop my grin.

"And then we can go wherever we want. The Hollywood Walk of Fame is close. I'd take you shopping on Rodeo Drive, but I think most stores will be closed by then."

Talk about expensive. "I don't need anything from Rodeo Drive." I set my hand against Latson's cheek. "I have everything I need right here."

He lowers his gaze to my mouth. "Where have you been all my life?"

"Where have you been all of mine?"

He gives me my favorite lopsided dimple smile before kissing me senseless. We may only have the next twenty-four hours together, but we're going to make them count.

~~~~

"Let me help you with that, darlin'."

"Thanks, Beau."

I hand our driver my guitar case as I haul myself up the steps of the tour bus. I keep my acoustic with me between cities because it gives me something to do besides watch movies and sleep.

"Y'all alone? Where are the boys?"

"They're on their way. You know how it is."

The fifty-nine-year-old ex-bull rider scowls at me. "If I told you once I told you a thousand times. Stop walkin' your tail out to the bus in the dark after shows. You hear me? It's not safe."

I reach up and playfully flick the brim of his Stetson. Beau has become a surrogate father of sorts. "You want to talk about safe? How can you watch the road wearing this thing? I can barely see your eyes."

"Are you sassin' me?"

"Don't I always?"

He hands me my guitar case with an exasperated sigh, and I grin. "Frowning like that with give you wrinkles," I warn him. "You need to keep that face pretty for the ladies."

He chuckles. "There's only one lady I'm interested in seein' and she's at our next stop."

"Then I'll go get comfortable." I adjust my backpack on my shoulder. "We can't be late for your date in Dallas."

He winks at me before I wander back to my bunk. The bus sleeps eight, and my "room" is below Roxanne's. When I first boarded the tour bus in L.A., my immediate thought was it looked like a motorhome on steroids. The front lounge holds opposing couches, a small table, a mounted flat screen, and a kitchenette. Our bunks are located in the middle of the bus, and another small lounge, along with the bathroom, resides in the back.

Pulling the curtain to my bunk aside, I toss my things on my bed. It's hard to believe I left Los Angeles three weeks ago. We just played Denver, and in an hour we'll be headed south to Texas. Time is flying, but I'm enjoying it. My only regret is I haven't seen Latson since the first show. We talk daily, and I've been waiting for him to surprise me again. I have to remind myself that he said his visits would be few and far between.

Before I get comfy in my sweats for the long ride, I grab my phone and send him a message: *Bye bye Rocky Mountain High. Hello Lone Star State.*

He responds quickly. *Say hi to the Cowboys cheerleaders for me ;)*

I scoff. *In your dreams.*

Footsteps and greetings to Beau at the front of the bus make me look up. The guys are here.

"I need a beer," Drew says, stopping at the mini fridge. He opens the door and pulls out a Miller Light.

"Me, too," Paul says as he plops down on the couch. Dean joins him and adds, "Me, three."

"Jen?" Drew holds the refrigerator door open. "You want one?"

"Sure," I say and catch the can Drew tosses me. It's Angry Orchard, my new favorite. "Thanks."

As quickly as Paul sat, he stands and looks around. "Where's the remote? I know there's a game happening somewhere."

Dean pulls the control from beneath his butt and turns on the TV. It looks like it's going to be another typical night on the bus. Beer and baseball until everyone gets tired and crawls into their bunks. Not that I'm complaining. I'm glad the guys save the parties for hotels, when we stay a few nights in one city.

Popping the top to my can, I ask, "Where's Roxanne?"

The boys look at one another and shrug. "I thought she was with you," Dean says, looking toward the back of the bus.

"Nope." I lift the curtain to her bunk. "She's not here."

"Well, your guess is as good as mine." He turns back to the television. Paul's found ESPN and they're recapping a Detroit Tigers game from earlier today. *Go team*, I silently think in support of my home state.

I set my drink down and open my backpack, locating the cozy clothes I left out of my suitcase. I walk to the bathroom and change, then brush my teeth and wash my face. I pull my hair back in a loose pony. It takes almost thirteen hours to get from Denver to Dallas, and that's if we don't stop. When I fall asleep tonight, I want to crash without having to wake up and wiggle out of tight jeans.

Just as I settle in my bunk with my guitar across my lap, I hear Roxanne's excited voice from the front of the bus. I lean to the side and stick out my head to see what's going on.

"Just make yourself comfortable; we have plenty of room," she gushes. "Boys. Ariel will be joining us for our drive. Please try not to be rude."

My eyes widen as I see Ariel standing behind Rox. She's hanging on to a small rolling suitcase with one hand and a large Coach purse, more like a duffle, with the other.

"There's no need to lecture the guys," Ariel says. "They know me and I know all of them. We're like family."

Dean leans forward in his seat. "What's going on? Is everything all right?"

Ariel rolls her eyes. "Just some dancer drama that I don't care to be a part of."

"Then kick them the fuck off your bus," Paul says with a wave of his beer. "That'll show 'em. Not that I care you're here." He grins. "If we have to be family, we can we be distant cousins by marriage and share a bunk."

Ariel laughs and Roxanne glares at Paul before turning to our guest with a forced smile. "Anyway," she says, "we have three available beds. Two next to Jen and I, and one next to dipshit over there." She jerks her thumb in Paul's direction. "Take your pick."

"Thank you so much," Ariel says as she starts to follow Rox toward me. "I couldn't take the bitching anymore. My moods haven't been the best lately. If I stay, it will only make things worse."

Roxanne nods with empathy. When the two of them make it to me, Ariel smiles. "Hello again. I hope you don't mind me crashing your party."

I shake my head. "Not at all. It's your tour."

Ariel selects the bottom bunk directly behind mine. She lifts her suitcase on to the bed and then peeks around the corner. "I was hoping we'd get a chance to talk. You know, get to know one another."

I can't stop my confused look. "Why?"

"Jen!" Roxanne scolds me. "If the headliner wants to speak to you –"

"Rox." Ariel puts her hand on our manager's arm. "It's random that I'd want to talk to her. Think about it. She's dating my ex."

Roxanne goes silent, then focuses on me. "I'm going to get comfortable, head to the back of the bus, and get lost in a book. Behave."

She turns on her heel and I look at Ariel. Her bottom lip disappears between her teeth to suppress a laugh, and I do the same. She starts to unpack, and I turn back to my guitar.

Time passes and Beau gets the bus underway. An idea for a new song popped into my head tonight before the show, so I mess around with notes and lyrics. Everything is gibberish right now, but that's how my songwriting usually starts. After a half hour or so of playing around, Ariel appears by my side. "Is this a bad time?"

My eyes swing to her. She's changed clothes, and her dark hair is piled in a messy bun on top of her head. With her hair off her face her features look exotic, something I hadn't noticed before. "No," I say and move back a little. "What's up?"

She crawls on to my bunk and faces me, crossing her legs. "Nothing really. Just lonely and bored." She glances around and her eyes land on Oliver's drawing taped to the wall. She smiles. "I bet I know who made this."

I'm about to confirm her thoughts when my phone vibrates. "One sec," I say and pick it up. It's a text message from Pete: *Hey, rock-n-roll queen. Where are you?*

I smile. *On a bus in the middle of nowhere. Where are you?*

Home in bed. I should be asleep, but I'm not. I'm worried out of my mind.

I frown and respond *Why? Is everything okay?*

Three little dots appear on my phone, indicating he's typing back. It must be a long message because the dots linger. I hope nothing is wrong with Jules or our family, although my parents would've called. Great. Now I'm starting to worry, too.

"Who are you talking to?"

I look at Ariel. "My brother. He's being vague and annoying."

"Older or younger?"

"Older."

Finally his message comes through. *Everything is fine. I'm awake because I have an expensive diamond ring sitting in my dresser drawer and NO IDEA HOW TO PROPOSE.*

"Is that all?!" My voice is loud. *You idiot!* I send. *You scared me.*

Ariel cocks an eyebrow. "Is something the matter?"

I sigh. "My brother needs help coming up with a way to propose to his girlfriend. They got married in secret and now he's backtracking. I told him I would think of some ideas for him, but I've fallen down on the job."

Ariel shrugs like it's no big deal. "That's easy. Have him do it at a show. Call them up on stage and have him surprise her. She'll love it."

My mouth falls open. It's so simple it's stupid. "How did I not think of that? Thanks!" I start rapidly typing while Pete responds to my idiot comment.

Calm your buns, I send. *Ariel Allyn is sitting across from me and she says you can do it on stage.*

He replies. *Are you serious???*

Yes. You should do it in Detroit, since mom and dad will be there. I grin. It's perfect.

You said Jules deserved epic and this definitely qualifies. Thank you Jen. Now I can sleep.

I make a face. *Because that's what's important, dork. I'll get back to you with the details.*

No, seriously. Thank you.

You're welcome. I set my phone down.

"Everything good?" Ariel asks.

"Yes. I'll work out the details with Dean later. I'll tell him you said it was okay."

She smiles. "I'm glad I could help." Her eyes go back to Oliver's picture. "His nephew drew this, right?"

I nod. "Oliver's a cool little kid."

"What is he now? Five years old?"

"Seven," I say.

She shakes her head. "I can't believe how much time has passed." Her eyes land on my guitar. "So, what are you working on?"

"Not much. I'm just messing around."

"I used to play, too, before I was told I could only sing." She gets sarcastic. "It's all about the image. I should demand some changes in my next contract."

I'm surprised. I was under the impression she could do whatever she wants. "Do you still practice?"

"Not much anymore." She tips her head. "I've been watching you play. You're good."

My cheeks flush. That's not unusual or anything. "Um ... thanks."

Ariel smiles, then looks down and studies her cuticles. "Look, Jen. I'm going to be honest." Her eyes meet mine again. "I don't have many close friends, but I'd like you to be one. When I talked to Latson, he said you're good people. I'm thinking of making some changes to my style. I'm sick of being a pop princess."

What? "How can you be sick of success? I mean, if it isn't broke, don't fix it."

She pulls her knees to her chest and wraps her arms around them. "I've been doing this for a long time. It's getting old; I'm twenty-seven. I need to grow as an artist. Hell, I need to grow as a person."

I'm silent. Does she think I can help?

Ariel sets her chin on her knees and continues. "I need a fresh perspective. I need to hang around someone normal. Someone who's still grounded."

I'm skeptical. "So, the dancer drama was a lie?"

"Oh no." She turns serious. "It's true. Some of those girls are straight up bat-shit crazy."

I snicker as my mind flashes to Heidi. Some of the groupies are, too.

"Anyway, enough about me." She lowers her legs and crosses them in front of her again. "Let's talk about you. Let me hear something. Play an original Jen creation."

Why not? It's not every day a pop star asks to hear your work. The song I wrote in Chicago comes to mind, the one about the couple on the beach. "Okay," I say. "This one's called "Fairytale". There might be a few changes, but it goes like this." I straighten my back, clear my throat, and strum the strings to find my place:

"When the fairytale ends
When it all falls apart
Who will pick up the pieces
Of our shattered hearts?
It can't be you
And it won't be me
Because unlike a fairytale
We were never meant to be."

I take my time and play the entire song, stopping only once when I get tripped up on the second verse. When I finish, Ariel has a glassy look in her eyes. She blinks to clear it and then quietly says, "Save that one for me."

"What?" I don't know what that means.

"I love it," she says. "If anyone approaches you about that song, tell them it's taken. Tell them you're saving it for me."

My eyes grow wide. "You would sing my song?"

She nods. "In a heartbeat. Show me what else you've got."

Chapter Twenty Two

"You'll never guess what the record company did for us." I shut the bedroom door so I can talk to Latson in private. "They upgraded our hotel room to a penthouse. A penthouse! Can you believe it?"

"That was nice of them." He sounds doubtful. "I thought the tour was only in Dallas for two nights."

"We are. Tonight and tomorrow, then it's off to Houston. But, we found out they upgraded us there, too."

Obnoxiously loud music starts to play from the interconnected penthouse living and dining rooms. Looks like our guests have arrived.

"What is that?" Latson asks.

"The party just started." I roll my eyes. "Dean and the guys got excited about the space, so they invited everyone to our room tonight." To be honest I'd rather curl up in the magnificent bed that's calling my name. "Did you know penthouses can have six bathrooms? And three bedrooms? I still have to share with Roxanne, but whatever. At least the guys get to spread out."

"I'm not worried about the guys," Latson mutters.

I won't let that comment slide. "What's wrong?" I sink down on to the bed and pull one leg beneath me. "You know, when I found out we'd been upgraded, I thought you did it. I thought maybe you would be waiting to surprise me."

He doesn't respond so I add, "I miss you."

"I miss you, too," he says. "I'm working on next month's schedule for Torque and booking the entertainment. Once everything is confirmed you'll probably see me."

"Probably?"

"You'll definitely see me."

Suddenly, the bedroom door flies open. Ariel shuts it behind her in a rush and leans against it. "There you are. I need your help."

I'm confused and my face shows it. Latson asks, "Is someone there?"

"Just Ariel," I say. Leaning away from the phone I ask, "What's up?"

She makes a zipper motion across her lips and gestures for me to end the call.

"Uh ... I gotta go," I stutter.

"Why?" Latson asks.

Ariel hurries past me and toward the bathroom. "I'm not sure," I whisper. "Ariel probably wants to talk." I told him about last night's conversation on the bus. "I'll call you in the morning, okay?" Now that we're in the same time zone it makes things a little easier.

"Okay," he says, uncertain. "But, Jen ..."

"Hmm?"

"Be careful. I don't like knowing there's a bunch of strangers hanging out in your room. Penthouse or no penthouse."

"Yes, boss," I say playfully. "Sweet dreams."

"Only if they're of you."

I end the call and walk over to stand in the bathroom doorway. Ariel is leaning against the counter, fidgeting. "Are you all right?"

She shakes her head no, then lifts her shirt. A box is tucked into the waistline of her pants. She pulls it out and shows it to me. "I can't do this by myself."

My eyes consume my face. It's a pregnancy test. "Are you sure?"

"Of course not." Her expression twists. "That's kinda the point of taking the test."

I step toward her. "What I meant was, it's a possibility?"

She scowls at the box in her hands. "Unfortunately, yes. For the record, Zach, one of my dancers, is not gay."

I close my eyes for a second and then reopen them. "You had unprotected sex because you thought the guy was gay?"

"No! I didn't think we'd end up sleeping together because I thought he was gay!"

She's flustered, so I walk further into the bathroom and shut the door. "Are you late?"

"Ten days." She bites her bottom lip. "I've also felt off. Emotional and exhausted."

"You could just be stressed," I say. "Traveling and performing aren't easy." I reach for the box and she hands it over. I read the directions. "You have to pee on the stick and wait three minutes. It doesn't sound complicated."

"No," she says. "The complicated part comes after."

I give her a resigned smile, and she takes a deep breath. "Okay. Let me do this and then I'll need you to hold my hand."

I give her the test. "Good luck."

Her face falls. "Thanks."

I leave the bathroom and head to the bed to wait. I can't believe Ariel might be pregnant. I also can't believe she feels close enough to share this with me. There's no way she can jump around on stage and fit into a cat suit with a belly. My mind recalls our conversation from last night; this is probably what she meant when she said she needed to grow as a person. She could potentially be a mother.

Ariel looks pale when she opens the door. "Three minutes?"

I grab my phone. "I'm setting the timer now."

She makes her way over to me and sits down. "Thank you. I had to tell someone. It was killing me." I offer her my hand and she takes it. "I couldn't say anything to my team. Not yet. If I'm ..." She hesitates to say the word and sighs. "Changes will have to be made."

We sit in silence as the music from the party pumps through the walls. I glance at my phone as the timer ticks down slowly. My stomach starts to knot for her and for us. Dean's put so much stock into playing; he'll be crushed if he has to cut things short.

Squeezing her hand, I ask, "How does that work?"

"What?"

"The changes."

She frowns. "There's a clause in my contract about medical conditions. Shows can be delayed or postponed, or, in the worst case, canceled." Her shoulders sag. "I'd hate to do that to the fans. Or the crew. People depend on getting paid for this tour."

I never realized that such a huge responsibility was placed on a headlining act. "So, you'll keep it?" I ask. "Not that it's any of my business."

"I kind of made it your business." Ariel looks down at her lap. "I don't know. It's easy to think you'll do something a certain way until you're confronted with it." Her eyes meet mine. "What would you do?"

"Me?" I haven't put much thought into it because I'm always careful. "I guess it would depend on my situation. If I could financially support a baby, and if the father wanted to be involved, for example."

She gives me a tiny smile. "Well, if you slip up with Gunnar, you know you're covered. He's been dedicated to his nephew since the day Oliver was born. It's part of why we broke up."

I never questioned their reasons. "Really?"

"Call me selfish, but I didn't feel like I could compete after he won custody and moved away. He was wrapped up in starting a new life, and I couldn't give him the time or attention he deserved. We agreed it would be best to call it quits."

At least she admits she was partly to blame.

Ariel leans over to check the remaining time on my phone. "Who would have thought one drunk night would lead to this?" She pauses. "Never mind. That was a stupid question. The probability is actually quite high."

Before I can agree with her, the timer goes off. We look at each other and she lets go of my hand. "Here goes nothing."

She straightens her spine as she walks away, and I stand in anticipation. When she disappears through the bathroom door, I start to pace. I feel bad for her. She made a bad decision, yes, but so did Zach. I silently wonder if he's going to be supportive, or if he's going to ditch her like Levi did Audrey.

When Ariel doesn't reappear after a minute, I go find her. It doesn't take that long to read one pink line or two. Peeking around the corner, I can tell by her expression what the outcome is without asking.

"Congratulations," I whisper.

She gives me a sad smile before a tear rolls down her cheek.

~~~~

All I want is a bottle of water, I think as I weave my way around bodies. It's been almost an hour since Ariel learned she was expecting and left the party. She said she was going to find Zach and break the news, so I decided to find the guys and make sure they were living it up. Little do they know all of this could come to an abrupt end, depending on how Ariel feels and what she decides to do.

"Excuse me. Pardon me. Sorry," I say as I finally make it to the wet bar. Some random guy is behind it, having dubbed himself honorary bartender. "Can I get a bottle of water please?"

"One water comin' up," he says and flips a bottle behind his back and over his shoulder. He catches it and presents it to me.

"Thanks," I say.

"Aww. Look, girls. The bitch is trying to come off as Snow White."

My body tenses at the sound of Heidi's voice. Slowly, I turn around and find her standing with her friends. "Well. If it isn't the old hag here to hand out more poison."

Her narrowed eyes bounce between me and the water. "Do you think you're above us?"

"No. I think I'm thirsty."

"Thirsty for Dean, maybe," one of her lackeys snipes.

Is she serious? "Oh, honey," I take a step toward her, "I wouldn't go there if I were you. Heidi knows there's only one man I'm thirsty for. Right, Heids?"

She doesn't like my cutesy nickname, and she crosses her arms. "Then how come we just saw you come out of Dean's room?"

My forehead pinches. Is she high? I look over my shoulder, in the direction I just came from. "Do you mean back there?" I point. "That's my room. Get your facts straight, sweetheart."

I refuse to interact with stupid, so I leave. I swear Heidi has nothing better to do than make assumptions about me. She should take a hint from *Mean Girls* and back the hell off. She could get hit by a bus.

A tour bus, to be exact.

Spying the sliding glass doors, I decide to make my way to the balcony for some fresh air. Just as I squeeze past the last few people in my way, I hear, "Hey. I've been looking for you." A hand grazes my elbow, and I turn to see a certain record executive smiling at me.

"Caleb? What are you doing here?"

He ushers me to the side, then leans against the wall. "I'm keeping an eye on my interests. How have you been?"

I can't help my skeptical look. "Things are good." What else can I say?

"Do you like the penthouse?"

I glance around. "It's nice. I'd enjoy it more without all these people, though."

He laughs. "Well, at least you have tomorrow and Houston."

"How do you know about Houston?"

He gives me a self-deprecating smile and my eyes widen. "You upgraded us?"

"Guilty."

Well, that was generous.

"Listen, Jen." Caleb shifts his weight. "I don't know what Gunnar's told you, but I want to make sure we're okay. I don't want any bad feelings between you and me. You're a crucial piece of Dean's band."

I'm confused. "And?"

"And he could be part of the Snare Records family again. I want him to be comfortable in making that choice."

He can't be serious. "Do you think I'm bad mouthing you to Dean?"

He puts his hands in his pockets and shrugs. "I'd like to think you're not."

I shake my head to clear it. I refuse to get involved in anything political. "You're overestimating my part in this. Yes, Latson's told me about your past, but I haven't brought it up to Dean. Why would I? You cut him off back then just like you did Latson. He doesn't need me to remind him."

"Precisely." Caleb pushes his body away from the wall. "I think he's moved on, and I'd like it to stay that way. The past needs to stay in the past. If you talk to Gunnar, tell him –"

His thoughts are cut short when Dean approaches. "Hey, man. How's it going?" He gives Dean a hearty slap on the shoulder. "Great show tonight, as always."

Dean grins. "I didn't know you were there. Can I get you something to drink? A beer?" He notices me. "Jen! Do you need anything?"

I notice the glaze in Dean's eyes. He's well on his way to having too much. "Nope. I'm good. Maybe you should put that bottle down and pick up one of these." I hold up my water. "You don't need a nasty hangover."

"You're probably right." Dean runs his hand through his hair. "It's good to have a voice of reason around. Don't you think, Caleb?"

Caleb looks at me. "As long as the voice can be trusted."

I have to stop my mouth from falling open. He wants to talk about trust? Please.

"Deeeean."

Oh, for the love of God.

My eyes meet the ceiling as Heidi whines Dean's name. She walks up behind him and hangs on his arm. "Can I borrow your cell? I left mine in my room by accident."

"Sure," he says and pulls it from his pocket. "Take your time."

She slides it from his hand with a sly smile. "Thanks." She gives him a quick peck on the cheek, and I inwardly cringe. I'm going to have to speak to this boy when he's sober about the company he keeps.

Dean and Caleb start to talk about tonight's show, so I take the opportunity to disappear. I step around them and head to my original destination: the balcony. I find a spot between some people and lean against the railing to stare out over the city. A smile forms on my lips as I remember sitting on the fire escape and doing the same thing with Latson. I don't know which direction I'm facing right now, but I pretend it's east. I telepathically send my thoughts to him, letting him know I miss him and things are getting complicated here.

I take my time and finish my water before heading back inside. The party is going strong, but I don't feel the need to socialize. Ariel's secret has me feeling a little melancholy, so I decided to find out if my bedroom door has a lock. I don't need Caleb finding me again, or, God forbid, Heidi. There's nothing more I can say to either of them that hasn't already been said.

When I reach my room and investigate the door handle, I smile when I see there is a lock. I twist it and shut the door;

Roxanne will just have to knock when she wants in. I sit on the bed and lie back on the pillows; I would change my clothes but not while there's a bunch of people here. Lock or no lock, no one needs to see me in my pj's. My phone vibrates against the nightstand where I left it to charge, so I pick it up. Immediately, worry sets in. There are a ton of alerts – all from Latson. I click on the text messages first, even though there is voicemail, too.

We need to talk. Where are you?
I left you a message. Did you get it?
Answer the phone please.
Are you avoiding me? Call me as soon as you get this.

What is going on? Quickly, I go to my voicemail. Latson sounds pissed:

"Jen. I just talked to you. How could you not say anything? I had to find out from Dean? What the hell?"
Then, twenty minutes later: *"Damn it!"*
And then, seconds ago: *"I'm sorry. I'm not mad. Just … call me."*

My stomach sinks as my head spins. I jump off the bed and leave the room, bent on finding Dean. What could he have told Latson to upset him? I make my way around bodies, even pushing a few out of the way so I can see. I spot Dean near the center of the room; he's still talking to Caleb. I march in his direction, then grab his arm without saying a word and pull him to the side.

"What the –?" He frowns. "What's the matter?"

"What did you tell Latson?"

He looks confused. "I didn't tell him anything. Why?"

"He's pissed at me for something you said." I let him listen to the message.

Dean looks legitimately confused and pulls his phone out of his pocket. "I haven't talked to him since early this morning."

265

I look at my phone and tap Latson's number, then hold my breath as it rings in my ear. He answers almost immediately.

"Jen." He sounds defeated, even sad.

"Hey." I wrap my free arm around my waist. "I just got your messages. My phone was charging. What's wrong?"

He lets out an annoyed breath. "You're still at the party? Really?"

Damn the music. "Yes. Why does it matter?"

"Because –" He stops talking and changes his tone. "Why didn't you tell me?"

"Tell you what?"

He's silent for a moment before he asks, "Are you really going to play this game? Why can't you be honest with me?"

I'm so lost. I wish he'd just come out and say –

Dean taps me on the shoulder. When I turn around, he looks white as a ghost. He holds up his phone, so I can see the screen. It's his text message thread with Latson, and the last thing sent is a picture. My breath catches when I realize what it is. It's a picture of a positive pregnancy test followed by the words:

Look what I found in your girlfriend's bathroom. Congrats, Dad.

Chapter Twenty Three

"Heidi," Dean and I say in unison.

"What?" Latson's voice sounds in my ear.

I open my mouth to explain as Dean says, "I'm on it." His eyes flash before he turns and walks away.

"Jen? Are you there?"

"Yes, I'm here." I start to make my way back to my bedroom. "Let me get out of this noise." I weave my way around bodies, and then shut the door behind me. "It's not what you think," I say when I'm alone. "I saw Dean's phone. He didn't send you that text."

"Then who did?"

I get sarcastic. "The one and only Heidi." God, that woman is a bitch. Not only did she invade my personal space, she involved Dean.

"Are you telling me there isn't a pregnancy test in your bathroom?" Latson sounds like he doesn't believe me.

"No, there is." I start walking in that direction. "But it's not mine."

He lets out a heavy sigh. "What is going on?"

I flip the light switch and see the test on the counter, next to the sink where Ariel left it. I don't feel right sharing her situation, but, then again, Latson knows she came to see me earlier. "Remember the last time we talked? Who interrupted us?"

"Ariel. So?"

"So?" I frown into the phone. "Put two and two together. The test isn't mine. I'm not pregnant."

Latson's silent, so I decide to elaborate. "Heidi and I ... we got into it tonight. She must have snooped around my room. I was with Dean and Caleb when she asked to borrow Dean's phone. I should have known she was up to something by the look on her face." I pause, thinking about it. "I'm sure she thinks she caught me hiding a secret." Well, I am hiding a secret. Just not my own.

Latson still doesn't say anything, and I start to feel uneasy. I wait a second or two before asking, "You believe me, right? You know there's no way the test is mine. We've been safe every time."

He finally responds. "Sometimes things fail."

His tone makes me wonder if he wants me to be pregnant. "Are you disappointed?"

"Yes."

My mouth falls open. "What?"

"Why were you with Caleb?" He clips his words. "Why is he there?"

So that's what he's disappointed about. "I wasn't with him," I explain. "I had no idea he was here until he pulled me aside and asked me not to bring up the past to Dean. He's worried you're filling my head and I'm sharing the details. I told him you weren't and I wasn't."

"I don't like him talking to you," Latson says. "I don't want him anywhere near you."

I want to tell him I can hold my own, but instead I say, "I'll try to avoid him, but I never know when he's going to be around. He seems determined to sign Dean."

"I'm sure he is," Latson snaps.

I wonder why Caleb wants Dean so badly, but I don't ask. Latson's agitated enough for one night. I wish he were here, so we could get lost in each other and forget the outside world.

"I'll make sure Heidi's taken care of," Latson interrupts my thoughts. "I meant what I said before. I can get her kicked off the tour, and I will. There's no reason for her to mess with you like this."

"I think Dean may have beat you to it," I say. "He went to find her." I'm quiet before I add, "She's in love with you, you know. That's why she acts the way she does. She wants you."

Latson scoffs. "Her actions aren't love. They're infatuation and greed."

I can imagine her reaction when she's forced to go home. If she's kicked off the tour, I'm sure she'll pay Latson a visit. Or two. Or three. "Maybe it would be better if she stays here and far away from you," I say.

"Do you think I'd let her get to me?"

"I don't know," I tease. "She was all over your lap the first time I met her."

Latson doesn't think I'm funny. "Seriously? You're going to throw that in my face when you're surrounded by guys?"

Whoa. "I was kidding."

"No, you weren't. You've brought this up before, when you thought Heidi and I were dating."

I get defensive. "What did you expect? She was all over you."

"What was I supposed to do? Shove her on the floor? I told you I was numb. I didn't care about anything back then, other than work and Oliver."

My stomach starts to knot. How did we start fighting? "I'm not doing this," I say.

"Not doing what?"

"Fighting with you. Heidi sent that picture to start crap and it's working."

Latson sighs and I picture him rubbing the tension from the back of his neck.

"I shouldn't have tried to joke about Heidi," I say. "I just know how she is around you."

He's quiet for a moment. "I'm sorry. I shouldn't have snapped."

Suddenly, there are three loud bangs on the bedroom door. I walk over and open it to find Dean. "Jen." He walks toward me with sympathetic eyes. "I can't find Heidi, but when I do her ass will be gone." He wraps me in an unexpected hug. "I can't believe she violated your privacy like that. I'm so sorry. How are you feeling?"

He sways a little, so I know he's still buzzed. "I feel fine. Why?"

"Is that Dean?" Latson asks through the phone.

"Yes," I respond.

"Because you're pregnant." Dean steps back and holds me at arm's length. Then, he smiles. "I'm going to be an uncle again."

Oh boy. "No," I shake my head, "you're not. The test isn't mine. Heidi's confused."

Now Dean looks confused. "But ..."

"Let me talk to him," Latson says.

I hand Dean the phone. "Your brother would like to speak to you."

While Dean talks to Latson, I plop down on the bed. How did this night get so out of control? First Ariel, then Heidi. Now Latson and I are snapping at each other, and Dean thinks he's going to get a new family member. *I'll take a do-over for $1,000 please, Alex.*

"Well, yeah. I agree." Dean paces back and forth. "Do you think I wouldn't? Yes, I promise. What? That's out of my control." He stops walking. "What do you mean? How's she involved?" His eyes grow wide. "Oh."

I tap my fingers against my leg and start to wonder how Ariel's chat with Zach went. She hasn't come back in tears, so I assume things are going okay.

"Yeah. I'll call you later. Yes … yeah. Here's Jen." Dean hands the phone back to me with a scowl. "I need another drink."

He really doesn't, but I don't say anything. As he leaves I put the phone to my ear. "Hello?"

"I wish I were there," Latson says, his voice more relaxed.

"Me, too."

"Heidi should be gone soon. You won't have to worry about her anymore."

"I'm not worried now. As long as you know everything she says is a lie, I don't care what she tries to pull."

"You shouldn't have to care about her at all."

I hear something shut. "What are you doing?"

"Checking on O. He's been faking sleep for Shark Week. I've caught him watching recorded episodes twice already. Both times it was after two a.m."

"It's summer." My expression softens. "You should let him watch the sharks."

"Easy for you to say. You don't have to deal with his grumpy butt the next morning."

I look at the clock. I wonder if there are any shark shows on now. "You know I'd be happy to deal with him if I were there. Tell him I'll try to watch some episodes so we can compare notes. What channel is it on?"

"The Discovery Channel. He'll like that."

I look around the room for the television remote and catch the time. I didn't realize it was so late. "It's almost three a.m.," I say. "I'll let you go so you can get some sleep."

"Now that I know I'm not going to be a father that should be easy."

I frown. Is he being sarcastic with me? "I'm sorry about tonight. Trust me. I'll always be honest with you."

"Don't apologize. What happened wasn't your fault."

"I know, but I still feel bad." I swing my legs off the bed and sit up. "I'll call you tomorrow, before we head to the arena."

"Alright." He's silent for a second. "Hey, Jen?"

"Yeah?"

"I ..." He stops. "I want you to know if you were pregnant, we'd make it work. I would respect any decision you made. I wasn't angry about a baby; I was angry about being the last to know."

My heart skips a beat. He wouldn't be upset if I got knocked up? "I understand. But, just to be on the safe side, I think we should still be careful." A small laugh escapes me. "I don't think I'm ready to be a mom."

His voice is quiet. "Well, for what it's worth, I think you'd be great."

He sounds disappointed, but before I can ask why, he says goodbye. "I'll talk to you tomorrow," he says. "Sleep tight."

~~~~

A week later, we're wrapping up our set in New Orleans.

"Thank you Louisiana!" Dean shouts into the mic.

The fans cheer, putting a grin on my face. The three of us join Dean for our usual wave goodbye, and, out of habit, my eyes dart to the groupie section near the front of the stage. The usual girls are there minus one. True to Latson and Dean's word, Heidi was kicked off the tour the day after she pulled her little prank.

I didn't see it go down, but I was told security escorted her out with Roxanne's help. Apparently Rox freaked when Dean told her Heidi was sneaking around our hotel room. She said if I see Heidi again I'm supposed to report it. So now, every time we play, I look for her. I don't expect her to show up, but you never know. She could actually pay to attend a concert for once.

As we head off the stage, Dean falls behind Drew and Paul to walk next to me. His eyes dart around before he asks, "Has she said anything?"

He doesn't have to tell me who "she" is. He's referring to Ariel. He knows she's pregnant because Latson told him the night of the text message. She hasn't made a formal announcement yet, and

Dean's worried about the tour. I don't blame him. He's got a lot riding on it.

"Nothing specific," I say as I stop to get stripped of my gear. "I know she's made a doctor's appointment. That's all."

Okay, that's not really all, but Dean could care less about her relationship with Zach. Since our trip to Dallas, Ariel has permanently moved to our bus. She travels with The Union and confides in me. She told me Zach supports her, but they're not in love. What happened was a one night stand, a drunken mistake, and Ariel still isn't sure what she's going to do. All she has decided on is an appointment when we get to Tampa. She grew up in Florida and has a local doctor there.

"You'd tell me, right?" Dean hands his guitar to a crew member and pulls out his ear piece. "If it's bad news, I need to know. I hate being blindsided."

"You and me both," I say, and it's the truth.

When I'm free of equipment, I follow the guys out of the backstage area. I don't know what their plans are, but I want to grab my stuff and head to the hotel. I'm hungry, and a hot shower and room service sounds like perfection. We're headed down the hallway to our dressing room when a small crowd gathered outside Ariel's door catches our attention.

"Interesting," Dean says as we get closer. He cocks a questioning eyebrow, and I shrug. It appears some dancers, along with some arena staff, are anticipating something. We pass the group and I try to eavesdrop. Unfortunately, everyone goes silent as we walk by.

"That was weird," Drew says when we enter our room.

"Think Ariel's having a diva moment?" Paul jokes, opening the mini fridge.

I doubt she is. I've haven't seen her be rude or demanding toward anyone. Then again, I'm not around her when she performs.

Grabbing my bag, I open it to find my phone. There's a message from Latson: *How'd it go tonight?*

I type back *Super fantastic as always* and hit send. Then, I hear an unfamiliar voice. "Jen? Jen Elliott? Where's Jen?"

I look up. Ariel's manager, Mason, looks stressed as he pokes his head into our dressing room. "That's me," I say, doubtful. I've never talked to him before.

"I need you," he says and rapidly gestures for me to follow him. "Bring your guitar."

"My acoustic?"

"Whatever you have. Just move!"

"Go," Dean says as he picks up my instrument and shoves it into my hands. "This doesn't sound good."

Confused, I do as I'm told, pulling the strap over my head as I follow Mason's tall, lanky frame down the hallway. We speed walk to Ariel's dressing room.

"I'm here. We're here. Let me through," he says as he parts the bodies standing in front of the door. He opens it and ushers me in ahead of him. When I step over the threshold, I look around Ariel's posh set-up and feel a pang of jealousy. Comfy couches, an adjacent room filled with racks of costumes, a counter filled with catered finger foods, and bottles of champagne complete the area. We're lucky if we get a bowl of pretzels and an extra folding chair.

"Ariel! I found her," Mason calls out.

A partially open door to my left opens further. It's a bathroom, and Ariel is sitting on the floor in front of the toilet. "Hey." She gives me a weak smile. "Did you know morning sickness doesn't only hit in the morning?"

My eyes consume my face, and I glance at Mason. "Yeah, I just found out," he says, crossing his arms and setting his jaw. "She's been puking for the last hour."

I look at my guitar and then Ariel. Does she want me to play her a song? I walk toward her and kneel down. "What can I do?"

"I need you to stall," she says. "I can't go on yet. I'm feeling better, but not one hundred percent. I still need to get dressed and fix my face."

"Stall how?" My brow furrows. "Do you want me to get the guys and go back on?"

"No." She shakes her head. "I mean, you can, but you already played your set. Does the band have anything else?"

"Not that we've rehearsed."

"Then you go," she says. "Sing "Fairytale." Sing "I Choose You." Sing –" Suddenly, she leans forward and dry heaves. "Sing whatever the hell you want," she says into the toilet.

She's lost her mind. "Are you insane? The people out there don't want to see me." I can hear the booing and catcalls now. My music isn't what they paid for.

"I'm asking a favor," she groans. She looks over her shoulder at Mason. "Where are my Saltines?"

He looks like he's losing his patience. Either that or he's so far out of his comfort zone he doesn't know what to do. He holds up his hands. "I put in a call."

My eyes bounce between the two of them. Couldn't my favor be to deliver the crackers?

"Please," Ariel pleads. "I just need some extra time."

My mind races. Going out on stage alone violates my cardinal rule. The idea doesn't make me happy. In fact, it scares the shit out of me. I'm not prepared.

"Jen. Think of it as a career opportunity," Mason says.

"You're on board with this?"

"I'm on board with anything that prevents a hostile audience." He looks at his watch. "And we're supposed to start the show in a few minutes."

I take a deep breath. Nothing like a little pressure to force you into a decision. "Okay." I stand up and look at Ariel. She wears a grateful expression.

"Thank you," she says before pushing her body off the floor and turning on the sink.

Don't thank me just yet, I think. She may still wind up with angry fans.

"Let's go," Mason says and opens the door. As soon as he does, he's bombarded with questions.

"Is the show canceled?"

"Is Ariel sick?"

"What does she have?"

"The show is not canceled," he says, raising his voice and his hands to push back the people. "Ariel had a migraine, but she's feeling better. We're running about twenty minutes behind. Go get ready." He grabs one of the arena personnel. "I need a mic at the front of the stage. Tell the crew there's been a slight change, we have an extra act."

The guy nods and starts talking into his headset.

"C'mon," Mason says and starts to lead me through the fray.

"Jen!"

I hear Dean and look behind me. He catches up to my side as we walk. "What's going on?"

"Ariel needs extra time. She wants me to stall." I give him a panicked look. "She wants me to play."

His eyes grow wide. "Are you okay with that?"

"Do I have a choice?"

The three of us make it backstage where I'm hooked up with everything I just took off. "Just go out there, introduce yourself, and play," Mason says as Roxanne comes running up.

"What in the hell is going on here?" Her eyes shoot daggers.

"Don't worry, Roxy. I'm not stealing your talent." Mason looks me over, making sure I have everything. "Last minute schedule change, that's all."

"Why?"

"Ariel's not feeling great. She needs a few more minutes." Mason looks me in the eye. "You're all set. I'll tell you when it's time to come off through your ear piece." He gives me a little nudge toward the stage. "Please don't suck," I hear him mutter.

Oh my God. Am I really doing this?

"I'm going with you." Dean grabs my hand, and I relax a little. He leads me toward the stage. "You've never performed alone before. What they're asking isn't fair. I'll introduce you and stay close."

"Thanks." I squeeze his hand.

We walk out on to the darkened stage and the lights come up a bit. Dean lets go of me and waves as he makes his way to the mic. I stare out into the arena as I follow him and notice every seat looks filled. They're waiting for Ariel.

Not me.

"Hello again, New Orleans," Dean's voice echoes. "Remember me?" He laughs and the crowd cheers. "I'm Dean McCarthy, in case you forgot." He jerks his head, telling me to move closer. "This here is Jen Elliott. You saw her earlier, too, when she wailed on rhythm guitar with me and the boys."

The people actually make noise for me, so I nod and smile.

"Ariel –"

The crowd erupts at the mention of her name. It's deafening. Dean grins and claps with them, then gestures for them to calm down.

"Ariel will be out in just a few minutes," he continues over the whistles and applause. "While you wait, she sent you someone special. She asked my friend Jen to entertain you. I promise you're going to love her."

He steps back, giving me the mic, and my head feels heavy. A low buzz sounds in my ears, and I start to feel nauseous. My heart pounds in my chest like it's trapped in a cage. *Don't faint. Don't faint. Don't faint.*

I manage to step up to the mic without keeling over. "Thanks, Dean. Hello, Louisiana." My voice sounds thick and tense. I force a smile even though my legs feel weak. "I'm Jen, and this is 'Fairytale'."

The people continue to cheer. Not like they did for Ariel, but at least the majority sound polite. Adrenaline feeds my nervous energy, so I close my eyes and strum my guitar. I feel like heaving. *I cannot throw up!*

The sound of the instrument centers me, and the buzzing starts to fade. My heart continues to race, so I concentrate on the feel of the guitar in my hands. It gives me confidence, and I let the first notes flow through my fingers and onto my strings. I open my eyes, then I open my mouth and ...

Sing.

Chapter Twenty Four

"Check this out." Dean extends his hand to show me his phone. He taps the screen and a video of me starts to play.

"You taped me singing?" I try to steal his cell from him, but he's too fast.

"Yep," he says and holds it close to his chest. He starts typing. "I'm sending it to everyone we know riiiiiiight ..." He draws out the word as his thumbs fly over the screen. "Now." He sets his phone down with a smirk.

I roll my eyes.

"Here we are." Our smiling waitress appears. We're seated at a high top table at a loud bar near the arena. She sets down four shots of Fireball, then hands out our other drinks. "I'll be back to check on y'all in a few minutes."

Drew and Paul waste no time reaching for the shots and passing them out. "To Jen!" Drew announces with his glass in the air. "On her first solo performance!"

"Hear, hear!" Dean and Paul chime in.

"You guys are dorks," I say, but raise my glass just the same. We down the shots and slam the glasses on the table.

"I think we should add your song to our set. At least in Detroit," Dean says. "Isn't your family coming to that show?"

I nod. "I'm not sure if that makes me more or less nervous. I almost passed out tonight." I've never felt a mixture of fear and excitement so strongly before.

"The more you do it the easier it will be," Dean rationalizes. "You did great. Even the audience thought so."

"They were being nice."

"They didn't have to be," Paul says. "I've played for a few evil crowds. Those motherfuckers can turn on you like that." He snaps his fingers.

I'm so glad that didn't happen.

"Who's up for darts?" Drew asks, eyeing an open board.

"I am," Dean says. "Five bucks says you lose."

"Five?" Drew scowls. "At least bet me enough to buy another beer."

"Fine. Ten."

Drew looks at me and points. "You're playing next."

I smile. "You're on." I haven't played darts in years, but my parents used to have a board in the basement. I was decent against my brothers.

Dean and Drew leave the table, and I take a sip of my Kamikaze. It reminds me of Latson and his party when we formally met. If I knew then what I know now, I would have jumped that man immediately and taken him up on his offer of a private tour. We would have had four more weeks together before I left. I sigh. Hindsight is always 20/20.

"Jen." Paul gets my attention. "I'm going to go hit on that blonde at the bar." He looks over his shoulder. "Will you be okay here for a minute?"

"Just a minute?" My eyebrows shoot up. "You think that's all it will take?"

"You know it is." He winks at me before he stands. "I'll be right back."

Sure, I think as he walks away. This isn't the first time I've witnessed his moves. If she shows any interest I won't see him until morning.

I'm just about to get up to watch Drew and Dean when my phone buzzes against the table. I lean over and read a message from Gwen: *I got Dean's video. You go girl! So awesome!*

I smile and reply: *Thanks. It was a last minute thing.*

Then, almost immediately, I get another text message from Jules: *Holy shit! Are you the headliner now? Congrats! Oh, and Pete says you were lip synching. Don't worry. I hit him for you.*

I laugh. I miss those guys.

Just as I'm responding to Jules, a smooth voice says, "Spectacular show tonight. I'm glad I caught it."

A body slides next to me and into Dean's seat. I look up and mentally groan. "Caleb."

"Jen." He flashes his perfect smile and raises his hand, calling over a waitress. "I'll take a Dewar's straight, please." He looks at me. "What would you like?"

My eyes dart to my nearly full glass. "I'm all set. Thanks."

The waitress leaves, and Caleb turns his body and attention toward me. He's dressed casually in a t-shirt and jeans; his dirty blonde hair left natural and un-styled. Unfortunately, I like this look on him. He appears approachable, more like a regular guy.

"I didn't know you could sing like that," he says.

I raise an eyebrow. "And I didn't know you were stalking Dean across the fifty states."

He laughs. "What if I am? I'm just doing my job."

"Really?" I skeptically glance around the bar. "I don't see any other label execs. In fact, I haven't seen anyone other than you since we've been on tour. Why is that?"

"Snare Records is Ariel's label."

"But Dean's a free agent."

He smiles. "Why are you giving me such a hard time? Don't you want Dean to get signed?"

"Sure I do. I'm just not sure you're the best choice."

Caleb loses his grin. "Because of what Gunnar told you?"

"Um, yes," I say sarcastically and take a drink. I may need another one of these if he's going to hang around.

"Look –"

The waitress interrupts him to deliver his scotch.

"Thanks," he says before turning back to me. "I'm trying to right a wrong here. What happened before shouldn't have happened, and I know that now. Gunnar isn't performing anymore, so I can't make it up to him. But I can try with Dean."

"Why the change of heart?"

Caleb plays with his drink, turning it around with his hand. "Because time tells stories. I realize what I did wasn't necessary."

I get snarky. "Well, isn't that big of you."

Caleb crosses his arms and leans against the table top. "How much do you know? What did Gunnar tell you?"

"He's told me enough," I say. "It's your fault he lost his career."

"That's fair," Caleb concedes. "But did he tell you he was there the night his sister died?"

No, I think and frown. "What does that have to do with anything?"

"Because he was caught on the security camera leaving her hotel room before she overdosed. There was speculation when the footage was released; hell, his own father accused him of murder." He moves closer to me. "I knew Gunnar didn't put the coke up Audrey's nose, but the bad publicity was impossible to ignore. It seemed the best thing for everyone was to let the band go."

I remember reading the headline about Latson's dad, but hearing it from Caleb still shocks me. As my mind wraps around his words, I say, "So, you're telling me Latson ended his career before you did."

"I'm telling you we're both guilty."

The man looks sincere. I can see where he's coming from, but it's undeniable Latson was a victim of circumstance. There's also the issue of Levi. "Don't you think your brother shares part of the blame, too?"

"That he does." Caleb takes a long drink and swallows. "That he does."

I study him. Something doesn't sit right. He flew all the way out to New Orleans for what? To see the exact same show? "Why are you really here?"

"I told you. Dean."

I raise my eyebrows. "And?"

Caleb smiles and shakes his head. "Fine." He places both hands on the table and sits back. "You."

"Me?"

"Yes, you. You intrigue me." He leans forward again. "You're the only woman in an all-male group. Someone who's never played professionally, but performs like she has her whole life. Someone who writes her own music and saves the day at the last minute."

I'm confused. "Saves the day?"

"Roxanne told me how you stepped up for Ariel. I wasn't expecting that. No one was."

Does everyone think I'm a bitch? "She needed my help. I have a heart, you know."

"That's not what I meant." Caleb shakes his head. "No one was expecting your performance. It was good. Really good."

I don't want to feel flattered by his compliment, but I do.

"Have you ever considered recording a demo? I could get you into the studio once the tour's over. We could see where it goes."

Is he serious? "I've never thought about being a singer."

"Why? What's your nine to five back home?"

I laugh and pick up my drink. "It's more like a six to two. I tend bar."

Caleb's eyes light up. "Selling music would earn you more. A lot more."

Of course it would. The idea is tempting, especially after tonight. However, there's no way in hell Latson would want me to work with Caleb. Plus, there's no guarantee my songs would sell. "Thanks, but I'd rather not get my hopes up."

Caleb leans into my personal space. "What's holding you back?"

I shrug, but don't move away. He's doesn't intimidate me.

"I know it's your boyfriend," he says. "Are you going to let him run your life?"

My jaw drops. "Excuse me? You don't know anything about us."

"I know the chance I'm offering is one in a million. You should take it." He pushes a loose piece of hair away from my face, his fingers lingering on my skin, before he whispers my ear. "Do you know what I mean?"

Oh, I know what he means. My eyes narrow. "You don't get to touch me. Ever. Is that clear?"

He pulls away. "Jen, I ..."

"Don't Jen me." I stand. "This conversation is over."

My phone starts to buzz against the table. I reach for it, but Caleb's faster. He holds it out of my reach and says, "Don't go. Let me explain."

"Give me my phone."

"If you would just wait a minute –"

"I said give me my phone."

"You don't understand what I meant."

"No, I understand perfectly what you meant." I try to grab my cell, but he stands and holds it hostage. "Damn it, Caleb! Give me my phone! I want to leave."

"What's going on here?"

I turn around to see Dean and Drew. Caleb answers, "Jen and I were just discussing the possibility of her starting a singing career. Weren't we, Jen?"

He smiles, but I can see the message lying beneath. He doesn't want me to say anything about what just happened. Little does he know the truth will be told once Dean and I are alone.

"Yep," I say, clipping the word and holding my hand out for my phone again. He gives it to me, and I look at Dean and Drew. "I'm headed back to the hotel. I'll see you guys tomorrow."

"I'll come with you," Drew says, giving Caleb a questioning look.

As we leave the bar, Drew sets a protective hand against my back. I glance down at my phone to see who called and realize the call connected. Caleb must have brushed his thumb against the screen when he picked it up. My heart drops.

It's Latson.

"Hello?" I put the phone to my ear. "Hello? Are you there?"

"You're with Caleb."

Shit. His words are a statement and his voice sounds flat. I say the first thing that comes to mind. "No, I'm not."

"Yes, you are. You're thinking about a singing career."

"No. I –"

"I'll let you go."

"No! Wait."

The line goes silent. "Latson?" No answer. "Latson?"

He's gone.

~~~~

"If it makes you feel any better, he's not taking my calls, either."

I shift my gaze from the ceiling of my bunk to Dean. "You tried again?"

"Just now. I left another message."

My face falls. If Latson won't answer the phone for his brother, my chances are disappearing by the second. It's been two days.

"He'll come around," Dean says. "He's sulking right now, but he'll snap out of it."

"When?" I ask. "Because this is killing me."

It is. I think it literally is. My stomach has been in knots ever since this whole thing happened. I have no appetite and sleeping is impossible. I keep thinking he'll text or call, and I'll be asleep and miss it. I've even been taking my phone with me into the bathroom when I shower.

"Hopefully he'll get his head out of his ass by the time we get to Tampa," Dean says. "Only a few more hours to go."

If that happened, I would welcome it. With open arms, trumpets, and confetti cannons. I know I didn't do anything wrong, but it feels like I did. All I want is the chance to explain what he overheard.

Dean's phone rings, and I nearly jump out of my skin. I get hopeful until I watch his expression twist. He sends the call to voice mail. "Caleb," he says.

"Asshole." I flop back against my pillow. "Is there any way we can rid of him?"

"I wish." Dean pockets his phone. "You know I'm only putting up with him until the end of the tour."

After I told Dean that Caleb tried to hit on me, he wasn't pleased. He confided that he never planned to sign with Snare, not with Sacred Sin's history. He's only tolerating Caleb to get through this tour. He said he has to be nice to him to avoid burning bridges; labels and agents talk. His main goal is to gain exposure, then shop his music.

"Latson knows, right? You told him?"

"In every message I've left."

I sigh. I hate that he won't talk to me. This is exactly like the time he overreacted at the hospital. It makes my heart hurt.

"I'll let you know if he calls," Dean says.

"Okay."

I roll over on my side and try to settle into my bunk. It seems Beau has us traveling at warp speed to Florida; I can feel it in the shimmy of the bus. I contemplate waking Ariel to ask her if Latson acted this way when they were together, but I know she hasn't been feeling well and she needs her sleep. There's nothing left for me to do, other than close my eyes. Instead, I find myself staring at Oliver's drawing. When did things get so complicated?

I feel a tap on my shoulder. "You up?"

I roll over and see Ariel. "Yeah. I thought you were sleeping."

She shakes her head. "My mind is racing."

"Same here."

"Move over," she says and nudges me.

I scoot to the side as Ariel sits down. She swings her legs up beside mine and lies back, so we're lying side by side. She pulls the bunk curtain closed. "You'd think they'd make these beds bigger," she says. "Rock stars get laid on their busses all the time."

I raise an eyebrow. "Are you speaking from experience?"

"Maybe."

I elbow her and she giggles.

We're quiet for a few moments before she says, "Things are stupid right now, aren't they?"

I nod in agreement.

"I'm knocked up and you're fighting with Gunnar. Neither should be happening."

"Amen, sister."

We stare at the ceiling. Although we're both dealing with issues, hers more life-altering than mine, it's nice to know I'm not alone. I'm sure she feels the same way.

"You know," she breaks the silence, "true artists would take their feelings and spill them into song."

I turn my head. "Like Taylor Swift?"

"Exactly."

I guess I'm not a true artist. "I don't feel like writing. All I want is a phone call."

"I hear you." She sighs. "All I want is to stop puking up everything I eat."

"You're having a girl," I muse. "My mom said I was the worst pregnancy out of four. I have three older brothers."

"You think? I like the idea of having a girl. I wouldn't know what to do with a boy."

"I think you'd figure it out. Moms are resourceful like that."

Ariel closes her eyes. "I still can't wrap my mind around the idea. I mean, I can't deny what my body is telling me, but it's still surreal." She looks at me. "How will I make it through nine months of this? How will I push out a baby? How?"

"With the help of powerful drugs."

She rolls her eyes and sets her hand on her belly. "That doesn't make me feel better for subjecting an innocent child to my poor parenting. I'm not sure I should have this baby."

"Stop," I chastise her. "The stork has never once delivered a baby and a handbook. If you decide to raise the little peanut, you'll do just fine. I know it."

"You think?" Ariel's expression softens. "It's hard to be logical when I'm so emotional."

"I know you'll do what's right, whatever you decide."

She sighs. "Thank you. That makes me feel better."

I frown. "I wish Latson felt better."

Ariel extends her hand to me, and I take it. She squeezes my fingers. "He'll call."

"Unless he doesn't." I can't help but imagine something awful, like him taking PTA mom Natalie up on her carpool offer. I shudder.

"He'll realize he overreacted." Ariel gives me an encouraging smile.

"I hope you're right," I say.

When we arrive in Tampa, Ariel heads to her doctor appointment in a rented Mercedes, and I head up to my room without Roxanne. My body feels drained when it shouldn't; I just spent the last nine hours on a bus. I need to pull myself together and focus on something other than Latson. We have a show tonight, and I need to concentrate.

When I get to my room, I open the door and fumble my way through with my suitcase, guitar, and bag. My exhausted eyes sweep the space like they always do and land on the desk opposite the two queen beds. A huge grin break across my face and relief instantly floods my body. I drop everything I'm carrying and skip over to a huge vase of roses sitting there. I bury my nose in the petals and inhale; there must be two dozen flowers here. Each one is a rich, velvety red and has a faux diamond set in the center. Eagerly, I find the card with my name on it and pry it open, excited and relieved to read Latson's words.

As quickly as the high came, the low crushes me. The flowers aren't from him.

My apologies for NOLA
Yours, Caleb

Chapter Twenty-Five

"I really think we should add "Fairytale" between "The Short Life" and "Over-Exposed". It would be a natural pace progression."

Dean tries to talk me into performing solo as the four of us enter our dressing room. We just finished opening at the Tampa Bay Times Forum.

"It would also give my voice a break."

He wiggles his eyebrows, and I shove his arm. "Pace progression my ass. You're just being lazy."

Singing solo doesn't bother me so much anymore; it's the attention I might get from Caleb. I don't want to give him any reason to talk to me, much less send flowers. Speaking of, I got rid of the roses by leaving them on an empty table in the hotel lobby. I didn't want them, and I definitely didn't want Roxanne to question me.

Stepping in front of the mirror, I pull out the bobby pins Mona buried in my hair. Instinct tells me to check my phone to see if Latson called, but I force myself to wait. I really don't want another dose of disappointment. In fact, I'd rather check it when I'm alone so I can mope in private. I don't know how long he plans to drag out the silent treatment, but I think it's been long enough.

"Hey, guys. Do you have a minute?"

I turn around to see Mason enter our dressing room. He looks stressed. "Is Ariel okay?"

He nods. "Everything's on schedule tonight." He glances over his shoulder, then shuts the door behind him. "I need to talk to you all about the rest of the tour."

His words grab Dean's attention. "What about it?"

Mason turns toward the guys. "Ariel's pregnant."

Paul's mouth drops open. "No shit."

"Yes, shit." Mason rubs his eyes. "I met her at the doctor this morning. She's six weeks along."

Drew blows out a heavy breath and Dean crosses his arms. "So, what does that mean?"

Mason's phone rings, and he pulls it out of his pocket to silence it. "It means she's made a few decisions. Number one, after seeing her ultrasound, she's decided to have the baby."

I smile. I had a feeling she would.

"The tour's fucked." Paul throws up his hands. "Unbelievable."

"Not so fast." Mason meets his eyes. "We'll have to cut some dates, but we'll finish the States. The international leg will have to be canceled."

I can feel Dean relax from feet away. "Are you sure?" I ask. "Ariel's felt awful."

Mason nods. "Her doctor gave her the okay to perform as long as she's feeling up to it. I'm going to look at the remaining cities tonight, get with the label, and decide what to cut. My guess is that we'll avoid multiple stays in one city."

Dean rubs his chin in thought. "How are you going to justify the cancellations? Are you going to make something up?"

"No. Ariel is going to announce the baby. She'll tweet the news tomorrow." Mason steps toward the door and opens it with a sigh. "She doesn't want to lie to her fans, or let them down. I'm headed to find Roxanne and break the news. I'll send you the revised schedule as soon as I have it."

When he's gone, all four of us look at one another. "I wonder who the father is," Paul muses, then winks. "I know it's not me."

I shake my head and start to pack my things. I won't be sharing that information.

Dean plops down in a chair next to me, so I ask, "Do you feel better about the tour now?"

"I'm a little disappointed things will be cut short." He gives me a small smile, and I give him one in return. "You should let Gunnar know," he adds. "With this news, you might get a response."

Since I'll be coming back earlier than expected, maybe I will.

I pull out my phone and try to hide my frown when I see Latson hasn't tried to contact me. I type out a message: *I know you're not talking to me, but Ariel has decided to have the baby. Some tour dates will be canceled. I'll be back before November.*

I want to add "If you want me back", but I'm too afraid of his answer.

~~~~

When I get to the hotel, I shower and put on Latson's t-shirt. It still smells like him, but not nearly as strong. I silently hope it's not a metaphor for our relationship; that it's not slowly fading away, too.

As I curl up in bed, the thought of losing him starts to take root in my mind. It's the last thing I want. I consider calling him again, since Roxanne is still with Mason going over the schedule, but I don't want to come across as hyper or clingy. I just want him to talk to me.

A knock on the door stops my thoughts. Confused, I walk over to see if Roxanne forgot her key. When I look through the peephole, I blink a couple times to make sure what I'm seeing is real. My pulse starts to race, and I can't get the door open fast enough.

"You're here." The words rush out of me.

In less than a second, I'm in Latson's arms. He holds me against him and I melt into his chest, inhaling his scent and feeling his heartbeat. He walks forward, pressing me back, until he shuts the door behind us. Without words, his mouth finds mine; his kiss is soft, yet urgent and deep. I return it with everything I have and run my hands up to his shoulders, feeling him relax beneath my touch. We stand in the middle of the room, connected, for countless minutes until he finally pulls away. His eyes meet mine for the first time, and I notice red discolors the whites. He looks tired, like he hasn't slept in days.

"I'm sorry I didn't call," he says.

I run my thumb over his cheek, across the purplish tint beneath his eye. "You were mad. I get it."

"I was at first, but ..." He shakes his head. "Something else came up."

His tone tells me something bad has happened. Immediately my thoughts jump to Oliver. "Is O all right? Where is he?"

"He's fine. Believe it or not, he's with my dad." Latson pulls me closer. "I'm a little freaked out about it."

My expression falls. "What do you mean he's with your dad? Did something happen with custody?"

"No." Latson pauses. "My mom passed away this morning."

Oh no. My eyes search his face. "Was she ill?"

"She wandered away from her room," he says. "She fell and hit her head."

I wrap my arms around his waist and hug him tight.

"I've been at the hospital the past few days. At first it seemed things would be okay, but she kept getting worse. The bleeding inside her head wouldn't stop."

My voice is muffled against his chest. "I'm so sorry. Does Dean know?"

"I just left his room. I feel like shit; I should have called him sooner. Everything happened so fast. One minute she was going to be fine, and the next she wasn't. Before I knew it, I was taking Oliver to say goodbye."

I look up at him. "How is he?"

"He cried, but not much. He held her hand and told her he loved her."

My heart starts to ache at the image.

"Then my dad distracted him with swimming and he was a seven-year-old again."

"Swimming?"

"My parents have a pool. My dad asked to spend some time with O."

Leaning back, I study the man in front of me. This is a huge step for him. "I can't believe you let him go."

"It's only until tomorrow night." Latson rests his forehead against mine. "When my father asked to watch Oliver, my first reaction was to take him and run. But O begged, and I thought of you."

"Me?"

"This is the first time my father has shown any interest in his grandson." Latson meets my eyes. "If you had been there, I know you would have told me to let them spend time together. You would have said it's the right thing to do."

I give him a gentle kiss. "You know me so well."

He almost smiles. "I also knew I needed to see you. I couldn't stay at my place alone. Not tonight. Not with Oliver where he is and the way I left things with you. The silence would be deafening."

"About that –" I start.

"Forget it," he says.

"No. I want to explain." I set my hands against his chest. "Caleb ambushed me. He said it was partly your fault Sacred Sin got dropped. I tried to leave and he stole my phone to make me stay. Dean and Drew came to my rescue, but by then you'd heard –"

"It doesn't matter." He puts two fingers beneath my chin and lifts my gaze. "Whose shirt are you wearing?"

"Yours."

"Who gets to kiss you?"

"You do."

"Who's missed you more than anything?"

I circle his wrist and move his hand, so I can lean in and hug him again. "You."

As I say that word, all the stress from the past few days melts away. I feel better, but a new hurt starts to grow. One for Latson and what he's going through.

"Come on," I say and lead him toward the bed. I prop the puffy pillows against the headboard as he takes off his shoes. It's just now that I notice he doesn't have a bag or a suitcase with him. "Did you bring any clothes?"

"I left my backpack with Dean," he says. "I'm only here for the night."

I wish he didn't have to leave so soon, but I know Oliver is weighing on his mind. Plus, arrangements need to be made for his mother. I crawl to the center of the bed and he joins me fully dressed. We scoot together, and I end up tucked against his side. He wraps his arm around my back, and I thread my legs through his.

"I don't think you know how much you calm me," he says.

I'm sure things haven't been easy. "Do you want to talk about it?"

"About what?"

"Oliver. Your mom. Whatever you want."

He's quiet. My fingers find their way to his side and trace patterns over his shirt.

"You know," Latson says, "I actually thought she was getting better."

My tracing stops. "Before she fell?"

"After." His arm tightens around my waist. "For about five minutes my mom was completely lucid. She asked about Oliver and his last day of school. She asked about the bar and Dean. I thought it was impossible for her to remember anything, but she was her old self. Her personality came back."

I give him a tentative smile. "Then what happened?"

"My dad came into the room. She called him by name and he dropped his coffee. She laughed and called him a klutz. I haven't heard that laugh in years." He sighs and runs his palm over his tired eyes. "A few seconds later she asked where Audrey was. As fast as she appeared, she slipped away again. The fall didn't help her disease. It couldn't."

"I'm sorry," I whisper.

"It was stupid to think she was recovering. No one recovers from dementia."

I lift my head and kiss the corner of his mouth. "There's nothing wrong with having hope."

His eyes meet mine. "I wish you could have met her. The real her, not the shell."

"Me, too." We study one another, until I say, "Although, in a way, I have met her. Part of her is in you."

Latson scowls. "You're wrong. She was a good person. I'm not —"

"Stop." I cut him off. "You're good."

He gets sarcastic. "Does a good person use his mother's illness against his parents to gain custody of his nephew?"

My mouth falls open. "What?"

"Does a good person fight with his drug addicted sister when he knows she will use any excuse to get high?"

I shake my head to sort out what he's saying.

"That's what I thought." Latson lets his head fall back against the headboard. "I'm not my mother."

No. "Hang on." I sit up and kneel beside him. "You couldn't love your nephew more if he was your own child. You give him everything. There was no choice but for you to take him. Your mother was sick and your dad works a million hours. He would've ended up with a nanny."

"Mrs. Gibson is a nanny."

I groan and let my head fall back in exasperation. How can he not see all the good he's done? "As far as Audrey goes, you fought with your sister. What brother doesn't fight with his sister? You had no idea she was going to OD. Knowing you the way I do, you were probably arguing with her to stop her from using. Am I right?"

The muscles in Latson's neck tense. "I confronted her the night she died."

"And?"

"Levi was in her suite. I knew there were only two things they could be doing: lines or fucking. Neither of which Oliver needed to see."

My eyes grow wide. Hopefully he showed up in time. "You were fighting with her because you cared about her. Not to provoke her."

Latson sets his jaw. "I knew she was unstable."

"Your heart was in the right place."

"I stormed out."

"You were pissed."

"If I had stayed she might still be alive."

"You don't know that."

"My father thought so. He said I killed her."

Defeated, I let my shoulders sag. "I don't understand how your father could accuse you of anything."

Seconds pass before Latson takes a deep breath and reaches for me. "You know we never saw eye to eye on music," he says as I settle into his side. "My dad was angry about a lot of things, and when he found out that I left Audrey after an argument, he said some really shitty stuff to get to me. When I got custody of Oliver, I cut him off."

"Until now," I say against his chest.

"No. Not until now. Until you."

I look up at him, confused.

"My dad pulled me aside when you were admitted to the hospital." He pushes my hair back from my forehead. "He tried to apologize and blame grief for his actions. I ignored him. I told him it was two years too late, asked him to take care of you, and left."

I can tell his father's words made an impact. "But you still listened."

"I've been thinking a lot about what he said."

Propping myself on my elbow, I lean forward and kiss him. "I'm glad." I hope things work out. If not for him, then for O.

I curve my body against his and, after minutes of silence, I start to fall asleep. Latson is tired too, and that's okay. His presence alone is comforting. I feel warm and safe surrounded by him, and that thought makes me realize just how hard I've fallen for this man. We don't have to do anything but be together, and I feel sated. Yes, he has some baggage and I hate the sad circumstances that brought him here tonight, but I'll do whatever it takes to make him feel better. I once told him his hurts are mine. I still believe that.

"Jen?"

I look up at him. "Hmmm?"

"Do you think you could come to the funeral? I'd really like you to be there."

"Of course. I'll talk to Roxanne about it tomorrow. Whatever you need."

Latson's eyes lock with mine before he cradles the side of my face. He leans in slowly and gives me a tender kiss. "You," he says. "I'm going to need you."

~~~~

The following week, I pack a small bag to take to Chicago. The funeral is tomorrow, and I'll be staying with Latson for two nights. Dean flew out ahead of me, to spend time with the family and attend his foster mother's wake. The Union won't be opening for Ariel in Atlanta because of our absence, but Dean and I will fly back together to pick up the tour in Nashville.

Opening the closet, I pull out the black dress Ariel helped me find. When I told her what had happened, she volunteered to go shopping with me for something appropriate. Being out in public with Ariel was a trip. She was in disguise, wearing a baseball cap and sunglasses, but a few people still recognized her. Before we left the hotel, she told me she wanted to visit a few baby stores, but we never made it. Luckily the madness started after we found what I was looking for.

I hang the dress up in the bathroom, so I can remove any wrinkles with the steam from a hot shower. I start to get undressed when someone starts pounding on the door like the hotel's on fire. I jump at the sound and race to open it.

You have got to be joking.

"I just wanted to let you know I'm back." Heidi crosses her arms and a shoots me a superior look. "I talked to Caleb."

My eyes narrow. I thought I ran the chance of running into her in Chicago, not Atlanta. My tone is acerbic. "I don't even want to think about what you did to get into his good graces."

I start to shut the door, but she slams her hand against the wood to stop me. "We're having a party tonight to celebrate."

"And?"

"You're not invited."

Does she think that hurts my feelings? I stare at her stupefied. "I'll be sure to write that in my diary later." I slam the door. Apparently, she feels vindicated. Fine. Whatever. Leave me alone.

When I get out of the shower, Roxanne is already tucked in bed, her face illuminated by her Kindle. I no more than tell her who's back when I understand the reason Heidi brought up the party.

It's happening in the room next to ours.

Loud music, laughter, and later, moans, filter into our room throughout the night. It's impossible to sleep, no matter how hard we try. When Heidi starts to scream Caleb's name, I'm fully aware of what she did – or will do – to stay on this tour. It's pathetic.

"That's it!" Roxanne jumps out of bed and rips the handset off the phone. "I'm calling the front desk!"

Like it will make a difference, I think. Not with Caleb involved. He'll probably toss some extra record label cash at the manager and continue his sexcapades. I bury my head beneath the pillows as Heidi starts up again. Good God, she has to be faking by now.

As predicted, the complaint to the front desk yields zero results. It's three a.m. and I have to get up in two hours. I'm dead tired and pissed as hell. It's almost as if they're doing this on purpose. I throw my blankets off and march to the door.

"Where are you going?" Roxanne sits up straight.

"To shut them up," I snap.

I pound on their door like Heidi did earlier. It takes a few times before the noise stops. Satisfied, I start to walk away when the door opens. Caleb stands there, half-naked, holding a sheet around his waist.

"Would you two keep it down?" I hiss. "People are trying to sleep!"

"Jen." He looks me over. "I didn't know you were next door."

"Does it matter? Just shut the hell up!" I start to walk away.

"Don't leave."

Against my better judgment, I turn around. "Did you get my flowers?" he asks.

He wants to discuss this now? I groan. "Yes. I gave them away. I don't want anything from you, Caleb."

Suddenly, Heidi appears behind him and shrieks, "You sent her *flowers*?"

"As an apology," he says.

She starts to pummel him with her fists. "No! No no no no!" He tries to block her. "She can't have you, too!"

"Calm down. Christ." Caleb moves and tries to ward her off. "What is wrong with you?"

I hear the distinct sound of a door open across the hall. *Fantastic,* I think. We're waking up the whole floor. "Guys!" I try to whisper-yell. "Knock it off!"

"You bastard!" Heidi continues to wail on Caleb's chest, her red hair a tangled mess. "How could you?"

"Nothing's going on!"

He lets go of his sheet to catch Heidi's flying fists, and it falls to floor. Oh, Jesus. I slam my eyes shut, but not before getting a full view of Caleb's naked ass. Their struggle stops and I hear, "You wouldn't dare."

"Watch me, asshole!"

A door slams and I open one eye. Caleb has been left in the hallway sans bed sheet. He faces the door, sets his hands on either side of the frame, and hangs his head. I can't help but notice that's not the only thing hanging.

My eyes find the ceiling and I sigh. "Would you like some help?"

He turns and faces me, covering himself with both hands. "Yes, please."

We look at each other, and I try not to laugh. This is ridiculous. We're standing a few feet apart and he's totally naked. I'm wearing nothing but Latson's t-shirt and my underwear.

"Come on." I turn to walk the few steps back to my room. No one deserves to be Heidi's victim, although he did bring it on himself by getting involved with her.

When I open the door, Roxanne sits up in bed. "What happened?"

"I stopped the sex."

Caleb follows me into the room. "Hi."

Roxanne's eyes bug out of her head. "So you brought him over here for more?"

I shoot her an "oh, please" look. I open the closet, find an extra blanket, and toss it at Caleb.

"Thanks." He catches it with one hand against his leg. "Can I use your phone?"

After he calls the front desk and apologizes to us, he leaves to meet someone with another key. I fall back into bed and close my eyes. Apparently he and Heidi have separate rooms, which I'm grateful for. I don't want to hear arguing or, god forbid, make up sex. I've seen Caleb in all his glory; I don't need any more to add to the visual. All I want to do is get some sleep. Tomorrow is going to be hard enough; attending a funeral is always sad. I want to be as alert as I can for Latson, and I can't wait to hug O.

Unfortunately, when my alarm sounds, it's way too soon. I've never been a morning person, but this feels especially torturous.

Forcing myself out of bed, I get dressed and catch a cab to the airport. When I make it to my gate, I take a seat and look up to watch some news channel playing on the TV. It's not long before my eyelids start to droop and I close them for a few minutes. Thankfully Pete is picking me up when I land and taking me to his apartment before the service. I hope he doesn't mind if I nap on the way.

"Excuse me? Miss?"

Someone nudges my shoulder. When I open my eyes, I'm face to face with a kind-looking elderly woman.

"Yes?" I say, my voice scratchy.

"You've been sleeping for quite some time," she says. "I wanted to make sure you didn't miss your flight."

"Thank you." I smile. "But my plane doesn't leave until eight a.m."

Her face falls. "Oh, honey. It's after nine."

It can't be. My eyes dart to the monitor behind the ticket desk. Bold white letters advertise the time and the temperature, along with the flight number and location. Instantly, my stomach knots. I'm not going to Topeka, Kansas. Panic starts to set in.

I missed my flight.

Chapter Twenty Six

I leap out of the cab as soon as it pulls up to the cemetery.

By the time the airline found me another seat to Chicago, I knew I would miss the church service. With a shaky voice, I called my brother and told him how stupid I was. He tried to reassure me that mistakes happen, but it didn't make me feel any better. He said he would send me the cemetery address and meet me there. After I changed clothes at the airport, I prayed during the entire flight that I could attend most of the graveside ceremony. When the plane touched down, my body was coiled with tension. Nothing moved fast enough; not my feet, not the cab, and certainly not traffic.

Now, as quickly as I can, I make my way toward the green tent and the people gathered around it. The closer I get, the more I realize everyone is standing in small groups and talking casually.

Damn it all to hell! Did I miss everything here, too?

A group standing off to the side breaks apart and it's then that Pete catches my eye. He waves and starts to walk in my direction, hand in hand with Jules. The whole Torque crew follows them, and, when we get close enough, Jules lets go of Pete and wraps me in a hug. "You made it."

"Not soon enough." I frown over her shoulder. "Did I miss it all?"

She steps back and nods. "We just finished."

My heart sinks. "How is he?" I look at Pete. "Did you tell him what happened?"

"I did. He seems ..." Pete rubs the back of his neck. "He seems pretty pissed, Little J."

A lump forms in the back of my throat. I knew Latson would be upset.

"You should ride with Kenzie and me to the dinner." Gwen rubs my arm compassionately. "There's room in my car."

"Thanks." I give her a weak smile.

"Jen!"

In the space between Carter and Felix I see Oliver running toward me. He looks adorable in his little suit and tie. I kneel down and the boys step aside, so Oliver can reach me. He throws his arms around my neck, and I squeeze him tight. "Hi, O."

"Uncle Gunnar said you were coming." He leans back. "What took you so long?"

"I got stuck at the airport," I say. "How are you? I'm sorry about your grandma."

He nods. "She was sick, but it's okay. Know why?"

"Why?"

"Because she's in heaven with my mom."

The lump in my throat gets bigger. "I'm sure she is."

"C'mon." He pulls on my hand. "I want to show you something."

I stand and look at Gwen. "Go ahead. We'll wait for you," she says.

Trailing behind Oliver, I follow him toward the green tent. I search for Latson and find him talking to Dean and a few other people. He stands with his hands in the pockets of his black suit, the jacket fastened by one button at the waist. I've never seen him dressed so formally, and it takes my breath away. To say he cleans up nicely is an understatement. The only thing I wish I could change is the sad, distant look on his face. I curse myself for screwing this up; I should have been here for him.

Oliver and I keep walking and, just when I think he's leading me to his grandmother, he takes me behind the green tent. As we pass by, I get an up-close view of the deep mahogany casket covered with a huge spray of every pastel rose imaginable. The finality of it hits me, and I swallow. Oliver stops in front of a headstone and points. "This is my mom," he says in a quiet voice. "This is where I come to visit her, although Uncle Gunnar doesn't bring me a lot. He might more now, since Grandma is here, too."

My breath catches. This is the last thing I expected him to show me. The August sun reflects off a polished gray stone etched with:

Audrey Jean Latson
Beloved Daughter, Sister, Mother
November 12, 1984 ~ April 9, 2012
"All you touch and all you see is all your life will ever be."
~ Pink Floyd

I crouch down and sit on the balls of my feet to study the intricate flowers carved around the stone. They look like Lily of the Valley mixed with Forget-Me-Nots. "This is a very special place," I say to Oliver. "Thank you for sharing it with me."

He smiles, then kisses his finger and touches the top of the stone. "This is what we do when we come here, so she knows we love her," he explains. "Uncle Gunnar says angels can see our kisses."

Without warning, tears prick my eyes. What an amazing thing for him to say.

"Oliver."

Latson's voice is stern behind me, and a wave of anxiety slides down my spine. I immediately stand, but he barely glances at me.

"Uncle Gunnar, look." Oliver's face lights up. "Jen's here."

"We have to go." Latson extends his hand toward his nephew. "We don't want to be late." His eyes dart to me when he says the word "late". They're cold. Colder than I've ever seen them.

"Okay," Oliver says and reluctantly shuffles towards his uncle. "I'll see you at the restaurant, Jen."

"'Kay," I say, my voice stuck.

As they walk away, I'm rooted in place. Latson didn't speak to me, much less look at me.

My heart cracks, and the fissure runs to my soul.

~~~~

Hours later, I'm curled up on Pete's couch. I don't think my body can get any smaller. Maybe I'm trying to disappear, or maybe I'm trying to hold my insides together. Either way, the feeling sucks. I'd give anything to go back in time and fix today.

"You should go talk to him." Jules sits by my feet. She places a mug on the table in front of me, and I give her a confused look. "Coffee," she says. "You didn't eat anything at the dinner."

She's right. All I did was push food around my plate.

"I wasn't hungry," I say. I'm still not. I hurt Latson, and I feel hideous.

"C'mon." She swats me on my ass.

"Ow!" I scowl at her. "What was that for?"

"Nothing is going to solve itself with you sitting here. He's right upstairs. Go. Talk. To. Him."

"I want to," I say. So badly.

"Then what's stopping you?"

I shrug.

Jules lets out a sigh. "They say never go to bed angry. You should at least go upstairs and apologize."

She's right. I wanted to apologize the minute I saw Latson at the cemetery. I wanted to apologize at the dinner. However, he was with family, and he wouldn't acknowledge me. "I think I need to give him some space. He just lost his mother." I sit up and reach for the coffee. "I'm not sure it's the right time."

Jules' voice gets quiet. "When you love someone it's always the right time."

I'm silent. I'm not sure if he loves me. He's never said it; but then again, neither have I.

"Think of it this way," she says. "If he had done something to hurt you, wouldn't you want an apology? Or at least words?"

I nod.

"So?" She prods. "Oliver should be in bed by now. Go."

I give her an uncertain look. "I think I should wait until morning."

She huffs, then grabs me by the arm and pulls me to my feet.

"Hey!" The coffee splashes. "You don't have to –"

She leads me out of the living room, then opens the door. She takes the mug from my hands and nudges my leg with her foot. "Go say you're sorry. I won't wait up."

Rolling my eyes, I step outside the door. Without another word she shuts it, and I'm alone.

Slowly, I make my way to Latson's apartment. It's not like I don't want to see him. It's the exact opposite. Every part of me aches to hold him. I want to do what I promised, to be there for him and take away his pain. The problem is he's angry, and I don't know if he wants to see me.

When I reach his door, I tentatively knock and wait for a response. When none comes, I knock again, only harder. I fidget as I wait. I guess he could be sleeping. It's been a long, difficult day. I would give anything to be asleep beside him.

Sighing at the thought, I turn to leave and stop when the door opens. Latson stands there wearing gym shorts and a t-shirt. No fun saying graces his chest, just the solid color blue.

"Hi," I say when he doesn't speak. "Can we talk?"

His face is impassive as he steps outside. He crosses his arms, glances at the floor, and then looks at me. "What do you want to talk about?"

"Today," I say. "I'm sorry about today."

"Me, too," he says, emotionless. "I buried my mother and my girlfriend wasn't there."

That hurts. "I'm sorry," I whisper. "I tried to be there. I really did."

"Did you?" He tilts his head. "Because it sounded to me like sleep was more important."

What? I'll kill Pete if he made it sound that way. "You have to know I didn't do it on purpose. I had a late night. I know it's a lame excuse, but it's the truth."

Latson nods, but doesn't look convinced. "Is there anything else you want to tell me about last night?"

I stare at him in confusion. His tone implies I did something wrong. "No. Heidi and Caleb were being obnoxiously loud in the room next to mine and I couldn't sleep."

"Bullshit," he snaps.

My heart starts to pound. "Excuse me? I'm not lying."

"Heidi was kicked off the tour."

"And Caleb let her back on." I study his face. "You can ask Roxanne. Heidi came back yesterday."

I try to step closer to him and he steps back. It hits me like a punch to the gut. "What's wrong?"

He lets out a sarcastic laugh as he shakes his head. "I just...I can't keep up with you, Jen."

"What's that supposed to mean?"

"It means I want to believe you. It means I want to have faith in what you say. But when I have proof otherwise, it makes me wonder what else you've lied to me about."

Hold on. "I've never lied to you."

"Yeah?" I don't like the look in his eyes. "You promised you'd be there today and you weren't."

My face falls. "I know and I feel awful. I fell asleep; it was an accident."

"You promised you'd stay away from Caleb and you haven't."

I frown. Are we back to that night at the bar? "I told you he found me and took my phone. I didn't find him."

"And last night? How do you explain that?"

I'm at a loss for words. I already told him Caleb and Heidi were next door. Does he think I booked the room? "I don't know what you're trying to say."

He lets out a frustrated sigh. "Have you been online today?"

"Why in the hell would I be online?" I've been riding an emotional rollercoaster ever since I woke up this morning; checking social media has been the last thing on my mind.

He reaches into his pocket and pulls out his phone. "It's all over the internet."

What is? Latson taps something on his cell and hands it to me. The minute I see the pictures all the blood drains from my face. Someone posted pictures of me and Caleb standing in the hallway. He's facing me, covering his junk, and I'm trying not to smile. The second photo shows us entering my room. How is this possible?! I read the caption and the hashtags: *The fun things you see on tour #groupielife #renegadetour #niceass.*

Oh my god. I heard someone open a door.

"I can explain." My voice is barely there. "I went over to shut them up. Heidi got mad about the flowers Caleb sent and she started hitting him and –" I'm rambling.

"Flowers?" Latson goes from incredulous to angry. "What flowers?"

Fuck. I can barely breathe. "Caleb sent me –"

Latson grabs his phone from my hand. "I've heard enough."

"But –"

"Don't." His eyes flash and his entire body looks tense. "You need to go."

I'm shaking. "Go where?"

"Anywhere but here. I can't talk to you right now."

I hate the way he dismisses me. "Please." I reach out and graze his arm. "Let's –"

He jerks his arm away and ignores me. He opens his door and walks inside.

"Latson." I step forward. "Wait."

He slams the door in my face.

I stand there, stunned. Tears burn behind my eyes and my heart threatens to pound out of my chest; I want to beat down the door and run away at the same time. Never in my life have I felt so helpless. Nothing I say will make this better. No apology will make this better.

I don't know how long it takes me to walk back to Pete's. When I get there I'm grateful Jules didn't lock the door. I try to make it to my bedroom without anyone noticing me. It doesn't work.

"Jen?" Pete sticks his head out of his room. "I thought you went upstairs."

I look down to hide my face. "I'm back. Goodnight."

"No." He steps in front me and his face fills with concern. "Why are you all red?"

"It's nothing. Just –"

"How'd it go?" Jules joins us, way too perky. "I didn't expect –" She stops talking and narrows her eyes. "What happened?"

I can't help it. The tears I was holding back spill over. Pete sets his jaw before pulling me into his arms. "What did he do?"

"Nothing. It's my fault," I say against his chest. "I messed up."

Jules rubs my back to soothe me. "It's okay. You'll work it out."

I close my eyes and remain silent. I can't bring myself to say I don't think so.

Chapter Twenty Seven

Oh, Ed. How I've missed you.

The soothing sound of my boyfriend's voice travels from my phone to my ear buds. He's kept me sane over the last three weeks, reminding me that everyone falls in love and everyone gets lost. I may be biased in thinking I get hurt more than others, but one look at my love life proves it hasn't been stellar. I'm grateful my pretend boyfriend hasn't abandoned me because I've needed him.

I've needed him ever since Latson slammed the door in my face.

With my eyes closed, I curl on my side in my bunk. We just left Pittsburgh, and Beau is driving us to Ohio. When we're finished playing Columbus and Cleveland, the tour will end in Detroit. My rock star life will be over two months earlier than planned. It's perfect timing really; Tricia called and my apartment is ready. I have a home back in Michigan.

Too bad my heart is in Illinois.

Sensing someone behind me, I roll over. Ariel pulls out one of my ear buds. "I need to interrupt your time with Ed for a minute."

She knows I'm obsessed. I sit up and scoot back, so she can join me. "What's up?"

"I'm staging an intervention." She pulls her legs beneath her and gets comfortable. "I miss your smile."

I look down at my lap. "Me, too."

"I think you should know," she pauses, "Dean and the guys are concerned."

"Why?" I frown. I've hidden my feelings pretty well on stage. So what if I don't go out to bars and parties? The tour's almost over.

Ariel tips her head. "When's the last time you played the Fender?"

Ugh. "Last week."

"Why?"

"Because I figured after two weeks of silence we were done." I pull out my other ear bud and wad the cords up in my hand. "Latson doesn't want anything to do with me."

Ariel studies me in silence and crosses her arms. "You know I disagree."

"Yes, oh Wise Sage." I roll my eyes. This isn't a new conversation. "I told you I wish things were different, but they're not. I lost his trust. There's no coming back from that."

"Your brother said he's miserable."

"Probably because Pete threatened his life." I knew my brother would stand up for me, but I didn't realize he would hold it over Latson every single day. Jules sent me a screenshot of the reminders on Pete's phone. Each day there is an alert *for Remind my boss he lost the best thing he ever had.* I don't think my brother's behavior is helping any.

"Let me ask you this." Ariel shifts her weight. "If Latson called you right now and said he was sorry, would you take him back?"

"Of course I would, but ..."

"But what?"

"We'd have to have a serious discussion about jumping to conclusions."

If Latson has a fault, it's thinking everyone is out to get him. I understand why he feels the way he does; a lot of close people have betrayed him. Yes, I missed the funeral, but he has to realize accidents happen. He can't hate me more than I hate myself for that mistake. On the other hand, the situation with Caleb was coincidental. Should I have stayed in my room and tried to ignore the sex-a-thon? Given the outcome, probably. However, I was standing up for myself and Roxanne. I won't ever stop defending what I believe is right, regardless of who is involved. Whether it's loud neighbors or Ariel's right to choose or Gwen's small chest, it's part of who I am.

"He does tend to think the worst," Ariel says. "He needs to move past the Caleb thing."

I nod. "I don't think it will be easy for him, though."

"I don't think anything worth fighting for is easy." She pats her still-flat belly. "Case in point, Lil Munchkin."

I smile.

"There it is!" She grins. "I knew you could smile."

"Only temporarily." I smirk on purpose.

She groans and then bites her lip like she has a secret. "What if ... what if I had news that might make it more permanent?"

I'm intrigued. "Keep talking."

"What are your plans after the tour ends?"

My shoulders sag. I'll be right back to square one. "To find a job so I can refurnish my apartment. Why?"

"If you say yes," she taps her chin, "I'd like to make you my primary songwriter."

I stare at her, stunned.

"I've talked to Mason, and he thinks my publishing company would take you on after hearing "Fairytale." If it works out –"

I launch myself forward and hug her.

"Ah!" She squeals.

"Oh my god, yes," I say over her shoulder.

She laughs. "Do you want to hear the rest?"

I try to contain my enthusiasm and lean back. "Sorry."

She smiles. "I'm not exactly sure how everything will play out, but there could be yearly advances on top of royalties. You'll have to discuss the business stuff with them, but I know several people in the industry who make a good living writing songs. I can't give you an exact amount of money, but –"

"I still say yes." Is this really happening? Is Ariel Allyn asking me to write songs for her?

"Excellent." She extends her hand. "So, we have a deal?"

I reach for her hand, but stop short. "Wait. You're not doing this because you feel sorry for me, are you?"

She gives me a pointed look. "Your songs will directly affect my career. I can't make a call like this out of sympathy."

"Noted." I shake her hand and let a smile sneak out. "Thank you."

She smiles back. "No, thank you."

"Time to celebrate!"

Paul leaps in front of us and we both jump. I smash my shoulder against the side of my bunk. "Don't scare us like that!"

"Gotcha." He winks.

Drew appears behind him with Dean. He grabs onto the bottom of Roxanne's bunk and hangs there. "We were eavesdropping."

My pulse races from the scare. "Are you bored?"

"A little."

Dean points his phone at me. "Jen Elliott! You've just been offered a new career! What are you going to do next?"

"Is this where I say I'm going to Disney World?" I hold up my hand to block the camera. "Are you recording this?"

"Damn straight I am."

"Stop! I look like crap. There are enough bad pictures circulating of me as it is."

"Hey. You might want to watch this one day," Dean jokes.

Roxanne appears from the back of the bus. "I'll get some drinks. What does everyone want?"

My eyes get wide. "You were listening, too?"

"It's kinda hard to avoid in this space," she says. "Besides, I finished the book I was reading. You want the regular?"

We nod and the guys follow her toward the front of the bus.

"So," Ariel pushes on my knees, "I think you should call Gunnar and tell him. It will give you something to talk about."

I shoot her a skeptical look. "Are you sure you didn't do this to be nice?"

"No, but it's a conversation starter, don't you think?"

"I think you're trying to play matchmaker." I find my phone. I won't text Latson, but I will send a message to Pete and Jules.

Dean reappears and hands Ariel a ginger ale. I get my Angry Orchard. My phone sounds with an alert and I look down. *No way Little J. Congratulations!* It's my brother.

Ariel's eyebrows jump. "What did he say?"

"My brother says congrats."

"You didn't tell Gunnar?"

"No."

She groans. "Why?"

"Because." How can I explain this? "Contacting him is all I have. If I call him now and he doesn't respond, it will kill me." I meet her eyes. "It will be confirmation, you know? If I put it off, it seems ..." I shrug. "It seems like I still have something to hold on to. Like I haven't burned my last bridge."

Ariel's expression falls. "I get it," she says. "It's your last card to play."

I nod. This fight, this break up, whatever it is, it's different. I've left guys before and they've left me. It wasn't fun, but it didn't hurt this much. I never felt like a part of me was missing. Losing Latson ... I feel like there's a huge hole in my chest. If I let myself think about him too much, it's hard to breathe.

"If you could tell him anything what would it be?" Ariel looks genuinely interested. "I need to know for when I find the love of my life."

The hole in my chest aches. If Latson is the love of my life I would hope we'd have a happier ending than a fight over a mistake and a misunderstanding. Since my apology didn't work, the only thing left to share is how I feel.

"I would tell him I love him," I say quietly. "It's the only thing I never got to say."

~~~~

"Come on, guys. I want a picture."

Rox, Dean, Paul, and Drew all gather around as I try to fit us in the frame. I've never been good at selfies; I don't think my arms are long enough.

"Let me do it," Paul says. "I'm taller." He takes my phone from me, and we all pose for a few fun shots. I've been taking a lot of pictures over the last week – my last week on tour. I'm going to miss these guys something fierce. I can't believe it's all ending tonight. After Ariel's encore, everyone in this room will go their separate ways.

"Send me some of those," Roxanne says. "I'll put them on Dean's website."

"Will do." I nod and start typing.

"So," Dean approaches me, "you using the Fender tonight?"

I look up at him and frown. "No. Why?"

"I don't know." He leans against my vanity table. "We're in your home state, your parents are here, and it's your last show."

I narrow my eyes. "Do you want me to use it?"

"Would you if I said yes?"

Why does he care? He hasn't over the past few weeks. "I guess so," I answer. The whole Latson thing is still a sore spot for me. I was planning to send the guitar back to him when I got home and settled.

"Good." Dean's eyes light up. "I thought you'd agree, so it's already backstage."

"What's going on?" Yes, I'm suspicious.

"You want to impress your family, right? Plus, it's the last show. I like the sound better."

"Now you tell me?" I make a face.

He smiles as Roxanne gets our attention. "All right, lady and gentlemen. Let's head to our final meet and greet."

The five of us file out of the room and down the halls of the Palace of Auburn Hills. I've been to countless concerts in this arena throughout my life; it's only thirty minutes away from my home. Never once did I think I'd be playing on stage here, though. The farther I walk, the more mixed my feelings become. Excitement, intimidation, a little bit of sadness ... they're all there.

When we enter the room to meet the fans, I spot my family right way. My parents faces light up when they see me; they wave and I wave back. My eyes find my brothers Adam, Josh, and Pete, then Jules ... then Carter, Felix, and Gwen. Holy shit. I wasn't expecting them. Adrenaline surges through me and my heart dares to hope a certain someone else is here, too. My eyes search the room, but they don't find him. I hide my disappointment. Did I really think he'd show up?

No. Not until I saw everyone else.

Roxanne and the Palace staff start to let people through to meet us like usual. Attendance has picked up during the tour like Rox had hoped; there have been at least a hundred fans, if not more, at the last several meet and greets. Mid-way through the signing, my parents make it to me.

"Baby girl." My dad looks at me out of the corner of his eye before opening his arms for a hug. I gladly sink into them. It's been months since I've been on the receiving end of a Dad Hug.

"Hey, Dad," I say against his shoulder before he steps back and holds me at arm's length. He looks me over, and I do the same to him. What the hell? "Who dressed you?" I ask.

He chuckles. "Jules got ahold of me." He looks down. "You don't like my jeans?"

"They have holes in them." They're distressed and ripped, very hip for a fifty-five year old English instructor. He's also wearing a vintage, little-too-tight Moody Blues tee.

"Let's get one with my girl!"

My mom's hand slides around my shoulders as she pulls me into a picture with her and Drew. She pops one knee and winks as Jules takes the picture, a total confident fan-girl pose. I look at my dad. "What did you feed her?"

"I'm just excited," she gushes and leaves Drew to hug me. "I'm so proud of you! This is so big time."

I smile. "It kinda is, isn't it?" She kisses my temple and leans away. It's then I notice she's dressed the same as my dad. "What's with the Moody Blues?"

"It's the first concert I went to with your father. We still had the t-shirts!"

"Let me get a picture of all three of you and then one with the boys." Jules starts ordering us around. My parents stand on either side of me and wrap their arms behind my waist. Jules raises her camera and says, "Say pickles!"

"What?" My mouth falls open just as she takes the picture. "Ugh. Take another one."

She takes a few shots, and then I pose with my brothers. "'Sup." Josh jerks his chin, trying to look like a badass. It doesn't work; he's a much more boyish version of Pete.

"I'll take that as a hello," I say.

"Way to go, Little J!" Adam tries to give me a noogie, but I jump out of the way.

"Adam!" I slap at him. "Would you act your age? Jesus."

"I don't think they're used to seeing you like this," Pete says. He slaps Adam on the back of the head. "Don't mess up her hair, dick face."

"Hey, now." My dad uses his stern voice. Coupled with his signature glare, it's enough to make my grown brothers behave.

Once my family steps to the side, I hug the crew from Torque and sign things for them. "You guys know you can get my autograph anytime. You didn't have to come all the way here."

"Mi amor." Felix's voice is smooth. "Montamos en el coche siempre para ti."

"Huh?" I frown.

"We all rode in your car." Gwen sounds as excited as my mom. "It was cozy but fun!"

"All five of you fit in my car?" My surprised eyes jump to Pete. "I thought only you and Jules were bringing it back."

I had to get my car from Chicago somehow, so the plan was for the two of them to drive it to Michigan for the concert. Then, after, they would take the train home.

"Road trip!" Carter grins. "Any excuse to see our favorite bartender."

Gwen elbows him. "Thanks a lot."

"What?" He shrugs. "She's your favorite, too."

"Okay, you're right." Gwen gives me a smile.

I feel a tap on my arm and turn around to see Roxanne behind me. She whispers, "I'm all for the family reunion, but we need to keep the line moving."

I nod and face everyone. "Okay, guys. I'll see you from the stage."

"We get to go to the after party, right?"

I nod my head and push Adam's arm. "Yes. Go. I'll see you later."

Everyone waves goodbye, and my parents give me a quick kiss. Pete lets the group walk ahead of him and then quietly asks, "After "Over-Exposed", right?"

"Yep." I grin my first legit grin in weeks. Operation Propose to Jules is officially in motion.

"Break a leg." Pete fist bumps me.

"You, too."

He starts to walk away, then stops. "Listen. I caught the look on your face earlier. I'm sorry Latson isn't here with us. I tried to talk him into –"

"Stop." I push on his arm like I did Adam's. "It's fine. Go have a good time."

Pete smirks like he doesn't believe me, then leaves through the exit. Before I turn around to meet the next person, I take a deep breath. The last thing I need right now is to get emotional. I have one more show to play, and it's important. After tonight, I can wallow in misery for as long as I want. It will make me happy.

Cardinal rule.

Chapter Twenty Eight

"Think what you want
See what you see
Deal with the lies that you think of me.
All I ever am
And all I'll ever be
Is the truth behind the lens
That you'll never see.

I'm over -exposed
And it's still not enough
I'm over-exposed
Your mind has me cuffed
I'm over-exposed
How much can I bleed
I'm over-exposed
To fulfill your need."

Drew beats the shit out of the cymbals to finish the song, and I hold the last note on the Fender longer than usual. Paul's practically diving off the front of the stage, and Dean's clutching the mic like he's trying to strangle someone.

Hey. It's our last show. Time to go big or go... Wait. We are going home.

The crowd roars for us. They sound louder than usual, probably because my family and friends are screaming the place down. They're only a few rows back, toward the center aisle on the main floor, and they've been going strong the entire set. I'm glad they're having a good time.

"Thank you!" Dean shouts into the mic. He wipes the sweat from his brow, then turns around and looks at me for the go ahead. I nod.

"So," he swings his guitar to the side, "I don't know if you all know, but ah...our rhythm guitarist hails from the Motor City."

Drew bangs the bass drum a couple times and the crowd cheers. I step forward and wave. I can see Jules, Gwen, and my mom jumping up and down.

"Jen's family is here tonight." Dean takes his mic off the stand and looks at me. "Would you like to do the honors?"

"Sure, Dean." My voice echoes through the arena. Suddenly, I feel like June Carter Cash on stage with Johnny. "If you'll all bear with me, I'd like to ask my brother Pete and his girlfriend Juliana to join me on stage. There's something we need to take care of that's long overdue."

Much to the confusion of my family and friends, my brother grabs Jules' hand and leads her away from their seats. The audience whistles and claps as a cameraman focuses on the couple and projects them on every screen in the place. When they get close to the stage, security escorts them over to me.

"What are you doing?" Jules asks through a forced smile. "I didn't bring my tambourine."

I laugh, remembering our conversation about our fake band. "I'm going to let my brother take it from here," I say and back away. I glance at Pete, and he gently takes both of Jules' hands. He stares into her eyes, and I hold the mic between the two of them so everyone can hear.

"Juliana –"

The crowd goes crazy as soon as Pete says her name.

"I can't remember a time in my life without you. You're my rock, my best friend, my voice of reason, and my partner in crime."

He drops to one knee and the fans grow louder. My eyes jump to my parents, and I see my mom hanging on to my dad's arm. Gwen, Carter, and Felix are hanging on to each other in anticipation, too. My attention falls back on Jules and her mouth is hanging open. She tries to cover it with one hand, but my brother won't let her go.

"It's time to formally ask you to be my partner in life," Pete says and scoots closer to Jules. "Juliana Louise. Will you marry me ..." He leans away from the mic. "Again?"

Her eyes get teary as she enthusiastically nods yes. The audience cheers, my band mates clap, and Pete jumps up, grabbing Jules and spinning her around. When he sets her down he kisses her, then reaches into his pocket and pulls out her ring. She gasps when she sees it and holds out a shaky hand. My brother slides it onto her finger, and it sparkles in the stage lighting.

"Congratulations you guys," I say into the mic and my voice echoes. "It's about time I got a sister." The two of them turn and make me the meat in a Jules and Pete sandwich.

"How long have you two been planning this?" Jules whispers in my ear.

"Since I found out you were *married*," I whisper back.

She leans away with wide eyes and I smirk. "Oh, yeah. I knew."

"Thanks a lot, Little J." Pete hugs me once more. "We'll never forget this."

Me, neither, I think. Despite how empty my heart has been, it swells with emotion for Jules and Pete. They have the real thing, and it's beautiful. Because of them I know true love exists. It's out there, and I can only hope one day it will find me.

~~~~

"There you are."

I hear Pete's voice and look over my shoulder. I wanted some time to myself, but I guess twenty minutes is all I'm allowed.

My brother exits the pool area of the hotel and pulls a patio chair next to mine. The scraping sound against the pavers makes me flinch. "There's one hell of a party happening upstairs," he says as he sits down. "Why are you out here all by yourself?"

I shrug. The outdoor patio at the hotel seemed like a nice place to get away and look at the stars. "It's a warm night for September. I wanted to enjoy it."

He shoots me a skeptical look. "And?"

"And I needed a minute," I say. "I can only watch mom try to do the "Wobble" so many times."

Pete laughs. "You can blame Jules and Gwen for that little show."

I roll my eyes, but still smile.

"Seriously, though," he sets his hand on my knee and shakes it, "What's wrong? The show was great. We pulled off the proposal."

"I know."

"Plus, you're going to write for Ariel and become a mega-millionaire." He grins. "By the way, I am your favorite brother, right?"

I snort. "You may be my favorite, but I wouldn't hold your breath waiting for millions." I look across the patio. "It just hit me, that's all."

"What did?"

"That it's over," I say. "The tour. Chicago. Torque. Hanging out with you guys. Latson and me ..." I rub my arms like I'm cold. "It's all over."

"Little J." Pete's voice turns empathetic. "If you want to come back to Chicago with me and Jules, you can. You don't have to stay here if you don't want to."

"And live in the same building as the man who hates me? I don't think so."

"Who said he hates you?"

My eyebrows jump. "I would think a month of silence screams hatred. He hasn't tried to contact me."

"Have you tried to talk to him?"

"No," I mutter at the ground. "I tried to apologize in person. He didn't want to hear it."

"It was a hard day," Pete says. "Maybe he's ready to hear it now."

I frown. Since when is Pete in Latson's corner? "Are you defending him?"

"No. I'm –"

"It sounds like you're defending him. He's mad at me over an accident, Pete." Well, two accidents.

"Listen. Did you ever stop to think that he –" Pete hesitates, then lets his head fall back. "Fuck it."

"Fuck what?"

He looks at me. "Both of you are messed up over this. I'm sick of seeing you sad."

I get sarcastic. "You've only seen me one day."

"You're forgetting the rest of the weekend when this whole thing happened. Not to mention I've had to listen to your depressed voice every time I call." He reaches into his pocket and pulls out my car keys. He starts to hand them over, but stops. "Before I give these to you, I need to know one thing."

"What?"

"When you said you loved Latson," he sighs, "did you mean it?"

I'm confused. "How do you know I said that?" I've only told Ariel how I felt.

Pete points at me. "If anyone finds out I told you this I'm going to say I don't remember because I was drunk."

Maybe he really is drunk. He's not making much sense. "Okay."

"Dean sent a video to Latson," he says. "It was from the bus. You can't see much, but you can hear voices. Ariel asks if you could tell Latson anything, what would it be? You answered that you love him."

My eyes narrow. Dean was recording me?

"So?" Pete gets impatient. "Do you really love him?"

"Of course I do. I don't profess my devotion for people if I don't mean it."

He hands me my keys. "You need to go home now."

"Home? As in –"

"Your apartment. And before you get mad, yes, I made a copy of your key."

My heart starts to pound. "Is Latson –"

Pete stands and pulls me to my feet. "Don't ask questions. Just go. I already gave too much away."

I take a step, then start to sprint toward the pool room doors. "Don't speed!" Pete calls out.

Jogging through the hotel, I burst through the front doors and into the parking lot. I have no idea where my brother parked my car, so after going up and down a few rows, I give up and push the panic button on my key ring. Once I find it, I jump in and head to the expressway. It's not long before I realize I ran off and left everything I own at the hotel. I don't even have my driver's license on me.

Shit. I'll have to make a trip back in the morning.

During the drive to my place, a million thoughts swirl in my mind. Is Latson really there? If he's not, something else certainly is. What it could be? Dean's covert video obviously made an impression, which reminds me of Ariel's expression when she asked me her question. Was she in on this, too?

When I pull into my apartment complex, I spot Dorothy right away. Latson is here. I park next to his car, then jump out of mine. Racing inside, I take the stairs two at a time until I'm outside my door. I raise my hand to knock, but stop when it seems weird. It's my apartment. Plus, it's almost three a.m. Latson's probably sleeping. On what, I don't know because I need to replace my furniture. The carpet, maybe? At least it's new. I need to stop rambling and just open the damn door already.

Placing the key in the lock, I try to be quiet when I turn the knob. I step inside and notice all the lights are off except for a strange blue glow coming from the living room. Closing the door behind me, I take a few stealthy steps until I'm staring in awe. Light from a fish tank I never had illuminates my place, and there, on a brand new couch surrounded by all new furniture, lies a sleeping Oliver snuggled against a sleeping Latson. After my rush to get here, my pulse slows to a steady pace. Everything about this feels right. I can see myself coming home to these two every day of my life.

Soft sounds coming from the corner lure me over to stand in front of the fish tank. A lump forms in my throat when I realize what's inside. Four seahorses are hiding amongst the seaweed and coral; two are a grayish color, one is yellow, and another is red. They float weightlessly, hanging on to the plants with their tails. They're gorgeous. I know this had to be Oliver's idea, and it makes my heart melt.

"Hey," a sleepy voice whispers as arms slowly wrap around my waist. "You're home early."

I fall back against Latson's chest and close my eyes, content to be there. He kisses the side of my neck before setting his chin on my shoulder. "Do you like them?"

I nod. "They're beautiful."

He holds me tighter. "I hope you don't mind we named them. O couldn't wait."

I smile and open my eyes. "What are they?"

"The two gray ones are Oliver and Uncle Gunnar," he says. "The yellow one is Ed, and the red one is Jen."

I stifle a laugh. "Ed? Really?"

Latson smiles against my skin. "I came up with that one."

I stare into the tank as he holds me. "Why am I red?" I whisper.

"For cardinal," he says. "I remembered your rule."

This makes me so happy. I turn around in his arms and wrap mine around his neck. He leans forward and sets his forehead against mine. "God, I love you, Jen. I'm sorry for everything. I don't ever want to lose you."

"I don't want to be lost," I whisper. "I love you so much."

He ducks his head and finds my mouth. My entire body reacts as my blood rushes through my veins. Out of all the kisses I've ever received, I never knew I was waiting for this one. It's full of passion, but it's not seductive. It's an apology and a declaration; it's longing and relief. It's everything I've always wanted.

One of his hands leaves my back and travels up my arm to circle my wrist. He leans back and moves my hand, pressing my palm over his pounding heart. "Do you feel that?"

I nod.

"It's for you," he says. "Only for you."

I look up and get lost in his eyes.

"C'mon," he murmurs as he steps back. He leads me past Oliver and into my bedroom, which I'm not surprised to see has a new bedroom set. He turns on a lamp for some light, and I run my hands over a thick sage comforter. "Why did you do all this?" I'm still whispering. "It's too much."

"You don't like it?" He looks worried. "Everything can be exchanged. I thought –"

I hold a finger to his lips. "I love it all."

He relaxes.

"But ..." I glance around. "What does this say?"

"What do you mean?"

"Do you want me to stay in Michigan?"

Latson reaches for me and wraps his arms around my waist again. "No. I mean, yes. I mean, I want whatever you want."

My brow furrows.

"Dean made it sound like you were set on staying here. I didn't know if that meant you never wanted to see me again or if you might be open to a long distance relationship. All I knew was I wanted things to be as easy as possible. I wanted your mind free to think about us and not material things."

I give him a tiny smile. "I only said I was staying here because I thought you didn't want me. I didn't have anywhere else to go."

His eyes grow hungry. "You'd come back to Chicago?"

"What's keeping me here?"

He kisses me again, and it's more intense than before. His tongue parts my lips as it searches out mine, and I mold my body to his. When I catch my breath, I say, "It's a good thing Pete will let me stay with him."

Latson meets my eyes and shakes his head. "No. No more brothers, or crazy groupies, or asshole record label execs."

I bite my lower lip. "About that ..."

He frowns.

"Ariel asked me to write for her. I said yes. I don't know how the industry works, but I may run into Caleb again."

Latson rests his forehead against mine.

"You have to know he has nothing to offer me. Not a career and certainly not himself."

Latson runs his hands to my shoulders and then buries his fingers in my hair. "I know. Everything that happened the day of the funeral ... seeing that picture on top of missing you ... it was too much. Please believe I trust you; I do. I know your heart, and it would never hurt me."

My mouth crashes down on his. I can't stop myself; his words are perfection. They're exactly what I needed to hear.

Latson turns our bodies and backs me against the bed. As his mouth zeroes in on my neck and my stomach flutters, I ask, "Does this mean you want me to move in with you?"

His words are muffled against my skin. "Hell, yes."

With those words, my hands start to roam his body. As I debate going for his shirt or his shorts, my instincts take over and decide for me; I find the bottom of his shirt and push it up. I don't get far however, because he steps back and finishes the job. I try to reach for him again, but as soon as my hands slide across his bare skin, he backs farther away.

"One sec." He gives me my favorite smile and jogs over to the door. He shuts it quietly. "I don't think we need an audience."

My eyes grow wide. How could I forget about Oliver? "We don't have to do this right now."

Before I can blink Latson's standing in front of me again. "We are doing this, and we are doing it now." One of his hands grips my hip, while the other cradles the nape of my neck. "I've waited too damn long for you."

I smile. "A month's your limit?"

"No." He pulls me closer. "Life kept me waiting too long for you. I'm never letting you go."

His words make my heart race, and I trace his bottom lip with my thumb. "Promise?"

His lips meet mine in a scorching kiss. "I promise."

Epilogue

One Year Later

"Jules. Would you stop fixing my hair? I love it."

I watch in the mirror as she plays with more strands of my "messy" twist. It's a very precise hairstyle to be labeled messy.

"It has to be perfect," she says, determined. "Everything about this day has to be perfect."

I sigh. "It looks great. You need to get ready. Nothing can happen today without you."

She stops picking at me and looks down at her satin slip. "I guess you're right. Pete wouldn't like it if I walked down the aisle half-naked."

"Or maybe he would." I wink at her and she playfully shoves me.

Jules leaves my side, and I look in the mirror again. I touch a few of the pearl pins she put in my hair. They're simple, elegant, and perfectly placed. Over my shoulder, I catch Gwen's reflection wiggling into her plum-colored bridesmaid dress.

"What time do we have to leave again?" she asks.

Jules beats me to answering her question. "Twelve-thirty. We don't have much time."

I shake my head and smile. My sister-in-law is the best, but she's taking this day so seriously I'm afraid she's going to stroke out before it's over. She's coordinated everything right down to the minute.

A knock on the door distracts me from Jules' potential need for an ambulance. She tries to race me to open it, but I leap off the vanity bench and beat her to it. Her eyes grow wide. "You don't know who it is!"

I stick out my tongue and open the door anyway. I'm not as superstitious as she is. When I turn to greet our visitor, a smile breaks across my face. "Hey! You made it."

"We did." Ariel wrestles with a diaper bag in one hand and a baby carrier in the other. "Can you take her for a sec? She's getting heavy."

"Sure." I reach for baby Piper and carry her into my childhood bedroom. She's so chunky and adorable; I just want to squeeze her. At five months old I already know she's going to be a heartbreaker. I am a little biased though; she is my goddaughter after all.

Setting the carrier on my old twin bed, I peer inside and use my baby voice, which I'm sure is annoying. "How's my girl?" Piper just stares at me and chews on her fist.

"Your girl is entirely too awake at the moment." Ariel drops the diaper bag. "I really hoped she'd be napping by now."

I undo the straps to her carrier and lift her out. "Let me talk to her," I say.

"I don't think that's a good idea." Jules rushes to my side. "What if she throws up on you?"

I make a face. "She won't throw up on me." I settle Piper against my stomach, her back to my front, so she can see what's going on. "Besides, she's one of us. We have to get a look at her dress." She's dolled up in purple, from her tiny headband, to her outfit, to her little tights.

"Speaking of dresses ..." Ariel gestures for me to turn around and I do. "You look stunning. Gunnar may pass out."

I smile. "Thanks."

"I thought the baby was here!" My mom rushes into the room and makes grabby hands. "Let me have her."

I roll my eyes and hand her over. It's useless to fight with my mom over Piper, or any baby for that matter.

"When are you going to convince these two to give me grandchildren?" My mom talks to Piper as she sets her on her hip. She looks between me and Jules. "I'm not getting any younger, you know."

Jules turns around and pretends to be interested in finding her heels while I put my hand on my hip. "One thing at a time, okay? And what's Oliver? Chopped liver?"

"You know I love Ollie to death," my mom says as she canoodles the baby.

Oy. Ollie. He loves the nickname. Me not so much.

"Limo's here!" my dad shouts up the stairs.

"That's our cue to leave," my mom says to the baby. She walks over and starts to put her in her carrier, and Ariel helps.

I do a quick check to make sure I have everything. Small clutch. Yes. Shoes. They're on my feet. Bouquet. Yes. I inhale the ivory hydrangea and purple calla lily mix. When I lift the flowers, however, I realize my wrist is empty. Shoot.

"Are you ready?" Jules asks from behind me.

"I just need a second."

She gives me an impatient glare.

"Go on." I shoo her away. "I'll be there in a minute."

She reluctantly follows everyone else downstairs.

I walk to the overnight bag I brought and search for the tiny blue box. When I find it, I pop the lid and pull out the silver bracelet Oliver gave me. Four charms dangle from the links: a music note, a heart, a guitar, and, of course, a shark. I slide it over my hand. Perfect.

Picking up my flowers again, I take one last look at myself in the mirror before heading out the door. My dress is vintage lace, but simple. It's ivory and sleeveless with a V-neck, plunging back, and a few rhinestones at the waist. I think it makes me look respectfully curvy and very 1920's.

"Jen! Come on!" Jules hollers.

Good lord, the woman is going to have a heart attack. It's not even her wedding day.

It's mine.

~~~~

The limo delivers us to Heavenly Scent Herb Farm, located in my hometown, at precisely one o'clock. I know we took a chance with an outdoor ceremony, but Latson and I wanted something natural and intimate. Nothing big city, since that's where we live and work. We opted for the Herb Farm because the grounds are gorgeous. Everywhere you look there's a garden or hanging baskets overflowing with blooms or hidden statuaries. There's even a waterfall next to the arbor where everyone will watch us say our vows.

"Okay, everyone." Jules directs traffic. "Girls inside to the bridal room and parents outside to great guests."

She totally missed her calling as a coordinator. That's why I asked for her help. Things would be a mess without her.

As we stay hidden from the guys and the guests, we take a few pictures and do some last minute touch-ups. I haven't felt nervous all day, but now, moments away from seeing Latson, I'm starting to get butterflies. I'm not anxious about the commitment; it's just some of the day's details have been kept secret from me. Ever since he furnished – then unfurnished – my apartment, Latson likes to surprise me. So far, all the surprises have been good, like a spontaneous trip to Seattle, tickets to see Mama Mia! (gotta love ABBA), and my proposal on the yacht he rented to cruise Lake Michigan. I did manage to surprise him with one thing: our rings. When he proposed, I shocked him by telling him to take back what he had bought me. I'd been thinking about it off and on, and when things were official, I got my first tattoo – around my left ring finger. He did the same, and we match.

Forever.

"It's time," Jules says, pulling me out of my memories.

"Good." I follow her toward the door and my father. "I'm ready to get this show on the road."

When I reach my dad, he takes my arm and then kisses my cheek. "You look beautiful."

I blush. What is it about dads and compliments? "Thank you."

As we follow the girls, he leans into my ear. "If he ever does you wrong, you tell me. I'll take care of it."

I hold out my hand, and he fist bumps me. Yep. My dad, the teacher, is a badass.

When we make it outside, I can hear the buzz of guests whispering and the sound of an acoustic guitar. It takes me a moment to recognize the song as "You and Me" by Lifehouse, and I stand on my toes so I can peek over heads to see who's playing. I can barely make out Dean's head by the officiant, and I realize it's him. My expression immediately softens and ... crap. I'm going to need tissues.

Gwen is the first to walk down the aisle, followed by Ariel, and then my maid of honor, Jules. She specifically instructed me to start walking after the music changed, so I chew on my lip and wait until I hear a pause. Dean begins to play "Marry Me" by Train, and I start to get a little shaky.

"Here we go," my dad encourages me and pats my arm.

When we step into view, everyone stands. There's less than a hundred people here, but it feels like an arena to me. My eyes bounce around the guests, and I pick out family members, Roxanne, Paul, and Drew. I find Kevin and Ashley next to Kyle and Addison and seeing them makes me smile. I haven't talked to them in ages. If I'm not mistaken, Addison's face looks a little puffy. I wouldn't be surprised if she's pregnant. I swear, it's contagious.

My dad starts to lead me forward and my eyes land on Latson's father standing in the row across from my mom. He smiles when he sees me, and I'm so happy he reconciled things with his son enough to be here. I know the relationship is important to Oliver and, as much as Latson won't admit it, he would be hurt if his dad missed today.

With all the thoughts jumping around my brain, I think I'm holding up pretty well. I'm walking in a straight line and everything, until my eyes fall on the two most important men in my life.

Standing at the end of the aisle, both Latson and Oliver wait for me. As we get closer to one another, my eyes stay glued on Latson. This man is trying to kill me. Who put him in that suit? It's lethal. It's cut perfectly to the plains of his waist and his chest, his shirt and necktie offset by the ivory handkerchief in his lapel pocket. His eyes swim in mine, and the only thing I can think about is running my hands through his hair and kissing him. My mind barely registers Pete, Carter, and Felix standing to his left.

When I reach the end of the aisle, the officiant asks who gives this woman to be wed. My dad looks at Oliver because this is their big line. O wanted a part in the ceremony and since he "found" me at the aquarium, we thought it would be appropriate for him to give me away, too.

My dad starts, "Her mother and I ..."

"... and I do, too," Oliver finishes.

The guests think it's cute and they laugh. Latson looks like he could devour me as he takes my hand and leads me forward a few steps. He leans into my ear and his scent invades my senses. "I don't have words to describe how gorgeous you look," he whispers. "I'm not letting you out of the room during our honeymoon."

The officiant clears her throat and smirks like she heard what he said. I squeeze his hand in admonishment and stand up straight. I can feel him laugh.

"Ladies and gentlemen. We are gathered here today to witness the joining of ..."

The officiant's voice fades away. I'm anxious to get to the "I do" part. We wrote our own vows, and I've been practicing mine for weeks. When it's finally time, I give my flowers to Jules, face Latson, and smile up at him. "Hi."

He grins. "Hi."

I take a breath and then his hands, squeezing his fingers. "So, here's the thing," I say. "When you came into my life, I wasn't expecting you." His eyes light up. "All I wanted was space to sort things out, and you kept getting in the way."

Laughter filters through the guests.

"Thank you for never giving up on me," I say. "Thank you for believing in us. Thank you for encouraging my dreams, even though it's sometimes hard for you. Thank you for allowing me into your life, for sharing your past, and letting me love Oliver." I look at our joined hands and run my thumbs over the back of his. "Thank you for showing me it's possible for one man to love one woman and be faithful to her without secrets and lies."

My eyes meet his again and they look glassy. I swallow the lump in my throat; I've never seen him tear up before. "If someone had told me I would have to lose everything I had to find everything I need, I wouldn't have believed them." I pause. "You make me a believer. You're my truth. You're everything I need, and I love you. I promise to love you every day of my life."

Latson clutches my fingers and then lets them go. He traces the side of my face with one hand before blinking to clear his eyes. "How am I supposed to compete with that?"

Both Jules and Gwen say "aww" from behind me.

I expect him to take my hands again to say his vows, but instead he steps away from me. "My turn," he says as Dean stands and hands him his guitar.

My knees go weak. He's going to sing?

Latson sits down and sets the acoustic across his lap. "When I tried to write my vows my mind kept turning them into a song." He gives me his dimple smile. "I guess that's the only thing I know how to put on paper." He sets his fingers against the strings. "I hope you like it."

Like there's a chance in hell I wouldn't.

He starts to play and the song stays instrumental for a few moments. When he opens his mouth to sing, I get lost in the smooth sound of his voice:

"Against the world
Guarded and numb
An unforgiving path was the only one
I questioned my choices
And doubted my heart
Until we crashed together
And never fell apart.

You broke down my walls
And cut my chains,
I'll use them to bind us together.
No words or tears can stop our flame
Fall with me into forever.

Funny how love comes off a myth
Until fate decides it's time
I didn't know I'd lost my soul
Until your blue eyes met mine.
You see things in me I've never seen
You've opened up my eyes
I vow to protect your giving heart
And love you until the day I die.

You broke down my walls
And cut my chains,
I'll use them to bind us together.
No words or tears can stop our flame
Fall with me into forever.

You broke down my walls
And cut my chains
Bind yourself to me forever.
There's nothing in the world
We can't do
As long as we're together."

When he finishes the song, silence falls around us. He studies my face, and I try to breathe; it's difficult when my pulse is pounding so hard. Our family and friends start to clap, but I'm not having any of that. What he just did for me, said to me, deserves more than polite applause.

I throw myself in Latson's lap as soon as he's rid of the guitar. He laughs and grabs ahold of my waist as I take his face in both of my hands. I plant the most inappropriate kiss that I can on his lips, but I don't care. He doesn't either because he gives it right back and his fingers start to roam.

"I guess we'll just skip to the end," I hear the officiant laugh. "I now pronounce you husband and wife. You can … keep doing what you're doing."

I hear the bridal party cheer, and I smile against Latson's mouth. We did it. "I love you, husband."

He holds me tighter to him. "I love you, Little Bird."

Acknowledgements

As a writer, it's hard to crush a character. Especially one you really like. In Sparrow, Jen was only supposed to be a blip – an ex-girlfriend to show Kyle's inability to commit since losing Addison. Boy, did she have other plans for me! To quote Kyle, the "cute, funny, and talented" bartender became a much bigger part of Sparrow than I had originally planned (I didn't see the twist with Derek until I was literally writing the chapter). While what happened to Jen in Sparrow was right for that story, it wasn't right for her. I owed her, and she let me know it, too. She's been living in my mind for the last year, questioning happily-ever-after's and wondering if she'd get hers. I'm happy to say she found her forever with Latson. I hope readers will agree that she finally got the love and attention she deserves.

With that said, there are a few people I need to thank for their support and encouragement:

My family. Thank you to Drew – fictional Union drummer to readers, but real-life husband to me. Thank you for being in my band, for your "fight" advice, and for finding the Pink Floyd quote. Thank you to my son, my Oliver inspiration, for being adorable and loving Nerf and Minecraft so much that O does, too. And thank you to my daughter who, like an agent, is always checking up on me: "How much did you write today, Mom? Only a paragraph? You need to get moving!"

My betas. Koz, Tartney, JFF, and Brooke. This was a long process, ladies. Thank you for sticking with me. I know receiving one chapter every couple weeks, sometimes once a month, is tedious. Thank you for your faith in Latson and Jen ("She needs to be married and have tons of Latson babies!"), and for your faith in me.

My Street Team. Jenn L., Barbie, Tracey, Sonya, Lisa, Retta, Jordan, Charlotte, James, Angela, Brianie, Sarah, Deanna, Lyndsey, Tami, Colleen, Lindsey L., Christina, Leann, Kendra, Ginelle, Shawanda, Tiffany, Aubrey, Breena, Lori, Michele, Gloria, and Mary Ann. Whether we're Facebook friends, in-person friends, or family, thank you for your never-ending support. Last but not least, a special thank you to Joelle – if it were up to her, the entire universe would know about my books. Her promotion is tireless, and I love her for it.

Dean McCarthy and the Union Set List

All of the songs written by Dean and played on the Renegade Tour were inspired by real books written by authors who have become good friends. If you're curious, check them out on Amazon:

To Hell and Back
By Leigha Taylor

Breaking Free
By S.M. Koz

The Short Life of Sparrows
By Emm Cole

Over-Exposed
By Julie Jaret

Out of the Blu
Coming soon from Jennifer Fisch-Ferguson

Of course, Dean has more than five songs, but, unfortunately, I couldn't fit them all into the story. Here is the rest of his set list:

Old No. 7
Tribute to my brother's old band.
Paul, in Cardinal, is my real brother who plays bass.

Arrow On The Doorpost
The Walking Dead. Need I say more?

Until the End of Forever
See Guardian by Sara Mack

Red Ribbon
Eclipse, my favorite book of the *Twilight* Series

Raven
In honor of my daughter's ice hockey team.
Those girls are some kick-ass chicks, just like Jen.

About the Author

Sara Mack is a Michigan native who grew up with her nose in books. She is a wife and a hockey mom on top of being trapped in an office forty hours a week. Her spare time is spent one-clicking on Amazon and devouring books on her Kindle, cleaning up after her kids and two elderly cats, attempting to keep her flower garden alive, and, of course, writing. She has an unnatural affinity for dark chocolate, iced tea, and bacon.

Connect with Sara:

On Facebook

https://www.facebook.com/sara.mackauthor

On Twitter and Instagram

@smackwrites

Website and Email

http://smackwrites.wix.com/saramackauthor

smackwrites@gmail.com

Other books by Sara Mack:

Sparrow

The Guardian Trilogy
Guardian
Allegiant
Reborn

Made in the USA
Monee, IL
23 December 2024

72103773R00193